THE DIVINE SWORD

Rita Chowdhury is an award-winning Assamese poet and writer. She is a former Associate Professor of Political Science at Cotton University in Guwahati and a former Director of the National Book Trust. An important voice in contemporary Assamese literature, she has written fifteen novels, including *Chinatown Days* (*Makam*), that paint a vivid picture of her strife-torn state. In 2008, she received the Sahitya Akademi Award for her novel *Deo Langkhui*.

Reeta Borbora is a practising lawyer and a translator from Assamese to English.

Praise for *Chinatown Days*

'Rita Chowdhury is an energetic and empathetic storyteller'

– Amitav Ghosh, author of *Smoke and Ashes*

'This masterful saga recounts the tragic history of the Chinese community in Assam and Bengal … an intense and compelling narrative that explores migration, identity, and the cruel boundaries of narrow chauvinism'

– Namita Gokhale, author and festival director

'A fascinating portrait of migration, memory and mixed antecedents … wide-ranging and historically valuable'

– Anjum Hasan, author of *History's Angel*

'Rita Chowdhury's gripping story of the Chinese community in Upper Assam gives the insider version of the events of 1962. It is a history that has rarely been told before … and how beautifully Rita tells it'

– Easterine Kire, author of *Spirit Nights*

'An important book … *Chinatown Days* weaves its careful magic across borders and communities, relocating within history our humanity'

– Janice Pariat, author of *Everything the Light Touches*

'Rita Chowdhury's *Chinatown Days* is an engaging, monumental work'

– Hansda Sowendra Shekhar, author of *The Adivasi Will Not Dance*

'[An] epic saga ... Rita Chowdhury reminds us that those who populate her novel are our people too. It's a powerful suggestion'

– Hindu

'Rita Chowdhury narrates an epic saga of almost unrelieved pain and anguish, spanning more than a century and several continents'

– India Today

'Chowdhury narrates [this story] with great sensitivity and scholarship'

– Scroll.in

'Rita Chowdhury's empathetic prose, full of energy and vigour delineates the author's urge to let the story be heard'

– Times of India

'Racy, readable and full of little human actions, thoughts and feelings'

– Week

'An engaging, monumental work'

– National Herald

'Poignant'

– Asian Age

THE DIVINE SWORD

A NOVEL

RITA CHOWDHURY

TRANSLATED FROM THE ASSAMESE BY REETA BORBORA

MACMILLAN

First published in Assamese as *Deo Langkhui* 2005 by Jyoti Prakashan
First published in English 2024 by Macmillan
an imprint of Pan Macmillan Publishing India Private Limited
707 Kailash Building
26 K. G. Marg, New Delhi 110001
www.panmacmillan.co.in

Pan Macmillan, The Smithson, 6 Briset Street, Farringdon,
London EC1M 5NR
Associated companies throughout the world
www.panmacmillan.com

ISBN 978-93-90742-36-3

1 3 5 7 9 8 6 4 2

Typeset in Baskerville MT Std by SÜRYA, New Delhi
Printed and bound in India by Replika Press Pvt. Ltd.

ONE

Twilight. The royal palace of Gobha, typically bustling with the activities and chatter of its residents, stands in eerie silence.

Tragedy has struck. Old King Sadhukumar has just arrived with his retinue after consigning the headless body of Mriganko, the prince of Gobha and king of Kumoi–Boghora, to flames. The kings and royal representatives of the neighbouring provinces stand alongside Sadhukumar, joined by countless subjects of Gobha.

The field in front of the palace is filled with citizens who are inconsolable over Mriganko's death. King Sadhukumar, after comforting all of them, meets a council of loyal and friendly neighbouring kings to discuss how to tackle any potential political challenges brought on by the valiant King Mriganko's untimely death. There is no other choice.

No. He cannot grieve his son's loss yet. If he breaks down, chaos will reign the kingdom. The neighbouring rulers are seething with anger at King Jokanko of Khola for killing Mriganko.

As the son of the Gobha king and later as the ruler of Kumoi and Boghora – two kingdoms under Gobha's dominion – Mriganko was part of various political councils. He had gained admiration for his valour, especially after setting up a kingdom in the distant land of Komota. He had grown to attain almost mythical status, much like his parents Konsari and Sadhukumar.

In the vast expanse of Gobha, and among the tribes to the north and south of the Brahmaputra, who has not heard of

Mriganko? All of Gobha and the other Laloong kingdoms were proud of him.

Now, the Khola king's act of assassinating Mriganko without any provocation has angered not only the neighbouring rulers but also the people of Gobha. They want to jointly attack his kingdom.

Moved by Sadhukumar's earnest pleas, they ultimately abandon the idea, instead choosing to cut all political and economic ties with Khola. The old king is disturbed by this decision, unwilling to subject Jokanko to distress.

Despite the Khola king murdering his only son, Sadhukumar holds no ill will towards him. He knows that revealing his reasons would instantly calm everyone, including the agitated kings and subjects. Yet he remains silent.

For Konsari, a woman who commands the respect and dignity of a queen without the crown, has forbidden him from making the truth public. Sadhukumar can defy her wishes, but he lacks the will to do so. With patience and political wisdom, he tries to persuade the crowd patiently to not see Khola as their common enemy or unite against it.

Gradually, the noise emanating from the crowd subsides. One by one, the neighbouring rulers bid their farewells.

By the time Sadhukumar says goodbye to the last king, discusses the customary *karam* rites of the deceased with the *loro* – the chief priest – and mounts the elephant towards the old capital – Amsai Marjong – dusk has given way to nightfall.

Inside the private bed chamber of the main palace, Konsari sits on a dishevelled bed. All alone. The expansive royal palace is cloaked in stillness. The mustard-oil earthen lamps burn here and there, seemingly imploring the oppressive darkness to go away.

In the light of lamps burning inside Konsari's chamber, the darkness of the night has dissipated. But it cannot take away the intensity of her suffering. Its traces are evident on her face. Throughout her entire being. It is as if her withered existence has been wrapped with a faded shroud of anguish. Konsari sits with her shrunken and withered hands embracing her knees, her head resting upon them. Her long tresses, once tied in a knot, now lie scattered over her shoulders. Partly undone.

Konsari resembles a discoloured portrait by a mournful artist. Coloured, yet devoid of colour. Alive, yet lifeless. She is exhausted by the burden of painful memories accumulated over countless years of suffering. Cold as stone. Motionless. Limp.

Until today, she has never been seen in this state. When she first set foot in the land of Gobha, Konsari had just reached maidenhood. Having spent so much time in Gobha, the beautiful young girl has now become a grandmother – *Abi* Konsari. Almost all the people from Gobha, Dimoruwa, Nelly, Bhuyan and other subsidiary and neighbouring provinces know of her. They regard her as a living icon – a wise and compassionate woman who has sacrificed her life for the welfare of society.

In times of crisis, the people approach Abi Konsari with the same faith and hope they have in their King Sadhukumar. Abi Konsari and *Deoraja* Sadhukumar's liberal and considerate attitudes have made this a powerful and prosperous kingdom. Similarly, under the joint leadership of Gobha and Jaintia, all the nearby provinces have co-existed harmoniously without major conflict. Recently, however, Konsari has somewhat detached herself from social responsibilities. She is now engrossed in reading scriptures and spinning yarn. Her political involvement has become limited to only the most pressing matters.

In fact, ever since Mriganko's return from Komotapur, Konsari's zeal for work has significantly waned. As if age, coupled with some painful experiences, has sapped all her desire to work.

Nevertheless, in some respects, she remains unchanged. Composed. Serene and cheerful. No one has ever seen her break down in sorrow. Or become paralysed by grief. With dignity and patience, Konsari has faced every catastrophe, endured every moment of acute suffering.

With her living alone in the main palace of Gobha, and Sadhukumar at Amsai Marjong, they seem to have transformed into two ancient fig trees – tolerant, enormous, unwavering.

The Tiwashas, residing in the vast region bordered by the Brahmaputra in the north, Dimoria in the west, Bor-amoli in the south, Khagorijan in the east and others, have nearly erased from their memories the stunning image of the youthful Konsari. They have forgotten that old Abi Konsari was once a delicate maiden. That she had possessed exquisite and incomparable beauty. A languid body that could allure even the gods in heaven.

The remnants of her ageless beauty are still visible upon her. Her golden skin, silky black hair reminiscent of a serpent's body, eyes as deep as a lagoon and the captivating stature of a fairy remain almost unchanged. Only her wrinkled skin tells the tale that her beauty is but a gilded reflection of the past.

She had felt very awkward when she first draped herself in the native Tiwa *kasyong phaskai.* Whenever she ventured outside the palace, passersby would stare at her and whisper: 'Look, look, she resembles a goddess – like a *gossani* – she's wearing our native clothes, our *banath-bathu.* But she doesn't look like a *mekdo*' at all. She resembles us Laloongs.'

Amused by these remarks, her maid-in-waiting Xunzira, the *margi khamsamai*, had chimed in: 'Do you know what the people are saying, *Pai*? They think you don't look like a mekdo'.'

'What exactly is mekdo'?'

'An outsider, a foreigner. They are so happy to see you in our banat-bathu. You look ravishing in it, Pai.'

Konsari had laughed and said, 'Wearing the native clothes is not enough, Xunzira. It is also necessary to speak the native tongue. I intend to learn from you.'

'Please don't embarrass me, Pai. I'm an illiterate, ignorant *khorla.* I am a khamsamai working for Deoraja, our divine king, to attend to your needs. What can I teach you?'

'No, no, Xunzira, you must not speak that way. Is there a distinction between high and low in your society? If I am your pai, your elder sister, then you are my younger sister. What do you call your younger sister?'

'*Nannao.*'

'May I call you Nannao?'

'Of course. But how can a khamsamai be referred to as a nannao? It will make the deoraja cross with me.'

'Don't you think your deoraja is above such trivialities?' Konsari burst out laughing.

'Where will you find a *mathinegiri*, a keeper of the land, like our deoraja? He, like the *syonai* that appears in the night sky to illumine the earth like day, has also illuminated our *mathi*, our land. We are blessed to have him,' Xunzira said, joining both her palms in obeisance to the deoraja.

However, those incidents occurred many years later, long after Konsari's arrival in Gobha. Soon, her son Mriganko had to leave for the *dekachang*, which housed the unmarried young men of the kingdom.

During the period before and after Mriganko's birth, Konsari had never worn the kasyong phaskai. She used to wear *riha, mekhela* and *chador* made from fine cotton yarn, the traditional Assamese clothing. Sadhukumar had them woven and brought from the nearby villages by Xunzira. The shimmering mekhela and riha made from *paat* silk, embroidered with gold flowers, their dazzling threads deftly obtained from the larvae of caterpillars fed with *panchopa* leaves. Each strand, each fibre retained its rich glory, neatly tucked inside the cane chest given to Konsari by Sadhukumar. The sheer mist-like chador imported from Manipur, wrapped with a coarse-yarned *eri* scarf, was also neatly folded and placed in the same chest. In one corner lay the bejewelled gold ornaments wrapped in cotton cloth, untouched to this day.

Konsari has not shown them to anyone until now. She herself hasn't looked at them either. Most of the people who've seen those clothes are no longer alive. Sadhukumar, the king of Gobha, is one of the few remaining. Even Xunzira has never laid eyes on them. But then, she had arrived in Gobha much later. Sadhukumar had found her after searching for an interpreter who spoke the Laloong dialect for Konsari. Xunzira's first glimpse of Konsari was of a woman draped in a Laloong *Mang-anthla*, riha and eri scarf.

Hesitant, uneasy and lonely. She had stared at Konsari in awe from the doorway, forgetting to even pay her respects.

'What are you staring at? Go, go to Her Highness. Do as I have told you, understand?' Sadhukumar had said from the threshold. 'Your Highness, this is Xunzira,' he said, looking at Konsari and greeting her. 'She's fluent in both your and our dialects. She'll be by your side and help with your chores. If you have any trouble, please let me know.'

Then, leaving Xunzira with Konsari, Sadhukumar had walked out. At that time, he lived in the main palace of Gobha. A few days later, he went to live in the palace of Amsai Marjong, where he resides to this day. Occasionally, Sadhukumar visits the main palace where Konsari now lives, but he never enters her private chamber. He exits from the hall itself, like a guest. He talks to Konsari only when necessary. As does she with him.

It is a peculiar bond – born out of a combination of respect, friendship and affection, distant yet close, close yet distant.

Konsari frequently visits Amsai Marjong. Whenever she encounters confusion, fear or struggles to find solutions to her problems, she goes to Amsai Marjong. It is as if the solution to every hurdle, every obstacle that Konsari faces lies with Sadhukumar, a man with a mind as deep and steady as the Brahmaputra. She feels sheltered. Secure. As if her task is only to take from him. If it weren't for Sadhukumar's generosity, Konsari, bestowed with the honour of a queen despite not being one in reality, would have long been buried in anonymity and disgrace. She would have had to give up her royal lifestyle and the perks that come with it.

In fact, Konsari had set foot on the soil of Gobha as Sadhukumar's property. Her future at the palace was dependent on his whims. How weak she had been. How vulnerable and defenceless. If he had wished, Sadhukumar could have demanded her desirable body, commanded slavish loyalty from her, usurped all that a woman possesses.

But he did not.

He had left for Amsai Marjong, leaving behind a lifetime of mortification and endless agony for her. Konsari should have been able to surrender wholeheartedly without fear of force. Sadhukumar had earned her trust after a long trial period. Nonetheless, Konsari remained uneasy, unable to express her liking and gratitude for Sadhukumar before him. She couldn't bring herself to say anything to him. She couldn't ask for forgiveness or love – nothing at all. In two separate palaces, thousands of futile nights passed by, thousands of days of solitude.

During this period, she became a living legend among the non-Aryans north of the Brahmaputra. It was due to her physical attributes, distinct from those of non-Aryans, combined with her remarkable past and selfless present, that her unique persona slowly emerged. Even today, among the Laloongs, Jaintias, Mikirs, Kacharis, or for that matter in any of the royal families, no woman can rival Konsari's splendour. The only exception is in the neighbouring Bhuyan kingdoms, where there are a handful of women like her, but they remain confined to the four walls of their homes. Never seen in public.

Not Konsari. No one could restrict her movements. As a prominent woman in Gobha, she actively participated in the affairs of the kingdom. The women of Gobha, as a whole, led unrestrained lives, engaging in various outdoor activities, including farming. This is why Konsari had captured everybody's attention. They all stare at her, speechless in awe. Her tall stature, molten gold-like complexion, aquiline nose and elongated eyes, while wearing a kasyong phaskai, had earned Konsari the title of an unparalleled beauty.

Earlier, Xunzira would often say, 'It's easy to tell you are a mekdo'. What is the point of wearing our banath-bathu and adorning your ears and hands with ornaments like the *throng-phaila* of the Laloongs, Pai? Can clothes and ornaments truly alter your appearance?'

Konsari would laugh in amusement and reply, 'Just wait and see if I resemble a Laloong or not. Make sure you keep showing me everything the right way. Don't forget to correct me if I make any mistakes, Nannao.' She had never considered Xunzira her maid. In Konsari's unfamiliar, sad and lonely life, confined among the previously unseen and unknown people of Gobha, Xunzira, who was of the same age and came from a frontier village, entered like a breath of fresh air. Their ability to communicate in their own language made Konsari feel as if the vivacious Xunzira was her closest relative.

Every night, Konsari's heart would race, wary of hearing the sound of Sadhukumar's approaching footsteps. She almost insisted that Xunzira sleep beside her. When she gazed at the sleeping figure of Xunzira sprawled out on the floor at night, Konsari felt as if she was with God.

After that, her days changed. Sadhukumar left to live at Amsai Marjong. Konsari abandoned the riha-mekhela in favour of the kasyong phaskai, transforming into a solemn, responsible and cheerful woman fluent in the Laloong dialect. Despite her best efforts to blend into Tiwasha society, donning native costumes and ornaments, it was clear that she was not fully integrated among the Tiwashas. She remained different – an Aryan.

Now, age has caught up with Konsari. She is lovingly known as the 'abi', meaning grandma. But regardless of her age, she exudes the quintessential Aryan radiance.

Aryan … Aryan … How many springs had gone by since this word had last been heard. Perhaps Abi Konsari can hardly remember how many *Sogra* festivals, *Langkgon phuja*s or *Yangly* phujas were celebrated on this land. The days when the word 'Aryan' frequently resonated now felt like a dream. Even the once mighty King Pratapchandra appears unreal. The existence of Queen Chandraprabha, the royal *Mahishi*, within the innermost recess of the distant fortified golden kingdom of Pratappur, seems illusory – a dream.

Mahishi … Mahishi …

Aryan … Aryan …

Those two words were uttered by King Pratapchandra with

the air of sacred chants. He lovingly called his newlywed bride 'Mahishi'. Filled with pride for his Aryan ancestry as a *Kshatriya*, he often introduced himself arrogantly as the supreme leader of the Aryans. His entire existence revolved around his kingdom and Chandraprabha.

Pratapchandra possessed the typical Kshatriya obsession with expanding his kingdom's borders. As a result, he, a descendant of the Aryan–Kshatriya king Dharmapal who had immigrated from Gaur, had grown his kingdom from Biswanath to Majuli. He earned the loyalty of those living along the banks of the Dikhow river. However, this passion had somewhat faded after his marriage to Chandraprabha, who seemed to have captivated him with her irresistible beauty.

Chandraprabha's silk attire, adorned with intricate motifs of gold and silver that shimmered like sunshine, her gold jewellery studded with precious gems and her complexion resembling molten gold, created an ethereal magnificence that had deeply enchanted Pratapchandra's heart. He refused to travel anywhere without his queen, often even adjourning royal assemblies to spend time with Chandraprabha in their private quarters.

How young Chandraprabha must have been back then! Their wedding took place shortly after King Sompal's death. As a new bride entering the inner quarters of Pratapgarh, she was a simple, compliant, gentle and naive young girl on the cusp of adulthood, having just left her adolescent years behind. Raised with the belief that a husband should be worshipped like a god, Chandraprabha would touch his feet every morning before touching her own to the ground. She considered it her sacred duty to serve him with utmost devotion, and dedicated herself to his service. Under the overwhelming love of the mighty Pratapchandra, her blossoming body unfolded into a fully bloomed lotus. Pratapchandra himself transformed into a doting husband, an impassioned admirer of his mahishi.

Perhaps the passion was a little excessive. The emotions were also a little excessive. At times, Chandraprabha, who had grown up in a more open-minded environment, felt stifled by her husband's love. She would often ask herself, gazing at her reflection in the gold mirror, 'Am I really so beautiful?', wondering why the king was so fascinated with her. Every intimate moment overflowed with Pratapchandra's unbridled passion, adoring gaze and gushing compliments. He would often tell her, 'I have seen many beautiful women, Mahishi, but none as captivating as you. You are unique. Extraordinary. Matchless. Are the fairies of Amaravati more gorgeous than you? Perhaps not.'

Though secretly pleased with such lavish praise, the maiden Chandraprabha would almost faint from embarrassment. 'I'm more fortunate than you, O Son of Aryans. Not many women have the good fortune to be married to a handsome, heroic king,' she would respond.

Chandraprabha's humility and contentment brought satisfaction to Pratapchandra. The pride of possessing and pleasing a sensual woman with his youthful manhood radiated on his face. He would tell her, 'You deserve the honour of being the empress of this vast empire, Mahishi. You are queen to the most powerful ruler, Pratapchandra. Through you, the descendant of King Dharmapal will enter this world, carrying forth the lineage of our glorious Aryan ancestry. Prepare yourself to bring even greater glory to the Jitari dynasty with your virtuosity and magnificence.'

Embracing Queen Chandraprabha, Pratapchandra drowned her in love. However, beneath that love, the arrogance of a Kshatriya male concealed a hint of insecurity. Some unjustified suspicion. Pratapchandra did not seem very sure about his own masculinity or his ability to satisfy her. On occasion, his excessively possessive nature revealed traces of suspicion, but Chandraprabha accepted it as an expression of his intense love.

Often, when the king would abruptly leave a royal assembly and enter their private chambers, Chandraprabha noticed a twinkle of amusement in the eyes of the servants. She had seen the queen mother's eyes fill with irritation and displeasure. Although it filled Chandraprabha with embarrassment, she couldn't help it. For she herself was completely overwhelmed by Pratapchandra's manliness and striking looks.

'Abi,' the voice of a margi khamsamai snaps Konsari back to the present. To another birth. To another life. Here, there is no Chandraprabha adorned in silk mekhela-chador. Only Abi Konsari, donned in the kasyong phaskai.

'Xunzira Asi has arrived,' the khamsamai whispers with her head bowed.

The words hit Konsari like a blazing arrow, swift and piercing. Though Xunzira is her contemporary, she is commonly known as '*asi*'. Xunzira had gradually become 'aunt' to everyone.

For many years now, Xunzira has been living as a companion to the queen of Khola, Gangavati, rather than in the palace of Gobha. She has been taking care of Gangavati's son Jokanko since he was a baby.

Konsari herself had asked Xunzira to assist Gangavati. At that time, she hadn't become 'abi'. But her dream of becoming an abi struggled to emerge from a bag of sorrow.

It feels as if a devastating thunderstorm has trampled over Konsari.

'Abi,' the margi khamsamai calls once more.

'Go and fetch Xunzira.'

'*Do*', Abi,' the khamsamai nods and leaves. Abi Konsari rises from the bed, absentmindedly tying her hair into a knot as she stands by the window.

The palace is devoid of activity today. The courtyard lies deserted. The grief-stricken people residing near the palace remain confined within their homes. Their beloved King Mriganko's headless body has been reduced to ashes. When the corpse was taken to the cremation ground – the *hathama* – for the funeral, it felt as if the entire kingdom was crumbling in anguish. The area around the hathama turned into a mountain of timber and bamboo offerings from the people. Initially, when *kengadi*, the appointed mortician, lit the funeral pyre, the crowd was still, overwhelmed with sorrow. But then tears flowed and chests were pounded with grief.

But Abi Konsari remained silent.

She sat motionless in her bedchamber within the palace of Gobha. Since learning of Mriganko's death, Konsari had remained in the same position, without eating or sleeping. An inexplicable emptiness had seized her movements, and she felt as if her will to live had vanished.

As the head priests of the villages, including the *loro, jela baro, chamadi's chang doloi* and *chaang maji*, arrived to discuss the karam with Konsari, they left without being able to meet her. Konsari continued to sit in silence.

If it hadn't been for Xunzira, Konsari would have sat there indefinitely. Hearing Xunzira's name seemed to bring her back to the present, yet a strange uneasiness lingers within her. Why has Xunzira arrived? What more can be said or done for Konsari? Hasn't her meagre source of happiness turned to ashes with the cremation of Mriganko's headless body?

Over the years, Xunzira had maintained a connection between Gobha and Khola. But it went beyond that – Xunzira was the bridge between Gangavati, the queen of Khola, and Konsari, the abi of Kumoi Boghora. She conveyed Konsari's affection, blessings and advice to Gangavati, and in return relayed Gangavati's conflicts, anguish and queries back to Konsari.

But what has Xunzira brought today? What is it? Is it the unburned head of the body that has just been consigned to flames? A gesture to fuel the sacrificial fire burning in Konsari's heart?

What is Abi Konsari to do now? How will she deal with Xunzira, the very person who had nurtured the murderer, Jokanko?

'Pai,' Xunzira's voice quivers, drawing Konsari's attention. Dressed in a faded kasyong phaskai, Xunzira looks worn out, her face clouded with misery. It seems as though countless tears and wails of anguish are ready to burst forth at any moment.

Konsari moves closer to Xunzira, shifting away from the window. Despite her sisterly love, Xunzira has never forgotten her position.

As she approaches, Xunzira sinks to her knees. 'Pai, I failed to make a human out of Jokanko – look what he's done. He has destroyed everything.'

The dam of tears give way, and Xunzira sobs uncontrollably. Konsari stands motionless for a long time, staring at her weeping figure. Let her cry. Let her cry herself out of the heartache she is burdened with, Konsari thinks, although with an inexplicable tinge of envy.

A margi khamsamai could express emotions freely in front of her mistress, lightening the burden of sorrow through tears. But as the abi, Konsari can never afford such a privilege. The people of the kingdom would follow suit, causing chaos. The agitated masses might even attack the relatively weak and sparsely populated kingdom of Khola. They could harm Jokanko's maternal family members as well. Years ago, Konsari had used immense patience to avert a looming conflict led by Sadhukumar. Now, she had to employ the same patience to prevent further bloodshed.

Gently placing her withered, flaxen hands on Xunzira's back, Konsari says calmly, 'Rise, Nannao. Stop crying.' A khamsamai places a floral-patterned carpet on the floor. 'Get up, Nannao, and sit on the *amsa*. Aikon, go fetch some water for asi. Or perhaps you'd like some *joo*, Xunzira? It will give you strength. Aikon, bring some joo – some rice beer – instead.'

'Shall I bring some for you, Abi? You haven't even had a sip of water until now,' the khamsamai says.

Konsari remains silent, and after some time, Khamsamai Aikon leaves the room. A while later, Konsari speaks slowly, 'Nannao, wipe your tears – look at your pai. Is there anyone more doomed than your pai? Have you ever seen your pai cry? You should stop crying. Don't you remember what I had told you when I left you in Khola after Jokanko's birth? "He is a boy without a father. There is no one like him in Laloong society. Bring him up with love and care, and teach him the ways of our people." I know you did your job well. Jokanko killed Mriganko, but it's not his fault, Nannao. He did not know the truth, did he?'

'I know, Pai, I know. Yet I want to curse him. I had also brought up Mriganko. Oh, how dear he was to me.'

'I know, Nannao. I know how you feel. That's why I believe you can understand everything. You should be by Jokanko's side during this time.'

'I don't have your endurance, Pai. My poor child had to die because of him. My *sajjoh* Gangavati is also gone. Cursing Jokanko until her last breath, she passed away, unable to bear this grief.' Xunzira breaks down in sobs once again.

'What are you saying, Nannao? Gangavati—' Konsari's voice chokes, as another wave of overwhelming sorrow crashes over her heart.

That beautiful girl couldn't bear the grief and left this world?

Countless memories and images of sad and happy moments rush through Konsari's mind. Like a rock, she stands near the weeping Xunzira.

After a while, the lithified Konsari comes to life again. She puts her arms around Xunzira, helping her stand, and slowly says, 'Wipe your tears, Nannao. Tell me what happened. Here – come sit next to me on the bed. Come.'

Helping her sit on the bed, Konsari calmly waits for Xunzira to collect herself. Finally, Xunzira looks up, not even attempting to wipe her tears, and says, 'Sajjoh Gangavati told him about you. About some of the old days, too. But Pai, she couldn't finish the story. She didn't even allow him the right to perform her karam. For the past two days, he has only been drinking joo and crying uncontrollably. He has gone mad and is talking nonsense. He said he would come to see you today. I woke up early in the morning and hurriedly arranged for an elephant to bring him here. The people won't spare him once he arrives, will they? They'll finish him. Besides, he is completely drunk. He won't be able to defend himself. In Khola, people have come to know everything. He hasn't even stepped out of the palace. He is just drinking and crying, drinking and crying.'

Before Xunzira could finish her sentence, uproar echoes from outside the palace.

Xunzira and Konsari exchange helpless glances as a breathless khamsamai rushes into the room. 'Abi, there's a huge commotion outside. People are saying the king of Khola is on his way here. Our guards have gone to kill him.'

Without saying a word, Konsari runs outside as if possessed. Xunzira follows suit. By the time Konsari reaches the scene, the palace guards have surrounded Jokanko and his bodyguards.

The king of Khola, intoxicated and sorrow-stricken, stands bravely, surrounded by his skilled bodyguards amidst the chaotic scene. Abi Konsari and Xunzira rush into the midst of the turmoil. 'Stop! Stop the fight!' Konsari cries out in despair. Jokanko, upon noticing Konsari and Xunzira, stares at them in silence, his weapon ready. It is a fleeting moment of distraction.

But he remains alert enough to narrowly escape a severe wound as a soldier's sharp *khangra* slips past his shoulder.

'Don't kill, don't kill!' Konsari and Xunzira scream simultaneously.

Soldiers on both sides cease fighting and turn back, stunned. Konsari runs frantically and grasps Jokanko's blood-stained hand. Then, looking at the soldiers who are rooted to the ground, she tearfully pleads, 'Don't kill him. Please don't kill him. He is one of our own.'

One of our own!

The guards stand motionless, forgetting to lower their weapons as they stare at Konsari. Jokanko gazes at her, his intoxicated, sleepless eyes filled with a storm of emotions.

Konsari says, in a calm and grave voice, 'Get off the horse, *Syu*.'

Jokanko mechanically dismounts, still looking at Konsari.

'No questions. All that is for later. Follow me.' She holds one of his hands and they walk into the palace together, leaving behind a crowd frozen in shock.

TWO

'*Aaiama* …!'

Jokanko winces in pain. Konsari's hand pauses as she applies an herbal paste to his wound. She briefly looks up at him before resuming. 'The bleeding has stopped somehow. Is it hurting too much?' she asks.

'No … what medicine is this?' he replies softly, keeping the unbearable pain to himself.

'Just bear it for a while. The pain will subside.'

Jokanko doesn't say anything, gritting his teeth as he watches Konsari, who is fully absorbed in smearing the herbal paste.

This is his Abi Konsari – lovely, affectionate and dignified – *his* abi. She lived so close in Gobha, yet he has never heard a whisper of her all these years. No one has ever told him about her.

For as long as he can remember, he'd known he didn't have a father. Until now. Not even in his dreams could he have imagined having relatives outside of Khola.

Was there anyone he could call his own, aside from his mother? There was Asi Xunzira, who was like his family. Perhaps even more so. But did his mother ever care about him? Did she worry about him?

Since he was a child, he had seen his mother keeping to herself most of the time. She didn't say much to him. Despite being the ruling queen, he noticed that she showed no interest in the affairs of the state. The head priests of the villages made all administrative decisions informally, seeking approvals from the queen when necessary. With trustworthy army chiefs and other officials, as well as a generally tight-knit society, operations sailed along smoothly.

But then rulers typically depended on priests to take decisions in their society. The priests, in turn, were expected to abide by the wishes of the elders. Without the support of the chaang dolois or chaang majis, who were the officers in charge of the dekachang, they were powerless. Almost all Laloong states followed this custom. The civilians were the rulers. This way, the kingdom managed to run itself tangle-free, despite the queen's apathy.

But even when she was alive, Gangavati lived as if she didn't exist. Leaving Jokanko in Xunzira's care, she seemed to have detached herself from the world, entering a mysterious realm of seclusion.

Xunzira had been there for Jokanko since he was a child. The young boy had never sought his mother's company. He loved her, but their relationship remained somewhat formal and distant. As he grew older, he realized he needed permission to visit his mother and had to approach her with a certain level of dignity.

This environment had significantly shaped Jokanko's upbringing. Unlike other children, he didn't spend his childhood in the *samadi*, the boys' camp. Instead, he trained under the army general, learning the art of warfare and weaponry. It was as if his youth had been spent in a military training camp, the royal child missing out on the typical lessons the boys learnt from their elders at the dekachang or samadi. Most of his knowledge about society, societal behaviour, culture, customs and the ways of life had come from Xunzira, who seemed determined to educate him in these matters.

Jokanko had found contentment in his isolated, nature-centric life, never questioning it.

But then, his dying mother had thrust a spear into his heart, leaving a multitude of unanswered questions tormenting him. The realization of his uncertain identity unravelled his sanity. The mere existence of a father, a brother, grandparents – possibilities that had never crossed his mind. No one had ever mentioned them, and he had never imagined having a sense of belonging to anyplace other than Khola.

Why had nobody told him? What was the secret behind his birth? Why had he never seen his father? Why had his abi and *azo* never visited Khola? Where was his younger brother? Who else was out there? Where were his kin?

Questions … Questions …

No, no, not questions. It still feels like hundreds of parasites are gnawing at Jokanko, eating away at his peace of mind, his sleep – as if his heart has been detached from his body, drowning in a river of tears. The notion of death looms over him, eroding his will to live, extinguishing his thirst for victory and the vibrancy of youth.

'Abi,' he calls, his voice heavy with sorrow.

'Yes, Jokanko.'

'There is so much that I have to ask you.'

'I know.' Konsari sets aside the bowl of medicine, places a few *joormoni* leaves over the treated wound and covers it with a pliant banana leaf roasted over fire. Tying a thin string made from the outer coverings of the banana plant, she says, 'You can ask whatever weighs on your mind, but first, rest. I'll send you some medicine to ease your pain and help you relax. I need to go out and address our people. They are feeling great pain and anger. If I don't explain everything to them, they might kill you.'

'Let them kill me, Abi. What is there left to live for anyway?' Jokanko asks solemnly.

Konsari takes a moment to look at him before sharing her thoughts. 'You are in the grip of grief, Jokanko. The joo has obscured your judgement and allowed these thoughts to surface. True courage is in living life to the fullest until the end. When you gain the knowledge you seek, you'll find your way. Do you know what I believe? Grief is like hyacinths floating down the river. You can choose to gather them to the side, which can feel overwhelming. Or you can step back, observe from a distance and gradually watch them drift out of your sight.'

Jokanko remains silent as Konsari leaves him. Reclining on the bed, he takes in the room's simple yet elegant decor. In one corner, a bouquet of *kuthimali* flowers is held within a vase, their faded petals still emanating a sweet fragrance.

This scent, common to the woods and villages in Khola, was familiar to Jokanko. Xunzira had taken charge of all palace matters, a responsibility Jokanko's mother had entrusted to her.

Why had his mother acted in this way?

What caused her indifference?

The loneliness?

What was the source of her sadness?

These questions had swirled like a whirlpool in Jokanko's mind. He had asked his asi but received no answers. In frustration, he had turned to joo, shouting at Xunzira and crying. Eventually, he had resolved to visit the kingdom where he had caused a commotion by slaying their king and met Abi Konsari there. He needed to the meaning behind his mother's spoken and unspoken words.

Jokanko knew the citizens or soldiers of Gobha might kill him on sight. Nevertheless, he had embarked on this journey. He understood that his own clan, generally mild and simple, could become ferocious when provoked. He had sensed the commotion inside the palace of Khola when they saw him riding away alone, but he had not let it deter him. Unanswered questions consumed his mind.

'Jokanko,' Xunzira's voice brings him back to the present.

'Oh, Asi.'

'Finish this medicine. Your abi sent it. Finish it and get some rest,' Xunzira says, extending the bowl to him.

Jokanko accepts the bowl and says, 'Asi?'

'Oy.'

'Can I ask you a question?'

'You've never needed my permission to ask a question,' Xunzira responds weakly.

'Asi, I never did. But everything has been turned upside down. I feel so alone in this world.'

'*Paba*, my love, you shouldn't speak like this,' Xunzira says, on the verge of tears. She holds one of Jokanko's hands in both of hers affectionately. 'Everyone is here. I am here. Your Abi is here. Deoraja azo is here. And many, many other kinsmen. The *korakhi*, the protector of this realm, Fa Mahadeo the sun god is here. Aai Basundhari and Aai Kalikha, too.'

Despite his pain, Jokanko smiles. Xunzira Asi is extraordinarily gentle with him.

'Truly, Asi, you are so kind. What would you do if you were to suffer like me?'

'I am not sure. Finish the medicine and go to sleep. You'll need a lot of strength to talk to your abi when she arrives,' she jokes.

This was Xunzira. Like a light-winged seed. She could sway in a gentle breeze. A few drops of water could merge her with the soil.

'Don't leave, Asi. Stay right here. I don't want to be alone,' Jokanko says somewhat awkwardly.

'Alright, then. Now finish this.'

Jokanko drinks the medicine in one gulp and drifts into slumber. Xunzira sits near him, her heart swaying with emotion. Meanwhile, Konsari is revealing the contents of the casket concealing the Khola king's identity in front of the anxious crowd that has assembled in front of the palace again.

By the time Konsari returns, it is midnight. Jokanko is in a deep sleep induced by the joo and also due to physical and mental exhaustion. Even in his slumber, he occasionally lets out soft groans. Xunzira, sitting on the amsa with her head resting on the bed, is fast asleep.

Watching the two of them silently from the doorway, Konsari's heart is on the verge of falling apart under the weight of love and grief. Besides them, Ratnasinha, Samol and Sadhukumar – who else in this world can she call her own?

But then, isn't the whole kingdom hers? All her subjects hold her the dearest of the dear. As does she when it comes to her people. But there is a deeper level of affection – one that only has room for those whose faces float before you on closing your eyes.

Until recently, there was Gangavati. There was Xunzira's husband, Phuleswar *barika*. Mriganko, too, and even King Pratapsingh. They've all held a special place in her heart.

Even though she had never met Jokanko, she also saved a large part of her heart for him.

And why wouldn't she?

Wasn't he her grandson? Her heroic grandson? More so, because Jokanko is the tragic result of a social custom, being ruthlessly forsaken as motherless and fatherless.

Although Konsari had been separated from him all these years, she kept herself informed of his upbringing, thanks to Xunzira. She loved Jokanko with all her heart. This was why she is able to forgive him, the man the people of Gobha were calling a murderer. Despite losing everything, she is still able to say to her nannao, 'What is Jokanko's fault?'

And Xunzira? She is an extraordinary woman indeed! Konsari has never witnessed nor heard of a Tiwasha betraying their masters. Perhaps the seeds of betrayal cannot sprout in Laloong blood. Xunzira's loyalty is unparalleled.

When Sadhukumar had first brought her to Konsari, she was a young woman whose parents had succumbed to an epidemic that ravaged her village and claimed many lives. She was one of the few survivors. It had seemed as though Xunzira and Konsari were in the same boat.

Sad. Disillusioned. Lonely.

Forlorn yet steady.

Disheartened yet cheerful.

Lonesome yet lively.

During those days, an instinctive kinship had formed between the two women. After she had spent a few days at the Gobha palace, the headman of her clan arrived to take Xunzira back. But she refused to go. By that time, she had transformed into Konsari's younger sister. Into her nannao.

Confused by Xunzira's refusal to go back with the *jelabaro*, Konsari had rushed to Amsai Marjong to seek Sadhukumar's advice. He reassured her, saying, 'The headman is fulfilling his duty as a leader of the tribe, Your Highness. If Xunzira is reluctant to leave with him, we should not force her. She understands your language, your ways and customs. You have also accepted her as your sister, which makes her one of us. Her responsibility lies entirely with us now.'

Konsari had returned, free of all worries. Xunzira stayed back, settling into her role as a member of Gobha's royal family.

When the topic of Xunzira's marriage came up, Mriganko was only two years old. There was no custom of child marriage in their society. As for Konsari, she had been married before reaching puberty. But her *borbiya*, or actual marriage, took place afterwards. On the other hand, Xunzira had remained unmarried even at the age of seventeen or eighteen, which was common for the girls in this society.

Sadhukumar had started to search for a suitable match for her, intending to get her married and then send her back. But Xunzira had bravely told Konsari, 'Pai, I will not leave you to get married. Please find me a *gobhia*, so that we can both serve you for the rest of our lives.'

'Who do you mean by a gobhia?' Konsari had asked, surprised.

'I don't know. Ask someone else,' Xunzira had responded and fled, red-faced with embarrassment. Later, Konsari had learned from others that while it was traditional among Laloongs for the bride to leave her home after marriage, the custom Xunzira had mentioned allowed the husband to live in his wife's house. A hardworking man was always preferred in such arrangements.

Phuleswar, an industrious young man, was chosen as Xunzira's gobhia. She moved out of the khamsamai quarters and into a house with him in the palace premises. It was there that their son, Samol, was born. When he had grown into a young man, Konsari had sent Xunzira to Gangavati. However, Samol chose to stay back and became one of the most devoted bodyguards in the kingdom, remaining by Mriganko's side.

Xunzira had not insisted that he accompany her. By then, Phuleswar had also passed away. Perhaps that is why this life change had felt welcome. Although Konsari never saw her shedding tears for Phuleswar, she could sense Xunzira's anguish. Konsari had hoped that once Xunzira reached Khola, her pain would abate upon the sight of the infant Jokanko.

Just then, the night sentry's voice rings out loudly, startling Konsari.

It is well past midnight now.

It had taken a long time to calm the agitated crowd.

A great deal had to be explained to all of them.

Truths that had never been shared with anyone in public.

The people listened to her in a daze, as if hearing a tale from a far-off land. They did not know whether to laugh, cry or feel angry. They sat in stunned silence.

'Don't harm him. Show him your love. What does he know? Would he have killed your king if he had known? Could he? He is consumed by deep sorrow, you know. Let the karam go on. We will invite the jelaboros, loros and dolois to discuss the next steps. We must tell the truth now. After the karam, we'll invite the barikas and come together,' she suggested.

Leaving the people in a sea of shock, confusion, grief and bewilderment, Konsari has come back to the palace. But nobody can see the inferno of grief blazing through her heart.

'Nannao … Nannao … wake up—' Konsari shakes Xunzira, who wakes up in a frenzy.

'Come on, get up quietly. Don't wake him. Come outside, I want to know everything that happened at Khola – I need to prepare myself to answer all his questions when he gets up, you know. But before that, I have to know everything, Nannao.' Before walking away, she places a hand over Jokanko's body.

'Ah, his body is burning,' she exclaims. Instantly, the face of the wounded King Pratapchandra, lying in the kingdom of Pratappur, his body hot with fever, flashes in front of her. She trembles at the thought of the fate that awaits them.

'We'll talk later, Nannao. Place an earthen jar of water with a hole in the bottom over his forehead to lower his temperature. Our healer must be notified first thing in the morning. The cut from the iron khangra is deep – medicine alone will not suffice.' She sits near the fever-stricken Jokanko, caressing his brow.

The wild roosters from the distant hills begin to crow.

THREE

'Asi.' Jokanko looks around – his eyes unfocused and red from the fever – uncertain of his surroundings. The pain from the knife wound is excruciating, and he feels extremely weak.

Jokanko slept under the light of the earthen lamps on stands. He recalls someone dripping water on his forehead. Someone forcing medicine – bitter and acerbate – down his throat at regular intervals. Someone else touching his shoulders with soft, wet fingers. His old dressing being removed and fresh medicine being applied. Whenever he groaned, someone caressing his brow, asking, 'Is the pain terrible?'

Who was the shadowy lady? Mother? No, not Mother; she is no longer here. She has left this world because of him, overwhelmed with grief. Before leaving, though, she had cursed him: 'The weapon with which you have committed this sin will not be within your reach in times of danger. When you die, you will not be able to use these sinful hands to drink water. You will die drinking water like a cow. You—'

'Asi, asi—'

He struggles to sit up. The pain is suffocating.

'What is it, Jokanko? What's wrong? Are you having a nightmare? Look, your asi, your Xunzira Asi, is right here. Sleep … go to sleep … don't get up.'

Exhausted, he collapses again. An anxious face is hovering over him. He trains his eyes on it. Who is it? The face looks familiar, but where has he seen it before? When?

Konsari wipes his face with a soft, damp towel, gently placing it over his eyes. He lets out a long sigh. Everything is growing clearer. His memories are coming back.

Two hot tears roll down his cheeks. Konsari wipes them away, her own eyes welling up.

Xunzira has already begun to cry quietly. Unwilling to let Konsari see her tears, she tries to hold them back. Ignoring her own grief, she sits beside the wounded Jokanko.

For four long days and five long nights, Konsari and Xunzira have stuck to Jokanko's side as he lay comatose from a fever. It has finally subsided today, with the wound showing signs of healing. But blood loss, coupled with the illness, has weakened him considerably. Besides the royal healer's medicine and prescribed diet, he hasn't eaten anything.

In the open space outside the palace, awnings are being built. The karam rituals are to begin the next day. The subordinate kings, their representatives and rulers of frontier kingdoms, such as the Mikir, Kachari, Jaintia and the Bhuyan kings, are expected to arrive. The village chiefs from all the Laloong villages, as well as Gobha's own villagers and members of its clan, are supposed to attend. King Ratnasinha was said to travel from Baidyagarh. So were boro jelas of various communities.

Those responsible for preparing the joo – rice beer – are cleaning and setting up large vessels inside the palace. The *kra-kurmis* – cooks – were scrubbing clean the large *midoohs* – cooking utensils – needed for the occasion. The barikas have gone to invite people for the karam.

Sadhukumar has been overseeing all the arrangements since his arrival. Even though he is heartbroken at the idea of performing his son's funeral rites, he maintains a calm facade, keeping his emotions concealed. He no longer sleeps inside the main palace, choosing to travel to and from Amsai Marjong, which leaves him with little time to rest. Every time he arrives, he asks about Jokanko, talks about important matters with Konsari and then leaves.

Konsari is the only one who knows why the deoraja decided to relocate to Amsai Marjong. But she has remained silent, as has the old king. The public was told years ago that he left to ensure the smooth operation of the vast kingdom. Since then, whenever he visits, he stays in the foyer and avoids the inner chambers unless absolutely necessary.

He had made an exception once, when Konsari was preparing to leave for Pratappur. They had a brief exchange after arranging the boats, men, elephants, and other necessities for her journey.

Those were days of distress.

These are also difficult times.

That is why Sadhukumar has returned to supervise the karam for his late son.

Mriganko was Sadhukumar's son indeed. Sadhukumar had publicly declared before the boro jelas, *sokha jelas, hari kunworis, loros* and *doskhol–barokhol* headmen while sitting at the *number*, with the little boy on his lap, that he had adopted Mriganko as his own. By now perhaps many people have forgotten that the prince was adopted.

'Abi,' Jokanko calls out. Konsari leans over him.

'Would you like some water?'

'Yes.'

Xunzira goes away and returns with a bamboo tube filled with water from an earthen pot. She hands it to Konsari, who pours it slowly into Jokanko's mouth.

'Does it still hurt, Jokanko?' she asks tenderly.

'A little. I could not feel it when I fell asleep last night.'

'It wasn't last night, paba; it's been four nights. Your body was burning with fever. The temperature has gone down today at last.'

For a while, Jokanko remained silent. 'Abi,' he says softly.

'What is it? Are you hungry?'

'My heart is filled with overwhelming grief, Abi.'

'I know, Syu. But don't torture yourself with these thoughts. Can anyone undo what has happened?'

'Abi, why did those incidents happen in the first place? Why wasn't I informed of anything? Why had I been kept in the dark? Do you think I would have done something if I had known ...' Jokanko's voice chokes with emotion.

'I know, Syu. You don't have to say anything. I understand your pain, as does your Asi. It's not your fault. Whatever happened was destined for us, in our *kharam*. I will explain everything to you. But first, eat something. You will feel better. How will you face grief or your enemies if you don't regain your strength?'

'I will never fight again, Abi. I will never fight ... never fight with anyone,' he cries.

Konsari wipes away his tears gently. 'It's alright, you don't have to fight. Now, try to sit up.'

As she helps him into a sitting position, Xunzira appears with steaming-hot, fragrant *tuloshi joha* rice, dry fish cooked in spinach along with a few other dishes.

Jokanko's stomach grumbles with hunger. His head is bowed in thanks to Abi and Asi. When he is hungry, he becomes agitated and weak. He dislikes all foods except rice. He insists on rice, even if it is simply seasoned with salt, alkali or herbs.

Xunzira is well aware of his preferences, having supervised the timely serving of rice at the Khola palace. She has continued the old practice during Jokanko's feverish state, cooking rice and keeping it warm over burnt charcoal until late at night. Today, she has prepared rice for him, even if he does not want to eat anything.

Such was the depth of her affection for him. Who is he to her otherwise? Is she more important to him than his mother?

After all, hasn't his mother cursed him before leaving this world, without any consideration for how he will bear its weight for the rest of his life? Xunzira, on the other hand, is feeding him piping hot rice with her wrinkled old hand.

And Konsari is gently fanning cool air over Jokanko's head. She isn't used to fanning anyone; usually, the margi khamsamais huddle to fan her. The fan makes an unusual sound when handled by unaccustomed hands. There is no rhythm to the breeze either.

Oh, he had such a caring abi!

Such a loving abi. Why didn't his mother tell him about her? Why didn't she tell him anything?

Xunzira leaves after gathering the utensils and wiping Jokanko's lips clean. The Khola king looks at Konsari, who is mixing something in a metal bowl in one corner of the room.

'Abi.'

'I'll be right there, Syu. Let me prepare your medicine.'

As Jokanko observes her, his heart skips a beat.

How different his dear abi is! He'd never seen anyone like her in Khola. Her appearance is so different. So striking. She is not wearing many ornaments – just a pair of gold earrings and a red-sandal necklace of pot-shaped beads. She wears a black kasyong phaskai, like every other Laloong woman, but even in this simple outfit, she looks stunning.

Such solemnity! Such composure!

To think his mother had kept him away from her. She had withheld the details of his birth, depriving her child of his land and family.

From childhood to youth.

All she has left for him is a seed of anguish. It has now birthed offshoots that have grown into a tangled web of suffering around him.

So, what is he to do now?

What is he supposed to do with his tainted hands? He had spilled blood on the borders of a sleepy village atop the Dhoumora hills with these. With a single stroke of his gleaming, sharp sword, he had severed Mriganko's head from his body.

Ah! How strangely calm King Mriganko had appeared in the face of his impending death. He had no way of defending himself against Jokanko's unexpected attack. His gaze had been fixed on his opponent before they became unusually calm.

Moments before his death, King Mriganko had recognized Jokanko. His eyes remained serene even after his lifeless body fell to the ground. The young king had closed Mriganko's eyes before he took the head along to show his mother.

Unbeknownst to Jokanko, his actions and the sight of the decapitated head would unleash a lifetime of agony for him. The evil spirits began to swirl in his veins, intoxicated with cruel excitement. He had been so consumed by his victories that he had failed to consider the devastating consequences of his actions.

'Are you still in pain, Syu?' Konsari asks, a bowl in one hand and the other on his brow. Jokanko stares at her, startled. He gently lifts her hand and places it between his own. Slowly and clearly, he asks, 'Who are you, Abi?'

Konsari locks her gaze on him, a sad and grim smile on her lips. 'I'm your abi. Is there anything else you need to know, Syu?'

Jokanko looks her in the eyes. 'Surely you understand whether there is a need or not, Abi,' he says, his voice dull and tired.

'You've asked a difficult question, Syu. From one point of view, it might be better if you didn't know everything – after all, what happened cannot be undone, can it? Then again, I believe that once you learn the truth, you might find some relief. You will also realize what needs to be done.'

'I have to know everything, Abi. I asked Xunzira Asi, but she refused to answer my questions. Please do not remain silent. The wound on my arm might have healed, but the wound in my mind has not. Do you realize, Abi, that when my mother saw my father's head in my hands, she cursed me through her tears? My afa and maah have died because of me. Do you understand the depths of my anguish?

Jokanko's emotions were unfathomable. With his life turned upside down by divine providence, his restless hands are now trying to unlock the closed doors of her heart. Memories that Konsari carefully filed away years ago are stirring a whirlpool inside her mind now.

She realizes she has no choice at this point. Jokanko needs to understand everything. She needs to tell him a lot more than what she did to the crowd outside. The devastated young man, desperate to discover his origins, needs her guidance to go into the past.

Konsari pulls her hands away from Jokanko's. 'Get up, Syu. Take the medicine. I am going to tell you everything.'

Jokanko downs the medicine in one gulp. After setting the bowl on a nearby wooden table, Konsari retrieves the silk mekhela and riha with gold embroidered flowers from a cylindrical bamboo box stored inside a cane chest in the corner of the room. She also pulls out a mist-like transparent chador wrapped in an eri shawl and a bundle of ornaments. Jokanko is watching her keenly.

She lays out the items in front of his unwavering gaze. 'You know, Jokanko, when I had first arrived in Gobha, this is how I used to dress. A large chest in my room at Pratappur used to be crammed with piles and piles of such clothes and ornaments.'

'Your home was in Pratappur? The one on the north bank?' exclaimed Jokanko.

'Yes, Syu, I was known as Chandraprabha back then. I was King Pratapchandra's wife.'

'And what about the king of Gobha, my *azo*?'

'I will have to dig deeper to answer that question, Syu. That story can be told another time. But first, you must meet your brother.'

'My brother? Where is my brother?' Jokanko tries to sit up, but Konsari forces him to lie down again.

'He is right here. Lie down. Do not get up. He has already arrived. Shall I call him?'

'Where does my brother live, abi?'

'A long way from here – in Komota. His name is Ratnasinha.' At this very moment, King Ratnasinha appears in the doorway. He looks at Jokanko with ruddy, intoxicated eyes and asks, 'May I come in?'

The Khola king stays quiet. He stares at Ratnasinha without blinking once.

A brother! *This* was his brother!

'Come on in, dear, come inside. This is your home. You are not a guest, are you?' Konsari's tone is tinged with sadness.

'I am a man without roots, not a guest.' Ratnasinha laughs, brightening his red face.

Ratnasinha's laughter appears to hold a deeper meaning. Jokanko has the impression that he is crying. He feels the weight of a heavy rock instantly lifting from his heart. It's as if this strikingly handsome young man, dressed clothes embroidered with gemstones, is reaching out to him from the depths of despair.

Outside, people have begun to cut down bamboo poles to make awnings for the karam. Jokanko and Ratnasinha sit down together with Xunzira, as Konsari begins her journey into the past.

FOUR

'Our great-grandfather Dharmapal came from Korno Suborno to become the king of Kamrup. He established the capital of Kamrup at Godondo Mountains, or Kuberachal, on the north bank of the Brahmaputra. Korno Suborno was actually a part of Gourh, earning him the moniker Gourheswar. Since he was the king of Kamrup, he was also called Kameswar or Kamrupeswar. The Jitari clan is well-known on both banks of the Brahmaputra and throughout the entire western kingdom of Gourh. Revered. Always keep in mind the glorious history of our dynasty in whatever you do, dear daughter-in-law,' says Yajnavati, the great queen mother.

In the bedchambers of Queen Mother Yajnavati, inside the royal palace of Pratappur, a teenage empress, Chandraprabha, is sitting on a gold-inlaid low seat. Behind her, the queen mother is coiling gold thread around Chandraprabha's long hair and twisting it into a knot. A silver tray with gold hairpins, a small gold comb and many other ornaments, including a *kopali* worn on the forehead, has been placed atop a wooden table with carved ornamental details.

Chandraprabha holds a mirror studded with precious stones and gems in her hand. Yajnavati invites Chandraprabha to her bed suite on most evenings, where the queen fashions her hair in various styles and imparts wisdom gained from her mother-in-law and her own experience. The queen mother talks about topics ranging from make-up and health to housekeeping and politics, determined to assist her son's newlywed wife in upholding the traditions of their dynasty and equipping her with a broad range of knowledge. The new bride has just crossed adolescence to step into her youth. Her marriage to Pratapchandra has brought her to Pratappur recently, so the queen mother also spends some of her early afternoons training Chandraprabha.

But not regularly.

Most of Chandraprabha's days are spent with Pratapchandra, her husband and the king of Pratappur. Whenever the king is in the capital, he prefers to spend his leisure time in her company, and if he has to go somewhere, he takes her along. Today, King Rajdhar of the neighbouring Bhuyan kingdom of Tembuwani has arrived, and Yajnavati is pleased that it will be late by the time her son returns from his official obligations. Pratapchandra and Chandraprabha had been away from the capital for the past few days, taking a royal tour of the kingdom after offering prayers at the Lord Mahabhairav temple. It has been days since Yajnavati has met Chandraprabha.

Weary of her solitary days, the queen mother is relieved to be in her daughter-in-law's company. After coiffing Chandraprabha's hair into a bun, the queen mother engages her in conversation. She deeply cares about Chandraprabha and sometimes feels that this simple girl with captivating looks is more like her own daughter than a daughter-in-law. Since Chandraprabha's arrival, the atmosphere in the royal palace of Pratappur has become joyful. Previously, the king spent very little time at home, and Yajnavati felt immensely lonely after the death of her husband, Sompal. However, things have changed now. She has found a companion with whom she can share her feelings, even though it can hardly be called sharing. Chandraprabha doesn't say much; she just listens. She listens attentively to everything her mother-in-law says and tries to obediently carry out her instructions.

Even now, as she looks into the gold mirror, the young queen keenly listens to Yajnavati, attempting to master the art of creating a chignon. Apart from asking a few questions, she remains mostly quiet. While adorning the neatly tied hair bun with gold hairpins, the queen mother remarks, 'Bhuyan Rajdhar from Tembuwani has arrived today; did you know, dear?'

'I did not, honourable mother.'

'Have you ever heard of his name?'

'I think I heard it once.'

'Well, Rajdhar's father, Chandibor, was Shiromani Bhuyan. During the reign of my grandfather-in-law King Tamrodhwaj, he established his kingdom at Tembuwani. My great grandfather-in-law King Dharmapal and King Durlav Narayan of the west were descendants of the same dynasty. King Durlav Narayan also adopted the title Gourheswar, which commanded a great deal of respect in those days, you see. Even the landless kings proudly wore the title 'Panch Gourheswar'. King Dharmapal and Durlav Narayan were mighty rulers, and there was a conflict and subsequent political alliance between Durlav Narayan and the Ahoms, who are now a formidable force upstream.'

'Honourable mother, if King Dharmapal became the emperor of Kamrup and established his kingdom in the Godondo Mountains, how did we come to settle here?' Chandraprabha asks.

'It's a long story, my dear. Even I am unaware of all the specifics. What I know is that King Dharmapal married Banamala, the sister of Moinavati, the queen of Manikchandra, also known as Pratapdhwaja, the king of Bengal. King Manikchandra had several queens. Durlav Narayan is the son of his first queen, Parvati. Although they were cousins, King Dharmapal engaged in a battle with Durlav Narayan after establishing his capital in Dharmapur, seeking to expand his kingdom. The entire region where the shrine of Lord Billeswar stands today was once part of King Dharmapal's kingdom. Eventually, Durlav Narayan and King Dharmapal reached a truce. Upon King Dharmapal's request, Durlav Narayan sent a group of high-caste and sub-caste Hindus, including brave soldiers like Chandidhar and virtuous Brahmin pandits, to settle near Kamrup.

'But you are aware, aren't you, of the Kshatriya rulers' strong desire to expand their kingdoms? Isn't my son Ramchandra the same? Well, Durlav Narayan assassinated Dharmapal and took over Kamrup Komota. The brave Chandibor crossed the Bornodi river and abandoned Kamrup. King Dharmapal's son, Tamradhwaj or Ratnapal, my father-in-law, moved further upstream and settled here in the village of Kanyaka. I have once before told you about Chandibor, who settled in Tembuwani and became known as Shiromani Bhuyan. His eldest son, Rajdhar, and second son, Gadadhar, ruled the kingdom from Tembuwani and Routa. During their reigns, the realm was not as vast as it is now. Ramchandra expanded our territory up to the Bornadi by defeating Gadadhar Bhuyan. He has also stretched our rule from Majuli in the south to Komota in the west. Where we now live used to be Nagshankar's capital in the fourth century. Ramchandra has fortified the capital, but governing such a vast region is not an easy task. I feel there is no need to stretch the territory any further. Don't you think so? It is only because of Minister Sogor's wisdom that Ramchandra has been able to smoothly govern the kingdom. If he plans another expedition, you must stop him. Make him understand. I will try my best.'

'As you wish, honourable mother,' Chandraprabha replies. Her hand and shoulders ache from holding the mirror for so long. She feels uncomfortable sitting in this position for hours, but she is not given the opportunity to express her desire to leave, nor does she dare to do so. Yajnavati can see her daughter-in-law's face reflected on the bejewelled mirror. The fading rays of the setting sun in the western sky fall on the sparkling, latticed metal ventilators and bounce back onto Chandraprabha's face. It radiates with the ethereal glow of a goddess. Yajnavati's heart brims with infinite bliss. She had chosen this beautiful maiden from a pure Kshatriya family as the bride for her son after an extensive search. Chandraprabha's exquisite beauty, feminine grace and admirable qualities have won the hearts of the king and all his subjects.

Pratapchandra's single-minded ambition to expand the kingdom seems to have subsided following his marriage. In fact, Yajnavati's painstaking effort to select a bride was intended to quell his ambition.

As a daughter-in-law of the Jitari dynasty, Yajnavati is well aware of the Aryan Kshatriya rulers' thirst for victory. She has heard tales about the passion for expansion, vanity and warrior instinct of the Gourh-Kshatriya Dharmapal and other rulers of the dynasty. She has personally witnessed the unfathomable loneliness and deep sighs of the proud wives of such men. Yajnavati has observed the same arrogance, hunger for conquest and urge to expand the empire in her son Ramchandra, who has earned the name Pratapchandra through his valour. Since her marriage, Yajnavati had realized that every male of the Jitari dynasty carries in his blood an overpowering sense of superiority as a Kshatriya and an Aryan. At the same time, they display extreme generosity. Incredible bravery. Unyielding obstinacy. Immense physical strength. Warfare abilities.

The overabundance of these qualities in her son has frightened the queen mother. Pratapchandra has extended his dominion southward to Majuli, near Pratappur. A sense of impending misfortune for her only son has rocked Yajnavati's motherly heart. To make Pratapchandra more family-oriented, she aspired to get him married, and she has succeeded. King Pratapchandra has indeed been bewitched by young Chandraprabha's beauty and charm.

But Yajnavati has also noticed an abundance in his attachment to his wife. While it is a welcome change from his earlier obsession with royal matters, the queen mother is concerned that this apathy can affect the security and development of the kingdom. She is irritated, too. Being used to the behaviour of her father-in-law and her husband, she finds her son's all-consuming fascination with Chandraprabha unsettling. She believes this weakness is unbecoming and unwarranted for a king from Dharmapal's dynasty.

Nevertheless, she does not harbour any ill will towards Chandraprabha. On the contrary, she feels affection for the young woman, especially when she notices her exasperation at her husband's overwhelming display of love.

'Mother, may I put down the mirror?' Chandraprabha asks timidly.

'Why? Does your arm hurt?'

'A little, honourable mother.'

'Alright. I'm almost done with your hair. Only the adornment remains. Did you observe how a bun is tied? It's not as complicated as it looks, is it? You can do it on your own. It makes the hair look lovely and bright due to the gold wires. Can you do it yourself? Or would you like me to show you again?'

'I can, honourable mother.'

'Try it later and show it to me. If it's done incorrectly, you can have it fixed,' says Yajnavati, carefully arranging the kopali along the middle parting to rest on Chandraprabha's forehead.

Then, pinning the gold and silver flowers on the bun, she continues, 'I'm not going to be here forever. I have to teach you all that I've learned from my mother-in-law. This knowledge has been passed down from one generation to another. You'll have to pass this on to your daughter-in-law. Beauty aside, an alluring wife must also be well-versed in many other arts. The art of retaining one's beauty and youth for as long as possible. The knowledge of politics. Come and sit in front of me now. Let me give you two beauty tips.'

Chandraprabha obediently follows as Yajnavati picks up a small silver bowl from the tray. Dipping some cotton wool in the yellow milk bowl, she gently wipes Chandraprabha's face, explaining, 'This bowl contains milk infused with strands of a rare flower. These strands have turned the milk yellow. It is not available here and needs to be collected from remote Kashmir. It is expensive to bring them here, so use it carefully to avoid wastage.'

'Yes, Mother.'

Yajnavati then dips fresh cotton wool in another bowl filled with water and red rose petals. Setting aside the used cotton wool, she wipes Chandraprabha's face, saying, 'These red roses do not grow here. They were brought from the far west by my father-in-law. I have heard that Togrol Khan Mallik Juzbeck brought these rose plants when he invaded Kamrup. They need to be nurtured with great care to keep them alive. Using this water to sponge your face and body will make your skin sparkle. Cleanse yourself with this milk and filament solution every morning and before bed. It will make your skin smooth and radiant like gold. Do you understand?'

'I do, Mother.'

'You should always maintain your appearance, dear. We women are always indoors. Even as the wives of kings, we have to adhere to certain dos and don'ts. Our ancestors derived pleasure from conquests, from hunting wild animals and birds. So does my son Ramchandra. The men of this dynasty are all alike. They find pleasure in conquering, whether it be a woman or a piece of land. When they face defeat or feel defeated, they become ferocious, losing control of themselves. Remember these words always. These men have always been fascinated by the outside world instead of their families. They are unaware of and unconcerned about how their women spend time inside the four walls. They never attempt to understand. As a result, it is crucial for women to remain attractive in all aspects. To maintain their youth, they should practise regular beauty care. You should also do the same.

'Yet your situation is a bit different. My son is captivated by your beauty, which is a promising sign. But like the other rulers of our dynasty, he is driven by his thirst for victory. Despite expanding the kingdom as far as Majuli, he is not content. This obsession is harmful. Chandraprabha, you should try to control this yearning. If possible, tell him that it is not necessary to expand the empire any further because what he has achieved is sufficient.'

'Honourable mother.' An elderly maid enters the room and kneels.

'Oh, Maghi! Where have you been? Why haven't I seen you for so long?'

'I was with her, dear mother. Then I visited the royal healer. Didn't Her Highness tell you?'

'No, but why were you with her? Where is Bokuli?'

'Bokuli accompanied me. She was the one who called me there. Her Highness wasn't feeling herself. Judging from the symptoms, I felt something had changed, honourable mother. So, I went over to summon the royal medic.'

'What is ailing you, my dear daughter-in-law? Why haven't I been informed?'

'It seems you are about to become a grandmother, honourable mother.'

Happiness rushes through Yajnavati. For a moment, she stares with wonder at Chandraprabha, who has lowered her head self-consciously, and then back at her old faithful maid. 'Are you certain, Maghi?'

'Well, it's difficult to say, honourable mother. Perhaps Her Highness feels embarrassed to tell you. But based on my experience, I would say yes,' Maghi replies thoughtfully, fiddling with her rosary beads.

The queen mother stays silent for a while before saying, 'If you're not sure, don't let anyone else hear about it, Maghi. The news will spread like wildfire. If Ramchandra learns of it, he'll make a fuss with rituals, offerings and whatever else he can think of. We will be humiliated if it's not true. Let some time pass to be absolutely sure, and then we'll break the news. I shall announce it myself. You don't have to notify Bokuli; just give her my summons. I shall deal with that irresponsible lass.'

'As you wish, honourable mother. I will send her right away.'

Old Maghi bows and leaves. Yajnavati affectionately places a hand over Chandraprabha's lowered head and asks, 'Are you uncomfortable, my dear? Don't be. You should relax. Once you are married, you are bound to become a mother one day. But, my love, don't tell Ramchandra. Not until I say so. Do you understand? It's too early to be certain. If it doesn't turn out to be true, he will be devastated. You are aware of how emotional he is, aren't you?'

'As you say, dear mother. I shall not.'

'Take care not to let your tongue slip. You can be quite restive at times, you know. The way you jumped upon noticing the bird-sized white butterfly the other day! You didn't see how Bokuli and the other maids were laughing, did you? After all, you are quite young, although usually quite composed. Your arrival has brought great auspiciousness to the palace, and everyone here adores you.

However, at times, you seem to forget your role as the queen and behave more like a young girl. Ramchandra may not always approve of your playfulness.'

'In all honesty, dear mother, there are moments when I do forget. My own mother used to scold me for this very reason.'

'It's because your mother comes from a good lineage. She was angry because she understood the constraints women often face. We are of a high caste, part of the royal family. We must uphold our dignity even if it means setting aside our personal wishes and desires.'

Yajnavati finishes adorning Chandraprabha's chignon with gold and silver flowers. After carefully placing the studded gold comb atop her bun, she turns Chandraprabha around to admire her. The young queen is dressed in a lavish yellow silk mekhela, paired with a beautifully embroidered riha. A deep red cotton chador, dyed with lac and boiled water, adorned with blue flowers, is elegantly draped over her. A silver girdle decorated with coral beads encircles her waist, with a stunning necklace extending down to her navel. Her dainty fingers sparkle with gem-encrusted gold rings, and a pair of bracelets adorn her wrists, while silver anklets enhance her ankles.

'You look magnificent! As enchanting as a fairy! Now, please sit attentively. Allow me to guide you through what is expected of you during these times. With the blessings of Lord Biswanath, everything will be just fine.'

Wrapped in a cocoon of awkwardness and hesitation, Chandraprabha keeps her head lowered. She knows her liberal mother-in-law loves her deeply. Still, the queen mother's sombre demeanour occasionally unnerves Chandraprabha for no apparent reason. She wonders if Yajnavati's presence is the reason King Pratapchandra does not shower her with constant attention, fearing he might neglect his royal duties altogether. Pratapchandra desires to see Chandraprabha decked in beautiful clothes and ornaments at all times, and her apparent indifference troubles him. He demands her undivided attention when he is in the palace. Thus, her mother-in-law's presence unwittingly becomes a source of comfort for

Chandraprabha. She discreetly stows away the earthen toys made by Kamrup potters, which she had brought from her mother's place, inside a wooden chest in her bedroom. On every available occasion, she retrieves them and immerses herself in play. During these moments, she does not welcome Pratapchandra's proximity at all. Sometimes, she wonders if the king envies her toy collection.

One day, she had playfully voiced her suspicions, 'You must be envious of my toys, aren't you?' Pratapchandra burst into laughter, but then his countenance turned serious. 'You are right – whenever I sense that you care about someone or something other than me, it ignites a fire in my head, Mahishi. I feel infuriated with you.' Her husband's seriousness had startled her.

'Pay attention to my words, don't disregard them,' Yajnavati calls out to her.

'Of course, honourable mother,' Chandraprabha meekly replies.

Yajnavati picks up a silver bowl from the intricately carved wooden table and pours a small amount of an oily concoction onto Chandraprabha's palm, applying the rest to her face. 'Autumn is approaching. You should wear this mask until spring arrives. Only then should you apply powdered sandalwood or pollen from the *keteki* flower to your face, which can also be applied to your lips to keep them supple.'

'What is in this pack, Mother?' the young queen asks, rubbing the aromatic concoction on her hands and arms.

'We extract the saps of ripe orange peel, yellow mustard flower and other herbs to make this salve. Next, we add raw turmeric juice and butter, and heat the mixture in an earthen vessel. Once it thickens, we combine it with aloe wood and sandalwood. My mother-in-law taught me this recipe after my marriage. Soon, you'll be passing it down to your daughter-in-law.' Yajnavati chuckles, making Chandraprabha blush.

The queen mother then reaches for a bamboo tube wrapped in a green leaf from a nearby cane table. She takes a few drops of aromatic oil from the tube and gently applies it to her daughter-in-law's smooth, prominent breasts, visible over her riha. After securing the leaf back around the tube, Yajnavati says, 'My son adores this scent. Do you have some of this with you? Use it regularly, even in bed. Apply sandalwood paste over your breasts. Do you understand?'

'I do, dear mother.'

Yajnavati smiles as she hands her the bejewelled mirror. 'Look, look at your beautiful self.'

Before Chandraprabha can respond, King Pratapchandra's anxious voice drifts into the room, 'Honourable mother.'

'Come inside.'

'Dear mother, Mahishi is not in the bedchamber,' the king says as he walks inside. When he notices Chandraprabha sitting near his mother, his glum face brightens.

'Do you expect her to be confined to the bedchamber all the time? Why did you leave the royal court?' Yajnavati laughs.

'I've temporarily adjourned the proceedings. I have a headache, dear mother. And I wanted to tell you we are leaving tomorrow morning for the inauguration of Mayapur, the new capital of Majuli. I'm taking Mahishi with me.'

'Indeed, she will go. What about me?' Yajnavati teases.

'Nothing could be better, Mother,' Pratapchandra replies enthusiastically.

'I was only teasing, dear. Chandraprabha, go attend to your husband. He is complaining of a headache.' She smiles knowingly at the young queen, who leaves with her head lowered, visibly embarrassed.

Inside the bedchamber, the king draws her close to himself. 'I've told you many times that when I don't find you here, I get very upset. Didn't I tell you to wait for me today? Why didn't you stay back?'

'*Maah* called me to do my hair. Should I have said no to her?'

'No, of course not. You look lovelier than ever, Mahishi.'

'It's because of her efforts.'

Chandraprabha blushes, dipping her face in her husband's chest. Reassured by this passionate interlude, the king later returns to the courtroom. Meanwhile, swaying with happiness and fatigued from pleasure, the queen sits down on the veranda outside her bedchamber, her mind filled with anticipation about her likely motherhood.

FIVE

Mayapur, the newly established capital, has been adorned in magnificent decorations. The vast island in the heart of the Brahmaputra is shining with joyous celebrations.

Kings and princes from neighbouring regions have been invited. Those who can't attend in person have sent their sons, subsidiary kings or representatives. Rows of temporary camps have been raised along the silvery sands of the river to accommodate the guests.

Autumn has arrived in Mayapur. The sky is blending with the water on the distant horizon, and the fragrance of flowers has permeated the lively atmosphere. The *kohuwa* plant's fluffy white flowers have wafted skywards to mix with the white clouds. The sweet fragrance of the *xewali* flowers has mingled with the dizzying scent emanating from the musk deer's navel. This spirited ambience has affected the people as well.

Chandraprabha looks resplendent in her attire. Her silk mekhela glistens with coloured threads and tiny golden flowers. The tightly wrapped narrow riha embraces her young, lissome body like a passionate lover, resembling a lushly growing banana plant. The misty, diaphanous chador from Manipur is draped around her body like a cluster of early morning fog spread across a flowery shrub – about to drift away in the heat of the sunlight any moment.

And Chandraprabha's face?

The keteki pollen seems to have lost its grip on her glowing rose petal-like face, sponged with milk and soaked with filaments of flowers imported from distant Kashmir. Her pearl-like teeth, glinting through Chandraprabha's red sandal seed-like lips smeared with the stain of *borhomthuri,* appear to challenge the pearls in her necklace. The rising sun seems to have stopped on her forehead. The colour from her thick chignon seems to have slid into her deep, elongated kohl-smeared eyes. Faint drops of fog seem to hang from her long eyelashes. A girdle of gold encircles Chandraprabha's waist. A pendant of pearls on her forehead. Her neck is adorned with a pearl and coral choker, and long necklaces and chains studded with gems. On all her fingers are precious gold rings that are linked by fine gold chains. Her wrists are decorated with an assortment of gold and pearl bangles. Long pearl earrings hang from her ears. The silvery white silk costume, the glitter of the ornaments and the gleam of the enamelled gold flowers have lent her molten gold-like striking form a shimmer. Her face gleams with happiness.

Chandraprabha is glowing.

Like the full moon sparkling in a lagoon's deep waters. As if a fairy has descended from the heavens after getting lost.

'Ah, so beautiful!' Chandraprabha and Pratapchandra both exclaim simultaneously. Then, they ask each other, 'Who are you talking about?'

'I am talking about you, Mahishi,' says the king. 'Whom do you mean?'

Chandraprabha gazes at the river. It's not her first time seeing it. While coming to pray at Mahabhairav, she has noticed the grandeur of the mighty Brahmaputra before. But today, it feels different – unique and unparalleled. It's like the fabled seas she's only heard about. Are the seas as beautiful?

'I've never seen the Brahmaputra look so picturesque before, O Son of Aryans,' says Chandraprabha, addressing Pratapchandra as he likes to be. The king takes great pride in emphasizing his Aryan lineage in all his words and actions. The recognition of his ancestry from others pleases him.

However, Pratapchandra's serious demeanour quickly gives way to laughter. 'Come on, let's go inside. You look so ravishing today, even the Brahmaputra might fall in love with you.'

Chandraprabha blushes, her heart swelling with happiness. 'I don't want the Brahmaputra. It's you I want.'

Pratapchandra's worries dissipate. His heart overflows with joy today. It seems the goddess of fortune has chosen to reside in his kingdom. There is prosperity all around him. He has a stunningly beautiful and extraordinarily talented wife in Chandraprabha. What more could he ask for?

Yet a trace of concern lingers. How could Mahishi think of someone other than him while in his company? Doesn't he satisfy her? In Mahishi's thoughts, isn't Pratapchandra the one who holds a special place?

'Why are your thoughts focused on the Brahmaputra instead of me?' Pratapchandra asks.

Chandraprabha is taken aback, bowing her head awkwardly, unsure of what to say.

'Speak, Mahishi,' Pratapchandra insists, looking directly into her eyes. Chandraprabha remains silent for a moment before gently responding, 'Perhaps your presence has made the river appear so beautiful, O Son of Aryans. Can one find happiness outside of oneself when one is unhappy within?'

Pratapchandra's mind clears instantly. 'Indeed, indeed. That's precisely why I love you so much. Your words lift my spirits. I am profoundly grateful to have you in my life, Mahishi.'

'So am I, O Son of Aryans. Deeply content. Complete.'

'Complete? No, you are not complete; you have not yet gifted me with the fruit of our conjugal life. You have to bring to the world the descendant of King Dharmapal's dynasty. Hurry up, Mahishi. Make it happen quickly. I can't wait to set eyes on my progeny. Mayamotto is the name given to me by the people of Mayapur. If I have a son, I shall name him Orimotto. Orimotto, the son of King Mayamotto. How does that sound to you?'

'That would be great, O Son of Aryans.' Though prompted to tell him about her impending motherhood, she stays tight-lipped, remembering the queen mother's words of caution.

Just then the doorkeeper's voice drifts in from outside. 'May I come in, Your Royal Highness?'

'Enter.'

The doorkeeper bows. 'The honourable chief minister wishes to meet you, Your Royal Highness.'

'Invite him in,' Pratapchandra commands, waiting for the doorkeeper to leave before saying, 'Mahishi, arrange your scarf properly.'

As the chief minister arrives and bows, an attendant emerges from the background and places a chair for him.

Not only is Sogor faithful and loyal towards the king, he also genuinely holds goodwill for him. Pratapchandra confides in him exclusively. Sogor has played a significant role in all of the king's successes. He is also one of the elite few with access to the inner sanctum of the palace.

'What is the news, Chief Minister?' Pratapchandra asks.

'All of the arrangements for the celebration have been completed, O Son of Aryans. People are eagerly awaiting both of your presence. The programme will begin as soon as you arrive.'

'We are ready as well, Chief Minister,' the king declares, rising to his feet. Chandraprabha follows suit.

As they exit the royal palace, Chandraprabha is filled with awe. Since arriving in Mayapur the previous night, she has not witnessed the outside world.

The path from the palace entrance to the sandy bank of the Brahmaputra river is adorned with carpets woven from strips of mat rush. Banana plants line the sides, while garlands of hibiscus, marigold and fragrant crepe jasmine flowers embellish the trees. Colourful bamboo poles, decorated with scraped flowers, stand between the plants. Wood and bamboo carvings of birds, animals and flowers embellish the trees and poles. Sunlight filtering through the banana leaves and garlands create a mesmeric mosaic pattern on the carpeted ground.

The king and queen step onto the carpet with the sound of blowing conch shells and *uruli,* a shrill sound made by the tongue, filling the air. Hundreds of drums rumble and boom.

The spirit of the spectacular carnival is starting to strike at

Chandraprabha's heart, which is swaying like an anchored boat hit by waves over and over.

She raises her sparkling eyes to look at her husband. He is dressed in an off-white dhoti woven with yarn derived from silkworms reared on the magnolia tree. A thin deerskin *parivesh*, studded with gems, is wrapped around his waist. His bare, raw-gold-complexioned torso gleams, and a folded silk *uttorio* embellished with coral beads is draped over his shoulders. A gold sheath containing a sword encircles his waist, and a bejewelled yellow turban dyed with safflower sap crowns his head. A gold necklace with beads shaped like myrobalam nuts shines on his bare, masculine chest. Gold and coral danglers sparkle on his neck, while his arms twinkle with armlets resembling *angad* and *keyur*. His fingers are radiant with gold ornaments studded with precious stones.

A young man walks alongside them, holding a white silk parasol bedecked with gems and pearls above their heads. Chandraprabha is spellbound. Pratapchandra bears a striking resemblance to Indra, the king of the gods. Wearing deer skin footwear and walking beside Pratapchandra on the carpet, Chandraprabha softly murmurs, 'O Son of Aryans, you look like Indra.'

Pratapchandra continues walking silently.

'What a gorgeous parasol, too! I've never seen anything like it before. Did we get it here?' she exclaims.

'It is from Pratappur, reserved for special occasions. King Bhagadatta was the first to use these parasols. It is said that Lord Krishna presented it to him. It was called *abhog chattra*. This is the *varun* chattra, a replica. Would you like to have one?'

'You know that I always travel in a *shibika*. I'd be scared to use such an exquisite parasol. I'm not an emperor, am I?' she laughs.

'Don't laugh. It's unbecoming.'

'Alright, I shan't,' Chandraprabha tries to speak soberly but can't help grinning as she continues walking over the carpet, as if in a dream.

Pratapchandra is accustomed to such festivals, but a powerful surge of emotion and delight has transformed the queen into a jubilant young girl again, eschewing the solemn behaviour expected of her.

The euphoric sound of hundreds of people cheering for Pratapchandra's victory reverberates all over Mayapur. 'Victory! Victory to Emperor Mayamotto!'

The seats for the neighbouring kings are arranged in two rows, with the king and the queen in the centre. As soon as Pratapchandra and Chandraprabha arrive, all the guests stand up to greet them. The raucous applause for the king nearly deafens Chandraprabha. She looks around in awe, having never before seen such a grand gathering or preparations for festivities. The sight of numerous kings sitting together, dressed in various kinds of outfits, is captivating.

'Why are you looking around? It is indecorous,' Pratapchandra says with tremendous irritation, though a smile lingers on his face. Chandraprabha becomes conscious and sits still, striving to maintain her poise.

The king signals to Chief Minister Sogor, who is seated at some distance, and poses a few questions about the festival. His face brightens with satisfaction at Sogor's responses. This festival in the capital of Mayapur holds great political significance. The neighbouring rulers of the south bank have openly acknowledged Pratapchandra's supremacy by participating in today's events. The king has abandoned his ambitions of expansion to the south due to its costs and considerable fatigue. Meanwhile, the Syukafa dynasty from Nora has become a formidable force, extending their frontiers towards the south bank. Pratapchandra wishes to avoid direct confrontation at present. Once he firmly establishes himself in Mayapur, he will consider expansion. Thus, he strategically uses the inauguration ceremony of Mayapur for political purposes, which has yielded a satisfactory response. The peace-loving Mikirs, Laloongs and the warrior-like yet non-aggressive Jaintias, divided into separate kingdoms, have accepted Pratapchandra's proposal of alliance. While a few small Kachari kingdoms have shown loyalty, the king of Dimabong has indirectly displayed rebellion against such amity, a matter not overlooked by Pratapchandra. Dimabong has risen as a powerful force, and its king, Gajaraj Bodosa, has distanced himself from the festival by sending a royal representative. Pratapchandra notes that, despite the formalities, there is a lack of absolute loyalty from this kingdom.

'Let us wait and see. Things will soon become clear,' Pratapchandra reflects as he sits back and enjoys the show.

Chandraprabha remains oblivious to everything, her wide eyes brimming with curiosity as she looks around. She enjoys the performances, momentarily forgetting her husband's instructions. Her spirit surges with delight, suppressing the impulsive flicker of adolescent impatience. The vigour of life force manifests within her.

'Now the honourable kings of the neighbouring kingdoms will offer their individual gifts to the Great Emperor Pratapchandra, His Majesty Mayamotto.'

Chandraprabha shifts in her seat upon hearing the announcement. Gifts? What gifts did the kings bring? Are there any gifts for her, too?

The session begins. Rulers approach Pratapchandra, greet him and present their gifts. As he accepts the offerings, the king engages in light conversation, maintaining a grave expression and a smile. The rulers are welcomed with neatly arranged betel nuts and leaves on the *bota* – a round silver tray with a stand. The gleam of the silver botas nearly dazzles Chandraprabha.

The queen gazes at the faces of all the kings, disregarding any restrictions. Each of them is fascinating to her, dressed in their unique traditional attires. Some have brought ivory, some salt and spices and some barks that enhance the flavour when chewed with betel nut. There are also lime, cinnamon, saplings of the Eaglewood tree – which are used to write manuscripts – spices prepared from roots of banana and *lai krantha* trees, dried fish, lac, musk, honey, gems, jewellery, cloths, bamboo baskets and many other objects which Chandraprabha had never seen or heard of.

She can't take her eyes off the gifts, her face beaming with immense joy and immeasurable curiosity. The king, noticing the light on her face, grows extremely irritated. He decides to privately give her a good piece of his mind for such childishness later and continues to solemnly accept the gifts. Each presentation is followed by a group of performers singing and dancing in their native traditions. Numerous kings are in attendance, including those from Khola, Borduba, Dimoruwa, Nelly, Beltola, Rani, Jaintia, Kachari and other kingdoms.

As she realizes no one has brought any gifts for her, Chandraprabha's spirits begin to dampen. Yet she continues to gaze happily at the scene in front of her.

'Now we invite the king of Gobha, Sadhukumar, to offer his gifts,' someone announces. Chandraprabha looks around.

Sadhukumar.

The name sounds different, not matching the other kings'. It sounds like her own name. She scans the rows of kings seated on either side, searching for the king of Gobha until a young man rises from a row on the right. Instantly, a group of young men begin to play native drums and sing songs, their melodies echoing through the festival ground.

Sadhukumar walks forward, cradling a half-grown deer in his arms. With a smooth, clean-shaven face, twinkling eyes, deep red lips and a strong, youthful physique, he commands attention. He is wearing a *muga* loincloth embellished with flowers at both ends, and a sleeveless floral-patterned black shirt proudly displays his muscular arms. On his head is a white cotton turban. Despite being a remarkably young king, he radiates an aura of charm and politeness.

'The king of Gobha, located on the south bank of the Brahmaputra. The honourable king's name is Luit, but he is widely known as Sadhukumar …' the announcer continues, '… a king beloved by his subjects, this philanthropic ruler has been affectionately named Sadhukumar by his people. We cordially welcome His Highness Sadhukumar to the festival commemorating the inauguration of this new capital of the vast realm of king of kings, His Highness Pratapchandra.'

As Sadhukumar approaches, Chandraprabha looks at the fawn in his arms with admiration.

After greeting the king, Sadhukumar pauses and presents a cane chest containing four sizable eri scarves and two bamboo tubes filled with fresh honey. He salutes Queen Chandraprabha and places the fawn near her, while his accompanying deputy takes hold of the animal.

'This is for the honourable queen. A token of love from the kingdom of Gobha,' Sadhukumar declares warmly. His laughter sounds like fragrant *sewali* flowers falling from the sky.

Chandraprabha is enthralled. Amongst the many kings and princes, only the king of Gobha has brought her a gift – a truly unique one at that. Overwhelmed with happiness, she exclaims, 'Beautiful. Beautiful, indeed. I love it. What a beautiful fawn!'

Sadhukumar smiles and explains, 'This is a rock deer, known as *mos orlong*. It is found in caves and requires careful attention. Someone must be trained to care for this fawn.'

'Please teach me. I shall take care of it. What a lovely animal. I have never seen nor heard of it before,' Chandraprabha says, her face glowing with a smile.

Nearby, King Pratapchandra's face darkens. Ignoring his wife, he declares, 'The queen is not serious, Deoraja. Are these tasks fit for hands that blister from touching cotton wool? Our chief minister can delegate the responsibility to a slave.'

Sadhukumar smiles politely but remains silent. Then he leaves.

Oblivious to Pratapchandra's irritation, Chandraprabha leans forward from her seat to caress the fawn.

'Now the king of Khola is requested to present his gifts before the king of kings, the great Pratapchandra, also known as Mayamotto.'

Upon hearing the announcement, the native Gobha boy hands the fawn to a slave standing nearby and leaves after saluting. As does the slave.

Chandraprabha continues to enjoy the festival, paying little attention to the other rulers who come to offer gifts. She is stealing glances at the fawn from a safe distance and then at Sadhukumar. Every time, their gazes lock.

But whose eyes are not upon her? Chandraprabha finds her eyes meeting those of everyone she turns to. None of them has ever seen a more beautiful Aryan woman. None of them has ever seen King Mayamotto's mahishi.

Everyone stares at her with a mesmerized and spellbound expression.

Even Sadhukumar. He, too, has never seen a woman like her. Is there a woman of such exquisite beauty in any kingdom in the vicinity, let alone Gobha?

Irritation gives way to rage. Pratapchandra's face flushes with suppressed rage, scorched by resentment, anger towards Chandraprabha and intense hatred for Sadhukumar.

Gripped with feverish happiness, Chandraprabha remains blissfully unaware. Unknowingly, she is about to summon dark clouds of disaster.

At the end of the festivities, Sadhukumar, along with the other kings, sits for political discussions. A marquee, with all sides open, has been erected on the sands of the Brahmaputra. The kings go and take their seats underneath it. Although Pratapchandra exchanges pleasantries with everybody, deep resentment fills him on the inside.

Unbearable! Intolerable!

Chandraprabha's image of wild happiness is unbearable.

Even as he sits in the formal assembly, King Pratapchandra is fuming and raging from within. Honey-sweet wine imported from Kampith is being served in sparkling bell-metal bowls. Smoked deer meat is served on flower-engraved bell-metal platters. Savoury meat of the whistling teal cooked in pungent mustard oil, thick liquid jaggery, pearl-white grains of rice cooked in tender bamboo tubes and a variety of other delicacies are being enjoyed. There is still time for supper. Thick mattresses of soft *simolu* cotton wool warmed in the sun are being spread out in the open, with stark white sheets woven by the local weavers covering them. The kings recline on large pillows. The cool, soothing breeze from the river, blending with the warmth of the hot mattresses and pillows, seems to make everyone inexplicably drowsy. On the sandy bank, illuminated by torchlight, young boys and girls dance and sing, their hearts flooding with happiness to the soulful tune of the *oinitom*.

Everyone is content.

Everyone is ecstatic.

Except for King Pratapchandra.

The king is bothered. The image of Sadhukumar offering the fawn to Chandraprabha flashes through his mind. As does the Gobha king's spellbound gaze and cheerful smile. And Chandraprabha's exultant expression upon receiving the gift.

Pratapchandra smoulders with envy. Despite showering priceless gifts from his travels abroad on Chandraprabha, bringing her expensive clothes and jewellery, he had never seen such a glow of contentment on her face … ever.

It is true that Chandraprabha had been content. But her excessive joy on receiving a deer from a non-Aryan king seemed unnecessary, disturbingly so. He can't express his anger at his wife publicly, who is busy in conversation with a few fellow queens. The king is looking at how these women touch his wife's gold-embroidered mekhela, her silk riha, the diaphanous chador, the gold-wired chignon and, of course, her exquisite jewellery. With the same curiosity, she, too, is fascinated by the intricacies of the queens' bright colourful costumes, which she has never seen before.

Chandraprabha expresses her vulnerability like a commoner. How annoying! Her behaviour has started to fuel anger and resentment within the king. His numerous gestures directing his wife back to the palace have been futile. It seems the queen has forgotten about her husband's existence.

And it is not entirely untrue.

Perhaps not only the king, Chandraprabha may have also forgotten about her own existence. She may have forgotten about the thrilling prospect of a child growing inside her womb. She may have forgotten about the queen mother's warning. Forgotten that she is the wife of a triumphant Aryan monarch. Forgotten that it is unbecoming for her to display such unrestrained happiness before her subjects.

The brightly attired men and women of the locality, their vibrant and colourful attire, decked-up dancing girls, the resounding merrymaking of the festival grounds, the unusual and varied gifts, the peculiarly dressed kings, queens and princes … and, of course, the fawn …

Oh, what a thrill … what a thrill … Stepping out of the four walls of the palace, experiencing the blue sky, white clouds, vast expanse of sand and blue waters, the beat of drums, the sound of horns and other unfamiliar instruments … witnessing dances never seen before … listening to songs never heard before …

Leaving the company of the queens, Chandraprabha walks along the riverbank with her chief maid-in-waiting, Bokuli, and the other maids, while the guards keep a close watch on them from a distance.

She walks close past the area where King Pratapchandra and the others are seated. She briefly glances at the crowned heads sitting beneath the canopy and walks away.

She doesn't truly glance at her husband, whose gaze is fixed on her.

Pratapchandra's face has turned bright red with fury. Resisting the urge to drag his wife back to the palace, he remains seated.

He has to give the royal heads company, doesn't he? He cannot afford to incur the displeasure of the neighbouring kings who have acknowledged his friendship. These kings may appear insignificant, but they are no less egotistical than the others.

Unable to keep an eye on his queen, Pratapchandra grows impatient. The effect of wine is adding fuel to the fire. Various misgivings are causing upheavals in his mind. Images of the smiling king of Gobha carrying the fawn, Chandraprabha's illuminated demeanour, her glittering, curious eyes, flash through his mind again and again.

'I'm going to sit here for a little while. Make the arrangements,' the queen declares.

It is nearly sundown when she sits down on the lonely sandy riverbank, where a carpet has been spread out for her.

'I'd like to listen to a song. Bokuli, you sing,' she requests.

The day's festivities have filled the maids-in-waiting with a longing to dance and sing. They, too, are dressed attractively and bedecked with ornaments. The presence of young men of their rank stirs the natural turbulence of youth within their hearts, creating a sea of surging waves. Bokuli is wearing a necklace made of crow's beads and snake's spine, and coral earrings hang from her earlobes. She is draped in a mekhela chador woven with eri yarn, dotted with floral motifs. Her eyes are smeared with kohl. Ivory rings adorn her fingers and gold-plated bangles her hands. Bokuli stands out amongst the maids. That she is the queen's favourite is evident.

Bokuli's old cane chest brims with gifts, tokens of Chandraprabha's affection. Things she had never even desired in her dreams.

Bokuli's heart will forever brim with love and gratitude for the queen. Restless by nature, Bokuli is known for her humour, candour and open-heartedness. She is no longer a bonded maid, as she once was; she has transformed into Chandraprabha's companion. At the queen's behest, she begins to hum shyly but soon joins in singing with all her heart. The other girls enthusiastically dance to the lively bihu songs, catching the attention of the guards, who gaze in awe from a distance.

Everybody seems to have forgotten about Chandraprabha. At one point, she rises in the midst of the girls' dance. Removing her deerskin sandals, she places her bare feet in the shallow water. She playfully draws up her mekhela to her ankles and stands on one foot, frolicking in the water.

A short distance away, Sadhukumar sits with his bodyguards, sipping joo. The soothing notes of a flute fill the air, complementing the slowly darkening river, the cool breeze and the serenity of the moment. Distant voices and the faint sounds of drums and pipes drift in from the banquet area, while the well-lit sandy riverbank echoes with the tune of bihu songs and the tinkling laughter of young women. The king of Gobha is on the brink of sinking into a profound trance.

At that very moment, the jovial laughter of the young women abruptly turns into screams of terror.

'Something is happening there,' remarks one of the guards.

'Stop playing the *paanchi*. Let me see,' Sadhukumar commands.

As soon as the flute ceases its tune, the source of the commotion becomes evident: someone has fallen into the river.

Sadhukumar swiftly rises and dashes towards the torch-lit area.

'The queen has fallen into the water. Oh my god … what will happen now … someone please save her …' a young woman wails.

Lowering the bow from his shoulder, Sadhukumar proceeds to the river.

Chandraprabha has slipped into the water and is gasping for air in the unfamiliar depths of the dark, waist-deep Brahmaputra.

The river near the shore is shallow, with no current or significant depth. Following the sound of the commotion, Sadhukumar reaches a struggling Chandraprabha and brings her safely ashore.

By the time Pratapchandra arrives at the spot, Sadhukumar is pressing his wife's back with his hands, helping release water from her stomach.

SIX

Inside the bedchamber of Mayapur palace, Chandraprabha is sitting on the ice-cold floor.

Stunned.

Stupefied.

After riding high on imaginary clouds during the festivities, she has landed with a thud on the cold, hard ground of reality, struck by her husband's blows.

The king's hysterical and furious voice spews forth poisonous, lava-hot words, reducing her to ashes. Her entire body bears the marks of countless wounds inflicted by his powerful hands.

What has got into Pratapchandra!

Once immersed in love, content and fulfilled, he has undergone a drastic transformation over a trivial incident! Where had this side of him been concealed all this time? Where was this monstrous, brutal, jealousy-driven and maddeningly furious Pratapchandra hiding?

Even now, after enduring prolonged hours of torment, he remains frenzied. Despite inflicting countless wounds upon his wife, the inferno in his heart refuses to extinguish itself. The king's frenzied voice echoes from his chamber, each word piercing Chandraprabha like a razor-edged arrow.

'I will not listen to a single word, Chief Minister! My wife is unchaste. Dreadfully unchaste. She has committed an unforgivable sin by touching another man. I despise her. I cannot possibly share a bed with an unchaste woman who has so shamelessly thrown away her dignity and self-respect by cavorting with another man. Our veins course with pure Aryan blood. No empress in the history of the esteemed King Dharmapal's lineage has stooped so low. Chandraprabha has brought the utmost disgrace upon the noble Jitary dynasty. She willingly exposed her wet body in front of bonded slaves and the lowliest of Mayapur's wretched masses. She literally emerged from the water in the arms of a stranger. Sogor, my head is on fire! I had poured all my love on this unfaithful woman, treating her like a veritable goddess. Can you see the magnitude of her betrayal? How she has trampled on my pride and the reputation of our dynasty! I hereby command you to take her and that insignificant king to the riverbank and cut them both to pieces. Serve their flesh to the hawks and crows. Why are you refusing to obey my orders, Chief Minister? You are but a subordinate officer of King Pratapchandra. If you dare defy my orders, I'll have you imprisoned as well. I shall hack you before I hack the two of them …

Pratapchandra is screaming like a possessed man, drowning out Sogor's soft, consoling words.

This part of the palace is isolated, and no one is permitted to enter without prior permission. The guards stationed at the entrance of this wing are particularly stern today under the strict orders of their king.

About three hours ago, the chief minister had rushed to the palace after being summoned by the king. Upon entering, he was shocked.

What a peculiar situation this is! The king, swearing on Lord Biswanath, has forsaken his wife and condemned both Sadhukumar and Chandraprabha to death. The chief minister is desperately trying to calm Pratapchandra, who is intoxicated and engulfed by uncontrollable fury. Repeatedly, he made efforts to convince the king to retract his command, saying …

'It was a mere accident, O Son of Aryans. While attempting to rescue the queen …'

But Pratapchandra cuts him off. 'Accident? Whom are you trying to fool, Chief Minister? This wasn't an accident; it was a deliberate betrayal by a dishonest woman. Aah! To think that I worshipped this woman's beauty, worshipped her virtues … what a fool I was! What a fool! I shall never forgive … never. Capture the king of Gobha and bring him here … right now.'

'It will be done … but please, be calm …'

Finally, Sogor manages to rescind the death sentence, but Pratapchandra remains resolute in his decision to forsake the queen.

'I must give up that unfaithful woman to that insignificant king … Let her fulfil her desire in the ramshackle royal dwelling of that worthless non-Aryan ruler.'

The chief minister helplessly comes outside to sit down in the palace lobby.

His understanding of the king of Gobha far surpasses Pratapchandra's. Sadhukumar embodies humility, sensibility, bravery, kindness and greatness. In his youth, the elder *khara panthais* affectionately referred to him as Sadhukumar, and this name has gained immense popularity, overshadowing his previous moniker.

The Gobha king enjoys widespread popularity throughout his realm. Along with twelve kingdoms that recognize its supremacy, the kingdom of Gobha maintains friendly relations with all its neighbours. Sogor is aware of the frequent gatherings of royal heads from the Laloong territories to address various political, economic and social matters with Sadhukumar. The Jaintia king shares a special relationship with the Laloong kingdoms, particularly Gobha. While the relationship with the Kachari kingdom is not hostile, it lacks warmth.

At present, many neighbouring royal heads have gathered in Mayapur. Sogor, a politically astute individual, understands that Sadhukumar's amiable nature and heroic act of saving the queen's life will earn him immense admiration among both the kings and the common people.

Sogor also recognizes the profound impression the queen has made on everyone with her beauty and simplicity. If she is forsaken and Sadhukumar insulted in relation to this incident, it may lead to dissatisfaction among the rulers and the populace of Mayapur. This could jeopardize the peace and open the door to ambitious neighbouring powers like the Ahom kingdom.

But who possesses the courage to offer counsel to the king? Whose words will he heed?

Nobody understands the emotional, egoistic, possessive king better than the chief minister. He knows when Pratapchandra is consumed by intense emotions and rage, it is impossible to rein him in. The king's character is marked by extremes – love and hate, charity and vengeance, hopes and desires, everything in excess.

Sogor has witnessed the king's emotional turmoil for hours on end. He knows that the queen, sitting in the adjacent bedroom, has overheard every word spoken by her husband. One can only imagine the storm of emotions engulfing the gentle, innocent and delicate Chandraprabha. If the queen mother were present, she might have exercised some influence over her son or at least prevented this unfortunate decision. The king is somewhat receptive to his mother's counsel.

What should Sogor do? What should be the next step? How can he resolve this situation?

After careful deliberation, he orders for Sadhukumar to be brought to the room adjoining the king's bedchamber. Pratapchandra is still there, drinking wine. It is hard to discern whether the king's anger has subsided at all.

As soon as the chief minister enters, Pratapchandra blurts out, 'Where, where is that petty king?'

'He will arrive soon, O Son of Aryans. At this late hour, it will take him some time to come here all the way from the royal camp. Moreover, he is unlikely to come alone. He will undoubtedly be accompanied by his bodyguards. Your Highness, if I may offer a suggestion—'

'Go on, speak.'

'If you do intend to give up the queen, do so discreetly. This capital is still new. Its security arrangements are not without flaws. In the event of a battle or a revolt, self-defence might be a challenge.'

'Who would dare revolt against me? Who would risk a battle against the mighty Pratapchandra? Tell me, who?' the king retorts.

'Of course, there may be none. But a small spark can ignite an inferno, O Son of God. Sometimes, even a tiny insect's sting can bring down a mighty creature like an elephant. This isn't just about your personal security. Please consider the political implications as well. I won't elaborate further. At this moment, you are restless and tired. In my opinion, a discreet separation is the best course of action. However, the decision is entirely yours.'

'Very well, but this unfaithful woman must cross my country's borders before dawn.'

Before Sogor can say anything, the king of Gobha appears at the doorway. 'For what reason, O King, have you summoned me in the dead of night?' he calmly asks with an undertone of surprise and suspicion.

Sadhukumar had been taken aback when he was awakened by the king's summons. But despite his surprise, he proceeded to the royal palace with his bodyguards. Upon entering the palace, hidden sentries had swiftly arrested his bodyguards, leaving Sadhukumar alone and unarmed. The accompanying spearheads gleamed menacingly as some guards escorted him to the threshold of the room where King Pratapchandra sat.

Filled with astonishment and fear, Sadhukumar couldn't fathom how saving the queen's life had aroused suspicion, jealousy and vengefulness in the king's heart – instead of gratitude.

'Please have a seat, King of Gobha,' Sogor welcomes him. But Pratapchandra exclaims, 'There is no need to sit here – take him away, Chief Minister. I don't want to talk to him.'

'Have I offended you in any way, Your Highness?' asks Sadhukumar, perplexed.

'Yes, you have committed a heinous crime. Criminals are not offered seats under my rule,' the king replies coldly.

'Who is the criminal, Your Highness? Is it me?'

'Yes! You have immorally touched the queen.'

The light vanishes from Sadhukumar's pleasant and innocent countenance. Stunned, he stares at Pratapchandra, whose face is now grotesque with anger. After almost an eternity, the Gobha king says in a calm and solemn voice, 'I was rescuing the queen from the waters … Your Highness, you are viewing the incident with jealous eyes. You must not.'

'A petty non-Aryan like you … Are you trying to teach me what I should and shouldn't do? How dare you?'

Sadhukumar holds the king's gaze for a moment. 'I have courage, Your Highness. I am not afraid to distinguish right from wrong. I am uncertain about the distinctions of Aryan and non-Aryan. I am a king in my own right, and my people have bestowed upon me eyes, ears, a mouth and heart far superior to yours. Fa Mahadeo has witnessed that I have not committed any sin. So why should I admit to an offence I have not committed? We do not distrust our wives, but it seems you do. Is it customary for Aryans to distrust their wives?'

'Insolent king, do you realize who you are talking to? I'm the great Pratapchandra of the Jitary dynasty, ruler of the vast empire stretching from the Bornodi to Majuli. If I hadn't given my word to Chief Minister Sogor, your impudent head would have met the ground with a blow from my *ashi.* You are a lowly, insignificant king of a land the size of a plate, where a shout from one end can be heard at the other. You have dared to touch the wife of the mighty Pratapchandra, to look at her with sinful eyes. I despise that base woman more than filth itself. You must take her away. Settle down to a happy family life with the filth of my country. I won't listen to any argument. You have to take Chandraprabha with you. Or else—'

'Or else what, Your Highness?' Sadhukumar calmly asks, looking into the king's eyes.

'Don't you realize? I will invade and destroy your land, and the blood of your people will flow like a river. Not only you, but your entire community must also pay the price of your sin. You have to take Chandraprabha with you. I've left my unchaste wife. If you do not obey, the waters of the Brahmaputra will turn ruddy with your and Chandraprabha's blood and flesh, and of your bodyguards. Go! Leave before I raise my ashi.'

The chief minister places his hand on Sadhukumar's stiff shoulder, signalling for him to leave. After staring at Pratapchandra for a few moments, the Gobha king follows Sogor out of the room. Standing outside the queen's bedchamber, the chief minister explains everything. Sadhukumar is still, his bloodshot eyes fixed on Sogor. After finishing, the chief minister puts his hand back on Sadhukumar's shoulder. 'O King of Gobha, isn't a beautiful woman a better gain than a bloody battle? King Pratapchandra is a stubborn man. He never strays from his words. Save your land, king. Take the queen with you. I shall make all the necessary arrangements. No one will be the wiser about who is in the boat at this hour.'

Removing the chief minister's hand from his shoulder, Sadhukumar replies placidly, 'I am not a coward, Chief Minister. I shall inform everyone. The fire of revolt will be ignited in Mayapur itself.'

'You cannot do that. The people know how fond the king is of Queen Chandraprabha. Consider your own people. Also consider the queen. What is the point of sending her back to Pratappur with the king? Will she be able to live there in peace? Won't she be driven to death by torment and insult? Take her away, King of Gobha. Take her away before an Aryan man's pride reduces everyone to ashes.'

Just then Chandraprabha appears in the doorway. Chief Minister Sogor and Sadhukumar stand motionless, as if struck by a thunderbolt. Someone seems to have wiped away the radiance from the moon, leaving behind dull clay.

Looking at her sad face, both men greet the queen, their hearts squirming with pain. Before they can say anything, Chandraprabha raises her hand and says in a steady voice, 'I've heard everything, Chief Minister. My husband's piercing words have perforated my entire being. In the last few hours, many harsh truths have dawned upon me. There's only one question I wish to ask the king of Gobha.'

'Please ask, Your Highness,' Sadhukumar speaks up.

'Will the people of Gobha forsake you if you carry Pratapchandra's wife and her disgrace to them?'

Slightly confused by the question, Sadhukumar responds, 'The people of my land are not so base, Your Highness. There is no room in their minds for such lowly matters. They will believe whatever I say and stand by me. There is no question of forsaking me. But why should I submit to such grave injustice? Why should you?'

'Didn't the chief minister say a beautiful woman is a better gain than a bloody battle? What is the point of getting lost in the sandstorm of truth and deception? I have lived in the royal palace of an Aryan king whose pride rested in his superior lineage, power and wealth. I have seen how a woman's dignity is razed to the ground over a minor matter. I, too, am craving release from this life of humiliation, King of Gobha. Please take me away.'

Exhausted by the festivities, tears, insult, shock and her impending motherhood, Chandraprabha kneels down before the king of Gobha.

There is still some time before the night comes to an end.

SEVEN

The nighttime Brahmaputra is solitary. The swish after swish of innumerable oars has created an eerie cadence in the heart of the foggy river. Above is a pristine autumn sky. And below, a misty sea. As if a milky river has been aroused by the sparkle of moonlight. As if a group of mysterious explorers were travelling down the river.

Carried by the downstream current.

The oarsmen alternate between rowing and resting. The brightness of the moon has dimmed. As has Chandraprabha's light.

Sitting in an ordinary *tangkhrong* boat canopied with palm leaves, she rests her head on her knees. Exiled, lonely, stunned Chandraprabha.

She is accompanied by two of Sadhukumar's bodyguards, sitting at opposite ends of the boat, who are keeping a close watch on her on the orders of the Gobha king.

Sadhukumar had perceived the shadows of devastation in her expressionless eyes. Chandraprabha had not wept. Nor uttered a single word. She could try to end her life by jumping into the Brahmaputra.

Apart from a handful of guards on board, only King Pratapchandra, Chief Minister Sogor, Sadhukumar and a few trustworthy soldiers know of Chandraprabha's banishment. No one else has seen her leaving. In the final hour before dawn, Chandraprabha was secretly placed aboard Sadhukumar's boat. She boarded calmly and steadily, her head bowed, without looking at or speaking to anybody. No words of grief or repentance escaped her lips.

Standing aboard another boat, Sadhukumar is watching Chandraprabha. She is still wearing the same clothes and ornaments from earlier in the day. The sight of her getting onto the boat, without so much as a look behind her, had made his heart twinge with pain and compassion for her. His blood is also starting to boil with rage. He wants to confront the grim-faced Pratappur soldiers and bring down the conceited Pratapchandra's kingdom.

Chandraprabha had looked up at Sadhukumar once as she climbed onto the boat. Her eyes dripping pure entreaty. To avoid bloodshed. It had slowly slackened his tight grip on his sparkling *langkhui*. He ordered the boats to set sail. At that very moment, Sogor broke down crying, disregarding his status, his dignity. He knelt before the queen, begging forgiveness. Chandraprabha's face had shown no reaction. Calmly, she responded, 'Please rise, Chief Minister. Wipe away your tears. Is it worth repenting a relationship that can be uprooted by a gentle breeze?'

'Please voice your protest, Your Highness,' Sadhukumar had exclaimed in exasperation.

'I shall not, King of Gobha. I cannot be unjust to the innocent people of another kingdom while fighting for my own justice. If there is no place for me in your realm, there is always Baba Brahmaputra. Why fear?'

Then she had taken slow, deliberate steps onto the boat. The utter rigidity of her decision had stunned Sadhukumar. And Sogor. And perhaps everybody else.

The solitary riverbank remained devoid of noise, commotion or the sound of whimpering. In grave silence, as if it were a routine occurrence, Queen Chandraprabha, the mahishi of the mighty King Pratapchandra, was exiled from her own country. She, along with Sadhukumar and his bodyguards, surrounded by Pratapchandra's armed soldiers, emerged from a secret emergency gate under the direction of the chief minister.

Sogor had forbidden entry into that section of the palace until they left. Everyone in the palace had sensed something serious was taking place. Even before the shock of Chandraprabha's drowning had worn off, a new wave of anticipation had swept through the palace, which no one questioned. No one said anything, afraid of committing an offence.

Everyone inside the palace was awake. But no one dared to come out of their rooms. They listened fearfully and attentively to the sounds of heavy footsteps, people rushing around and doors opening and closing. The booming voice of King Pratapchandra faintly reached their ears.

Eventually, all the sounds ceased, and a profound silence enveloped the palace. Exhausted from the events of the day, most of the occupants had fallen asleep by the time Chandraprabha boarded the boat.

And King Pratapchandra?

The combination of wine, exertion, rage and excitement had lured him into a deep slumber. Chandraprabha had glanced at his sleeping face for a moment before leaving her chamber.

Chief Minister Sogor and Sadhukumar had witnessed the playful, teenaged queen suddenly transform into a composed woman replete with the wisdom of life. Their hearts were pounding with helpless anger and boundless agony. The Gobha king is sitting quietly on his boat now – agitated by a mix of sorrow, fury and humiliation. Not only Sadhukumar, the bodyguards are also sitting similarly on the other boats.

A group of young men. Disciplined yet unrestrained by fear. They had set out for Mayapur singing and rejoicing, never imagining that they would return unhappily with the divine-looking wife of King Pratapchandra.

The thirst for battle surged in their veins. Their weapon-wielding hands are fidgeting.

Silently they sit.

Restless and humiliated.

Their anger burning red.

But powerless.

They are bound by the interest of security and sovereignty of Gobha.

A feeble force against the mighty Pratapchandra's brutality.

Trapped by Chief Minister Sogor's diplomatic reasoning.

Lost before Queen Chandraprabha's will and Sadhukumar's resolve.

Yet no one doubts Sadhukumar. No one despises Chandraprabha. On the contrary, their hearts scorch with pain on observing the radiant queen sitting still.

Just the day before, they had seen her moonlit happy face. Camp after camp in Mayapur could talk about nothing except the beauty and simplicity of the queen, and the magnanimity and hospitality of the king.

Now, the fairy-like queen sits like a commoner, her head bowed on a boat, devoid of the comforts befitting a royal.

The soldiers are bewildered. In their society, too, laws punish adulterous men and women. In fact, it is deemed essential to preserve the social fabric. The chief priest holds the authority to punish an infidel man or a woman. But the accused can defend themselves at the trial. If lacking evidence, the accused can swear upon the *tuloxi* plant on their innocence and the trial is adjourned for some time. The Tiwaliboongs believe that if someone falsely swears on the tuloxi, something bad is bound to befall that person. If their innocence passes the test of time, there is no punishment.

The Laloong society thrives on faith and trust.

Thus, the young men are frozen in shock by the events in Mayapur.

What kind of individuals are these? What society is this? Can a relationship survive distrust, suspicion and lack of faith? Can a society endure such conditions?

In Laloong, women enjoy freedom. They are respected. They hold certain rights. No woman of Chandraprabha's age is considered eligible for marriage in their society.

Unlike what they heard in Mayapur, child marriage is not part of their customs. No man has the right to subject a woman to torture or abandon her at his whim. The Tiwashas may lack wealth, but they possess discipline. The society's leaders administer justice impartially. No woman is ever punished by unilateral consideration.

'We understand how to forgive,' Sadhukumar silently contemplates. 'When one commits a minor offence or breaks a rule driven by emotions, they are penalized with the resposibility of organizing a communal feast, allowing them to rejoin society as one of its own. But how could Pratapchandra, who took pride in being an Aryan king, punish them unilaterally, denying them the chance to defend themselves? What kind of justice is this? What kind of masculinity? Or bravery? How could a benevolent ruler abandon his beloved wife over unfounded suspicion? How can he lead with such a mindset?'

Over the Brahmaputra's mid-waters in the last hour of the night, Sadhukumar swears by Fa Mahadeo: 'I shall cherish your Mahishi, King Pratapchandra. I shall crown her with respect and dignity in my kingdom. I shall help her forget the pain she endured on your soil. Gobha may lack the wealth of Pratappur or Mayapur, but it abounds in love. It possesses simplicity. Faith. Humanity. Your vanity shall be vanquished, King Pratapchandra. King of Gobha Sadhukumar shall defeat you.'

'Deoraja!' a guard's cry echoes from another boat. 'Her Highness has fallen down. She is not responding.'

Sadhukumar jumps to the adjacent boat. He sees Chandraprabha lying unconscious under the canopy. Sitting down beside her, Sadhukumar stares unblinkingly at the queen's pale face for a while. He requests in his native tongue, 'Bring me some water to help awaken her. She has endured a great deal, and it may have taken a toll on her.'

A bamboo tube filled with water is quickly brought to Sadhukumar. Carefully, he sprinkles the water. Chandraprabha shivers, gradually opening her eyes. It takes her a moment to reorient herself to reality. She sits up unsteadily and looks at Sadhukumar with fearful eyes, questioning his intentions. Had he come over to assert the authority he had obtained from Pratapchandra? Did he plan to violate her womanhood in the middle of the Brahmaputra?

'Go to sleep, Your Highness. You are not well. There are bananas, packaged boiled rice and water on the boat. Try to eat something to regain your strength. I shall sit outside. If you need anything, please call me.'

Placing the bamboo tube near her, Sadhukumar leaves.

With a sigh of relief, Chandraprabha drifts back to sleep.

It is early morning now.

EIGHT

'I can't believe it, Maghibai. How can this be true? Can the Brahmaputra truly summon Her Highness, our queen, in a dream? And even if it did, would His Royal Highness give away his ethereal queen to the river?' Bokuli exclaims, agitated.

The mood in the capital of Pratappur has turned gloomy. People are consumed with grief. It has hardly been a few hours since King Pratapchandra entered the palace. The capital, no, the whole kingdom is abuzz with the news that Queen Chandraprabha has not returned. It is being said that the queen was pulled into the Brahmaputra while waiting in the shallow waters by the shore. Later, the Brahmaputra had appeared in the king's dream and commanded him to offer his wife. Disobeying would result in the destruction of the entire kingdom. For the well-being of his people, King Pratapchandra was forced to part with his most beloved queen.

Chief Minister Sogor, with the king's permission, has shared this tale to calm the public outrage over Pratapchandra's actions. While many of the people accompanying the king, who had witnessed Chandraprabha's fall into the water, are recounting it themselves, no one has mentioned her being offered to the Brahmaputra, as Sogor has claimed. The news has spread like wildfire. Many believe it. Others do not. As it passed from mouth to mouth, anecdotes have been woven into the story. The queen has become the subject of intense discussion throughout the kingdom.

Inside the palace, however, a deafening quiet prevails. Servants speak in hushed tones, nobody daring to comment or grieve loudly. King Pratapchandra's demeanour suggests there is more to Chief Minister Sogor's version, but nobody knows what it could be. Fear of incurring the king's fury and committing felony is keeping them silent.

Except for Bokuli.

She had accompanied Chandraprabha to Mayapur, and stayed by the queen's side until the moment Sadhukumar pulled her out of the water. Even as Chandraprabha had been carried to her bedchamber, Bokuli had keenly observed the crimson flush of rage appear on King Pratapchandra's face.

Soon after, on the orders of the chief minister, everyone had been commanded to leave. The massive teakwood door to the inner sanctum of the palace was ordered shut.

Bokuli had disregarded orders to stay in her room. Her love for her queen drove her to seek information about Chandraprabha. Seeing soldiers in the palace, fear overcame her and she vowed to perform a sacred ritual for Queen Chandraprabha's safety. She didn't know what happened after that. The chief minister, upon discovering Bokuli, had roared at her, after which she ran for her life through the main entrance.

So she refuses to believe this bizarre story. Nevertheless, she has stayed silent. It was only when the queen mother, by way of old Maghi, the messenger, sought to uncover the truth that Bokuli began to open up. Yet as she narrates the events, her emotions grow fervent and tears flow freely – a mix of grief, anger and despair.

'Softly, softly – speak softly, Bokuli – if someone overhears, we're done for – please, don't cry,' old Maghi pleads fearfully.

Bokuli screams in response. 'Who should I fear? Let the king cut me to pieces or banish me. Either way, Bokuli will not live in this sinful palace any longer.'

'I request you, say no more, Bokuli – anything could happen. We are lowly people. Why should we poke our nose in matters concerning kings and officers? You're still young, so you can take risks. My hair has turned grey with experience. So, I remain quiet. Don't say anything – whatever you saw or know – keep it to yourself, understand? Now, let's go to the queen mother. She grows impatient. Bokuli, promise me you won't speak a word to anyone,' old Maghi persuades, finally coaxing Bokuli. Together, they make their way to Queen Mother Yajnavati's chambers.

Yajnavati anxiously awaits old Maghi's arrival. The news of Chandraprabha being offered to the Brahmaputra has left the queen mother stunned, much like many others who are struggling to believe the tale. She hasn't had the chance to meet her son and verify the details. Barely conscious, the inebriated Pratapchandra fell asleep the moment he entered the palace.

In the past, whenever the king returned from his travels, he promptly visited his mother. However, this time things are different. Yajnavati has discovered that Pratapchandra has been awake for some time, yet he remains confined to his room. Eager to uncover the truth, she sends Maghi, her oldest and most loyal maid-in-waiting, to fetch Bokuli.

Old Maghi and Bokuli enter, paying their respects. Yajnavati erases every trace of anxiety from her face as she speaks in her usual solemn tone, 'Bokuli, tell me everything without concealing a single detail.'

Queen Mother Yajnavati listens without batting an eyelid. Slowly, her worried expression becomes grave. After sitting silently for a long time, she says to the weeping Bokuli. 'Don't breathe a word about this to anyone. If the news spreads, royal dignity will suffer, and state administration will weaken. You are a mature girl. Keep everything to yourself.' She then turns to Maghi. 'Send someone to inform Ramchandra that I wish to see him.'

Before Maghi can respond, a maid enters, announcing, 'Chief Minister Sogor wishes to meet you, honourable queen mother.'

When Yajnavati returns from her meeting with the chief minister, she finds her son in her chamber. It is evident that a tempest of immeasurable suffering, immeasurable lack of self-control, immeasurable disorder has torn him apart. His face is devoid of softness, despite his customary neat attire and combed hair. It lacks the regal glow. The usual regal charm.

He looks strained and ill. His eyes appear sleep-deprived and intoxicated. The lips are parched.

His posture and facial expression show clear signs of fatigue and apathy. Profound loneliness and delusion.

The Pratapchandra driven by insatiable rage and consumed by an urge for revenge has vanished. Since returning to the kingdom, his agitation has gradually subsided. Countless memories disturb him, striking at the core of his heart.

Ah! Mahishi.

How sorrowful, how still Chandraprabha's face had seemed. When she was brought back to the palace, ill from drinking the waters of the Brahmaputra, Pratapchandra had stood near her sleeping bed – how exhausted her eyes had looked.

Had he noticed any traces of guilt or fear in those eyes? Was there any evidence of an unfaithful woman's transgressions? A murky truth?

At that moment, it seemed as though he had seen it. But why does it now feel like he had seen nothing?

Mahishi had attempted to sit up on noticing Pratapchandra's presence. She had said wearily, 'You are unhappy with me, aren't you? But to be honest, I hadn't gone very far. I didn't realize it was so deep there.'

Listening to her words, the fires of envy and suspicion burning within Pratapchandra had flared up. He had struck Chandraprabha with harsh words, inflicting wound after wound to assert his authority over her.

Now he remembers – the look of profound astonishment that had filled his mahishi's eyes.

Without making any attempt to defend herself from her husband's onslaught, she had stared at him in bewilderment. Just stared. And then, she had burst into tears.

Chandraprabha hadn't uttered a single word of protest, nor any to defend herself. Even after Pratapchandra had screamed for her to apologize countless times, she had remained silent. She had only cried and cried.

But those tears could not douse the flames of vengeance, hostility, jealousy and distrust blazing inside Pratapchandra's heart. Instead, they ignited the fire even more fiercely. The intense urge to tear apart both Chandraprabha and the king of Gobha began to swirl in his mind. If the chief minister had not intervened, he would have had them both turned into food for the fish.

Sogor had forcefully taken the sword from his grip. They had both gone to an adjacent room where the chief minister convinced the king to abandon his plan.

Pratapchandra had expected Mahishi to break down upon hearing this news. He anticipated her falling at his feet, unwilling to live the life of a woman abandoned by her man.

However, she did not appear.

Pratapchandra waited and waited, filled with anticipation, until he eventually passed out from the effects of wine. In the meantime, Chandraprabha had left. She had left with the non-believer, the non-Aryan king of Gobha.

She rejected the power and opulence of her own lord and master, the mighty son of Aryans, Pratapchandra.

By the time he woke up, it was already noon.

The sandy shores of the river Luit were now empty. The guests and invitees had all left.

All that remained after the festivities were the remnants of the celebration and the vacant camps.

Pratapchandra did not ask anyone about anything, and no one spoke to him either. Lunch was served to him, and arrangements were made for his bath.

As the king paced back and forth outside Chandraprabha's bedroom, his heart raced. The calmness he experienced after eating was momentary, and the sobering light of day brought emotional turmoil. It was as if the wall of hatred he had built against

Chandraprabha was developing a crack, leaving Pratapchandra confused and anxious. Seeking answers was impossible. Just then Chief Minister Sogor arrived, signalling their departure.

As he prepared to mount the regally bedecked elephant, the king suddenly came to a halt. He stood in silence, staring at the nearby elephants and Bokuli, who stood at a distance.

Mahishi? Where was Mahishi?

'Please mount, O Son of Aryans, for the auspicious moment to begin the journey will pass,' the chief minister urged, also surprised by his reaction. Then, in an instant, it dawned on Pratapchandra.

Mahishi had left. She had been given away to Sadhukumar, the king of Gobha.

The return journey had been filled with loneliness and anguish. The conflict between his hatred and distrust of his wife and his deep love for her had torn him apart.

'Ramchandra.'

He starts at the sound of his mother's voice. Instantly, King Pratapchandra stands up, assuming a criminal and subordinate stance. Turning to his mother, he forces a smile and says, 'You called for me, honourable mother?'

'Yes, Ramchandra. Sit down, you look completely drained.'

Pratapchandra sits, lowering his head, waiting for his mother's question.

The queen mother observes him. Is there any point in asking this man anything? A man mourning the loss of his wife?

It is clear that he is not happy after abandoning her. He seems shattered.

Yajnavati knows her son well. She had witnessed Pratapchandra's intense attraction and possessiveness towards Chandraprabha. She could imagine the mental turmoil of her deeply sentimental son on regaining his rationality after being lost in a moment's passion.

Is this man, who deserted his wife due to unfounded suspicion, worthy of forgiveness? Worthy of solace? Worthy of support?

Absolutely not – the queen mother's conscience revolts. Remembering her expecting daughter-in-law Chandraprabha's quiet, innocent, bright face, her heart aches with sorrow.

Chief Minister Sogor had told her everything, after which the queen mother spared no words in her reproach.

'Why did you do this, Sogor? Why did you give away my kingdom's Lakhimi for no reason?'

'I was helpless, Queen Mother. There was no other way to avoid imminent battle, bloodshed and disgrace.

'No other way? Why not? In countless complex situations, I have seen you come up with suitable solutions. Even as a skilful politician, you failed to save the innocent queen? You sent her to a foreign land with an unfamiliar man to protect your own kingdom? What kind of politics is this? It is an affront to the valiant Kshatriyas. They march into battle, swearing on their mother's milk. Women are revered as symbols of power, knowledge, wealth – so how could these same Kshatriyas outrage the dignity of the queen? Where was your ashi? Where were the soldiers of this kingdom? Why didn't you capture the frenetic king and bring him back here? Why did you add to his insanity with wine?'

'I am a loyal servant of the king, Queen Mother. I would never have the audacity to defy his command. I, too, am suffering. But I am powerless. I managed to prevent Her Highness from the death sentence, averting a political catastrophe. I admit the shortcomings in my duty towards humanity and the flaws in my manhood that you have pointed out. I am ready to accept any punishment for this offence.'

Though she understood his reasoning, the truth was difficult for the queen mother to accept. Filled with incredible anger towards her son and the chief minister, she returned to her chambers.

'My son, are you now baffled by your irrational decision?' The question pierced King Pratapchandra like a spear. Perplexed, he looked up at his mother.

What kind of query was this?

What kind of a horrifying question was this?

Pratapchandra had expected his mother to either mock or praise him. What was this instead?

Living within the confines of the palace, from where did a royal woman derive such introspective power? Is this the authority of motherhood? Is this the surplus power bestowed upon women by nature?

'What is the basis for your assumption, honourable mother?' The words escaped his mind in the form of a question.

'I am your mother, my son. If I cannot understand what is going on in your mind, who else will? Tell me, isn't what I have said true?'

Pratapchandra remained silent for a moment before speaking in a weary voice, 'I may not be baffled, honourable mother, but I'm certainly scorched with suffering.'

'Scorched with suffering! It means you are confused, Ramchandra. This confusion arises from the depths of your mind. Do you have any idea what kind of woman Chandraprabha is? Do you truly believe Chandraprabha is capable of adultery? Your excessive love and emotion have led you to make the wrong decision.'

'How can you say it's wrong, honourable mother? I saw their intimacy with my own eyes. I witnessed their attraction and weakness for one another—'

'That was a delusion, my son,' the queen mother interjected. 'I am certain your vision was wrong. The decision was wrong. Your analysis was wrong. Your anger was wrong. You are guilty of unjustly punishing Chandraprabha. You have abandoned your virtuous wife without justification and based on false suspicion, my son.'

'How can you be so certain? You weren't present in Mayapur, were you? Did you have the opportunity to observe her conduct?'

'I may not have witnessed anything firsthand, and I may not have been present in Mayapur, but I know the truth. How can the woman carrying your child in her womb and about to give birth to your heir degrade her own dignity? How could she betray her husband?'

Pratapchandra is left speechless, his eyes fixed on his mother in disbelief. He is thunderstruck by her words.

What revelation is this? What reasoning is this? Was Mahishi expecting a child? While Pratapchandra, consumed by suspicion and anger, was closely monitoring Chandraprabha's every move, was she carrying his child in her womb? The descendant of King Dharmapal?

It has now become glaringly evident.

Everything has become clear to Pratapchandra. The source of his Mahishi's happiness is now evident. The enraged queen mother continues, 'I knew something like this had happened. You made a grave mistake, Ramchandra. A colossal blunder. Your distorted mind tainted Chandraprabha's purity. You have paved the path for the downfall of our dynasty. Haven't you heard of the Pandava and Kaurava clans? How the suffering of the innocent Draupadi brought ruin to a once prosperous kingdom? How the lineage came to a halt? By succumbing to your Aryan pride, you have cursed our own lineage. Who gave you the authority to do this? Just because she is your wife, you think you can elevate her or abandon her at your whim? What have you done, Ramchandra? You have handed over our goddess of wealth to another before she could even give birth to the heir of our dynasty.'

Pratapchandra's gaze softens as he observes his mother's mounting rage and emotional turmoil. Rising from his seat, he gently takes both of her hands in his own and hesitantly adds, 'Honourable mother, tell me that you are saying these words to torment me. Tell me that all of this is false. Chandraprabha was not pregnant, honourable mother. If she had been, I would have known.'

'How could you possibly know, Ramchandra? I had forbidden her from sharing the news with you until it was confirmed. With your restless nature, you would have disclosed it to everyone. To spare ourselves any embarrassment, I'd intended to wait until I was absolutely certain. What have you done, Ramchandra? Have you, like your namesake, also exiled my Sita-like daughter-in-law?' Pratapchandra is staring at his mother, motionless. All his anger has turned into tears.

Kneeling next to his mother, Pratapchandra starts to cry. 'I've made a grave mistake, honourable mother, a grave transgression. What should I do now? Let me go, right away. Let me bring my mahishi back from Gobha. I shall prostrate myself at Sadhukumar's feet, if necessary. I shall fall at Mahishi's feet and beg forgiveness.'

'Impossible. You've made it known to everyone that she was offered to the Brahmaputra. Bringing her back is now out of the question. This mistake cannot be rectified. Once a royal mahishi has been given away, there is no way of getting her back. Gather yourself, my son. You will have to live without Chandraprabha. There is no way out. Go. Return to your room.'

Pratapchandra rises, leaving his grief-stricken mother behind. With faltering steps, he walks out. To a lifetime of isolation. A lifetime of remorse. Of anguish and despair.

NINE

'Drink this *kakhir*, Your Highness. If you don't eat properly, Deoraja will be unhappy with me,' Xunzira says, offering a bowl of milk to her pai.

Chandraprabha, in the final stages of her pregnancy, is sitting inside her designated room in the palace of Gobha. She is worn out from both mental and physical fatigue. Xunzira's heart sinks as she observes Chandraprabha's pale face. It hasn't been long since she was brought to the palace of Gobha. Immediately after the Lungkhon Misawa festival, celebrated for the prosperity of the land and its people, the king had sent men to bring Xunzira from her home. She had later learned that they had searched extensively for her due to her knowledge of the language, customs and manners of the mekdo' people from the north bank. At that time, Xunzira had been grieving the loss of her parents and relatives in an epidemic. She had come to the palace at the request of her clan's headman, the jela baro. The plan was for Xunzira to nurse the pregnant queen until the birth of her child and then return home. Chandraprabha had no knowledge of the Tiwaliboongs' language or customs, nor did she have any other means of communication. She could not speak to anyone in the palace other than Sadhukumar, relying on gestures and signs to communicate with everyone. Xunzira had been instructed to stay by the queen's side and help her.

It hasn't been long, but in this short time, Xunzira, who is nearly Chandraprabha's age, has become her most loyal companion.

The queen is stunning, but also deeply depressed. What an extraordinary wife she had been. Some evil king from the north bank had punished her for no reason and banished her into exile with Deoraja Sadhukumar.

What a despicable man.

Did such a fairy-like, beautiful and virtuous woman deserve to be treated in this manner?

Xunzira's heart fills with compassion whenever she thinks of Chandraprabha. She takes excellent care of her, trying to keep her happy by singing, telling stories and whatnot. Nowadays, the queen occasionally laughs at Xunzira's words before descending back into gloom.

Sadhukumar, distressed by her sadness, had once summoned Xunzira and asked, 'Why can't you keep Her Highness happy, Nannao?'

'I try my best, Deoraja. Yet she remains depressed. Only Her Highness knows about the depth of grief inside her.'

'And we understand it too. That's why you have been brought here. You must take good care of her. Look after her with love. Teach her our language and customs, so that she can manage when you are not around.'

'Is she going to be here forever, Deoraja?' Xunzira had asked.

'Of course. Why not? Our society has embraced her, shown her affection. You are aware of everything, aren't you, Nannao? Now she is one of our own. Look after her well. Ensure she eats properly. Attend to her needs. Her life was once luxurious in the palace of a powerful king. Look at where she has ended up: in the kingdom of a poor ruler like me.'

'Why should we call ourselves poor, Deoraja? What do we lack?' Xunzira had protested.

'You are right. What do we lack, Nannao. We have love in our hearts. We don't know how to think evil. We don't know how to be evil. We can certainly look after Her Highness with great affection. Tell me, can't we?'

'We can, Deoraja. The queen is so good. She never fusses about the comforts of life.'

Xunzira reveres Sadhukumar as if he were a god, because he calls her Nannao. She holds him dearer than her own. Could there possibly be another king like Sadhukumar? Perhaps not, not in all the villages, not in all the samadis of the kingdom. His goodness surpasses that of any other panthai. His affectionate nature extends to everyone, tirelessly working for the welfare of all.

How deeply he cares about Her Highness's comfort! He leaves no stone unturned in his quest to ensure Her Highness's well-being. He visits the queen often, asking if there is anything she requires. Most of the time, however, he communicates through Xunzira, seeking information from her and guiding on how to fulfil the queen's needs. Xunzira has noticed that whenever Sadhukumar requests to see Her Highness, the queen seems to recoil in fear. It's beyond her comprehension to understand this reaction. After all, Sadhukumar is not a tiger, is he? Will he eat her up?

One day, Xunzira had mustered up the courage to ask the queen about it. But she had seemed more terrified by her question. Timidly, Chandraprabha had replied, 'Why should I be afraid? How can I be fearful of the person who has given me shelter?'

'Then why do you drag your feet when Deoraja wants to meet you?' she persisted.

'I feel embarrassed to appear before him in this condition, you see.'

Xunzira could tell from her expression that there was more to her fear.

Sadhukumar, like Xunzira, had noticed the queen's hesitation a while ago. Perhaps this is why he did not visit her as much anymore, preferring to talk to Xunzira instead.

'Drink the kakhir, Your Highness. It has become cold,' Xunzira reminds Chandraprabha, who is sitting absentmindedly with a bowl of milk in front of her.

'I don't feel like it, Xunzira.'

'Even if you don't want to, you must drink it. None of us drink kakhir. Deoraja has brought a cow and a calf along with attendants all the way from Bhuyagaon, just for you. Moreover, must you starve the child in your womb?'

'What do you know about a child in the womb?' she chuckles, causing Xunzira to blush with embarrassment.

Chandraprabha can't help loving this innocent young girl, who took care of her every need and worked tirelessly to keep her happy.

Behind all the care and affection, she can sense the genuine warmth Xunzira has for her, along with the attentive supervision of the king of Gobha.

Who doesn't adore Chandraprabha? Everyone in the palace regards her as their most revered guest, speaking to her with love and respect, and attending to her every need.

It felt as though she had stepped into a whole new world upon her arrival in Gobha. Life here seemed miles away from her previous existence in Pratappur. After sailing from Mayapur and disembarking on the south bank, the weary, exhausted and traumatized Chandraprabha had arrived at the palace of Gobha on the back of an elephant. The sun was still setting, casting its golden hues across the surroundings. At first, Chandraprabha had gazed silently at the unfamiliar structure before her. Then her attention had shifted to the women and children who observed their new guest with timidity. A strange feeling of apprehension had overwhelmed her.

She had arrived in this foreign land carrying the weight of infamy. Would this land also subject her to torment? Would it reject her, treating her as an outcast due to her status as a deserted wife? Would they scorn her because she was a foreigner, given away by Pratapchandra to Sadhukumar? These thoughts filled her with a sense of unease.

In her previous life, Chandraprabha had been praised for her beauty, and she had shared many passionate and amorous moments with Pratapchandra. It is for this reason that she is plagued by the sharp claws of fear. Will Sadhukumar treat her the same way her husband did? Will he assert the authority bestowed by Pratapchandra on her?

Chandraprabha is unfamiliar with this society and its men. In her mind, men were synonymous with her husband. As she stood outside the Gobha palace, the fear of losing her dignity gripped her.

The king of Gobha had escorted Chandraprabha inside and provided her with a room to rest while he spoke to his family members in their unfamiliar language. She had heard them utter strange words like *do'*, *abra*, *aai*, *aaya* and so on, without understanding their meanings. But now, thanks to Xunzira, she had come to understand how those words expressed surprise, grief, astonishment and agreement.

Over time, she learned many more things. Gradually, all of her fears have dissipated.

Except for one.

Chandraprabha continues to be terrified of Sadhukumar, despite never perceiving any signs of lust in his actions or expressions. Instead, she witnesses his admiration and respect towards her.

Despite this, the slightest noise at night sends tremors through her body. She startles at the imagined sound of Sadhukumar's footsteps, even though he sleeps in a separate room. The sleepless nights and growing pregnancy exhaust her. She longs for rest constantly, but Xunzira forbids it, encouraging her to explore the world outside the palace. To observe grains being ground in the mortar. To watch weavers weaving cloth on a handloom. To see how delicious dishes are prepared using herbs in the kitchen. To see how the fish are dried over the hearth. To see the overgrowth of the betel nut trees and betel leaf creepers in the rear garden. To explore the edge of the pond.

'You have very beautiful hair, Your Highness,' Xunzira remarked, bringing Chandraprabha back to reality with a smile.

'Really? And what about yours? It can even outshine the darkness of the night.'

'We use alkali extracted from burnt bamboo sprouts to wash our hair. It is beneficial to hair quality. Since you've started using it too, your hair is improving. What did you use before, Your Highness?'

Chandraprabha's mood dampened. As if scenes from the palace of Pratappur had infiltrated her mind in an instant.

'Could you share, Your Highness? We can give it a try.'

'We would use soap-nut tree seeds and a variety of herbs. Also, we washed our hair with a black pulse. I must admit, I'm not knowledgeable about these matters. The maids-in-waiting would bring these ingredients and help in washing my hair. You know what? We even used to fumigate our hair with burnt incense.'

'Why did you do that?'

'It gives the hair fragrance. Unlike you all, we never used mustard oil as it would make our hair sticky.' Chandraprabha laughed, and Xunzira joined in.

'When Deoraja arrives today, I'll ask him to bring us some incense sticks. He will immediately agree. He will get anything for you, including the *sanai* from the sky. He promised to bring fragrant timber on his way back from attending the *jongkong* phuja. Even musk. I shall burn the fragrant timber and blow its smoke into your hair. There is no need for incense. What will you do with the musk, Your Highness?'

'Musk? Who said I need musk?'

'Nobody. He just said that he will get it for you.'

Chandraprabha's mind filled with irritation. Why was Sadhukumar acting like this? How did he come to know whether she used musk in her beauty routine? What was the need for such unwarranted attention? Why was he so invested in her well-being? Did Sadhukumar consider her as his wife? Was he anticipating the arrival of her child?

'Could you please explain your use of the musk? It's quite rare. Sometimes, our royalty breaks it into pieces and uses small bits as a kind of medicine. Is that what you do?'

'Yes, that's right. By the way, what is the jongkong festival, Xunzira?' Chandraprabha asked, trying to shift the conversation to ease her growing frustration and anxiety.

'Ah, the jongkong festival? It's our religious celebration, meant to safeguard our cattle and other livestock from harm and ensure their well-being. We've had a good harvest, so we pay homage to both old man Pothor and old woman Pothor.'

'Who are they?'

'They are our harvest deities. A bountiful harvest ensures our sustenance. During the festival, we also invoke blessings from our ancestors, old man Thom and old woman Thom. If all goes well by the grace of Phradeo, I will take you to witness the festival after the birth of your child. It takes place in Agon, the eighth month of our calendar, and will be celebrated again next Agon if everything goes as planned.'

'Who is Phradeo?'

'Fa Mahadeo. Our principal god. Our priest says he is the master of all beings. He is also called Xos Khoider, the protector of the paddy seedlings. He's the one who bestowed upon us the customs for our festivals and ceremonies, tools for farming, musical instruments and banath-bathu for the dancers. He provided us with cattle and poultry.'

'Xunzira, you seem well-versed in religious matters and faith,' Chandraprabha compliments.

'Knowledge of these matters is widespread among our people. During religious festivals in our prayer hall, we hear about these things. Once you've given birth, I'll take you to the sacred shrines of Moha Deoxaal and Boxundhori Thaan, Your Highness. At Moha Deoxaal, we worship our god, Fa Mahadeo. You might not understand the priest's chants; we don't fully grasp them either. They chant from memory, handed down through generations. You don't have long before your delivery, do you?'

'I don't know, Xunxira.'

'Of course. How would you. You don't have your maah or your mother-in-law here. You don't even understand what our elderly women are saying. I shall tell you after asking them.'

'No, no, please, Xunzira. I'd feel embarrassed.'

'Alright, I won't. Only if you drink the kakhir, though.' Xunzira's eyes sparkle playfully. Even the queen can't help laughing.

Just then an eager young boy approached and stood on the doorway, delivering some message in the Laloong dialect.

'What's he saying?' Chandraprabha asks, surprised.

'He says our soldiers have captured a spy from a kingdom on the north bank. They've tied him to the tree near the palace where the elephants are kept. Deoraja is there. He says that we can watch if we'd like. We'll be able to see him if we go out; there's already a large crowd gathered,' Xunzira explains.

The queen's heart quickens. Could it be a spy from Pratapchandra's kingdom? Why would a spy from Pratappur come here? What kind of information were they seeking?

She stands up, suddenly out of breath and exhausted.

She had been feeling this way a lot recently. Xunzira had asked someone and found out that it was because of the child in her womb. For some time now, Chandraprabha has been experiencing the gradual movements of her child inside her. Despite the fatigue and discomfort, the child's gentle motions have brought her a newfound sense of liberation. She has been advised to walk cautiously, and there are several restrictions imposed on her, such as not going out after dark. Since Chandraprabha spends most of her time sitting or resting, Xunzira makes an effort to take her on walks.

'You shouldn't be sitting and resting all the time. Expectant mothers in our community are quite active; they even grind grains with a mortar and pestle because it can benefit the child. Should I get you a mortar and pestle too?' Xunzira playfully teases, her words warming Chandraprabha's heart.

What was her connection to these people anyway? She was nothing more than a wretched woman, cast away by her husband, with no family to claim her. She wasn't a queen, rather a mere refugee in Gobha. Yet she was treated with such care and concern, both for her well-being and the welfare of her unborn child.

How strange are the people of this kingdom!

How simple!

How upright!

How honest!

How logical!

How else could she have found such a welcoming sanctuary?

Shortly after entering the palace of Gobha, Sadhukumar had summoned all the chieftains of the kingdom. The clan's borjela, dolois of villages like the hari kunwori, *chokha* borjela, loro and *hadari* had gathered in a large assembly.

Chandraprabha had also attended the meeting. The headsmen had questioned King Sadhukumar and his bodyguards in front of her. While she hadn't understood their questions, she could understand a lot from their expressions and body language. She had noticed that the people would occasionally become excited, astonished and then sad. With Xunzira's help, they had also asked Chandraprabha a few questions, which her margi khamsamai had then translated for them.

Throughout the proceedings, she hadn't perceived any hints of contempt or mistrust in their eyes or on their faces. On the contrary, as the assembly concluded, she noticed reverence and affection directed towards her.

Sadhukumar had explained the outcome of the assembly to her: 'Our people have embraced you as one of their own, Your Highness. You are welcome to live here with respect and dignity. Our society stands by you. They are deeply disappointed with Pratapchandra. You can reside here without fear, considering this your own kingdom and home. We apologize for having to subject you to this trial, but in our society, no decisions are made without everyone's inputs. Even as king, I must abide by the collective will. In our kingdom, society reigns supreme.'

While these words had provided Chandraprabha with a sense of security, she couldn't help but sense another unspoken message hidden in Sadhukumar's thoughts. With a heavy heart, she had left the assembly, already beginning to feel the effects of her anxiety, which she couldn't reveal to anyone. She was haunted by the thought that Sadhukumar might appear at any moment and propose marriage to her. The mere idea of sharing a bed with another man sent shivers down her spine.

As a woman trained in the Aryan culture, she had grown up hearing religious preceptors' instructions and tales of chaste women. Even though her husband had given her away to another man, how could she accept the other man as her husband? Does she have the strength to resist such an unfair offer from Sadhukumar? Ending one's life while carrying a child in the womb is a grave sin. So, what will she do? What?

When he appears before her, he exhibits the same reverence for her as he had in Mayapur. But she has noticed pure, unadulterated love in his eyes! Unfathomable admiration!

For how long would she be able to resist his love? And how?

'Walk slowly, Your Highness, the light is inadequate here,' Xunzira advises.

Chandraprabha, who has come out with Xunzira dreamily, starts. What is she here to see? Who has she come to watch? The spy who has come from the north bank? Why? Why is she feeling this interest?

Is she still harbouring any expectation? For Pratapchandra's appeal? Is she anxiously waiting to return to her husband's home? Unconsciously?

Never.

Never.

Never.

She has left Pratappur forever. She has no affection left for her irrational husband Pratapchandra.

There is, however, something nameless, vague. An emotion stuck in her mind. The child's movements in her womb remind her over and over that she is Pratapchandra's wife. That she is the mother of his unborn child. That she is still wearing vermilion in the parting of her hair. That she still wears the ornaments she wore when she was banished. Everything else has been removed and set aside: the gold wires for her bun, the gold hairpins, the gold comb, the gold and silver flowers, the gold kopali on her forehead and the girdle.

At her core, Chandraprabha has always thought of herself as an Aryan. She cannot abandon her roots, the foundation of her existence.

'Look, Your Highness, look, there – that's the man. Strange! Why is Deoraja thrashing him? Why is he so upset?' Xunzira exclaims animatedly.

Chandraprabha stares in astonishment.

It is true.

Sadhukumar is fuming with anger. His calm, gentle, rational face has turned bright red with rage.

Sadhukumar appears so strange! Exactly like Pratapchandra.

'Why did you come here? What brings you to this kingdom? What do you want to know? Is it to gain information about the exiled queen? Go and tell your king that Chandraprabha is dead. She is not in the kingdom of Gobha. Go and tell your king to never send a spy to this kingdom. Else, we will sacrifice them before Goddess Kalikha and drink his blood. What does he think about the people of Gobha? Or about the king of Gobha? Scared? Weak? A king for name sake, with no military power? Tell him to fight his way into Gobha for any news he wants, if he has the strength and courage. Don't come like a thief.'

Right and left, Sadhukumar is flogging the young man, tied with the rope used for fastening elephants. The normally composed king of Gobha seems to have lost control of himself.

'Xunzira, go, call the king of Gobha and tell him Her Highness is calling him. Go, go.'

Staring speechlessly at Chandraprabha for a second, Xunzira takes to her heels.

Chandraprabha is watching.

Xunzira says something to the king.

Sadhukumar comes to an instant halt. Then, after spitting on the ground with great contempt, he returns with sombre steps.

'You called for me, Your Highness?' he asks calmly, with no trace of anger on his face.

'Yes, I did. Please come to my chamber, king of Gobha. I wish to ask you a few questions.'

Sadhukumar looks shocked to hear such a proposal from Chandraprabha, who had previously only given answers to questions posed to her. He comes to a halt and stares at Chandraprabha, as if trying to understand something. Then he says calmly, 'Please proceed, Your Highness.'

Standing face to face in the bed chamber, Chandraprabha asks, 'What is the meaning of torturing an ordinary spy so severely, Deoraja?'

Sadhukumar stands still in astonishment. 'What is the cause of your concern for an ordinary spy, Your Highness?'

'Because he is a spy from Pratappur, Deoraja. I've heard you're not a ruthless ruler. Until now, you have never punished anybody with your own hands. Even in the midst of the difficult situation in Mayapur, you had remained calm. Why are you so irritable today? How come you are not able to control your anger?'

'For your sake, Your Highness. For your sake. You were banished on false accusations without any trial; what information does he need to gather through a spy? Is he going to reclaim you? Will he make you his queen again?'

'What makes you object even if he does? What if he's being repentant, or if he wants to learn about his wife's well-being? Why should you be so frenzied?'

'Let him collect information. But not by stealthily sending a spy. You have your own dignity, Your Highness. I'm not sure what your status was in Pratappur. But you have a respectable status in this land. The locals consider you as one of their own. Nobody has the right to insult you, Your Highness. Not even King Pratapchandra.'

'It is only an insult if you believe so, king of Gobha. I suspect another reason for your unwarranted excitement.'

'Other suspicion? Which other suspicion, Your Highness?' Sadhukumar asks, astounded.

'You know very well what the suspicion is. I don't feel secure in this palace, king of Gobha.'

'Don't feel secure? But why?'

'Because I am an Aryan woman. A Hindu woman. We are incapable of accepting a second husband.'

A second husband? He keeps staring at her until gradually, the picture in the queen's mind becomes clear. 'I can understand, Your Highness,' he pronounces each word haltingly, enraged by this humiliation.

'It's important for you to understand, Deoraja. I'm about to be the mother of King Pratapchandra's child. I have great respect for you. I am grateful for your courage and generosity, for providing me with a safe refuge. But I owe you nothing more than that. Please do not waste your time and energy on worthless dreams.'

The humiliation, coupled with endless torment, is causing turmoil within Sadhukumar. As the upheaval comes to an end in his mind, a sharp smile appears on his lips as he says, 'I understand, Your Highness. I understand everything. I had not realized. I must confess, I had not understood anything. We lack the intelligence to think crookedly. You, on the other hand, belong to the esteemed Aryan race, possessing superior knowledge. Yet I must say, your twisted thoughts have wounded me. You may hurt me. But I implore you, do not harm yourself with needless fear. We hold you in high regard. We admire you. But we do not covet. Our society does not teach us to be greedy. Do not judge our society based on the views of yours. Such a decision would be erroneous, Your Highness. Fa Mahadeo knows my intentions. I swear on him, you can live here without any fear for as long as you wish. This palace is entirely yours. If you wish to go back to Pratappur, tell us and we'll take you there with honour. I swear on Fa Mahadeo that I shall never spend a night in this palace, ever. I shall never step inside unless absolutely necessary. I will move into the palace of Amsai Marjong today itself. Rest assured, Your Highness, as an honourable guest of our kingdom, you shall never want in security.'

Without waiting for Chandraprabha's response, Sadhukumar leaves with steady steps. In the bedroom illuminated with mustard oil lamps, Chandraprabha stands stupefied, overcome by agonizing mortification – motionless.

TEN

The newborn is crying.

Chandraprabha's newborn. Xunzira has tired herself trying to soothe the baby. Today, she has gone to bathe in the pond next to the palace, taking her clothes along for washing.

Xunzira is furious.

Is Her Highness planning to wash her own clothes? What will Deoraja think of Xunzira if he finds out?

'Let me wash them, Your Highness. You can go and bathe afterwards,' she had insisted.

'No need, Nannao. Haven't you been washing clothes all these days? I should never have allowed a maiden to handle my laundry. Today, the baby will be taken outside. Let me perform the rituals, Xunzira. There's nothing to worry about. You can take care of him.'

With those words, Her Highness had left. However, Xunzira made arrangements for other women to accompany Chandraprabha. Xunzira specifically told them to wash the clothes at any cost. She herself was weary from the demands of babysitting.

A newborn infant, only a few days old. Can it stay away from its mother? Before Xunzira reached the edge of her patience, Chandraprabha entered.

'Troubling you too much?' she laughs.

'For sure. He's been crying and crying. How could he not? He's still an infant, and he gets hungry from time to time. Here, let me feed him some kakhir … no, wait … you just bathed, and the milk in your breast is cold. The baby might catch a chill, Pai. Let me get you something to eat. Should I bring a bowl of kakhir?'

'No, Nannao. Not milk. Get some rice grains for me to chew on. I shall eat once the ritual is over,' Chandraprabha says, taking the baby from Xunzira.

Cajoling the baby, she waits for Xunzira to return.

Since the baby's birth, paddy husk was being burning inside the room, following the advice of experienced women in the palace. Garlic pods and mustard grains were frequently thrown into the fire to ward off evil. Both large and small knives were placed under Chandraprabha's bed. She was being nourished with mud-water fish, pepper, papaya, parboiled rice and other lovingly prepared dishes. The women, including Xunzira, were religiously and genuinely concerned, diligently attending to the care and needs of a new mother in her post-natal stage.

They've done everything within their capacity during these days, right from the birth of the infant until now. Even today, two women accompanying Chandraprabha had washed all her clothes with alkali despite her protests. They even bathed and washed her hair.

Chandraprabha's heart has softened by her boundless love for the women of the palace and Xunzira. Her head is bowed in infinite gratitude.

What does she need to do to repay them? How can she reciprocate their love and respect?

If her own mother or mother-in-law been with her, could they have done anything more?

And the darling Xunzira …

Is she any less a sister to her? It is for this reason, Chandraprabha now calls her nannao, meaning younger sister. She has also taught Xunzira to address her as *bai*, which means elder sister. Xunzira uses 'pai' instead of 'bai'.

It sounds wonderful.

Chandraprabha is overjoyed.

Out of love and gratitude, she pays heed to whatever they say.

'Take, Pai, take.'

Xunzira, clearly out of breath, opens her palm and hands her pai a few grains of rice. Putting the grains in her mouth, Chandraprabha sits down to breastfeed the baby.

'Let me go and watch the ritual. It's about to begin.'

'Alright, Nannao, go.'

The palace has received a makeover today. Since the baby will be taken out of the palace for the first time today, the walls have been plastered with mud. Water infused with tulsi leaves and dog's-tooth grass is being sprinkled to purify the entire palace. All the clothes have been washed and cleaned.

The jela baro and *hetari*, accompanied by the chief priestess, the *hari kuwori*, have arrived to conduct the clan's religious rites. Today marks the customary ceremonial cleanliness day, intended to remove defilement resulting from the birth of an infant.

Xunzira enters the courtyard. On the easternmost side of the neatly plastered courtyard, the elderly ladies sit with hari kuwori, keeping an earthen lamp burning over a pile of tender banana leaves. Nine bedecked bamboo bows and arrows are placed on another pile of banana leaves. Five betel nuts and leaves are arranged behind the earthen lamp.

Standing nearby, Xunzira observes the ritual preparations. After some time, the hari kuwori says in her own dialect, 'It's time to bring the mother and child.'

Before anybody can reply, Xunzira almost runs inside with excited steps.

The baby has gone to sleep.

Dressed formally, Chandraprabha sits near the child, adorned in a pair of finely woven riha-mekhela made from delicate cotton yarn. She has tied the white mekhela with red flowers above her bustline and tightly wound the riha several times around her breasts and waist. Over it, she has draped a floral chador crafted from eri yarns. Sadhukumar requested these clothes to be woven and brought from a nearby village, while the eri chador was woven by the women of the palace.

The winter chill has yet to recede, and the spring bihu festival must be approaching. This location, nestled at the foot of the hills, retains the lingering cold. Chandraprabha has lovingly preserved her gold beads, the flower-engraved silk riha-mekhela and the ethereal, transparent chador brought from Manipur inside a cane chest. She has also kept the ornaments she used to adorn her hair. She still wears ornaments on her hands and in her ears.

Habit.

Faith.

An unadorned married woman is considered unbecoming and even ominous, according to her deeply rooted beliefs. However, since her arrival in Gobha, these convictions seem to be loosening their grip on her.

The women here also wear ornaments, but it's more for beautification than any strict rules. Chandraprabha was initially surprised to see married women here without vermilion, as she knew it was considered an ill omen back home. Gradually, she's come to question the validity of her own convictions.

Nonetheless, she lacks the will to move around with a bare forehead. Only Sadhukumar knows where he gets the fruits of vermilion. Even now, the seeds are being dried and stored for her. Chandraprabha will not need more for a long time.

Thinking about Sadhukumar makes her unhappy. Her heart fills with deep shame and humiliation. She has had misgivings about his intentions too! She has dreaded him since. She is so mean! So distrustful! So selfish!

Since that day, Sadhukumar has not spent a single night in the palace. Even when he comes on urgent business, he always leaves from the outside. He has never visited Chandraprabha. Every time Sadhukumar arrives in Gobha, she cringes in shame, writhing under the sharp pangs of guilt.

While the things that the Gobha king supplies from afar are not essential to the Laloong women, they are for Chandraprabha. Yet they seem to thrust her into the pits of agony. They gnaw at her peace of mind, her sleep at night.

'Pai, the chief priestess is asking for you and the baby.'

Chandraprabha gets up, hearing Xunzira's happy voice. She looks down at the sleeping infant.

'But he is sleeping.'

Chandraprabha lifts the baby and wraps him in an eri scarf. The jela baro rises as she emerges from the room. He brings a pair of betel nut and leaf, a few grains of rice, basil leaves and *doob* grass arranged on a pile of banana leaves. Placing it at the doorway of Chandraprabha's room, he then returns, trims some of the baby's hair and lays it over the banana leaves.

'This should be placed inside a shell smeared with cow dung and affixed to the main door later.'

The hari kuwori says something in the Laloong dialect. Chandraprabha looks at Xunzira. 'What is she saying?'

'She says to lift the baby with its head facing east, Your Highness.'

The borjela takes an egg in his hand.

'Now Fa Mahadeo, Ma Kalikha, Ma Kamakhya and other gods will be worshipped, Your Highness,' Xunzira repeats in a low voice. The jela baro has now started chanting the mantras.

Chandraprabha is captivated as she listens to these unfamiliar chants and observes rituals she has never witnessed before. The jela baro then raises a small white pigeon and announces, 'Your Highness, this young pigeon shall be offered to Fa Mahadeo.' Xunzira explains his chants to her in a hushed tone.

Then the jela baro holds the pigeon in his hand and begins to chant quickly and melodically:

> *Aa Ram ishwar phorbhu hojadeo mahadeo. Oye Ma Kalikha-Kamaikha. Nago sewa reedong-phuja reedong. Nithao reedong-niban reedong. Tassoon tine phara. Kharu kharu jala-kharu kharu boroine osana. Na-ne niom thaido-niti thaido. Beboor niti-niom manegere. Nago bhag osdong-jog osdong. Sewa osdong-phuja osdong. Thol moori thol aro jiew moori jiew. Hebe kisa siyap laigare suntosh honga. Hebe nunaiba. Nunai sajogo ma-ne logsonge. Thira rakhana-jirai rakhana. Choklowo afott-pigini/chikai laigare. Berowgo osasi ossao ooi phorgbu hojadeo mahadeo. Oye Ma Kalikha-Kamaikha.*

The jela baro slashes the young bird's neck with a single blow and drains its blood onto the banana leaf. Chandraprabha shudders, her eyes closing involuntarily.

'You must not close your eyes, Your Highness. It offends the gods,' Xunzira whispers.

Startled, Chandraprabha opens her eyes.

It offends the gods!

The gods must not be offended.

If evil befalls her son, how will she survive? She unwittingly joins her hands and prays to Lord Biswanath.

Isn't Fa Mahadeo her Lord Biswanath? Will not Xunzira's Fa Mahadeo accept Chandraprabha's prayers?

The hari kuwori chants mantras. She invokes the blessings of Ma Kalikha-Kamakhya and other gods for the well-being of the mother and child. Chandraprabha tries to listen to and understand the prayers intently.

Slowly, her mind grows calm and peaceful. Happy and blissful. As if she is one among the people of this land. She feels joyful. Immensely joyful. She seems to have discovered her roots. As if, at the end of a period of prolonged, distressing, sleepless days and nights and perturbing fatigue, she is finally returning to a life of stability.

'*Aa Ram ishwar phorbhu hojadeo mahadeo. Oye Ma Kalikha-Kamakhya …*' In the name of God Shiva, Ma Kali, Ma Kamakhya …

The hari kuwori is chanting in the same tune as the jela baro.

Chandraprabha becomes completely absorbed in praying for the well-being of her child, inside her mind.

The chief priestess picks up the bow and arrows, chanting the mantras faster now: '*Phurbone sewlo chokolowo afatt-pirini. Hebe pla-chelene logchonge chikai lime. Poschimone deo lo pschima lime. Uttorone dep lo uttora lime. Thirai rakhana-jirai rakhana. Chokolowo deo pitri santosh hongo. Oye hojadeo mahadeo. Oye ma ghordeo ghorgossani. Kalikha-Kamakhya.*' Imploring the gods and goddesses to remove all evil from the directions of north, south, east and west, and to keep the baby safe.

Holding the baby's hand on the arrows, she releases seven arrows in seven directions. Then she aims an arrow at the sky, but instead of releasing it from the bow, she places it in the baby's hand and says something in the Tiwa tongue.

'What is she saying?' murmurs Chandraprabha.

'She is saying, "My child your battle will always be outside". If it was a girl, she would've said, "Your battle will always be inside,"' Xunzira explains.

The priestess takes the arrow from the child's hand and places it over the banana leaves.

In the meantime, the unmarried and married women begin to lift large urns filled with pepper-flavoured joo-*sa* wine and place them on the courtyard. They also start arranging the bowls into which the joo-sa will be poured in front of the women sitting in the courtyard.

The priestess speaks something in the Tiwa dialect and smiles at Chandraprabha.

'What is she saying, Xunzira?' Chandraprabha asks, confused.

'She has asked you to go inside with the baby, Your Highness.'

Feeling peaceful and happy, Chandraprabha gets up.

At that precise moment, Sadhukumar and his bodyguards come to a halt in front of the palace. The sound of horses trotting echoes all around.

Chandraprabha's heart gives a thud. Keeping her feelings to herself, she comes back to her bedchamber with composed steps.

A little later, Xunzira enters. 'Pai, would you like some joo-sa?'

In one hand, Xunzira holds a bowl, deftly knitted with narrow strips of bamboo. In the other, a light meal platter.

'Joo-sa? No, Nannao. I have never tasted anything like this before. I feel scared.'

Putting down the platter on a cane table, Xunzira laughed. 'It's merely rice water, Your Highness. We are all drinking. It is delicious. It's got pepper powder in it. They are not prepared every day. We usually only drink joo-*magra*. Joo-sa is more delicious. I've brought a little for you in this *draan*.'

Chandraprabha stares at the bowl in Xunzira's hand with surprise. 'How did you keep joo-sa in this bamboo bowl, Nannao?'

'It's possible. It has been crafted with great skill. Look, this is the outer part of the bowl. Inside, there is another bowl made of bamboo. Both have been affixed with glue extracted from bamboo shoots. Once dry, this glue never melts, even in water.'

'Strange. Really strange. I'd never seen anything like it before, Nannao.'

'How would you? Deoraja has instructed that your food be served only in bell-metal plates and bowls. Who will show you all this?'

'You must show me, Nannao. You must. I like everything about you people. I am keen to learn and understand everything about you all.' Chandraprabha says earnestly.

Setting the draan aside, Xunzira takes the baby into her own arms. She holds the dish towards Chandraprabha, asking, 'What is the point of learning? You are not going to be here, are you?'

'What makes you think I'm not going to live here forever, Nannao?' Chandraprabha asks, surprised.

'It is apparent, looking at you.'

It is as if she has dealt Chandraprabha a tight slap.

It is apparent from looking at you!

What does Xunzira mean by this!

It's apparent from looking at Chandraprabha that she is merely a guest of a few days. Does she really seem so detached? Does she really appear so unconcerned? Like a guest?

Suddenly, Chandraprabha's eyes well up with tears. She says, her voice trembling, 'Don't think like that, Nannao. Where shall I go leaving you all? Who else do I have?'

'I always say the same thing. I tell everyone at the palace – our queen, our pai, will never leave us. She will be here forever. But no one believes me, you know.'

'Why don't they believe you, Nannao?' Chandraprabha asks sadly.

'Because you don't wear the kasyong phaskai like our women, you haven't learnt about our ways, you don't speak our tongue, and you wear vermilion and stay away from everybody, looking sad and forlorn. I've told them – what do they know about the agony in my pai's heart – do they expect an expecting woman to dance at the Magro Misawa festival instead of feeling sad?'

'What is Magro Misawa?' She couldn't help laughing at Xunzira's anger.

'It is the dance of our Magrowali clan. It is also called Muinary Kanthi Misawa. Young men and women from different clans form pairs to dance together. Before I came here, I used to dance too. They play the *tumding* and *togor* drums, as well as a *muhuri*, which is like a flute. It's where I met Phuleswar.'

'Who is Phuleswar?' Chandraprabha asks, a bit surprised.

'I won't say. I feel shy.'

'Come on, tell me. No need to be shy.'

The young maid smiles and lowers her head. Just then, a young girl appears and speaks to Xunzira in their native language.

'The deoraja is requesting permission to see you, Pai,' she translates.

Permission!

Chandraprabha feels ashamed and guilty. She depends on the ruler of this kingdom and the people for their love, respect and acceptance. She regrets doubting the ruler's integrity.

Sadhukumar could have responded to her hurtful words or sought revenge, but he didn't. With a confident smile, he had left Gobha with his dignity intact. He'd defeated Chandraprabha, and now he's seeking her permission. It's like another insult.

Pratapchandra had asserted his masculine supremacy by casting his wife aside, a woman who stood still without seeking forgiveness from him.

But Sadhukumar did nothing of the sort.

'Should I tell Deoraja you're on your way, Pai?' Xunzira asks eagerly.

'Oh yes, Nannao.'

'But you haven't eaten anything.' Xunzira stops on her way out.

'Let me meet him first.'

'Have some kakhir, Pai, or you might feel unwell.'

'Alright, I will. You can go.'

Xunzira leaves and Chandraprabha drinks milk, covering herself with an eri scarf. Then she picks up her sleeping son.

Orimotto.

She can't let go of this name.

On a romantic night King Pratapchandra had named his dream child, Orimotto. How can Chandraprabha resist giving him this name? Yet she's thinking of asking the people of Gobha, especially Sadhukumar, for another name.

Chandraprabha is slowly trying to find a new identity in this kingdom. Will she be the abandoned wife of King Pratapchandra or an integral member of the Tiwasha society? How much of her own culture and traditions will she keep?

What will she get by holding on to her culture?

Where is her society now? The society had exiled her at the command of one man.

Remembering that incident sets her blood on fire. A fierce fire begins to burn deep within her. At the core of her heart. A strong desire for rebellion courses through her veins.

But what's the point? What's the use of clinging to memories of her origin, tradition and past? What's the use of holding onto her identity when it has deserted her, when it's been erased from the land she once called home? What's the use of wearing her native dress, speaking her native language and clinging to her individuality if she ignores the society that has welcomed her with open arms, love and recognition?

Her son, King Pratapchandra's heir, will grow up in this society. She will never be able to teach him her own traditions, customs or culture. Can these lessons be taught in a school? Can they be conveyed through words alone? Can they be taught without examples?

When Orimotto grows up and sees his mother in the riha-mekhela attire with vermilion, won't he have questions? Won't he feel like a stranger? Will he be able to fully embrace this society as his own without an identity of his own?

Should she take Orimotto away from this society and send him to the capital of Pratappur? Should she hand over the Aryan-Kshatriya descendant and flag-bearer of Dharmapal's dynasty to King Pratapchandra and the Queen Mother Yajnavati?

Could she? Could Chandraprabha stoop so low?

Never. Impossible. Chandraprabha can never kneel before King Pratapchandra and seek his forgiveness or favour.

This society is much better. It has given her dignity, which she never had in the palace of Pratappur. She has found solid ground here.

What did she have in Pratappur?

Did she have her own identity, authority or dignity?

Never. If she did, Pratapchandra wouldn't have expelled her. She could have challenged him.

She could have obtained justice.

Demanded a fair trial.

She won't go back. Chandraprabha will live here. She will wrap herself in the threads of this society and be reborn. She will shape Orimotto.

With firm and serious steps, she goes to meet Sadhukumar in the outer lobby of the palace. The king rises to greet her. 'Your Highness, forgive me for disturbing you at this untimely hour.'

'Please do not hurt me with such harsh words again, Deoraja. I am ashamed of my behaviour. I seek your forgiveness,' she says sadly.

'Kindly do not speak like that, Your Highness. It stings. It is true that your words had wounded me, but I realized you are not at fault. I didn't know many things, and you suffered because of my ignorance. Please don't dwell on it.'

'You had to move far away to live in Amsai Marjong. It pains me a lot, Deoraja.'

'Don't worry, Your Highness. It's still my kingdom, no matter the distance. I came here to discuss two important matters with you,' Sadhukumar says.

'Please go ahead.'

'I am concerned about your son's future, Your Highness. I don't know what you're thinking, but I have two conclusions. If you want to take him back to Pratappur, I'll go to King Pratapchandra with my head bowed. His anger must have subsided by now, and he might accept both of you. I'll swear on Lord Mahabhairab and tell him the truth. However, it's your choice. You are our revered guest, and your wish is our command. Before I discuss the second matter, I need to know your decision.'

Sadhukumar's thoughtfulness and tolerance have cleared the last dregs of uncertainty. Chandraprabha remains quiet for a moment.

Finally, she looks up and says with deep emotion, 'I have thought long and hard, Deoraja. I realize there's no reason to leave this society. Let my son, Orimotto, grow up like other children here. Give him a name from the society, or any name of your choosing. He wasn't born a prince but as the son of a poor refugee woman from another kingdom. Let him grow up this way. This culture will teach him how to live as a good human. It's for the best, Deoraja. I'll also give up my identity and become one of your people, adopting a new name.'

Sadhukumar, moved, fixes his stare on her. 'Please don't feel deprived, Your Highness. Gobha and its people stand with you. As for the other matter, our society has granted Orimotto the authority to lead our clan. With your consent, we'll perform the adoption ritual at the nuber, and he can ascend to the throne of Gobha.'

'What are you saying, Deoraja? You intend to ordain the son of the conceited, irrational king who insulted you as your heir?'

'King Pratapchandra is the one who is irrational and conceited. I am not, Your Highness. I shall fulfil my own responsibility.'

'Please, Deoraja, don't consider such a thing. While Orimotto may be adopted into your clan, please do not think of making him the king of Gobha. It's unfair, extremely unfair, to deny your own sons the throne and give it to the son of an enemy from a foreign country and clan. Please don't put me through such anguish, Deoraja,' Chandraprabha's voice trembles with pent-up emotion.

The king's face is radiant now. He gives Chandraprabha a moment to gather herself before saying, 'In a way, you are right,

Your Highness. It would be unfair to crown your son as king at the expense of my own sons, but that would only be unfair if I were to have sons. I swear to Fa Mahadeo that I will never have a family. I will inform our society of my intentions and, with their and your approval, adopt your son as my own.'

Surprised, Chandraprabha continues to gaze into the king's eyes. Tears well up within her, seeking an escape, like floodwaters breaking free.

ELEVEN

Lali hilali lai o' dear father
Lali hilali lai.
The simple laloong was abducted.
While singing hilali.

The courtyard is filled with elders sitting in neat rows. Their unified singing brings the *lali hilali* song to life. As one row finishes, the opposite row begins their repartee of singing. People gather around the elders, and in the centre, Aai Khamari Konsari occupies a special seat.

No. It is not Chandraprabha.

It is Aai Khamari Konsari, whom the people of Gobha have honored as the mother – the first lady of the palace of Gobha. She dons a black kasyong phaskai adorned with red and yellow floral motifs. A silver chain graces her neck, and silver bangles and earrings adorn her wrists and ears. Her long, black, alkali-washed hair is tightly tied in a top knot without a middle parting. Her bright golden face is free of the vermilion dot or *regha* lines. Her deep, wide eyes are untouched by kohl.

A different, one-of-a-kind face.

A different woman.

A different personality.

Konsari is wearing her finest dress today, woven for her by

Xunzira. From threading the yarn, colouring the thread, to weaving, the young maid did it all on her own.

To teach Konsari. To train her.

Xunzira had dyed the cotton threads using indigo leaves and blackberry rinds. The yellow and red hues were obtained by grinding the roots of the *haju* tree in the mortar and boiling them in hot water. The technique surprised Chandraprabha.

'Try to get used to it, Pai. We learned by watching our mothers at work,' Xunzira had said.

With her help, Chandraprabha has gradually learned many local practices and embraced them.

When Konsari first began twisting the yarn, she used mud reels. But a few days later, Xunzira presented her with one crafted from tortoise shell.

'Only women from royal families and high-ranking officials use this for twisting the yarn. We use reels made of mud,' she had explained.

'Where did you get this? It looks new.'

'I asked Deoraja for it. Does using a mud reel suit you? Deoraja had it fetched immediately.'

'You are a naughty girl. You shouldn't have bothered the king. What must he be thinking?'

'What would he think? Deoraja loves you a lot, Pai. He respects you so much.'

Konsari's blush escaped her nannao's notice.

These days, she finds great pleasure in twisting the yarn. In her bedroom, alongside her own clothes and those of her four-year-old son, Orimotto, a cane basket for storing eri and muga cotton cocoons also occupies a place in one corner. Another addition to her collection is books. Sadhukumar has supplied Konsari with several books written on the barks of the *saanchi* tree. He has provided reeds for writing, inkpots of myrobalan seed sap, other colouring herbs and heaps of blank barks of the saanchi tree to write on. When Konsari reads the books in her leisure, the other women of the palace regard her with awe. The children, too. They boast about her in front of others. Konsari radiates with a new appearance and identity. Whoever looks at her becomes spellbound. They bow in profound reverence.

Even now, the respectful looks of the people and the elders occasionally move her. She does not look at anyone, instead watching the ritual with great interest. Today is the *monsho* phuja, a ceremony to cleanse the clan of the defilement caused by the birth of children over the last few years. The members of the clan are prohibited from holding rituals for the dead in public if they do not perform this ceremony.

Sitting alongside the elders, singing lali hilali songs, are children ranging from ages one day to four years, awaiting purification. Also seated in this group is Arimotto.

Over the past four years, Konsari's son Orimotto's name has changed to Arimotto, simply by way of word of mouth.

Konsari never voiced any objections. She was not unhappy with the change in the name bestowed upon her son by Pratapchandra. It was the wish of the people, which she would never disrespect.

On the day Konsari announced her decision to join this society, Chandraprabha also decided to never go against its wishes, interests, customs or traditions. After receiving the name Konsari with blessings from the clan's elders, she removed the red vermilion dot and sandalwood paste from her forehead. She started studying the dialect, rituals and practices of her new community. Slowly, she transformed herself.

With Xunzira's help, who is a dedicated teacher, Konsari has learned a lot. Her nannao's enthusiasm surpasses hers, telling her about everything she knows. And for anything else, Xunzira collects information from others and shares it with her.

At this moment, too, Xunzira, sitting on a mat next to her, asks, 'Pai, are you enjoying the lali hilali songs that our elders are singing?'

Konsari smiles warmly and replies, 'Yes, I am.'

'Pai, did you know that the Lali, Hilali and Lai were three sisters?' Xunzira asks excitedly. 'Abi Ajoi told us.'

'Really? Do tell me the story.'

'I don't know much about it, Pai. My abi said that these three nannaos and pais loved one another very much, but fate had them separated. Lali, believed to be the founding mother of our neighbouring Mikir tribe, holds a special place. It is said that the Boro-Kacharis trace their origins back to Hilali. And Lai, the youngest nannao, connects us Laloongs as we are her descendants. That's why, during the monsho phuja and other celebrations, we sing their praises. We even find joy in singing lali hilali songs while sowing and harvesting paddy. It's a cherished tradition. Now, let's wait and witness how the elders guide the boys in their captivating dance among the people.'

'What about the girls kept inside the nuber? Will they also be expected to dance in a similar manner?'

'Yes. They will sing first and then gracefully dance. The hari kuwori will be their guide, while the borjela and the *xorujela* will lead the boys in their dance.'

'Well, then let's watch and listen attentively. Enough talking for now, Nannao. You are very chatty.' Konsari laughs.

'I must admit, I really enjoy talking, Pai. Look at our darling child. How he stands out. He will grow up to be really handsome.'

'I hope you, too, give birth to a boy. He'd make an excellent companion for Arimotto. Your time is approaching, isn't it?'

Xunzira blushes with embarrassment and delight, her heart feeling contented.

These days, Xunzira lives in the nearby village of Gawolia, alongside the king's attendants, bodyguards, maids and servants. This way, they are able to respond to calls immediately. Xunzira makes regular visits even now, despite her busy household responsibilities alongside her husband, Phuleswar. Her primary job remains catering to Konsari's needs. But Konsari spares her from many tasks due to Xunzira's growing weight, insisting she sits nearby for a chat.

'Everybody says that I'm going to have a boy, Pai. It appears that I've lost a significant amount of weight and there are other symptoms. At times, it fills me with fear.'

'With the blessings of the *burha goxai*, everything will be fine. Don't let fear consume you, Nannao. You mustn't be afraid.'

Suddenly, Xunzira can't contain herself as she exclaims, 'There, there, look! Now the boys are going to dance. Look!'

One by one, the elders rise from their seats, each taking a child in their arms. The sawkhajela cradles Arimotto, whom Sadhukumar introduces to society as his adopted son. The one who commands respect.

Carrying the children, the elders make their way to the centre of the crowd, instructing them to dance in joyful circles. In the sawkhajela's arms, Arimotto also cheerfully shakes his arms and legs to the lively music.

Lole lah lole bah lala heloia lai
Bah lala heloia lai
Hei lali lang lehe lo bai hei
Lali lang lehe lo bai
La la heloia lai

Konsari is watching, enraptured.

The monsho festival is nearing its conclusion. The harmonious chorus of women inside the nuber and the gathering of excited men outside reach a crescendo, filling the crowd with wild enthusiasm.

In an open area not far from the courtyard, a group of about a dozen men skilfully craft bowls from banana plant stems. These bowls will be used to serve food and joo-sa to the attendees at the end of the festival.

In the temporary kitchen shed with a dried plantain-leaf roof, the fragrant *malbhog* joha rice simmers in large *mihdoos* or vessels, supported by clods of earth. The crowd's excitement grows with the enticing aroma of ginger-infused curry, powdered rice and pork meat cooked to perfection in large mihdoos by the *kra-koormis*, the chefs employed for public banquets.

The wooden *draans* used for drinking wine and the plates made from banana tree sheaths are wiped clean and neatly stacked on banana leaves. The women serving at the feast place strainers over bamboo *doraparis*, prepared with joo-*lauor* bowls in hand, ready to serve the refreshing drink. The *khoosa-khangsi* and *kahi-pathi*, the plates and bowls used for serving the loro, borjela, chokha jela, hari kuwori, doloi, elders of the clan and village leaders are scrubbed to a golden shine and arranged on a *khata* made of green bamboo strips.

The festive atmosphere, filled with aromatic delights, buzzing excitement and vibrant colours, lights up the nuber and its surroundings.

'Please hold the child,' a chokha jela approaches Konsari. She immediately stands up, and with a smile, the young priest extends Arimotto towards her.

'We have named him Mriganko. How do you like it?' he asks.

'A very beautiful name.'

'The people also like the name you have given him. That name will also remain. May Hojaideo bless him. May Podolmaji protect him from all perils. This child will grow up to bring glory to his clan. He will be renowned all around.'

Offering silent prayers to the gods, Xunzira reaches out her hands to hold Arimotto. However, Konsari resists and says, 'No, Nannao. He is heavy. It's not good for you.'

'Alright, Pai. Then let me take him out for a stroll, holding his hand.'

'Well then, go.'

Caressing Arimotto's head before letting him go, Konsari remains seated. The people hold this beautiful and affectionate foreign woman in high esteem, seeing her as a fairy-like figure. Konsari is well aware of the admiration showered upon her, and it fills her heart with love and gratitude towards these people.

Mriganko. Mriganko.

Konsari repeats the name silently within herself. It is indeed a beautiful name.

Arimotto and Mriganko.

Two names given by two kings. One name is bestowed by an arrogant king for his future descendant, and the other by a compassionate king to elevate the identity of the son of an unfortunate woman in society.

What a contrast!

The people of Gobha were quite surprised when they first hear the name Orimotto. Even Pratapchandra had not fully explained its meaning to Chandraprabha. Later, after much contemplation, Konsari had figured it out. When Pratapchandra captured Mayapur, he was given the name Mayamotto. 'Ori' means enemy. Did Pratapchandra intend to name his son 'Orimotto', signifying the conqueror of enemies?

Who knows.

Xunzira had asked, 'What kind of a name is Arimotto, Pai?'

'Why do you people say Arimotto? It is Orimotto.'

'Ori is a tongue-twister … Ari is simpler for everyone. Do you know what people are saying?'

'What?' Chandraprabha had asked in surprise.

'They say your son's head and chest resemble the *ari* fish, also known as the catfish. So they think his name is Arimotto. Why did you choose this name, Pai?'

Chandraprabha realized that she has strayed from the topic at hand. She hadn't fully transformed from Chandraprabha to Konsari yet. The preparations for her transformation had only just begun.

'Ma.'

Arimotto comes running to hug her, bringing her back to reality. She takes him into her lap and sees that the boy is holding a bow in one hand and a floral pouch full of pebbles in the other.

'Where did you get the bow, my child?' she asks, looking at Arimotto's bright face.

'Deoraja gave it to me.'

'Deoraja?'

'Yes. He just arrived. He is supervising the arrangements in the banquet area,' Xunzira says.

'Can this young child handle the bow? He also brought pebbles.'

'The *pathuri* bow is only used to shoot birds with pebbles. It's for learning how to shoot with a bow and arrow. The string you see here is the *khunkura*, made from the bark of a special tree. It's attached to a bow used with arrows,' she explains expertly.

Konsari laughs.

By then, Arimotto has started taking out the pebbles from the pouch and counting them one by one. 'Siwantha, siwanning, silantham, siwanobroi—' One, two, three, four …

Konsari lifts Arimotto in her arms and rises to her feet. The festival has come to an end, and the crowd moves towards the feasting area. She steps out of the nuber, carrying Arimotto in her arms, her heart filled with joy and deep contentment.

TWELVE

On a cold winter evening, young Arimotto rides a horse along a narrow path nestled between vast paddy fields. The mist-covered tracts of land shimmer under the moonlight, while numerous fireflies, known as *khang-jang*, twinkle like tiny lanterns. The stars themselves seem to have descended from the heavens, playfully dancing on the empty ground.

The harvest is complete.

The silence of the village deepens, as the weary villagers lay fast asleep after a day's hard labour, with a shrill, relentless chorus of ji-ji from the *kaoling* insects.

Years ago, on one bitterly cold winter evening, Arimotto had come to this area to live in the dekachang. As per tradition, the young unmarried panthais and the elder families dismantled the old samadi and erected a new one. This is the rule. The ritual took place every six years. The newly formed khara panthais admit young boys over the age of ten, while bidding farewell to the *khorkia* panthais who have spent twelve years in the samadi. This passage is commemorated through the *kheljuwa*, a special ceremony. When he was ten years old, Arimotto, too, was led to the samadi by Deoraja, to join the newly formed khara panthais.

To this day, Arimotto calls Sadhukumar 'Deoraja', not 'Fa'. As a child, he had heard the word from Xunzira Asi, and it had stuck in his mind. And it sounds especially endearing in a child's voice. Deoraja's love for Arimotto knows no bounds. Before he had joined the samadi, the king always brought something for the boy on his visits to Gobha. In those days, the deoraja even arranged for people to teach Arimotto the skills that a king's son should possess. Brahmin Acharya Prabhakar Bidyanidhi from the north bank of the Brahmaputra taught Arimotto how to read and write. Even during his time at the samadi, the boy spent most of his days away. The kingdom's major general, who took Arimotto under his wing, taught him about politics, handling weaponry and various aspects of warfare.

Arimotto has now become fit to be a ruler. His personality and demeanour reflect the radiance of royal training. During his early days at the samadi, the older panthais had taught him and his companions various crafts. He has studied the craft of cane-bamboo and cultivation here at the samadi. He has learned every rite and ritual, as well as the customs and conducts of their society.

More than twelve years have passed in this way. The panthais have once again dismantled the samadi and constructed a new one. In the process, they have learnt how to build houses. Under the direction of the elders, the samadi's heads – the chaang doloi and chaang maji – have been relieved of their responsibilities, and new office bearers have been elected.

Arimotto is now the chaang doloi. It has been six long years since he assumed command and became the samadi's most beloved leader. Today marks his last night at the samadi. The loro along with the village elders have met the new office bearers.

The construction will start afresh the day after tomorrow. After praying to Fa Mahadeo, Charibhai-Charikora and other deities, the loro and hadari will go to the woods to cut timber for the central pillar. All the young men of the samadi will follow, as well as the elders' group.

A temporary shelter has been erected to stay for the one week required to complete the new construction. All the panthais are going to shift to the new house tomorrow.

As soon as the meeting was over, Arimotto had left for the

Gobha palace where Deoraja awaited him with a surprise gift: a horse.

A stout white horse.

A dream object of every Laloong panthai. Holding the reins of the horse in his hands, Arimotto had laughed joyfully. So had his mother, Xunzira Asi and the others who stood nearby.

'As soon as you leave the samadi, you will be crowned the king. At first, you will be ordained king of Kumoi and Boghora,' Deoraja had said. Arimotto was caught off guard.

'So soon!'

'Not soon at all … have I not grown old … how long shall I rule this kingdom? I can retire only when you become capable of taking over Gobha.'

'Being a king is not enough. You will also have to marry soon,' Xunzira said.

'Oh, Asi!' Arimotto went red with embarrassment.

'It is true. How can you not perform *phahdewa* after leaving the samadi? Only the mad ones do that.'

When she became aware of Sadhukumar's presence, Xunzira clapped her hand over her mouth and stopped. Then she fled.

Deoraja had laughed his heart out. Konsari laughed, too. Even the self-conscious Arimotto could not control his laughter.

Now with a light heart, Arimotto is returning, riding on the horse gifted to him. As he approaches the samadi, the faint sound of drums grows louder. The thunderous boom-boom of the khram played by the panthais shatters the silence of the misty evening.

The activities inside the samadi reach their peak only after the villagers have gone to sleep. Once they finish their tasks in the paddy fields, the panthais celebrate at night, while the elders impart various skills, including dancing, singing and playing musical instruments like the drum and flute. As a rule, no bachelor over the age of ten is allowed to live at home, and those who try to do so face societal punishment. The young men at the samadi are the pillars of society, enlivening the silent nights with song, dance and laughter, while also vigilantly ensuring the safety and security of the village and the kingdom.

He dismounts as he reaches the samadi. This is the only *chaang ghar*, a house built on a raised platform, in the village. The roof is slanted, touching the ground on both sides, leaving the other two sides open. The front segment of the one-roomed samadi, called *numaji*, is used for religious festivals. Standing there, Samol is playing the flute.

Xunzira's only son and Arimotto's most loyal childhood friend, Samol, is about to become a khorkia panthai. When he hears the sound of a horse trotting, he removes the flute from his mouth and gazes outside with curiosity.

'Chaang Doloi,' he exclaims, 'What a beautiful horse! Where did you get it?'

'Deoraja gifted it to me. First tie the *kora* and give the horse some water, too.'

'Did you go to the palace? We were wondering what happened. The chaang maji told us you had been summoned. It was to give you the horse, wasn't it?'

'Yes. Something else, too. I'll tell you about it once you're free.'

Arimotto ascends to the samadi clad in his thenus-tagla.

Standing on the numaji, he looks inside. The officers are sitting on the *nukthi*, a sitting area, engrossed in discussions about the new samadi and the upcoming Khel Juwa festival scheduled to begin from the day after tomorrow. Occasionally, the young officers laugh playfully. To the left of the nukthi, a few panthais are sitting over wooden planks around the square earthen stoves set up for cooking. The panthais to the south are crafting bamboo and cane vessels, flutes and other musical instruments. A few sparks from the kitchen fire escape into the darkness, creating a mysterious gleam. The reddish-yellow glow of the blazing fire illuminates the work-engrossed panthais' strapping, grown-up bodies and their naive, child-like faces.

'Chaang Doloi, what took you so long to come? You were gone since the afternoon,' says the chaang maji sitting on the nukthi.

'Don't say anything. Something significant happened today.'

'Hah! What happened?' everybody calls out.

'I received a kora today from Deoraja,' Arimotto announces, entering the nukthi area.

'Ha,' everybody shouts, astonished and delighted.

'Really? *Chotlo*?'

'I swear. *Chot.* It's true. I never imagined that I was summoned to the *noh* to fetch a kora.'

'Oh my gossai, he gave you a kora?' Huruma Baroi almost screams in joy and amazement.

'Why not? He is a king's son. Moreover, he loves the chaang doloi so much,' says the chaang maji.

'Where have you kept it?' the *re pasari* asks.

'I have brought it with me. Samol is tying it up.'

'Hey, let's go take a look,' the chaang maji cries out.

'Can we ride on it, Chaang Doloi?' the korai maji asks.

'Why not? All of you can. Does the fact that it has been given to me imply that it is solely mine? It's yours too. Go and call all the khara panthais as well.'

As soon as the word gets out, the langkhon phuja dance begins inside the samadi. Jumping and squealing with delight, the young men rush down helter-skelter to the courtyard.

Everyone surrounds the horse, running their hands over its body. The loud comments and cheers of the boys echo through the still darkness of the village.

At one point, Arimotto says, 'Come on now, let's go up. We have to finish all the work. And we must wake up before the *phurimoso* rises. Come, come.'

Everyone follows the rule of the samadi to obey the chaang doloi.

Those who had been working with the cane and bamboo sit down near the kitchen fire, while the pupils learning under the *khram ojah* move to another corner to continue with their music lessons.

The accumulated noise of *khram panthais*, *khram pangchi* and *khram khujura* enlivens the samadi once more.

'Tonight is the last night,' the *bhetta maji* says, sitting in the nukthi.

'It's really sad,' the re pasari laments.

The khorkia panthais sitting in the nukthi feel their hearts heave.

This is the last night of the twelve-year-old samadi. Nobody will be able to sleep a wink tonight, especially the khorkia panthais.

How can they? A week from now, as soon as the construction of the new samadi is complete, the Jhanjhuwa festival will begin. It is the final festival of the elder khorkia panthais, during which rice grains are ground. After that, they will leave the samadi forever and return to the village to live with their families, to marry and start their own families.

When Arimotto first arrived at the samadi, his mother's reaction went beyond crying, even though she didn't shed any tears. Her overwhelming display of love had deeply touched both Arimotto and Xunzira Asi, bringing tears to their eyes.

He gradually got over the pangs of separation from his mother and his home. The activities, training sessions and liveliness of the samadi transformed Arimotto from a mother's baby to an independent, courageous, competent young man, well-versed in warfare.

Arimotto's royal investiture ceremony is going to take place as soon as his stay in the samadi is over. The panthais at the samadi are aware of this fact. Apart from respecting Arimotto as a chaang doloi, the panthais also look up to him as the future king. They take great pride in having a future king as their companion at the samadi.

'May I serve you some joo-magra, Chaang Doloi?' Samol's voice draws Arimotto's attention.

'Yes, you may.'

'Some bird meat, too?'

'Which bird?'

'*Aarli* duck.'

'Alright. Have all of you eaten?' Arimotto turns towards his companions.

'Yes, we have. It's delicious. But we could not relish it at all. We are feeling depressed, chaang doloi,' the chaang maji says.

'What can you do? It is a social custom. Besides, do you want to be a bachelor forever? You're dying to be a gobhia at Khumdela's house the moment you get out of here, aren't you? You are already waist-deep in her love,' Huruma laughs.

'*Eeh, ye-e-e,* chotlo? Really?' the re pasari asks, surprised.

'He is keeping it a secret, you know,' Huruma replies, deftly evading the blow the chaang maji had aimed at him.

Samol, who had entered with a wooden bowl to pour joo and a banana leaf to serve the whistling teal meat, leaves in a flash after placing both the bowl and the leaf on the floor.

The khara panthais are not allowed to partake in amusement with the khorkia panthais or even laugh around them.

All the other khorkia panthais sitting in the nukthi fall upon each other, laughing. Arimotto also enjoys the banter between Huruma and the chaang maji, smiling every now and then. At one point, when the argument becomes too much for him, he exclaims with mock anger, '*Aaahri.* Why are you causing such a commotion? Please keep quiet.'

'Hey … the *paakraja* has forbidden you from creating a commotion. Keep quiet,' the korai maji says, pretending to be scared and comparing Arimotto to a lion.

'Of course, paakraja will forbid it. To him, any discussion about girls is like talking about ghosts and evil spirits,' the chaang maji says.

The samadi rumbles with everyone's laughter.

'I wonder when we'll see our paakraja's better half,' says Huruma.

'… at the right time,' Arimotto answers.

'When are you going to be ordained king, Chaang Doloi?' Huruma asks.

'Deoraja said, immediately after the Khel Juwa festival.'

'But you will need a queen, won't you? A regular girl won't suffice. I'll go around asking where to find a queen. Just wait,' says the chaang maji. Then, as if remembering suddenly, he exclaims, 'Aa, *aabra,* it really escaped my mind. There is one in the kingdom of Khola – Queen Gangavati.'

'*Aayy*. Right, right. It is the Khola queen's custom to tow in a gobhia. Our paakraja will not be eligible,' Huruma remarks.

'Why not? What difference does it make for a king to be a gobhia? He can live there occasionally. I've heard she is quite lovely. The korai maji had seen her at the Jonbeel mela. Come on, say something – isn't it true?' the chaang maji says.

'It is true. Gangavati appears to make it a point of attending the fair. I'd gone there only to have a look at her. Chot … a beautiful woman. I'd seen her exchange eri cloth for colourful beads from the Jaintias. I believe she loves wearing those beads. Very reserved. She doesn't seem to look at anybody.'

'From where did the korai maji collect so much information, ha?'

'His fiancée is from Khola. He has learned all of this from her. Do you know what he says? He'll elope with her as soon as he gets out of the samadi.'

'You all seem to be talking a lot about khorlas these days,' Arimotto chuckles.

'Didn't I warn you? To him, talking about girls is like talking about ghosts and witches. Why shouldn't we talk? Do you expect us to be like you – whetting our *thrual langkhui* on the whetstone instead of thinking about girls? We have more fun thinking about girls than by sharpening our swords on the *sarih*.'

Once more, explosive laughter shakes the samadi.

Arimotto laughs as well. Even at that moment, a few khara panthais are learning how to play the khram. Others are dancing to the beat. In one corner, a few of them are busy organizing nets, spears, bows and arrows. A few others are making beds in the sleeping area.

Sipping joo, Arimotto sinks into his dream world. 'When I become king, I shall make my kingdom larger. Immense. I shall collect lots of revenue and keep my people happy.'

Youthful dreams of claiming power hover on his drooping eyelids due to the joo's effect. And surfacing on and off is the misty silhouette of the unknown queen of Khola, Gangavati, a renowned beauty who enjoys wearing beads from the Jaintia hills.

THIRTEEN

The major general's voice startles Gangavati, who is deep in discussion with the village chieftains. She turns her head to acknowledge him.

'Your Highness, you had summoned Huruma. He is here now,' the major general says.

'Tell him to wait. I am coming. Have you informed the barika and the *khurinols*?'

'I have, Your Highness. Barika has gone to notify the loro and hadari, and they should be arriving soon. The khurinols have started steaming the sticky rice in the kitchen. Although they might be a little late, they will come,' the major general replies.

'Good. Please go and supervise the arrangements in the hall. I have already greeted everyone. Let me know in advance when the royal representative of Gobha and the king of Kumoi–Boghora arrives.'

'It will be done, Your Highness,' the major general leaves with a bow.

The capital of the kingdom of Khola is bustling with activity. The kings of all the Laloong kingdoms are gathering for the annual assembly. Along with the provinces that acknowledge the supremacy of the king of Gobha, chiefs from other neighbouring kingdoms have already arrived. The durbar mainly focuses on discussions about politics, border security, revenue collection and diplomatic ties among the Laloong states.

At the end of the assembly, the king of the friendly kingdom of the Jaintias will be honoured. The annual festivities are hosted by one of the Laloong kingdoms. This year, Khola was in charge of organizing the assembly, thanks to King Sadhukumar's encouragement.

However, the old king would not be present today, despite giving permission for the durbar. Instead, his son Arimotto, the newly ordained king of Kumoi and Boghora, would attend. Although Gangavati was invited to Arimotto's coronation ceremony, she couldn't attend due to an important discussion regarding a border dispute with the neighbouring Beltola kingdom.

Gangavati had heard much about Arimotto and his mother, Konsari. Like her subjects, she admired and respected them. Konsari had taught the Tiwaliboongs valuable skills and was revered in Gobha. Gangavati had always longed to meet her but her responsibilities as the queen left her with little time for such visits.

Recent acts of aggression from the Garos, a tribe descending from the mountains, had led to discussions among the neighbouring kingdoms. Smaller ones like Looki, Rani, Beltola, Chaygaon and others had joined forces to defend these attacks. Dimoruwa, which was larger and more powerful, shared close ties with Gobha, Jaintia and Khola, leading to frequent political exchanges.

Although the kingdoms from Pandu to the border of Kolong coexisted peacefully, the Bhuyans living at Pandu, Guwahati, Looki and Ouguri desired larger realms. Khola, thanks to its geographical location, held significant political importance in the region. Gangavati had to constantly engage in diplomatic exchanges while managing the internal affairs of her kingdom. Currently, she is busy making arrangements for the inter-kingdom council, set to begin today in the capital.

Arimotto is supposed to arrive as the chief guest of the durbar, and Gangavati is eagerly waiting for him. A daughter of one of Khola's emissaries, who occasionally works in Gangavati's palace, had once eloped with a young man from Gobha. When she visited Gangavati, she'd sung praises of Arimotto, mentioning that the king had promoted her husband to an officer.

'Back at home, there is a lot of talk about you, Your Highness. My man told me that in the samadi, everybody said that you and King Arimotto would make a wonderful couple,' the girl had said shyly.

At the time, Gangavati had told her to keep quiet. Now, recalling the girl's words makes her laugh. At the same time, she feels a nameless, jittery emotion descending upon her.

Even during his royal installation, people had been discussing Arimotto's appearance and virtues. It had all reached the queen's ears.

Khola is a small kingdom, not subordinate to Gobha, due to their friendly relations with the Jaintias. Gangavati's diplomatic skills have allowed her to maintain amicable relationships with both Gobha and Jaintia, as well as other neighbouring kingdoms. However, the rise of the Kachari king, Gajaraj Bodosa, has raised concerns among the nearby states, especially the Laloong chiefs. They have become worried about their safety and sovereignty due to the growing ambitions of the Kacharis. And so, the conference today holds further political importance.

Gangavati has been busy preparing for this durbar for several days. The capital Khola has been scrubbed and polished with materials sent from all its villages. The dolois from each village had been invited through the barikas to attend the inaugural session.

All the dolois have arrived by now, and there is still time for the conference to begin. Everyone is trying to use this opportunity to discuss other concerns about the kingdom. The event will start only when King Arimotto reaches, and the Jaintia king is expected to arrive towards the end of today's session.

Gangavati has assigned specific groups of people to entertain the guests in the meantime. Numerous cottages have been erected for the guests. The young men have fearlessly gone fishing in the Kolong, despite the intense winter chill. The women and girls skilfully catch fish that have drifted downstream using the *ha-pisi* herb paste as bait. These fish are then dried for future use.

In village after village, the sound of pounding echoes as rice is ground to prepare powder, cakes and flat rice for the upcoming

Magh Pisu festival and for bartering in the Jonbeel mela organized by the king of Gobha. Various rice delicacies are being prepared to cater to all the visiting royals and their guards, sentries, servants and maids.

Under the supervision of the dolois and the loros, the young men from the samadis fetch banana trees and wild bananas to feed the large number of elephants expected to arrive with the kings. Tasks are distributed among the panthais. Swine collectors gather swines. Fowl collectors collect fowls. Wild deer, wild birds like waterhens, wood pigeons and green pigeons are collected. Wood collectors gather firewood. Individual groups of men and women are assigned tasks such as preparing spices, alkali and extracting mustard.

Meanwhile, the kra-koormis have finished preparing joo-sa, joo-magra and joo-*lampha* separately. After preparing joo, these kra-koormis are now cooking various dishes over a blazing fire burning beneath earthenware made to support the massive vessels. The panthais and young girls, along with the drummers and flute players, are to look after the guests and greet the kings. Gangavati is also at the main entrance. Only after all the kings have reached does she go down to talk with the dolois milling about nearby.

She will go out as soon as Arimotto arrives.

'Please allow us to take your leave now, Your Highness,' says the *bordoloi*, rising to pay his respects.

'Yes. You may leave.'

After the dolois depart, Gangavati exits the assembly hall. Outside, the barika, Huruma and the khurinol are waiting.

'The royal representative of Gobha, king of Kumoi–Boghora is on his way, Your Highness,' the barika informs her.

'Alright, I am heading to the gateway. Please accompany the bordoloi, who is already on his way. Follow him.' Bowing before Gangavati, the barika leaves.

'You had summoned me, Your Highness?' asks Huruma, who is in charge of supervising the village roads and drinking water during the festivities.

'Yes, I had. The gateway looks messy, with the flowers and leaves strewn about. It's almost time for the young king of Gobha to arrive. Send Hurumphali to clean the area. There could be a water shortage in the kitchen. Make arrangements for some water.'

'Any other command, Your Highness?'

'No. You may leave. Oh, one other thing. Inspect the interior and exterior of the durbar hall thoroughly. Check to see if all the decorations are perfect. Also, examine the pathway leading to the levee.'

Huruma leaves with folded hands.

By the time Gangavati discusses the supply of joo and betel nut with Khurinol and reaches the gateway, the caravan of decorated elephants carrying the young king of Gobha and his officers and guards has arrived at the gateway.

Arimotto is sitting atop an elephant.

Beautifully attired panthais and khorlas are standing at the entrance that is bedecked with bamboo carved to look like flowers, leaves and banana trees, and they greet Arimotto and his retinue. The panthais' drumsticks set the long khrums rumbling to life. The khorlas, clad in bright red, yellow and black-and-white kasyong phaskai, are softly tossing fistfuls of marigold petals from small bamboo baskets. A symphony of myriad buffalo-horn pipes blows in unison. The capital of Khola resonates with cheers for Arimotto's victory. The moment Gangavati appears at the gateway, all the elephants sit down at once.

Arimotto descends from his elephant. Raising her curious eyes, Gangavati looks at him.

Arimotto is wearing a waistcloth, or thenus, woven with muga silk with floral borders running from waist to ankle. His chest sports a black cotton tagla studded with gold beads. A necklace of gold *cheomoni* beads adorns his neck. Gold ear-studs decorate his ears. A turban-like *phaga* of muga silk is wrapped around his head. With his golden complexion, slender, robust and tall physique, elongated deep black eyes, pointed nose and crimson lips, Arimotto emerges like the son of God.

His regal posture, solemn countenance and profound gaze leave no room for doubt – he is a valorous young king with all the qualities befitting a ruler.

Gangavati steps forward to welcome the king.

Her slender form is elegantly adorned in a pair of vibrant black-and-yellow kasyong phaskai, fitting snugly. Her hands, neck and ears glisten with beads acquired through trade with the Jaintias, a rarity among the Laloong women. As far as Arimotto can recall, he has never witnessed anyone donning these unique adornments before.

Despite being clad in a traditional Laloong outfit, why hasn't Gangavati worn any traditional jewellery on such a significant political durbar? Is it because of her love for Jaintia ornaments, which he had heard about at the samadi? The answer comes to Arimotto instantly, based on the political wisdom he's obtained from Sadhukumar.

The Jaintia king has been invited as a special guest for today's durbar.

That is the reason. Arimotto finds himself captivated by Gangavati's diplomatic skills. Her beauty and personality fascinate him.

Following his royal ordinance, Sadhukumar had advised Arimotto, 'You must preserve all that is your own. You must not abandon your traditions. However, you must not adhere to traditions in the manner of an old-world conservative. Society moves forward with a little give and take and understanding. If you hold on to your tradition and remain aloof from others, you will eventually become a loner.'

Gangavati appears to be aware of this mantra. From whom did she learn it? As soon as this question came to his mind, Arimotto laughs at his own foolishness. Which ruler of this region didn't know about it? Whether Mikir, Laloong, Jaintia – which king has ever fought with whom? There could have been a quarrel between two brothers within the kingdom. This quarrel might have resulted in the division of their kingdom, but other than that, when and where has there been a battle?

Sadhukumar had said, 'Please remember the song about the three Lali Hilali sisters, Mriganko. If the offspring of these three sisters fight with one another, who will gain from it? Never quarrel among yourselves. If necessary, give up the land itself. Subjects are greater than the kingdom. Sustaining mutual goodwill is greater than the kingdom. You must respect your elders. Do not work like a fool who does not pay heed to others. One day you are going to be the king of this vast realm. Apart from the subordinate provinces, the others also hold Gobha in high regard. Their people are close to us. They are also our own people. Always remember that. Your noble path will inspire others to follow in your footsteps.'

Sadhukumar had shared a lot more wisdom. Although he lives in Kumoi, Arimotto often visits Amsai Marjong. While he lives with his mother in Gobha's central palace, he spends most of his time with Sadhukumar. The older king has taught him how to rule a kingdom. Although Arimotto doesn't agree with everything Sadhukumar says, he has no desire to conquer other kingdoms in the region. Instead, he wants to expand their reign. He dreams of making the whole region more powerful politically and economically, like the developed countries in the east and west. He plans to announce these ambitions in the future, as revealing them now would meet with opposition from his parents. They prefer a slow and peaceful approach to development, while Arimotto likes a faster pace. He loves the thrill of his horse galloping at full speed on the smooth, wide roads between Kumoi, Boghora and Amsai Marjong.

After taking over Kumoi and Boghora, Arimotto is gradually expanding the military force. He is collecting information about the activities, military power and geographical positions of the kingdoms on either bank of the Brahmaputra from east to west. He will decide in which direction to advance his expedition only after the preparations have been completed.

'Would you prefer to rest for a while before going to the durbar, Your Highness?' Gangavati's words suddenly reach his ears.

'No, let us proceed to the durbar itself.' He smiles solemnly. They walk side by side, followed by the drummers and guards.

Inside, Arimotto is struck with admiration again. The kings sit on attractive flower-engraved chairs carved out of rock, arranged in a square. As soon as Arimotto enters, all the kings rise from their respective *orlong khamlis* and greet him. Outside the durbar hall, the sound of khrums slowly fades. In the southern row, three differently shaped and curved orlong khamlis have been placed. Bouquets of fragrant *gutimali* flowers adorn the four walls. There is a latticed centre table made of rock decorated with a few more bouquets. In between, flower-engraved bamboo tubes, beads sewn with yellow, black and white threads are also placed. The kings, too, hold in their hands similarly decorated bamboo tubes. They all sit down after the greeting. So do Arimotto and Gangavati.

'Where did you get the lovely beaded tubes, Queen Gangavati?' he asks in the middle of the ongoing session, sipping water from one of the tubes.

'They were made by our boys. I brought the beads from the Jaintias and asked them to decorate like this. Khola is a very small place, and we struggle with revenue. How else can we express our love for you all?' Gangavati says politely.

'Apparently, the people of Khola know quite well how to express their love. Since they have a queen like the goddess of wealth,' Arimotto laughs.

Gangavati's cheeks redden. She steers the conversation to politics, saying, 'Please address the matter of our revenue and tolls, Deoraja. Any suggestion from you will be accepted. The toll from Sohori is falling short for us. They thrive in agriculture, trade and commerce. The proximity to Mohong market and Gobha makes us hesitant to pressure them. We fear they might cut ties. Your attention to this during the durbar would be extremely helpful.'

Gangavati's political analysis takes Arimotto by surprise. Ignoring the praise from a handsome king, this beautiful woman is busy discussing the affairs of her kingdom.

Strange.

What he heard at the samadi is true.

The queen of Khola has no interest in young men. She is only concerned with her kingdom.

'She is like me,' he marvels.

Instantly, he remembers something else that was brought up at the samadi – Gangavati and Arimotto would make an excellent couple.

'You are not paying attention to me, Deoraja.'

Startled, he replies gravely, 'I am. I shall raise the issue.'

The durbar has begun.

The rulers who have arrived from various kingdoms are talking about their own problems, including inter-state complexities. Arimotto and Gangavati become engrossed in a political discussion.

FOURTEEN

The people are coming out, leaving their villages deserted. Except for the mothers with infants and the infirm, there is perhaps not a single elderly person left. Young boys and girls, as well as healthy old men and women, are moving forward in groups through the paddy fields, clapping hands in a particular rhythm and singing. Songs that make the body sway. Pervading the almost dark, numb winter dawn, wave after wave of the shrill cheering chorus is soaring to the skies. And spreading across the fields towards the distant sleepy villages.

There will be community fishing at the Jonbeel fair today. The villagers will step down together into the waters of the Jonbeel lake to enjoy a day of fishing.

The annual mela has been set up on the shores of the lake. It is the eve of the Magh Bihu festival of the king of Gobha. This festival is celebrated in Gobha when the tenth Assamese month draws to a close.

The festive fever has gripped the people. With harvest season over, it is time for everyone to celebrate. After bihu ends, cultivation will resume. Apart from the khrum–pangchi, everybody will go back to their livelihoods.

The eastern sky is gradually brightening.

Endless rows of people belonging to different tribes, clad in traditional costumes made of cotton, silk, eri and muga in a variety of colours and designs can be seen on the fairground and the paths leading to it.

Drowning out the din and bustle, the colourful, cheerful atmosphere of the bright morning, the highway echoes with the sound of countless khrum and buffalo horn pipes.

People walking along the pathways and the highway turn their heads around in curiosity.

They come to a halt.

And then, the clapping, cheering and singing abruptly ceases.

The crowd descends to gather in the reed-covered fields wet with mist.

The king is coming.

The king of Gobha.

Today, the royal officers will collect toll from the fishermen in the presence of the king of Gobha.

'The deoraja has arrived quite early today. What is the matter?' a man hauling a fishing net over his shoulder asks.

'Don't tell me you are not aware? This time the durbar is held in Khola. They say all the kings are coming to the fair to watch community fishing.'

'Chotlo? But I heard that all the kings went back at the end of the durbar yesterday.'

'Did you hear it in your sleep while you were drunk on joo?' another joins.

'No, no, not in his sleep. He must have heard it while sleeping with his wife,' yet another man chimes in, continuing the wordplay.

A group of people from the same village burst out laughing. Several young men squeal loudly.

'Shut your foul mouth.' Deeply embarrassed, the newly married man says angrily.

'Oh, look how he flares up at the truth. Do you sing lali hilali songs while lying in bed at night?'

'No, no. He performs the sogra dance in the *khoom-khatih* dress.' The villagers laugh in unison once again.

People standing nearby exchange smiles. The bachelors cheer

merrily. Even the young women carrying fishing tools, such as the *jakoi*, giggle with their hands over their mouths.

Just then the sound of the barika's khrum drifts over the din of laughter.

'Good people, please listen. The deoraja is on his way. Move away from the road.'

On hearing the barika's cry, the crowd forms a line on either side of the highway.

The elephant carrying the messenger and the khrum player passes by.

'Are the other kings on their way as well, barika?' someone shouts from the crowd.

'Yes, yes. The neighbouring kings will also arrive. The Jaintia king, too. So is the queen of Khola.'

As a barika of Khola, he announces his queen's name.

'It's going to be a great day. We'll be able to see so many kings together,' the people chat amongst themselves.

'We'll also be able to see the new young king of Gobha.'

'I have seen. Very handsome. A robust panthai, I must say. One must be fortunate to have such a king.'

'What flaws do you see in the old Deoraja that you keep harping on about fortune? In my opinion, having a noble person like him is a blessing.'

'Right. The new king could be strong. He could be handsome. Let him sit on the throne of Gobha. His work will prove whether our fortune is good or bad.'

'He's good, really good. We've heard of him. Wait and see if he really works for the welfare of the people. After all, he is Konsari Pai's son.'

'That's true. With a mother like Konsari Pai, how can he not work for the good of the people?'

'It seems the young king will live in Kumoi. Not Boghora. Now he spends most of his time in Amsai Marjong. Later on, he will shift to the palace of Kumoi.'

'Is it? Where did you hear this?'

'I went to Gaolia. There, I heard this news.'

'Good, good. So be it. As long as the people are happy.'

'Ho – yaaaa – they are here – they are here …' Several people from the crowd cry.

'Don't create a commotion. The deoraja will be offended. The royal guests are there, can't you see?' a man who sounds like a village head says loudly.

Suddenly the people, agog with excitement, fall quiet. They look eagerly at the distant procession of elephants.

Gradually, the long line of animals advancing while resonating the villages with the sound of khrum and pipe becomes visible.

The people in the nearby fields watch in awe this rare scene.

A row of innumerable bedecked elephants. The first few carry on their backs the khrum, pangchi and buffalo horn players. Followed by elephants carrying the guards and soldiers. Behind them is the Jaintia king.

The king is followed by three elephants carrying his bodyguards.

Riding on the next elephant is young King Arimotto.

Three elephants carrying Arimotto's bodyguards follow him. Then there is Queen Gangavati. Another line of armed bodyguards. The king of Dimoria comes thereafter. Some more bodyguards, followed by the king of Nelly. In this manner, king after king, each accompanied by their respective bodyguards, proceeds in the lineup. In their midst are the elephants carrying khrum, pangchi and buffalo horn players on their backs. Last in the row are the officers.

To the people standing on the paddy fields on either side of the highway, everything appears like a dream. The fragrant kuthimali flowers, red hibiscus and colourful leaves adorning the elephants, the glitter of gold and silver inlaid seats on their backs, the kings positioned on elephant-backs and the shining armours reflecting soft sunlight blind the villagers.

Acknowledging the obeisance of the long line of people kneeling on the paddy fields, the long row of bedecked elephants passes by.

Gangavati moves ahead, looking all around.

The queen of Khola attends the Jonbeel mela every year. The multicoloured crowd, the varied merchandise and the ecstatic thrill of the environs of the carnival delight her. The open banter and zest of the fishermen and fisherwomen transport her to another world. The paddy fields in the autumn to winter transition, the thick mist and the festive days provide a unique sense of fulfilment.

Gangavati had planned the three-day interstate durbar around the fishing festival of the Jonbeel mela. During these days, nature is at its tranquil best. Cultivation is at rest. The granaries are replete. Jungles are less dense. Assembling durbar at this time is convenient in every way. On each of these nights, Gangavati has organized entertainment for the guests. Musicians from far and wide have been invited. As a part of the entertainment package, Gangavati has arranged for a banquet on the banks of Jonbeel lake today. It will allow guests to enjoy the carnival as well as watch community fishing. Simultaneously, there will also be discussions about politics. In keeping with the tradition, the Jaintia king and the king of Gobha barter gifts on this day. Every year, the Jaintia king comes down to the valleys on the eve of Magh Bihu and visits the Jonbeel mela. Gangavati knows that the Jaintia king's presence would be politically significant. Apart from the extensive preparations needed for the guests' comfort, Gangavati has spent lavishly to keep them all entertained. She wants to please the neighbouring rulers as well as the kings of Jaintia and Gobha in order to improve and cement their political relationships.

A friend of her father, the Jaintia king looks upon Gangavati with fondness. Sadhukumar feels the same way. This time, the prince of Gobha, Arimotto, is here. And while trying to establish a good relationship with the young king, she has developed feelings for him.

Arimotto is not arrogant, and he does not seem too reserved either. He knows exactly how to socialize with others while maintaining his dignity and gravity. Gangavati had spent the whole of the previous day and far into the night in his vicinity. In this time, both the young king and queen have been able to build a rapport. The fact that they are almost of the same age has helped spark a friendship. Now and then, Arimotto utters a double entendre, which causes Gangavati to blush. She can neither assume a serious demeanour while dismissing it as the banter of a fickle young man, nor can she make any comment while accepting it as a serious political statement. Gangavati is befuddled by these exchanges. Like Arimotto, whose youthful mind flickers from under the king's robe, she too longs to reveal her jubilant self time and again, keeping gravity at bay.

The elephants have stepped into the waters now. The surroundings have come alive with sounds. Gangavati absentmindedly looks around. A herd of elephants are crossing a small river. A winter river. Almost devoid of water. A little distance away, a buffalo-herder lets his fat, robust buffalo sharpen its horns on the sandy slopes of the riverbank. Moving its head from side to side, the buffalo is plunging its horns hard into the sand dune. The sandy soil slithers from the impact. The oil-smooth hide of the animal shines in the early morning sunlight.

A fighter buffalo. It will go to the buffalo fight held around Magh Bihu, for sure, that Gangavati has arranged to entertain her royal guests. Almost all the participants have by now arrived from Baropujia. The king, on his own, has taken this responsibility. Gangavati is confident about this part of the presentation. She is hopeful about today's program to go well. The royal guests will depart tomorrow shortly after the buffalo fight.

Analysing the various aspects of the durbar deliberations and the political issues she intends to discuss with Arimotto, Gangavati moves along. By the time she reaches, sunlight brightens. A misty canopy forms from the vapour. The procession slows to a noisy halt in front of the rows of tents lining the shores of the Jonbeel lake.

Arimotto dismounts. All the other kings and officers join in, as do the panthais with their khrums, buffalo horns and other instruments. The Jaintia king has not yet come down. As is the tradition, Arimotto formally welcomes him.

Gangavati descends using makeshift bamboo and wood stairs set up near the elephant. She wears a traditional long black *manganthla* skirt dotted with red and yellow motifs and a muga riha that is draped over her body. In her ears are the traditional stone-studded *jangphai keroo* earrings, on her neck a *junbiri* and a creeper-shaped gem-studded pendant called *biri* brought all the way from upcountry. On her forehead dazzles a bright kopali, the parting of her hair covered with the sparkling *xirpota*, along with broad *gaamkharu* wristlets, shimmering peacock-tailed *nejia* and lotus-shaped *podumkoli* rings.

People line up in front of the camps to welcome the guests, and the crowds on either side of the road stare in awe at Gangavati and Arimotto. It appears as if the sun has just emerged after bathing in a river of molten gold. Gangavati admires Arimotto, who is dressed in a *mejankori* silk thenus, a tagla speckled with red and gold beads, and a yellow silk phaga studded with gold beads. He, too, stares at Gangavati, both sets of eyes full of fathomless admiration. After alighting from the elephants, they walk towards each other.

'You look gorgeous, Queen of Khola,' Arimotto mutters.

'Oh, Your Highness!' Gangavati turns red in the face.

'In fact, I am concerned about Khola's security,' he continues gravely, as they walk together towards the Jaintia king.

'Why, Deoraja?' Forgetting her shyness, Gangavati becomes anxious. From a shy maiden, she instantly transforms into a responsible ruler.

'Because of the goldmine at Khola,' Arimotto says, looking worried. He walks beside Gangavati with measured steps to welcome the Jaintia king. To the onlookers, it appears as if both are engrossed in a serious political discussion.

'A goldmine? But there is no goldmine at Khola,' Gangavati expresses in surprise.

'There is, indeed. I shall tell you. Later. Let us first make the Jaintia king comfortable in his camp,' Arimotto says, without looking at Gangavati.

The courtyard in front of the camps is filled with the sound of countless khrums. Arimotto and Gangavati come to stand near the elephant atop which the Jaintia king is sitting. Soon, he alights.

After the euphoric reception, all the rulers sit down in a neat row on seats placed in front of the camps. Gangavati, Arimotto and the Jaintia king sit in the centre. In front of the row of seats, a colourful *aanthla* mat has been spread across a long bamboo counter. On top of the counter are bamboo tubes, studded with beads. Bouquets of kuthimali flowers and colourful leaves have been arranged in carved tubes of stout *bholuka* bamboo.

On one side, the officers and panthais are sitting on a different bamboo bench draped in a colourful aanthla. One of the panthais is playing a pangchi. The flute's melodious tune caresses the tender hearts, complementing the early, pleasant morning. The fog hasn't dissipated properly, yet. Groups and groups of people are getting down into the waters of the vast Jonbeel lake in front and are already beginning to fish. The sweet songs of the fisherwomen blend with the rhythm of the fishing tools and nets. The intermittent cheers from the crowd beckon the joys of leisure. The joy of garners bursting with harvest. The joy of indulgence.

Young khorlas, attired in colourful kasyong phaskai and silver jewellery, begin to pour pepper-flavoured joo-sa from the draans into the bead-studded bamboo tubes. A little further away, a few women are grilling fish around a fire. They are serving the guests piping hot grilled fish, fresh from the Jonbeel lake, on banana leaves. There is no meat today. It's a day for fish only.

Behind the campsite, inside a cooking shed, preparations are going on for breakfast, comprising steamed sticky rice, delicate rice flakes, tender rice, curds prepared from buffalo milk, jaggery, grilled sweet potato, rice steamed in bamboo tubes, parboiled pounded rice, black lentils cooked with wild garlic and so on. Noise from the Jonbeel mela wafts in. Everything is submerged in a nameless sensation.

'You had mentioned something about the security of Khola, Your Highness?' Gangavati asks Arimotto, who is sitting next to her.

He looks at Gangavati. For a fraction of a second, his eyes twinkle with amusement. With his eyes, he gestures towards the kuthimali flowers in front and says, 'Strange! These flowers have no fragrance.'

'What do you mean?' Gangavati asks.

'Is the panthai playing the pangchi?'

'But of course. What are you trying to say, Your Highness?'

'I thought you hadn't smelled the kuthimali fragrance. You haven't heard the pangchi yet.'

'I cannot understand anything.' Gangavati becomes baffled.

'Of course not. Do you know anything other than your kingdom? You are a strange khorla indeed. Does any young khorla worry about her kingdom in such an environment?' Arimotto's eyes sparkle with laughter.

Gangavati becomes serious. She says after a brief pause, 'I am not merely a woman, Your Highness, I am the queen of Khola. My priority lies in the welfare of the people. At least for me.'

'Have I offended you? I, too, am a king, Queen Gangavati. The king of Kumoi and Boghora. The prince of Gobha. Twelve kingdoms like Khola fall under Gobha. The welfare of the people is a priority for me as well. But I am also a panthai. I know how to derive pleasure even while working for the kingdom.'

Gangavati tenses. Arimotto is upset! A small kingdom like Khola cannot survive by offending Gobha. A few moments pass in awkwardness. Then Gangavati speaks in a humble, remorseful voice, 'I apologize, Your Highness. We do not have a strong army like yours. We have to survive bearing in mind the Jaintia kingdom above and the neighbouring states like Rani, Dimoruwa and Beltola. I've already told you, we are weak in trade, forest resources and revenue. These reasons alone are enough to keep us so fearful and worried. And then, taking advantage of my status as a khorla, the other kings want to dictate terms to me.'

Arimotto's roaring laughter catches the attention of the other kings, who are sipping joo and watching community fishing, as well as the bodyguards and officers. Everybody stares at Arimotto in surprise, then, realizing that it is impolite to exhibit curiosity, goes back to watching fishing blankly.

Gangavati's face and ears begin to heat up.

'It seems the young prince of Gobha has found a good reason to laugh.' The elderly Jaintia king chuckles.

The Jaintia ruler has become very fond of this young prince. He is also pleased with the hospitality of the queen of Khola.

'I have been teasing Queen Gangavati,' Arimotto says, his tone respectful while speaking to the elderly, powerful Jaintia king.

'It's better not to rag the queen of Khola. She is a firebrand.'

Gangavati relaxes between the two men's easy banter. Yet at the same time, an unknown sensation rocks her inner self. She has finally understood what Arimotto is trying to express. In the past two days, he has occasionally said a few things of this sort, which Gangavati thought she understood but didn't. In the midst of serious political discussions, those words seemed to relate to politics.

'A goldmine at Khola,' Arimotto had said. Where is the goldmine? Only now has it become crystal clear to Gangavati. Today she is wearing a golden muga riha. She has adorned herself with gold ornaments.

Gangavati looks beautiful. Arimotto is insinuating that some ruler may invade Khola and seize her. As soon as she realizes it, a hot flush of blood flows to her cheeks. It takes quite some time for her to transform from a shy maiden to a queen.

But Arimotto has spoken the truth. Gangavati looks radiant today, and she is aware of it. However, she is not the type to be obsessed with her appearance. The majority of her day is spent on matters relating to her kingdom's progress and border security, among other things. A considerable amount of time is also spent on arms training. Gangavati utilizes her leisure hours in reading. She has already finished the few books in her native dialect.

Meanwhile, a teacher from Komota has visited Gobha several times and taught Arimotto how to read and write in Sanskrit and in the language flourishing in Kamrup. He has also left behind some books for the prince. It is very important for the kings to read and write various languages to maintain a good relationship with their neighbours. It would be sufficient if the couriers knew, too. But the king of Gobha has engaged a teacher from Kamrup for Arimotto. The same teacher, on his way back, had stayed as a royal guest at Khola and had taught Gangavati how to read and write. She, therefore, spends her free time reading and writing.

Gangavati has never experienced interest in any panthai. No panthai dares to behave with her in the manner a panthai treats a khorla because she is a queen. They regard her with awe and respect. As a result, no one has been able to impress Gangavati, until now. She has not considered anyone worthy of her.

For the first time, a panthai has created ripples inside Gangavati. Arimotto, just like the fisherwomen who unsettled the waters of Jonbeel repeatedly by thrusting their jakois, has ruffled in the still waters of Gangavati's heart through his intelligence, good looks and personality. Are there similar waves in Arimotto's heart, too? During intervals between serious political discussions, why did Arimotto use words with double meaning?

Gangavati has spotted the admiration in Arimotto's eyes. No woman ever makes a mistake in understanding it. She becomes immersed in her thoughts. The officers from Gobha are by then collecting toll from the fishermen on the lakebank. The khorlas dressed in multi-coloured banath-bathu are beginning to serve refreshments to the royalties in bowls and dishes.

'Aren't you going to barter eri cloth for Jaintia beads today?' Arimotto's words startle Gangavati, who is absorbed in thought.

'How did you know that I barter Jaintia beads, honourable king?' she asks.

'From this.' Arimotto laughs, pointing at the beaded bamboo tube.

'Oh.'

'When I was in the samadi, the other panthais told me many things about you. They had also told me that every year you visited the Jonbeel fair to barter eri cloth for Jaintia beads.'

Suddenly, Gangavati is reminded of the words spoken timidly by the newly married khorla, who had come to work in the palace of Khola. All at once, her heart flutters with an unknown sensation. Concealing her thoughts, Gangavati smiles without saying anything. After remaining quiet for some time, Arimotto asks, 'Would you like to hear what else my companion panthais had said?'

'No, I don't want to.' Gangavati blushes self-consciously.

'Why?'

Before she can respond, an officer comes up and says something in Arimotto's ears. Immediately, he transforms from a playful panthai into a serious king.

'Queen of Khola, it's time to exchange gifts with the Jaintia king.' Arimotto rises.

Two groups of officers approach from opposite sides.

The Jaintia king stands up, too.

The khrums come to life. And the buffalo horn pipes.

First, Arimotto makes his offerings: two enormous teeth of an elephant. A bundle of eri cloth. A few long and wide aanthla scarves designed with variously coloured threads, two bholuka bamboo tubes, flower-engraved and filled with honey, a few colourful draans, two wickers full of raw fish, two wickers full of dried fish and a trapper elephant. In return, the Jaintia king presents two baskets full of oranges, two wooden tubes full of dried bamboo shoots, colourful cloths, a latticed wooden box full of multicoloured beads, wooden serving spoons, folding knives, a few pine wood tubes filled with oil and many more gifts.

Afterwards, the Jaintia king embraces Arimotto, who is about his son's age. Arimotto returns after greeting him. One by one, the kings rise and offer their gifts to the Jaintia king, who reciprocates by giving gifts to each of them. On behalf of the king of Gobha, his officers offer wickers of raw fish, softened rice, aanthlas and eri shawls to all the kings. Later, everyone walks to the Jonbeel fair.

At the Jonbeel lake, fishing is still in full swing. The fairground is bustling with people from different communities who have brought goods to barter. They sit in rows, displaying their wares in front of them. The Laloongs from the valleys and others have brought a variety of items, including rice cakes stuffed with sesame, *sandoh* (wet rice parched and pounded into lumps), steamed cakes, dried fish, shawls woven with eri yarn, golden muga yarn, white silk yarn, oranges, herbs, spadix of the banana tree, handicraft items made of bamboo and wood, multicoloured bedspreads and aanthlas, among many others.

While the festivities continue, Arimotto presents a chest of beads given to him by the Jaintia king to Gangavati. She is watching a performance of wooden birds dancing when she hears him speak. Gangavati laughs heartily and jokes, asking if he would give away his nation's assets just because she likes Jaintia beads. Arimotto replies that while giving away might not be right, if it brings back twice as much, why not?

Arimotto gazes into Gangavati's eyes confidently, and she blushes but candidly points out that donating to the unworthy could incur loss. However, Arimotto assures her that she is not unworthy, and he doesn't see any likelihood of loss. Their playful banter continues, and Gangavati agrees to accept the beads, knowing that there is a gold mine in her kingdom.

Just as emotions stir within Gangavati, her bhitor maji arrives to inform that lunch is ready to be served. Both Gangavati and Arimotto return to their respective tents.

The Jonbeel lake is now cleared of all fishermen. A sense of calmness settles over the surroundings.

FIFTEEN

The elevated Rongchuwa ground near the palace and the durbar site is packed. Crowds have arranged themselves into rows on three sides of the ground, leaving the centre vacant. Some are standing to ensure they don't miss any part of the spectacle.

A huge bamboo-and-straw awning stands on the eastern side, providing restful shade. Arimotto, Gangavati and the kings of Dimoruwa and Nelly are sitting in the centre of the first row. Gangavati is wearing a dark green kasyong with yellow and red flowers, paired alongside a bright yellow phaskai adorned with red motifs. An eri scarf woven in the indigenous Laloong design is draped across her shoulders. Arimotto is in a silk thenus and a deep red tagla, with an eri scarf patterned with colourful motifs. A silk phaga studded with coral beads adorns his head, lending him a celestial aura surrounded by a swarm of butterflies. All of the citizens are captivated by the two stars in their midst.

This day marks the end of the durbar. The Jaintia king had left after returning from the Jonbeel mela, and the previous night's entertainment programme had been a grand affair. Dancers and drummers from the Mikir hills, Rani, Beltola, Pandu and Guwahati had performed various mythological plays. Meanwhile, *ojapali* puppeteers and singers from Komota unveiled a captivating array of songs, dances and performances, many of which were previously unseen and unheard of.

Visitors from distant kingdoms have been staying in nearby villages to attend the evening's events. It is a cultural tradition to welcome any guests seeking refuge for a night as gods. Over the past three days, these visitors have become the villagers' brethren, all of them sipping freshly made joo and enjoying the festivities together.

Early this morning, all the kings had gathered at the durbar hall to go over all the resolutions reached in the past two days. After lunch, everyone walked over to the Rongchuwa ground.

It was time for the buffalo fight. Typically, they were just a fun activity for young buffalo keepers. So, if someone wanted to participate in the real contest, which offered handsome prizes, they had to travel to Baropujia where it was patronized by the royal family. Gangavati had never witnessed a buffalo fight before. She didn't like seeing the animals being forced to fight for entertainment and had heard terrifying things about these contests. But as the queen hosting the durbar, she is obliged to attend. She uneasily sits down near Arimotto, her discomfort slowly transcending the buffalo fight now.

Arimotto had similar feelings. When he had first arrived at Khola, he had been regarded by the queen as a valuable, unyielding piece of gold. Over the past two days, though, he had swifty displayed his political acumen, demonstrated a free-thinking approach to ruling and helped create a friendly atmosphere with light-hearted jokes while upholding dignity.

Unspoken feelings had culminated in a surprising discovery of love. Despite engaging in mere casual conversation, a bridge had formed between the two of them, carrying a rainbow of emotions.

A shiver runs through Gangavati suddenly, making her blush without any reason. No one around them has noticed the passionate whirlpool building between the young king and queen.

Suddenly, her thoughts are interrupted by the sound of drums and cheering. Two buffaloes, ready to fight, have entered the field, led by their respective keepers. The animals look restless amidst the cacophony of drumming, cheering and shouting from the crowd.

'Did you know the two sticks held by the keepers have first been sanctified at Mayong?' Arimotto asks.

'Really? Does everybody do that?'

'Yes. Have you noticed the oily hair and foreheads of the buffalo keepers? The oil they use is also purified through incantation.'

Gangavati is regarding the two men with the curiosity of a teenager.

Striking their respective animals, the keepers try to make them move forward. The buffaloes lower their heads, gearing to fight.

'I don't like animal fights,' she blurts out.

'Why?' Arimotto turns to look at her.

'I don't like fights in general.'

'What if someone comes to fight after seeing the goldmine in Khola?'

'I shall ask him to stay back as a Gobhia,' Gangavati replies, blushing.

'Such courage. What if he refuses?' he smiled.

'I can't beat you at words, honourable king.'

'My name is Arimotto. My friends call me Mriganko.'

'Mriganko. I didn't know.'

'You think this name complements my personality, do you? Does "Arimotto" remind you of the head of an ari fish?' he laughs aloud.

Forgetting to behave like a solemn queen, Gangavati also laughs open-heartedly.

And then suddenly, as if by magic, she feels at ease. The heavy walls of Gobha's might and the queenly obligations of hospitality have come down.

'This is the way you should laugh. It makes you look like a khorla,' Arimotto says seriously. 'I was bored of watching the queen manage the loro, barika, doloi and kra-koormi.'

'Now?'

'I don't feel like watching the buffalo fight.'

'Me neither.'

Yet they keep sitting.

The Rongchuwa ground has come alive with the commotion and wild, shrill laughter of the people. The two robust buffaloes are becoming excited. Both the keepers have freed the *naki* cords from the animals' noses at the same time. The buffaloes, moving rapidly, forcefully collide with each other's heads. They repeat this action several times before backing off and then charging again, trying to thrust their horns into the other's ears. The loud noise every time they crash into each other adds to the intensity of the fight. Both buffaloes are becoming increasingly combative, and their keepers growing agitated, jabbing their sticks on the ground and shouting at their animals.

The crowd are reaching a crescendo of excitement. Even the royal guests, usually composed and dignified, are showing signs of restlessness. Some are almost standing on their seats, clenching their fists and hitting the arms of their chairs in the heat of the moment.

Arimotto is sitting still. But even his lips are beginning to stiffen. His expression has hardened. His arm muscles look visibly tense.

Gangavati is starting to feel unsettled. She wants to leave now. A timid girl scared of fights is trying to force herself out from within the Khola queen, known to be proficient at warfare. Suddenly, a loud, excited clamour spreads across the Rongchuwa ground. One of the buffaloes is bearing down on the other with its horns. With great force, it is tearing apart the oil-smooth, sturdy thigh of the other buffalo. One of its legs is turning bright red with blood. Wounded, the other buffalo is starting to retreat. Seized by murderous passion, the winning buffalo is trying to knock down the injured buffalo.

Suddenly, after taking a few steps back to defend itself, the wounded buffalo turns around and begins to charge in the direction of Gangavati and Arimotto. Forgetting everything, the queen stands up. Just then Arimotto's warm, heavy hand firmly clasps hers. The crowds in the field are yelling now. Numerous guards are chasing after the buffalo. It has to be driven away to another direction before the animal rampages through everything. Spectators on the southern side are scrambling to flee in panic. The royal guests are being shielded by the soldiers. Amidst this commotion, nobody is paying attention to Arimotto and Gangavati.

'Sit down. Don't worry,' he says in a deep, calm voice. The

queen looks into his eyes, an unfamiliar emotion shaking her to the core.

'Sit,' he says again, with the same intensity. It is a single word, yet it feels like an epic has just been narrated. As Arimotto releases her hand, Gangavati sits down again. Transformed. Exhausted. Stripped of her armour.

One of the keepers holds the wounded buffalo down. He inserts the naki cord through its nose and tugs the animal. They come to a stop near where Gangavati and the others are sitting. A boy takes out some leaves from a bag, and the buffalo keeper rubs them into a paste between his fingers before applying them to the animal's wounds.

Gangavati looks at the field where two more men are preparing to bring their buffaloes down. The commotion in the field has subsided. Arimotto sits to her right, appearing solemn and composed again, as if nothing has happened.

Feeling shy, Gangavati instead turns her gaze to the buffalo keeper, who is tending to his hurt animal.

'What is the buffalo keeper using?' she asks.

'Spinach. It can also be used to treat all kinds of human wounds. Although I don't know what is used to heal a wounded heart,' Arimotto laughs.

'Why must you know?' Gangavati fixes her eyes on him.

'Mustn't I?'

'No.' She is smiling, though her eyes are wet.

'Now that the durbar is over, I shall leave in a while. Of course Khola is a sovereign kingdom, but if you think of another way of building an alliance with Gobha, I shall be delighted.'

'I shall consider it, Your Majesty.'

'My name is Mriganko. Could I expect to meet a khorla instead of the queen when we meet next?'

'I can't say that right now, Your Highness.'

'No need. You can tell me when I meet you as a panthai.'

Gangavati lowers her head. A battlefield of buffaloes is descending upon her heart now.

SIXTEEN

'A courier messenger has arrived from Kumoi–Boghora, Your Highness,' the bhitor maji informs Gangavati, who is busy deliberating a border issue with the royal representative from Beltola and her major general in the secret counsel room.

Even though Khola has managed to avoid any major border conflicts with its neighbouring western kingdoms, certain disputes crop up from time to time. To maintain cordial relations with the Koch kingdom's territories, the queen often dispatches missives and gifts. Since Khola is under the patronage of Gobha, other small kingdoms such as Rani, Looki and Beltola also try to keep peace. Typically, they all try to resolve petty issues through deliberations, exchanging gifts, messages and so on. Khola has never engaged in battle with any of them until now.

'I shall be there soon. Arrange for his food and rest,' Gangavati gravely instructs the bhitor maji. She's feeling restless now. While the envoy from Beltola is unaware, the major general has picked up on it.

The major general has served Khola since the days of Gangavati's father. She has known the general since she was a child, and her trust in him is like that of a family member. On the other hand, the major general has also heard about Gangavati's recent meetings with the young prince of Gobha from the queen's loyal bodyguards, who report everything to him.

While these have been strictly tagged as political meetings, the major general isn't oblivious to Gangavati's inner feelings. There are also no restrictions on pre-marital relationships in Khola society. Gobha is an extremely powerful kingdom, and their cordial relationship with it has improved Khola's revenue structure, along with raising its political clout. With King Bodosa's rise, smaller kingdoms like Laloong, Mikir, Bhuyan and other neighbouring domains have united under Gobha to safeguard their realms. In fact, during the durbar, they collectively agreed to establish a combined armed force to counter any potential aggression from the Kachari king. Queen Gangavati has held multiple meetings with the king of Gobha outside the capital to implement this decision.

But the major general does not know how much closer Gangavati and Arimotto have grown during these meetings, and he won't try to find out. While their society may occasionally cast a shadow on emotional connections between a young man and a young woman, this resistance isn't insurmountable. As far as the rulers of their kingdoms are concerned, it especially does not hold much weight.

Once their discussion with the Beltola missive is finished, Gangavati sends him to rest. Then she turns to the major general. 'I have something special to discuss with you, General. King Arimotto of Kumoi–Boghora wishes to expand their kingdom. I'm on my way to deal with his courier. Tomorrow at this time, I shall go over the details with you. I have decided our position on the matter, but I must consult with you before talking to the loro and dolois.'

'As you wish, Your Highness. I shall report here tomorrow,' the major general said and left.

Feeling restless, Gangavati steps out for a walk. She and Arimotto have met several times by now. Between talking about their political agenda, the prince has been slowly transporting her to a land of fantasy and dreams. With every encounter, her fascination seems to grow, her love becoming deeper. Arimotto's pervasive charisma has imprisoned her, like no other king she knows could.

Not only has she found a committed lover in him, but in Arimotto's words and actions Gangavati has also discovered the qualities of an ambitious, benevolent, victory-hungry ruler. She has perceived manliness, arrogance and pride. Never had she met such a man before. In their vast kingdoms, just like their citizens, rulers were generally peace-loving, too. They believed in governing their realms as per tradition, free of disputes and complexities. Arimotto was different. Unique.

But Gangavati never forgets about Khola for a moment, even when immersed in love. She is quick to bring up an issue concerning her people at the cost of ruining a romantic moment. Arimotto, too, freely expresses his desire to expand his kingdom to her.

'What is the use of expanding it, Mriganko?' she had asked him when they met the last time. 'It is wiser to live in peace like the present.'

'No, Gangavati. From what we've heard from the spies about King Bodosa's activities, it was essential for us to unite under one banner. We have come together. That's a good thing. But our weaponry and military powers cannot grow by depending on agriculture and forest resources alone. How many weapons can we make from the iron we get from Komarjan? Moreover, the accord for elephant-trapping with the Jaintia king is going to reduce our revenue from elephants. If we enlist the panthais from paddy fields into the army, then who will work in the fields? The greater our kingdoms, the better. We can collect tariffs from our subsidiary lands to keep our realms secure. The Mikir kings have also consented to our proposal.'

'Where do you plan to expand the kingdom? It is pointless to initiate a conflict with the Kacharis; they are our neighbours, after all. The Ahoms have significant influence in the eastern regions. If the Ahom king joins forces with the Kacharis, particularly Bodosa, and launches an invasion, how can we hope to fight them with our modest army and weaponry? The Ahoms are also in discussions with the Naga Hills, and I've heard of a skirmish there. Would they risk hostilities with the Ahoms for our friendship instead of the Kacharis? Probably not even the Deuri Chutias. Or the Morans. The Ahoms have solidified their loyalty by marrying their daughters to them. We could gain by expanding our kingdoms, but given both the geographical lay of the lands and the Ahoms' diplomatic skills and military strength, it would be wiser to abandon this idea entirely.'

'I know. This is why I plan to move westwards.'

'Do you mean Rani? Beltola? Looki? Chaygaon? The southern kingdoms are our allies. Things are different in Pandu and Guwahati, where we have neither allies nor enemies. But I can't let you fight the kingdoms of the southern bank. We live in peace. We prefer to live in peace.'

Her words had worried Arimotto. After some contemplation, he said, 'I won't attack the southern kingdoms, nor will I make them our subsidiaries. But their loyalty is crucial. If they refuse, I'll have no choice but to take action. You can't stop me. I will send an emissary to discuss this with them. If I don't win their loyalty, what is the point of marching north? It's meaningless to advance with a trail of enemies in our wake. As we advance north, the kingdoms of the south bank on the way must pledge their allegiance. Then I'll head to Komota, as it is currently vulnerable. I'll secure my position there first, as it boasts a significant number of elephants. It shares a border with the Bhot kingdom, offering access to wood and a wealth of other resources. Their proximity to the Koch and other Bhuyan kingdoms has made them more advanced than us in various fields. I've heard they're even acquiring the latest arms and weaponry. The farther west I venture, the more opportunities I'll gain, the more I can learn. It will also help me better develop our kingdom.'

'You are an unusual ruler, King Mriganko. Deoraja Sadhukumar is much more reasonable,' Gangavati had despaired.

'True, he is better. This is precisely why the Dimabongs are trying to seize our fertile land. I believe in progress. By expanding the kingdom, I shall make Gobha powerful. The prosperity of Gobha translates to prosperity for our clans and prosperity for all, Gangavati.'

'*Khroomdong*, Your Highness.' Samol, who was sitting in the guest house, stands as Gangavati enters.

'Khroomdong, Samol. Please, take a seat,' Gangavati says. 'What *pathra* have you brought?'

Samol is in charge of the samadi now. He also frequently delivers letters between her and Arimotto, making him almost a friend to Gangavati. Yet he always remains reserved, speaking only when necessary. He is composed, reliable and loyal. In response to Gangavati's question, he retrieves a letter from his tagla before saying, 'He seeks your response.'

Not wishing to open the letter in front of him, Gangavati rises. 'Please, have something to eat while I draft a response.'

Samol doesn't respond. Just as she's about to leave, leaving him in the care of a khamsamai, he says, 'I need to return early. I'm not supposed to be away from the samadi.'

'I'll write it right away. Enjoy some refreshments.'

With the letter in her hand, Gangavati heads to her room thoughtfully.

In the past, Mriganko's letters used to stir up excitement in her. But today, they also worry her.

After reading the letter, Gangavati's anxiety deepens.

Mriganko has decided to embark on his victorious expedition immediately after Bohag Pisu, the new year that begins in spring time. Meanwhile, the envoys who visited the kingdoms on the southwestern banks of the Brahmaputra have returned. Everyone has agreed to maintain loyalty and friendly relations with Gobha, offering help when needed. Right after Bohag Pisu, the Gobha prince will invade Komota, currently ruled by King Durlovendra, the grandson of the mighty Durlov Narayan and son of Indra Narayan.

Durlovendra is a weak king. His grandfather's once vast and powerful Komota has dwindled into a small, powerless kingdom. Many of the Bhuyans, who had migrated from Korno–Suborno and became feudal lords during Durlov Narayan's rule, are now independent rulers themselves. As such, once Arimotto gains control of Komota, he intends to seek a peaceful allegiance with Durlovendra first, to avoid bloodshed. He will resort to military action only if the king declines.

The letter conveys Mriganko's desire to meet her before starting his expedition in a few days, somewhere outside the palace, in a private setting.

Deep in thought, Gangavati begins to compose her reply.

SEVENTEEN

Komotapur.

King Arimotto of Komota is having a meal inside what used to be the elegantly decorated residence of its former chief minister, Nilakanta.

For the past two years, Arimotto has been using the house as a makeshift royal residence. The work is underway to build Baidyagarh, a new capital with a three-tier land-and-water citadel and adequate security arrangements. The construction of the fort and the residences inside it has been completed, with just the streets left to be cleaned. The transition from temporary dwellings to the citadel has begun. Ponds, lakes, army camps and quarters for the key officers, royal medics, attendants, maids-in-waiting and other personnel have been built. The citadel includes armouries, stables for horses and elephants, community kitchens, as well as vast grounds, vegetable and flower gardens, a Shiva temple and much more. The royal palace stands at a considerable distance from these developments, a self-contained realm with its own flower gardens, lakes, armouries and other necessary amenities.

Baidyagarh is scheduled to be inaugurated in fifteen days, with the auspicious moment determined by Robi Chandra Sarma, a renowned astrologer from a neighbouring kingdom.

In preparation for the inauguration, Arimotto is on his way to Gobha. His plan is to bring his mother, father and Gangavati to the ceremony. During the past two years, Arimotto could only visit Gobha once. In this time, he has had various new experiences in trade and commerce, armours and weaponry, languages and dialects, customs and principles. He's eager to put all this newfound knowledge to use in Komota, so that Gobha's name becomes recognized far and wide.

Despite regular correspondence with Gangavati and his mother and father through letters, Arimotto often feels restless living away from them, his homeland and his people. He longs to visit Gobha, but he knows leaving a newly acquired kingdom for an extended period would be unwise.

Can letters ever satisfy the intense yearning born of profound love?

Finally, the days of waiting are drawing to a close. The capital is now established with sufficient security measures in place. Arimotto can now bring his parents and Xunzira Asi for a brief visit. It's also the perfect time to bring Gangavati to Baidyagarh, not merely as a visitor but as his wife and the queen of Komota. Arimotto has decided to reveal his intentions regarding Gangavati to his mother the moment he arrives in Gobha. After a simple wedding, he plans to bring everyone back to Baidyagarh. Following a short stay, they will return to Gobha. Samol, who is not married yet, will remain in Baidyagarh. Arimotto will entrust him with authority over Komota, while ruling from Gobha himself.

Arimotto is certain that Gangavati will never permanently leave Khola to reside in Baidyagarh. Her profound love and sense of duty to her kingdom never cease to amaze him, further deepening his affection.

She is truly remarkable. Unique.

'Sometimes, I believe you'd rather part from me than your kingdom, Gangavati,' Arimotto had remarked during an intimate rendezvous by the banks of Kolong before he embarked on his journey.

'It is a ruler's duty to love their kingdom, Mriganko. Don't you love yours? It's for the sake of your kingdom that you're preparing to travel so far, isn't it? Have you stayed for my sake?' Arimotto had been left momentarily speechless.

Her words held undeniable truth. Arimotto couldn't dispute them.

His thirst for victory eclipsed his affection for her. His dream of ruling of a mighty, expansive empire drew him away from Gobha to Komota. The dream is on the verge of realization. He now commands the defeated king's armed forces and their extensive armoury. A significant number of battle-hardened soldiers and most of the royal command have recognized his authority.

All of this became possible due to Nilakanta's backing. Within a few days of Arimotto's invasion, he had yielded. He and his daughter Ratnavali knelt before the new king, offering betel nuts and betel leaves on a bell-metal tray. Arimotto had felt uncomfortable initially, but then the former chief minister had explained his decision. 'Turning my back on King Durlovendra and submitting to the enemy king is an act of betrayal, Your Majesty. It warrants a death sentence. Yet I'm compelled to commit this crime to safeguard my daughter. I am helpless because of this motherless girl. Where can I take such a beautiful young girl, Your Majesty? This place is fraught with danger for someone like her. I am a father. My daughter's safety has left me defenceless, so I've decided to surrender. If you believe my betrayal outweighs a father's duty, then punish me. I shall accept it unconditionally. I have only one request: my daughter's safety should not be compromised.

Won over by this candid admission, Arimotto had allowed the former chief minister to live at his own residence in Komota with full honour. But Nilakanta had refused, vacating the house for the new king, to go live in a small house outside the complex. Arimotto could have lived at Durlovendra's palace had the latter not set it on fire before fleeing the kingdom.

Nilakanta has not been reinstated as the chief minister; that role has been taken up by Samol. The responsibility for the kingdom's security has been placed in the hands of trustworthy officers from Gobha. Instead, Nilakanta has been given the role of caring for the horse stables, a duty he performs diligently and contentedly.

Arimotto is pleased with the former chief minister's dedication and attention to the king's comfort and well-being. As a native of this region and a man of vast experience, Nilakanta has become increasingly indispensable thanks to his prompt solutions to issues of the state. Their relationship has developed into something like a familial bond. Ratnavali often visits to perform various tasks. She prepares meals for Arimotto that he had never tasted before. Initially, she wanted to cook in the palace kitchen, but Samol refused.

Though the new chief minister's unwavering loyalty prevents him from opposing Arimotto's decisions, he keeps a watchful eye on the father and daughter's every move. Only after a thorough inspection does he permit the items brought by Ratnavali to enter the residence. They in turn lack the courage to defy his orders.

Having witnessed Arimotto and Samol's close relationship, Nilakanta has also come to understand the king's profound trust in his chief minister. So he obeys Samol's every directive without question.

Even now, he stands with his palms joined at a short distance from Arimotto, who is eating. The reserved and sombre Samol stands guard nearby as per the protocol.

Before serving the king, the chief minister tastes everything brought by Nilakanta. There is no misgiving about the food prepared by the royal cooks as the people of Gobha do not possess the venom of treachery in their blood. But the intimacy between the former chief minister and the king often exasperates Samol. And Nilakanta's oily devotion to the king makes him suspicious.

The former chief minister is also promoting his beautiful daughter. Both Nilakanta and Ratnavali are frequent visitors to the royal residence. The daughter brings Arimotto delicious snacks and specially prepared meals, tending to his needs. Even today, the pair have come to the palace with food for Arimotto, who is preparing to return to Gobha. Samol has not failed to notice the flicker of happiness on the king's face at their displays of hospitality.

The happiness irks him, but Samol doesn't have the liberty to freely express his thoughts. Despite their friendship, Samol has maintained the respect and loyalty of a khara panthai. Arimotto may have elevated him to the highest rank in his kingdom, but Samol never forgets his origins as the son of a barika and margi khamsamai. He never oversteps his bounds, simply observing Nilakanta's supercilious modesty and concern and Ratnavali's flirtatious movements.

While savouring the food, the king often discusses politics with Nilakanta. He enjoys Ratnavali's liveliness and playful banter, yet he never gives her an opportunity to cross boundaries. Arimotto is used to interacting freely with women from Gobha, but he always maintains a distance from Ratnavali as women in this society do not enjoy the same status. They remain veiled, subordinate to men, imprisoned in a fortress of customs and restrictions. The local girls can never imagine joining men in the traditional dances like the Muinary Kanthi.

Before he left, Sadhukumar had told him, 'Go if you want to. Remember one thing: You can win nations with weapons, but you can never win the hearts of people with weapons. Wherever you go, wherever you are, abide by the rules of that society. Abide by their customs. Respect them. Only then can you become a true ruler. Never abandon what is your own, but do not disrespect what belongs to others.'

Arimotto has taken Deoraja's advice to heart. He has adopted many of Komota's practices, which reflects in his attire – a thenus with borders and a short-sleeved floral shirt tailored by skilled men from the west. Around his shoulders is a neatly folded silk scarf bordered with red motifs, and a silk turban fringed with strings of pearls sits on his head. In his new outfit, Arimotto looks entirely different. The experiences of the past two years, the confidence of victory and his zeal have made him more radiant, dignified and determined than before.

Not only has he started to put into practice the skills, tools and modern administration techniques imported from the west, but he has also begun to introduce them in Gobha. His progressive mindset and enthusiasm have made him popular in Komota, and his worthiness has been recognized by the kingdoms on the southern banks, Gobha and the neighbouring regions. New administrative approaches have begun to spread in the southern regions as well. Arimotto's popularity is also attributed to his qualities as a good administrator – liberal and tolerant. He has never attempted to challenge the prevailing societal customs and norms of Komota to impose his own faith and beliefs. Instead he strives to assimilate himself into this culture. Under his leadership, no soldier has disrespected the modesty of any woman from Komota during or after battles. Despite numerous opportunities, Arimotto has never taken advantage of his intimacy with Ratnavali. His deep love for Gangavati keeps him devoted to her, ignoring other women.

'Should I serve some more curd?' Ratnavali asks, with a bowl of curd in her hand.

'No, I don't like *toi*.'

'You call milk "toi"?' she giggles, staring at the king in awe.

Arimotto becomes serious.

'Why are you laughing? We call milk "*saah*". Sometimes "*kakhir*". "*Toi*" is made from kakhir. Why do you call curd "*doi gakhir*"? Just say "doi". People on the south bank call milk "*gakhir*" and yogurt "doi". Not "doi gakhir", like here.'

'That's why we don't like people from the south bank. They don't know anything. We call curd "doi gakhir", and milk is known as "*phuita gakhir*". The girl burst into giggles again.

'Phuita gakhir.' Arimotto laughs too. Nilakanta, standing nearby with folded hands, is watching the expression on the king's face pointedly. He has witnessed Arimotto's physical strength, fighting skills, zest and valour. The former chief minister is a power-hungry man, craving authority and a life of luxury under royal power. He is also an inveterate politician – cunning and dexterous.

He knows the king will not remain in Baidyagarh indefinitely. Arimotto is destined to become more powerful. Nilakanta has learned of the king's intention to annex the Bhuyan kingdoms that gained independence during Durlovendra's reign. He knows the Bhuyan rulers fear Arimotto's ascension. Despite belonging to the same clan, there is no unity among them, making it easy for Arimotto to gain supremacy. He has become popular among the Boro–Kocharis and Jogis in the Bhot foothills. In the west, although the Kochs have risen to power, they have not yet become aggressive. In the small kingdoms of the west, monarchy continues to prevail. The former chief minister also understands that Arimotto's kingdom will expand further if he is not strategically opposed, by hook or crook.

While Arimotto is powerful, he is not ruthless, but liberal and straightforward. He has not oppressed or exploited anyone despite his victories in battle. He is trying to bring about peace through harmony.

Nilakanta has discovered only a few weaknesses in Arimotto: he is easily influenced, trusting, likes being complimented and has a weakness for alcohol. He is also somewhat conceited and unwavering in his decisions.

However, none of Nilakanta's plots have succeeded yet. But this won't do. A relationship between Arimotto and Ratnavali needs to be developed. Otherwise, they will not be able to oust Samol as the chief minister. Regardless of his devotion and loyalty, this king from the south will never completely trust the feudatory lord from the north. Nilakanta can never attain the power he enjoyed during the reign of Durlovendra. He has turned into a frenzied fox, though nobody can sense it from his appearance. He is slowly approaching Arimotto with careful movements.

'A Brahmin from Fingua Kunwar's kingdom has arrived. He claims to be acquainted with Deoraja.' Although the bhitor maji addresses Samol, Arimotto – who is about to pick up a betel nut from the bell-metal tray after finishing his meal – turns to look. As does Nilakanta.

A Brahmin acquainted with Arimotto!

The king's brow wrinkles. There is only one Brahmin from Komota whom he is familiar with – Acharya Prabhakar Bidyanidhi, who had travelled to Gobha to teach Arimotto to read and write. But Acharya Bidyanidhi had gone to Kashi. Has he returned?

'What did the Brahmin say his name was?' he asks.

'Prabhakar Sharma Bidyanidhi,' the bhitor maji says.

Arimotto's face brightens.

Noticing his expression, Nilakanta grows worried. A Brahmin from Fingua Kunwar's kingdom! Why is he here? Could there be a note with him from Fingua? If so, what could it be? What message could the neighbouring king Fingua Kunwar send to Arimotto?

'Ask him to sit, Samol. I shall be there soon.'

Picking up a betel nut from the tray, the king says to Nilakanta, 'You may leave now. The inaugural festival of Baidyagarh must be nothing short of perfect. Make arrangements for Kamrupia drummers, and ojapali and puppet dance performances. Ensure the neighbouring Boros participate in the function as well. I shall bring our own dancers and drummers on my way back. There must not be any flaws while making invitations. Discuss everything with the chief minister before proceeding. Make no decision on your own. My mother and father are likely to attend the festival. They might visit the temples of Kamakhya, Dirgheswari and Pandunath. Once they are here, they will also visit the Billeswar temple. Have everything arranged.'

'Your wish is my command, O king of kings.'

Nilakanta walks out with Ratnavali, pensively. On his way, he resolves to meet the Brahmin from Fingua Kunwar's kingdom. A different political strategy is beginning to take a faint shape in his mind.

EIGHTEEN

Konsari enters the Amsai Marjong palace after dismounting from her elephant. She's returned after a long absence.

Every time Sadhukumar visits Gobha, sleep eludes her. Severe mortification eats away at her soul. She writhes in shame at her own vulnerability.

It is an unusual relationship. They are not husband and wife, yet they are closer than spouses. Konsari is regarded as the queen. Arimotto is both Konsari and Sadhukumar's son. He also knows them to be married. Nobody has ever told him otherwise. Though he grew up with them living in two separate palaces, it had seemed like a natural arrangement. Perhaps this is why he has never raised any question about it.

And if he had any questions, perhaps the serious and introverted Arimotto has simply kept them to himself. There has always been a very cordial friendship between his parents. Earlier, Konsari used to remain tense all the time, anticipating questions from her son. She would worry about being interrogated by the Gobha people. Things have calmed down now.

Her youth passed in a blur. Sadhukumar remained unmarried. His singular devotion to Konsari is known to everyone within the palace, as well as the chieftains living outside.

Is Konsari blind?

Has she not detected the love glistening in Sadhukumar's eyes?

Has she not discovered her own self? After being won over by the Deoraja's magnanimity, has not a lagoon of love formed deep within Konsari? Where is Pratapchandra in that lagoon? For that matter, where are the waves of Queen Chandraprabha's wonderful, enthralling days following her marriage?

True.

Konsari, too, by holding onto Sadhukumar's divine love, has spent her youth in solitude. Her devotion is not conveyed through her expression but is manifested in her actions. She has immersed herself in Gobha society. Her unique bond with the Deoraja remains unsullied. For a relationship that defies the norms of decorum, everyone looks to them with reverence. Even though the Tiwa society typically does not hold unmarried men in high esteem, the people have made an exception for Sadhukumar. And Konsari's active involvement in governance as the king's representative and her commitment to the welfare of the kingdom have lent her the status of a revered figure.

The memories of Pratappur are slowly fading away. The intense flames of hatred are dwindling, and the pain and disgrace of separation have subsided. Cleansed by the affection of Gobha, Chandraprabha has transformed into Konsari. Her child has now grown strong enough to establish a capital in Baidyagarh.

However, Konsari's heart grows restless at the sight of her son. It's as if Pratapchandra's reflection flickers on and off in how he moves, how he looks, how his lips move. She has found echoes of Pratapchandra's over-emotional, arrogant demeanour in Arimotto. She can also sense the same Aryan–Kshatriya thirst for victory in him. How has this happened, despite Arimotto growing up as a Tiwasha boy at the samadi?

He hasn't visited Gobha in over two years, now reigning over the distant kingdom of Komota. Once again, Sadhukumar has been tasked with overseeing Kumoi–Boghora on the south bank, effectively managing it with the assistance of the dolois and loros. Konsari had long anticipated that Arimotto wouldn't permanently return to Gobha. Can a king, having tasted victory, be content with conquering just one kingdom? Is it possible for the thirst for victory to be quenched so easily? Arimotto will continue his conquests, she realizes. She had witnessed the insatiable yearning for conquest in the mighty Pratapchandra. After all, Arimotto is his son. Can upbringing erase the innate battle-thirst ingrained in one's blood? Never entirely.

Nevertheless, he is not Pratapchandra. Gobha's soil is part of him. Perhaps that is the reason Arimotto has expressed his wish to rule Komota from Gobha in a long letter to his mother before arriving himself.

'Your Highness.'

Sadhukumar's voice wakes her from her reverie.

'How have you been, Deoraja?'

'Why this question all of a sudden? Am I looking awfully aged, Your Highness?' Sadhukumar chuckles.

'I see the king has also mastered the art of twisting words these days,' she laughs as well.

'One has to learn a lot when one is in despair, honourable queen. It is difficult to describe how I have been. Forget about me, Your Highness. A man matured at the samadi. A body toughened by the sun's rays. But have you ever spent time in the sun? It pains me to watch you burn in Gobha's sun. You've travelled all the way on elephant-back. How far can a sunshade be effective? You must be exhausted. Rest for a while after eating something. But you must take the initiative. It's a bachelor's palace. There are no maids-in-waiting here.'

Konsari looks at Sadhukumar. 'Do you consider Fa Mahadeo to be a heartless, cruel god, Deoraja?'

'Of course not. Why?' he asks, a little surprised.

'Can't an oath, sworn on Fa Mahadeo, be broken? More so, if it had been sworn hastily, in misery?'

'It can. But Laloongs never break oaths. Not even the ones sworn hastily in misery.'

'Even if it hurts others?'

'When an oath is sworn for someone's well-being, it is unfair to feel hurt by it, Your Highness.'

'Whose well-being, Deoraja? Arimotto's? What has enabled him to become the king? Isn't that all there is? Would he have undergone suffering in this kingdom if he had not been a king? Is this kingdom anything like Pratappur? Ever since I set foot on the soil of Gobha, your life has turned upside down. It pains me a lot when I think about it,' Konsari says gloomily.

'You have a big heart. That is why you speak in this manner. There are no margi khamsamais in this palace because I don't have a wife. That is all there is to it. I think, no, if I say what I think, it will reach the phurimoso god's ears. Please proceed to the guest quarters, Your Highness. Rest a little. Let me summon the bhitor maji – he will supervise everything.'

Sadhukumar goes out without affording Konsari any opportunity to speak. In fact, he doesn't so much as goes out as he flees.

At least, that's how it seems to her. Looking at his disappearing figure, Konsari walks out of the lobby with tired steps, holding back a sigh of grief within her. After resting and having food, she returns to see Sadhukumar, who is waiting for her.

'You have arrived suddenly. What is the matter, Your Highness?' the Deoraja asks.

'Am I not supposed to visit if nothing is wrong?' Konsari laughs.

'You are trying to take pleasure in hurting me, aren't you, Your Highness?' the king says with a smile.

'I don't have the power to hurt you, Deoraja. I am here to discuss something special.'

'Please speak.'

'I have received a letter from Arimotto. He has set up a capital and a fort in Betona. He wishes to take you and me along to the inaugural ceremony. He is likely to arrive in a day or two.'

'Good. But this time he must be told quite clearly: there is no need to expand the kingdom any further. Let him appoint someone to rule Betona as a tributary king and return to Gobha. Let him settle down to a married life and live here.'

'He has expressed the same will. But even if he lives here, he will go on expanding the kingdom. I wonder why things happened this way. I had tried to dissuade him even before he left for Komota. He didn't pay heed to my words.'

'He will listen to you, Your Highness. He is a young man. It is the age to dream big. Once he is married, he will settle down.'

'I think so, too. I had even considered discussing his marriage as soon as he arrives. But the loro visited me this morning. After listening to what he had to say, I didn't know what to do. So I came to see you immediately.'

'What did he say?'

'Something very strange, Deoraja. He said Arimotto has fallen in love with the queen of Khola, Gangavati.'

'Mriganko? With Gangavati? From whom did the loro hear this?'

'It seems many people have heard about it. A doloi, from one of the villages on the banks of Kolong, has submitted a complaint to him. So the loro has to call for a trial.

'Of course, he must. Even the king must listen to the dolois.'

'It is a bad situation, Deoraja. The loro said that both Gangavati and Arimotto must be present at the trial. He has asked me to write to him. He said the people are extremely offended because the clans of the queen of Khola and yours are the same. Is that true?'

'It is true, Your Highness. But if both Mriganko and Gangavati really love each other, won't they feel hurt? I'm sure they did not know about their clans. I know Gangavati. She is a very mature khorla. And Mriganko is really tenacious. But come to think of it, Mriganko was not born into the clan. Surely people will not object if this is explained to them.'

'It is not the right thing to do, Deoraja. You adopted him as your son and accepted him into your clan. You have elevated him to the throne of a vast kingdom like Gobha. You chose not to marry in order to make him king. Can all of this be forgotten simply because it will cause him pain? Breaking the society's customs using the logic of past incidents, in my opinion, is a crime.'

'Mriganko is very persistent, Your Highness. One can't tell what he will be up to if he is hurt,' Sadhukumar says ponderingly.

'You think so because you love him a lot, Deoraja. He has grown up at the samadi. He is familiar with the society's customs. If he decides to break rules, there is no reason for regret. Also I have accepted this society as my own. I have nurtured him in this society. He does not know about my past. I do not wish to lend him a new identity now.'

'But Your Highness, don't you think he should be told the truth some day?'

'Why, Deoraja? Tell me, why must he be told? The blood of King Pratapchandra courses in him. What else is there of Pratapchandra? He has been nurtured by the soil and water of this land even before he saw the light of the world. He has been given a society in which to grow up. Showered with respect. What if the people of Gobha hadn't accepted him? What would have been his predicament? Or mine?'

Sadhukumar stares with surprise at Konsari's animated expression. Since stepping onto the boat at Mayapur, she had broached the topic of Pratapchandra only once before. It had torn Sadhukumar to pieces at the time. She has never shown signs of depression, anger or hatred. Instead, Konsari had steadily transformed from the fragile, miserable Chandraprabha to the solemn, affectionate Konsari, dedicating herself to the Gobha society.

'Tell me, Deoraja, silence will not suffice ...'

'What can I say, Your Highness – your observation is also mine. But the truth concealed under Mriganko's identity is also true.'

'True, but meaningless. Surely you know why it is meaningless, Deoraja? You saw, didn't you, when I was put in a boat and chased away with a group of unknown young men in the dead of night, for no crime of mine? Didn't you see what my position was in that kingdom?'

'I did, Your Highness. Thinking about it makes my blood boil even at this age.'

'It is bound to. Since you are a human being. You are not barbaric like Pratapchandra. I have closely observed both the societies I have lived in, Deoraja. When I compare them, I feel mortified about my past,' she paused.

Sadhukumar remains silent. After a while, Konsari speaks again, 'I was living very happily in the palace of Pratappur. It was more comfortable than here. Pratapchandra loved me deeply, always at my side, praising my beauty. I felt fortunate to be his queen and was proud of my role. But one small incident turned my reality into fiction. He chased me away without a chance to explain myself, never once considering me. What kind of bond is that, Deoraja? I was Pratapchandra's puppet, discarded in anger. I've never held resentment against him because I understand his anger and state of mind. Those days are like a dream – a mix of happiness and sorrow that I've shut myself off from venturing into. Before coming here, I never truly grasped my identity and dignity. I only saw myself as Pratapchandra's wife, believing in the enduring bond of marriage. I never imagined such a foundation could crumble with a single blow. That's why I was initially speechless. Pratapchandra asked me to apologize and struck me. I refused because I hadn't committed any wrong. Why should I apologize? Why should I apologize for something I didn't do? He would have taken me back in his arms had I asked for forgiveness. I understood the value of my identity and love gained through marriage, Deoraja. So, I accepted the sentence of banishment. It's only here that I've realized a woman is entitled to rights and dignity. I've seen that no Pratapchandra could exist in this society. The women are just as firmly rooted to the soil here. With this understanding, I've entrusted Arimotto to this society. He must follow its rules and live within it. I'll never let him rule this society with the identity of Pratappur.'

Listening silently, Sadhukumar looks into her eyes. His eyes shine with the radiance of divine love. He replies gently and gravely, 'I understand, Your Highness. Your judgement of right and wrong is absolutely sound. Everything you've said is correct. But will Mriganko understand? He might take Gangavati to Komota. This society won't accept their marriage under his current identity. He can't continue to be king either. Nevertheless, that's not our main concern. He's already established his own kingdom.'

Konsari continues, 'I don't doubt that he might do it. He's a stubborn young man. Once he loves someone, it's unwavering.

He might abandon this society. But if he leaves like that, how could I stay? I'll never leave, Deoraja. While I won't be punished for another's offence, I fear everyone will condemn my past identity. They'll blame me for introducing betrayal and defiance here. Even if no one speaks, I'll know, and I can't bear it. I won't tolerate it. I'll ensure this relationship doesn't take root. I'll make him understand, and if he doesn't, I'll talk to Gangavati.'

Konsari rises, then continues, 'Allow me to take your leave, Deoraja.'

It is evening, and she has come alone, without any bodyguards. Travelling by elephant, she would only return at dawn. The old king wants to ask her to stay back, but he cannot bring himself to do it.

So he walks her to the gateway and looks on until the elephant disappears out of sight.

NINETEEN

In a secluded spot along the banks of the Kolong on the outskirts of Khola, Gangavati sits alone on a rock. There is no radiance on her face today. No peace in her heart. For the first time ever, she finds herself at the crossroads of truth and deception, right and wrong.

From birth to her youth, fear had been an unfamiliar feeling to Gangavati. Her path had not always been smooth, but it had remained straightforward. After losing her mother as a child, she had been raised in the palace by her father and a wet nurse.

Her father, the king, was a composed and affectionate man who adored Gangavati. Despite losing his wife at a young age, he never remarried. Gangavati grew up displaying the same maturity as her father, always composed and undemanding. There was never a raised voice or a quarrel in the Khola palace. Her father's royal officials, reliable and sincere, still serve the kingdom today. When Gangavati ascended to the throne after her father's death, she encountered no difficulties in ruling the kingdom.

Perhaps it was her upbringing in the solitary palace that had made Gangavati introverted, sombre and rational. Her busy schedule, packed with lessons from the teacher from Kamrup, weapons training and other activities, may have also played a role in shaping her character. Loneliness never had a chance to take root in her mind. Her days and nights were spent governing the kingdom, learning, writing and honing her skills with weapons. She was mostly happy. Even content.

After meeting Mriganko, these feelings had taken deeper roots within her. Her heart connected with his without any confusion or apprehension. He had entered her life as if it were destiny. She could never have imagined that one day she would find herself at the mouth of a river clouded with indecision.

Such an astonishing scenario had never crossed her mind. Mriganko is a Tiwasha, as is she. Mriganko is the ruler of a kingdom, as is she. When the chief priest arrived at the Khola palace, he informed her that they were both from the same clan. Then he left, having read Gangavati's fate.

Marriage within the same clan is against custom, against society. Illicit. Impossible.

That was not the decision of the trial assembly. But she could predict their verdict, couldn't she? On hearing the loro, Gangavati initially became still, as if struck by lightning. Setting aside a ruler's demeanour, a restless woman had emerged.

'You have heard incorrectly. We could never be from the same clan. I would have known otherwise. The jela baro might know. I'll summon him right away. Please ask him, respected loro.'

'I intend to, but not here. It must be done at the trial assembly. It's the rule. I have received a complaint, and I am compelled to call for a trial. I've come to summon you to the trial assembly. Discussion is prohibited. In the case of others, a barika is dispatched to summon the accused. However, I have come myself. You are the queen of Khola, venerable, loved by the society as well.' Despite his grave voice, the loro's words reflected profound sincerity.

'What should I do now, honourable loro?' Gangavati had asked, after remaining quiet for a long time.

'You should be present before the trial assembly, Your Highness. You are aware of the rules of our society. The society can even try a king, on a complaint. They do. I am compelled to try you. You, too, are not above society. Nor am I. If you do not attend the trial assembly, the dolois will have you removed. If I refuse to proceed with the trial, I, too, will be dismissed. I am unable to predict the outcome of the trial at this time. I can arrive at a decision only after hearing everyone. But one thing is certain: marriage within the same clan is forbidden. This rule is rigidly abided by in the Laloong society.'

The chief priest had left after that, casting Gangavati into a sea of uncertainty and turmoil.

The trial assembly will convene tomorrow. However, this is a preliminary meeting, almost private. The loro will sit down with the clan's borjela, chokha jela and hari kuwori to adjudicate the issue. The loro is unwilling to set up a public trial and humiliate Gangavati and Mriganko, the pride of their clan, benevolent rulers of the society.

But not outside of society. Within.

The rulers do not have the power to degrade society through royal authority. Nobody does.

Mriganko and Gangavati would have to sever their relationship. They'd need to atone by hosting a banquet for the people; otherwise, they will be shunned by society and have their royal authority seized. Inevitably, they would be forced to abandon their societies and kingdoms and leave.

Both of them are well aware of this rule and its implications. Gangavati is becoming restless, terrified of losing Mriganko. He is expected to arrive today from Komota and will meet her at the palace before leaving for Gobha, as stated in his previous letter. But before he could arrive, she went out in the evening darkness with her most loyal elephant keeper. On the way, she dispatched a trustworthy bodyguard to wait for Arimotto on the western border, instructing him to bring him to the banks of the Kolong.

Gangavati has been eagerly awaiting this moment for so long, her heart heavy from the agony of separation and glowing with the joy of meeting Mriganko again. But the loro's words had shattered her dreams. Even now, his words seem surreal and untrue. Until this morning, Gangavati had never heard that the royal families of Khola and Gobha belonged to the same clan. But who would have told her? Is there anyone she could consider family?

Living in the palace with some margi khamsamais, Gangavati does not attend any of her clan's festivals or celebrations, nor does she feel inclined to do so. No one takes offence at the fact that she is an unmarried queen, which is why she never learned about her relationship with the royal family of Gobha from anyone.

She wonders what she would have done if she had known about the relationship. Would she have declined Mriganko's proposal and ignored his charm? Also, what would Arimotto have done if he had known? Would he have bowed before the rules of society and turned back from the sacred land of love?

As she frantically asks herself these questions, Gangavati feels exhausted. Mriganko is on his way, impatient to meet her. There is no other option; she must break this terrible news to him with confidence and quell his ecstatic fervour.

The trial is scheduled to begin tomorrow afternoon, and he must also be present. The loro has informed Gangavati that he has asked Mriganko's mother, who resides in Gobha's palace, to ensure his presence. Though unsure of his reaction, Gangavati can hazard a guess based on their intermittent meetings throughout their long relationship. She knows his obstinate, over-emotional, ambitious, liberal and desperately courageous nature.

Waiting alone on the deserted banks of the Kolong, Gangavati grows restless. She ties the elephant to a tree a little distance away, and the elephant keeper waits out of her sight. Once the sound of a horse grows close, the elephant keeper stands up.

Arimotto arrives alone, with the bodyguard sent by Gangavati sitting behind him. He had been somewhat puzzled and worried on reading the letter delivered by her bodyguard at the border. He has been wondering what exactly she could not disclose in Khola's palace, why she has invited him to the desolate shores of the river. Gangavati is not a woman who craves shallow physical intimacy. He has never found her to be lustful. So, is she in jeopardy? Is there any personal danger?

Arimotto is certain that there is no possibility of any political crisis, otherwise Gangavati would not have ventured out of the security of Khola's palace. Anxiously, he stops upon seeing the elephant. A man standing nearby salutes him and points towards Gangavati. Leaving his bodyguard behind, Arimotto proceeds ahead.

'Mriganko.'

Gangavati steps away from the rock and calls him. Her mind pulsates with pure love, but the fear of an uncertain future is palpable – an ocean of agony within her.

On the outside, she appears calm, and Arimotto moves closer. Looking into her eyes for a moment, he places his hands on her shoulders and says, '*Ainoh.*'

She is deafeningly silent, her eyes clouded with tears, her voice muffled by a flood of words. Arimotto draws her close. Their passionate, burning lips meet, and they are swept away by a dam of love that has ruptured.

Gangavati has no energy to resist Arimotto, feeling restless due to his prolonged absence. After overcoming all confusion, fear and uncertainty, unrestrained love takes over her body and mind.

By the time Arimotto becomes calm, the moon is up in the sky. In the pale light of the lifeless moon, holding Gangavati in his arms, his face resting in her open hair, Arimotto says, 'Speak, Ainoh … tell me about you … how did you spend all these days? All these nights? Have you suffered a lot?'

There is a long silence before Gangavati says sadly, 'Yes, Mriganko. But a lot more suffering is waiting for us.'

'More suffering? What suffering, Ainoh?' He turns Gangavati's face towards him.

'I shall tell you, Mriganko. I've called you here just to tell you.'

Trying hard to hold back tears, Gangavati is growing agitated with infinite agony. Arimotto's fingers stop moving over her hair. After a moment of stunned silence, he enquires, 'What is the matter with you, Ainoh? What kind of pain are you talking about?'

Gangavati is crying, leaving his rayon-woven shirt soaked from her flowing tears. When she grows quiet, Arimotto wipes her tears with his shawl and, sitting face to face, says softly, 'Now tell me, Ainoh – what has happened? What made you call me?'

She raises her head and tells him everything.

Each word from her turns into a poisoned arrow, piercing Arimotto from all sides. He sits stunned, still as a rock. He is aware of the consequences of a relationship within the same clan, but he can't decide what to do next. Should he abandon Gangavati and follow society's verdict, atoning with a banquet for the people? Or should he abandon both society and kingdom and flee with Gangavati? Could he live without her?

Which should he choose: social norms or his heart's desire? Which would make his life harder?

The soundless waves of Gangavati's weeping strike at Arimotto's heart. In the darkness of the riverbank, fading light of the dying moon and solitude of the deep night, he sits with Gangavati in his arms, surrounded by the sounds of the forest. He remains still for a long time, contemplating his choices. Then, lifting Gangavati's face with both hands, his voice full of emotion and clarity, he asks, '*Khaboo*, tell me, do you love me enough to abandon this society only to live with me?'

For a moment, Gangavati becomes confused. Could she live away from the society she has never left since her birth? Could she go away with Arimotto, ignoring the customs she has known and followed since childhood? But she can't imagine a life without him, having realized this fact after a two-year absence. What if she doesn't go?

She could still maintain her position in her own society by hosting a traditional banquet. But would that life bring her the satisfaction she desires – the intense fulfilment of living with the man she loves?

She cannot survive without Arimotto.

Holding Gangavati's face in his hands, Arimotto asks, 'Ainoh, tell me, what are you going to do? We've come this far without knowing anything about our clan. All this time, we believed our love to be real. Now that we know about our clan, will our reality turn into fiction? Will our love cease to exist? I cannot live without you. Can you, Khaboo? Tell me, can you?'

A flood of emotions is about to overwhelm Gangavati.

Removing her eyes from his emotional and impatient gaze, she takes his hands off her cheeks and rests her face on them, breaking down once again.

'I cannot, Mriganko.'

Arimotto wraps his strong arms around Gangavati and says determinedly, 'Let the people assemble. Let there be a trial. I shall speak the truth and not conceal a single thing. But I shall not submit to society's verdict. We shall go away to Baidyagarh. We shall never return to this society. Tomorrow night, wait for me in the same location where you instructed your bodyguard to wait. I shall take you to Baidyagarh on my way back from Gobha. Now, let's go. It's nearly dawn. Go to the palace before daybreak. After I see you off, I shall go see Maah.'

Gangavati tidies her tousled hair. Then both of them make their way to where the elephant and horse are tethered. The wild fowls crow to signal the final hour of the night.

TWENTY

There hasn't been any rain for days in Gobha. The fields, the trees and shrubs are all parched. The waters of the Kolong and Kopili have receded, revealing the stones in their beds. The fresh paddy shoots are losing their bright green colour.

Amidst the vast expanse of the drying paddy fields, Arimotto's horse gallops with incredible speed, scattering the highway's dust. The horses of the bodyguards have become exhausted, trying to keep pace with the king's ride.

His face flushed with rage and agitation, Arimotto is riding a silver-saddled horse with a tight grip on the reins. The humiliating events of the day, arguments with his mother, followed by the growing arrogance and determination in his mind have hardened his ruddy, gold-toned face.

He is en route to remote Komota, with a solemn vow never to return to the confines of this society or the sprawling Gobha empire. There was no opportunity to bid farewell to his mother; she had already departed the palace in Gobha, presumably to visit his father in Amsai Marjong.

Arimotto has often seen his mother turn to his father when challenges arise. He doesn't quite comprehend why his parents don't reside together, but he knows there is no strife between them. It seems they maintain separate palaces to ensure the smooth administration of their vast empire. Having observed his mother's equal involvement in governing the kingdom, this explanation makes sense to Arimotto. It's as though his parents have dedicated their lives to the welfare of the realm, with the conventional roles of husband and wife diminishing in significance.

However, Arimotto could never adopt this approach. He is not inherently self-sacrificing. While he is dedicated to his kingdom and his people, this commitment does not overshadow the needs of his personal life.

He needs Gangavati.

Without her, his life is worthless.

He had told his mother this in clear words. 'The loro has summoned me to the trial. I shall go. But I shall speak only what is true. We did not intentionally wrong anyone. Despite belonging to the same clan, we are distant. Were men born in this world belonging to different clans from the beginning? Maah, who knows where we've all come from?'

'You are right. But now we live in a society that we've created. Certain rules must be followed for its smooth functioning. You and Gangavati are leaders of this society. If you break the rules, how can our society operate successfully?' his mother had said.

'Had we known beforehand, we wouldn't have broken any rules, Maah. We are not so cruel. But we went ahead not knowing anything. How could we possibly go back? And what are rules, Maah? Don't new rules emerge from broken rules?'

Arimotto had a long debate with his mother. By the time they finished, it was morning. Afterwards, he had gone to attend the trial held at the nuber. Gangavati had been sitting in the courtyard with her head lowered. She hadn't even looked at him. Deoraja had arrived a little later. On noticing his father, Arimotto had felt concerned about his mother. He had no idea where she could have gone.

Soon, the trial began. The discussions and Gangavati's tear-stained face seemed to have propelled nature's most furious hurricane, the Bordoisila, into Arimotto's heart. It had ravaged the carefully tended garden of logic and deliberation he had nurtured.

He and Gangavati had both spoken the truth.

After hearing from the borjela as well as Sadhukumar, the loro had pronounced the verdict.

'This marriage is taboo. This relationship is also forbidden. It must be broken off. Nobody is above societal rules. No one has the right to cross the line, to tear the fabric of society. The sin must be atoned by hosting a feast for the headmen of the clan. The two must kneel down in front of society by placing the elephant keeper over the elephant or by putting a betel nut over a betel leaf on a tray. No one else, except for the headmen of the clans, will be invited to the feast. It should be kept private, as far as possible. Every effort should be taken to prevent private information about the clan coming out.'

The loro had ended the trial with his long speech. Nobody had the authority to comment on the loro's decision. Not even the king.

Arimotto also remained silent.

Gangavati, too.

He had no idea what was going through Gangavati's mind. However, his mind was filled with arguments and debates opposing the trial assembly's decision and reasoning.

On his way from the nuber to the main palace, accompanied by Sadhukumar, Arimotto began thinking, 'There is no one above society. Surely God is above society. If not, then why do people from this society worship the phurimoso god? Why do they believe he is superior to all other gods and goddesses? Even the sun god had unwittingly engaged in a relationship with his daughter. Despite committing such a grave crime, why was the god, who was hiding away in shame, accepted in the assembly organized by the Brothers of the Four Directions in the presence of all the gods? Even when the sun god had refused, why was he cajoled into attending the assembly? Why was he not tried and punished? Why wasn't he counselled to atone for his transgression? Is it because without his light and heat, all plantations would perish? Because there would be no agriculture? For self-interest?

There was no light in the universe because the sun god had hidden himself, embarrassed by his relationship with his daughter.

The universe had become cold, without the heat of sunlight. Trees and crops had begun to wither. Men and animals had begun to die. Is this why the Brothers of Four Directions absolved the god from the social customs to fulfil their needs and interests? Why didn't the two cocks, Langtha–Langthi Raja, sent to fetch the sun god, tell him such a relationship was blasphemous?

Arimotto had not committed a crime of this magnitude.

He'd merely fallen in love with a girl, not knowing she belonged to his clan. He would never have pursued the relationship had he known.

But having loved a girl with all his heart, would Arimotto succumb to societal customs and back away?

Would he do that?

Would he abandon Gangavati to maintain his social status?

Never.

He believes in God, as well as the four Brothers, so Arimotto will leave with Gangavati, abandoning society. He will live with Gangavati in the faraway Baidyagarh. There, Arimotto, with his own might, will establish a vast kingdom like Gobha. Arimotto apprised his father, Sadhukumar, of his decision.

His father, unlike his mother, had not tried to obstruct his way by building a barrier of arguments.

Sitting in the lobby of the main palace, his father had only said, 'You are not a small boy. You are truly a king. I shall not oppose your decision, which you have made logically and thoughtfully. But you will take away Gangavati by giving up your land and society. Gangavati is your responsibility. Take good care of her. I'm not going to pass judgement on what's right and wrong. But there's something I'd like to say: perhaps I can live without you, but can your mother? Who does she have, besides you?'

'But you are here, Deoraja. As long as you are present, my absence will not matter. I am not leaving to die. I shall live happily and peacefully in Baidyagarh. Would you all be unhappy if I lived happily?'

Sadhukumar had not replied to Arimotto's question.

His eyes moistened.

On his way out, noticing his father standing alone with a sorrowful face, Arimotto's heart had filled up with despair and tenderness. But those emotions had not been powerful enough to change his decision.

Abandoning Gobha, Arimotto had shrugged off all feelings of weakness from his mind.

He would never care about anyone.

No one.

It is not possible to live without Gangavati.

He has to let the kingdom go.

Let society go.

Let his parents be his past.

Arimotto must have Gangavati as his own.

Could anyone survive if their heart is taken away?

The night's darkness is gradually thickening. It is the second hour of the night by the time Arimotto, followed by his retinue, reaches a particular purging cassia tree on the western border of Khola.

Upon reaching, he dismounts from his horse.

The yellow petals of the flowers appear like a yellow aanthla carpet, spread under the tree. Tying the horse to the tree blooming with flowers, Arimotto comes to stand in the middle of the road. The sound of the horses trotting behind him cuts through the stillness of the night.

Roused from deep slumber, the villagers living on either side of the highway are straining their ears, listening to the sound of the horses.

In this region, horses are a rare sight, and the primary means of long-distance travel is the elephant. For shorter distances, people typically rely on walking. The women from royal families and high-ranking officials have adopted the *dola*, a type of carriage, although it is not the most comfortable mode of transport.

The elephant holds a special place as the most practical carrier in this area, given its ability to navigate the numerous small brooks, rivers, streams and ditches. During the rainy season, when lakes and rivers swell with water, boatmen offer their services to ferry travellers across for a nominal fee. Additionally, locals often use *sakos*, long poles crafted from bamboo or timber, which they lay across streams to facilitate crossing. Villagers have become skilled at utilizing sakos to traverse these waterways.

Now the streams and rivers have dried up.

But it is not the dry season.

They have dried up due to the severe drought.

That is why Arimotto has been able to travel on horseback. Or by the time the ferry man woke up and the horses were ferried across the river, it would have been dawn.

Not a single ruler between Kolong, Kopili, Dhanshiri and Jamuna owns a horse. As for common people, it is out of the question. No royal power from the west possessing a cavalry has ever set foot in Khola and Dimoruwa until today. If anyone is riding a horse, it has to be Arimotto.

The curious people, roused from slumber, return to sleep.

Arimotto must be on his way to Komota.

Everyone knows he lives there. Arimotto is not only the prince of Gobha, but also the king of Kumoi–Boghora. He is the future ruler of the subsidiary kingdoms, loved and respected by all. The people of Khola, Dimoruwa and Nelly consider him their most dependable and trustworthy refuge. Arimotto has brought numerous novel ideas from Komota, introducing uncommon things through batches of men dispatched from there. Modern weapons, implements of cultivation and other items have been built using iron extracted from Komarjan. The latest processes of cultivation have been taught, and seeds of new crops have been transported. Last year, when locusts attacked the crops, Arimotto saved the people from an impending famine by bringing them insecticide. Is it possible not to love Arimotto and wonder about his well-being?

Standing in the middle of the road, Arimotto looked around in the pale light of the moon. Extensive paddy fields lay on either side of the road, with villages nestled amidst them. The sleepy villages and fading paddy fields seemed to have drowned in sorrow in the dim moonlight. Absentmindedly, Arimotto gazes at the villages from the road.

Gangavati should arrive here soon. From here, they will leave for Komota, and Arimotto and Gangavati will become husband and wife by performing phuja at the Ma Kamakhya temple atop the hills of Nilachal, south of the Brahmaputra. They will then cross the river to reach Baidyagarh. After standing for a long time, Arimotto looks at the sky, feeling restless.

The waning moon is slowly brightening.

The night has deepened.

Arimotto is worried. Why hasn't Gangavati arrived yet? She isn't supposed to take so long. Has she encountered any opposition along the way? Has she been imprisoned in the palace of Khola by the major general and the dolois upon realizing she was leaving?

As time passes, Arimotto grows increasingly restless. Should he go back to the Khola palace? If Gangavati has been imprisoned, he has the strength to free her. He still has an army of capable soldiers at his disposal.

Voices of people from the nearby villages can now be heard. Arimotto grows alert. In the villages drowned in darkness, one could see, here and there, glows from the burning of ironwood seeds and mustard-oil lamps.

Have the people realized Arimotto is here? Have the panthais in the samadi become alert after spotting the army of soldiers under the tree? Or is the army of Khola marching through the paddies, preparing to obstruct him?

The bodyguards are now keenly attentive, and their weapons sparkle in the moonlight. At that moment, a number of earthen lamps glow in the courtyard of a house in the nearby village. In the moonlight, Arimotto and his men can see many human silhouettes. Within a few moments, some male voices begin to sing in unison:

Bayu raja, Bayu raja, nokha palai laba.
Au horlo nokha phid sadali simai lawa.

Arimotto feels a tremendous burden lift off his chest, and the bodyguards relax, putting down their weapons. The men of the village, both old and young, are singing '*nokha changa kit*', invoking rain through the song. A flicker of a smile spreads across Arimotto's face.

Memories of a similar incident from his days at the samadi resurface. Back then, he and his friends had stolen a pounding pedal from a household in the village. The morning after, hearing the housewife's ranting about not finding the pounding pedal, Arimotto and his friends had burst into laughter. A week later, carrying shovels and metal rods in their hands and a mortar borrowed from a family, they had visited every household. Placing the mortar in the courtyard, they had danced round and round singing '*nokha changa kit*' while digging the courtyards with shovels, metal rods, ploughs and other tools. They had all been drenched to the skin from the water splashed at them by the people of the houses.

Listening to the villagers singing '*nokha changa kit*' momentarily distract Arimotto from the long hours that have just passed. However, he is soon brought back to reality. 'Deoraja,' the bhitor maji says, 'It won't be long before daybreak. Her Highness has still not arrived.'

Arimotto snaps out of his reverie immediately. Why hasn't Gangavati arrived yet? He can't wait any longer. She must be in trouble. They must find out what has happened. Untying his horse, he says, 'Let's go back. Her Highness might be in danger. If necessary, we shall attack Khola's palace and bring her out. Let's go.'

As he mounts the horse, the bodyguards prepare to proceed towards Khola. At that very moment, in the distance the silhouette of an elephant shimmers in the moonlight. 'She has arrived, she has arrived, Deoraja,' the bhitor maji calls out. Arimotto comes to a halt, waiting anxiously for the elephant to reach them.

However, when the elephant approaches, Arimotto is puzzled. Where is Gangavati? The keeper and the bodyguard who escorted him the previous day are now sitting on the elephant. As the bodyguard approaches Arimotto, he gets down from the elephant and salutes.

'Khroomdong, Deoraja,' the bodyguard greets him.

'Khroomdong. Where is your queen?' Arimotto asks anxiously.

'Inside the palace. She has sent a letter for you, Deoraja.'

From inside his tagla, the bodyguard takes out a letter along with a hollow stem of a papaya tree filled with fireflies and extends it towards Arimotto. As he reads its contents beneath the gentle moonlight and the flickering fireflies, Arimotto's worry and anxiety give way to anger and despair. This isn't merely a letter; it feels more like Gangavati hurling a fiery molten iron bowl forged by a blacksmith directly at Arimotto's face: 'I have given it much thought, Mriganko – it is not possible for me to go away with you, forsaking my kingdom and society. Please forgive me.'

TWENTY-ONE

Arimotto reclines upon a comfortable wooden chair, carefully crafted with vibrant images borrowed from the Bhotpahar hills. Adjacent to the chair, on a beautifully embellished wooden stool is a handcrafted terracotta drinking vessel, and a second terracotta bowl brimming with joo. The bowl is being continuously replenished since Arimotto's arrival in Komota. Seated close by, Samol, his heart heavy with sorrow, gazes upon Arimotto's fatigued and mournful face, his own throat constricted by the weight of grief.

Though Arimotto has not yet shared any details with Samol, the bhitor maji has already given him a complete account. Samol and Arimotto, having grown up together and spent six years side by side at the samadi, have seen each other experience myriad emotions. But never had Samol seen Arimotto in such a state – overwhelmed by despair, seeking solace in joo to escape his existence. What, he wonders, has Queen Gangavati done?

How could she torment someone like Arimotto!

How could she betray him!

Samol's agitation is mixed with anger and disapproval for Gangavati, along with compassion for his king, but he keeps his expression grave and impassive as he waits for Arimotto's orders. Despite being the chief minister, Samol remains close to the king, delegating responsibilities to loyal subordinate officers. In Arimotto's company, he turns into a khara panthai again.

Today, Samol is sitting on the floor near the king at his request, with his eyes closed. Arimotto's sombre, exhausted voice jolts him back into attention.

'Samol.'

'Deoraja.'

'With so many people in this world, why did Fa Sindai choose me to suffer grief, leaving aside all others?'

'It's fate, Deoraja. Can anybody erase the writing of kharam?'

'You are right. Even the stars must have fallen from the sky at my birth.'

'Please do not say so, Deoraja. It hurts.'

'You are hurt? Why are you hurt, Samol? You are not even from my clan.'

'Why is one's clan important, Deoraja? Does one's clan provide the heart that grieves? I am the son of an ordinary khamsamai and a barika. Yet you have showered me with so much love.'

'You must not speak in that manner, Samol. Is there such a thing as big and small in our society? You have learnt all this after coming here. Don't bother. Don't learn anything bad.'

They remain silent, as if exchanging feelings. Arimotto takes the bowl of joo in his hands once again.

'Deoraja.'

'I know what you want to say, Samol. I must not drink joo, isn't it?'

'Yes, Deoraja, please don't drink anymore. A meal of your favourite fish made in alkali and *tangkhrai* without oil is ready for you. There's also grilled fish and pork cooked in sesame. A boro-kachari cook has prepared them. Please eat, Deoraja. You have not eaten anything since you arrived.'

The shadow of a smile spreads across the king's lips.

'You are talking just like Xunzira Asi. Like her, you are trying to tempt me with mouth-watering dishes, aren't you? You know, don't you, that I have no one in this world? I have abandoned everybody, Samol … my mother, my father. I swear on the waters of Luit, I swear on Fa Mahadeo, that I shall never go back to become the king of Gobha.'

'Why won't you go, Deoraja? That land is our own place. It is where our own people live.'

'Whether they are blood relatives or not, Samol, it hardly matters. Love makes them your own. By extending love, we can make even distant hearts our own. But there's one thing you must understand, Samol: in the end, no one is truly your own. No one. Rules reign supreme above all else. It's the rules that can make your loved ones seem distant, and, in my case, they already have. My Gangavati, whom I held dear as my very own, left me because of these rules, Samol. She left me to face my solitude in Baidyagarh. But I won't succumb. You'll see. I won't let myself fall. I'll prove to Gangavati that I can thrive without her, even more joyfully and serenely than before.'

'Deoraja, Nilakanta and his daughter have come to visit,' the bhitor maji says from the doorway.

Arimotto stares at the man for a while before solemnly replying, 'Send them in. Samol, ask someone to remove the bowls of joo. Nilakanta and his daughter will be offended. They are not like us.'

Samol gathers the bowls himself and leaves the room with a grim expression. Nilakanta and Ratnavali have rushed over in excitement. Ratnavali wants to see the king's parents and the bride, and her father wants to offer his greetings and hospitality to the family.

But Nilakanta comes to an abrupt stop once he enters. He can sense Arimotto's indifferent, weary demeanour. 'Your parents did not accompany you, Deoraja?' Ratnavali exclaims.

'No, they did not,' Arimotto replies coldly, without even looking at the girl.

'And—' she hesitates.

With eyes reddened from drinking joo, the king gazes at Ratnavali. 'And what?' His gaze makes her step back two paces.

Nilakanta bows to Arimotto. 'We've come to pay our respects to you, O king of kings. Nothing more. Please, Your Highness, take some rest. You've just arrived after a taxing journey. Ratnavali, you've offered your greetings, haven't you? We can chat with the king later. Please, relax, Your Highness. I can always return to inform you about the capital's inauguration.'

As Nilakanta and Ratnavali prepares to leave, Arimotto calls out to them, 'Wait – there will be no capital inauguration. Summon the religious instructor, Acharyadev. We will enter the capital after the sacred fire ritual. No other celebrations are needed.'

'As you command, Your Highness.'

Without much ado, saluting Arimotto, Nilakanta exits thoughtfully. The celebration has to take place, as his political design is directly linked with it. He plans to foster a friendship between Fingua Kunwar and Arimotto.

Nilakanta's association with the neighbouring king Fingua Kunwar has deep roots, as the latter was a close friend of Durlavendra, the former king of Komota. Their relationship extends beyond being loyal subjects to one another; it is on the verge of being cemented through marriage between Ratnavali and Fingua Kunwar.

Nilakanta had observed Fingua Kunwar's growing closeness to Ratnavali and, feigning ignorance, encouraged it to flourish. He had become excited about the prospect of marrying off his daughter to be the queen of the neighbouring kingdom. But the former chief minister was content with living off the success of others during Durlovendra's rule. He had no aspirations to ascend to the throne.

Also, he knows he lacks the mental strength, valour and other skills required to become a king. Even becoming the chief minister of Komota was beyond his expectations. Now that he serves in Arimotto's kingdom, Nilakanta holds a position as an ordinary officer. While he has managed to get closer to the king through flattery and skilled conversations, he knows his rise will be limited to his current status. Arimotto will never trust him as much as Samol, the son of a maid-servant.

Living under such a king seems futile to Nilakanta, and he questions what he would gain from all his effort and flattery. Initially, he had plotted to assassinate Arimotto cunningly with the aid of a few soldiers loyal to the former king. However, Arimotto's unwaveringly loyal, vigilant soldiers and officers from

Gobha thwarted Nilakanta's every attempt. Eventually, Nilakanta changed his approach, submitting himself before Arimotto, along with his family. His main objective thereafter has been securing a future for his daughter, Ratnavali.

Nilakanta has made every effort to win over Arimotto with the help of his daughter's beauty, and he has met with some success. The king is pleased with Ratnavali's culinary skills and hospitality. Arimotto enjoys his sweet conversations with her. And slowly, Nilakanta inches closer to Arimotto.

He has no military power at his disposal, so he relies on diplomacy. Fingua Kunwar possesses both military might and a charismatic personality that can sway people. He excels in the art of diplomacy, and harbours grand aspirations and immense ambitions to expand his kingdom.

Together, they have planned to overthrow Arimotto and reclaim Baidyagarh. Nilakanta is aware that the king will not remain there forever. After his marriage, he plans to return to Gobha, leaving Samol in charge. This has given them the right opportunity to seize Baidyagarh during the king's absence.

However, Nilakanta faces challenges within Baidyagarh. He is isolated and lacks trustworthy allies. The people who hail from Gobha distrust him, and the locals also dislike him due to his arrogance and insolence during Durlavendra's rule. In his quest to learn the fortress's ins and outs, the former chief minister risks potential exposure and capture.

To overcome these obstacles, Nilakanta has devised a plan to foster a friendship between Fingua Kunwar and Arimotto. He wants to gain access to crucial information about Baidyagarh's interior, its arms and ammunition. He plans to obtain this information from soldiers, officers and slaves accompanying Fingua, as well as by befriending a few locals.

With this goal in mind, the former chief minister had asked the king to invite Fingua to the inaugural ceremony. Arimotto has agreed, seeing it as an opportunity to foster goodwill with the neighbouring kingdoms. During the king's absence, Nilakanta had visited Fingua to lay out their plot. But Arimotto's early return without his parents and bride have disrupted their plans. Nilakanta had never imagined that Arimotto would cancel the inaugural ceremony, which would render his efforts futile.

As he leaves with Ratnavali, he tells her, 'Don't go near the king now. Go home. Don't come here until I tell you.'

'Why, Father?' she asks, surprised.

'Perhaps the king is unwell. He may get irritated if you approach him. Now leave.'

Ratnavali goes away, as her father proceeds to the royal guest house.

Inside the guest house, sitting on a mat, Prabhakar Sarma Bidyanidhi is reading a book placed upon a wooden prop-up, a *thoga*. When Nilakanta enters and bows, he looks up. Blessing him, the Brahmin offers him a seat and asks, 'Tell me, gentleman, what news have you brought?'

'There is no news, Acharya. I have come to you with a problem.'

'Problem? Do I have a solution to it?' The acharya smiles.

Even though he does not know what is going on inside this shrewd politician's mind, Prabhakar Sarma is not ignorant of his frame of mind. Nilakanta's excessive flattery irritates the acharya. Being aware of the intention lurking behind such flattery, it also amuses him. Acharya Prabhakar had taught Arimotto. The king reveres and honours him as a guru. He knows that is the reason for Nilakanta's fawning.

'The solution lies with you, Acharyadev,' Nilakanta says humbly.

'Then I must tell you, mustn't I?' the acharya laughs.

Nilakanta senses the tone of sarcasm underneath the guru's laughter. His insides are scorching with severe hatred. But there is no way for him to show his anger.

Nilakanta joins in the laughter as well.

'But the problem is really complicated, Acharyadev. The king has cancelled the inaugural ceremony. He has directed that only the ritual of sacrificial fire be performed.'

'Why?' the acharya asks, surprised.

'I do not know the reason, Acharyadev. The king seems depressed. He does not wish to talk. Before leaving for Gobha, he ordered me to make all arrangements after a discussion with you. Accordingly, I have completed all the arrangements as directed. The drummers and puppet players from Kamrup have already been invited. The ojapalis, too, have arrived. Rehearsals of the two plays *Battle of Lava-Kusha* and *Babrubahan* are in full swing. The temple dancers from Billeswar Devalaya have accepted our invitation.'

'I did not ask you to invite the *doluhainas* of Billeswar, Nilakanta. They are women who have been offered to the deity of the shrine. They are not public entertainers.'

'But, nowadays, audiences are entertained only when there are a few female dances of this kind. Even at the royal festivals, female dancers perform. The young men enjoy it, too. I have seen female dancers, myself. Worthy entertainers, I would say, Acharya.'

'Nilakanta – temple dancers are not ordinary dancers. They are virgins. Servants of god. Their names should be taken with respect. At times, I am irritated by your predilection, Nilakanta.' Acharya's face turns crimson with anger and exasperation.

Nilakanta becomes cautious. The acharya must not be upset.

'Please forgive me, Acharya. We belong to the most ordinary class of people. We believe whatever we see. Nowadays, the temple dancers are not respected as they once were, Acharya. People everywhere consider them to be fickle women.'

'This kind of mindset should be condemned. I have visited a number of Shiva temples. Most of them contain infrastructure for doluhainas to offer ritualistic worship by dancing before the idol of Shiva. But nowhere have I witnessed any of them being affronted by indecent comments. These topics are not worthy of discussion. Come to the point, Nilakanta.'

'I have already told you what the problem is, Acharya. After the arrangements are almost completed, how can His Royal Highness say there will be no celebration? If the ceremony is called off after all the preparations have been made, everything will be spoiled.'

'Surely there must be some reason. It's the king's order. Better not to argue.'

'But Acharyadev, invitation letters have already been sent to all the prominent people in this kingdom. A letter inviting Fingua Kunwar as the chief guest has been dispatched. If the ceremony is cancelled, everybody will be displeased. There will be complications in governing the kingdom, Acharyadev.'

'The king is intelligent. He understands politics. Put these arguments before him.'

'If he refuses to listen to me, Acharyadev?'

'It's been barely two hours since the king has arrived from Gobha. He must be exhausted. We should wait.'

'No, Acharyadev, he will never listen to me. It would be better if you explain this to him.'

'Alright, I shall, but let's not hope he will listen to me.'

'Not hope, Acharyadev, I have faith. He will never disregard you.'

'Alright. I shall talk to him. Now it is time for my evening prayers. I am unable to spare you any more time. Please forgive me.'

'Please do not send me to hell by asking for forgiveness, Acharyadev. You are a father figure to us, godlike.'

'I have understood.' Closing the book, Prabhakar Bidyanidhi gets up.

After paying obeisance, Nilakanta walks out, feeling both irritated and worried.

TWENTY-TWO

Baidyagarh.

The new capital of Komota, secure with a three-tiered land fort and a river-deep trenched water fort. In the interior of the capital, a strikingly magnificent palace has been constructed with bricks and matured wood of the sal tree.

The city has been adorned with rows and rows of garlands – of golden yellow marigolds, snow-white *kathondas*, gardenias and blood-red hibiscuses along with vermilion-dotted mango leaves. Rows and rows of earthen mustard oil lamps glow from every wall in the capital.

Either side of the pathway leading to the palace has also been lit up with two rows of such lamps. Baidyagah has been transformed into a dreamland in the bright silver moonlight. The inner complex of the capital is resonating with the sound of drums played by the drummers of Kamrup. Chief Minister Samol is welcoming Fingua Kunwar into the capital. On a ground inside the fort, the invitees of the kingdom, officers and residents of the capital are sitting in front of a group of puppet players.

The puppet show has not yet begun. It will, as soon as King Arimotto and Fingua Kunwar take their seats.

After participating in the day-long programme and resting a while in the guest house, Fingua Kunwar has just arrived.

He will go back after spending some time in King Arimotto's palace and watching the puppet dance.

The puppet players are going to present King Harishchandra's tale. The capital has turned clamorous with the crowd's excited murmur, one of the puppet players' singing and the Kamrup drummers' drumming.

In the frontyard of the palace bedecked with flowers and bright lamps, Arimotto is sitting in wait for Fingua Kunwar, upon a wooden seat curved by carpenters of the west and draped with a silk-cotton-wool-stuffed rug wrapped with a colourful cloth brought over from Bhotpahar. A little distance away, Nilakanta is standing, wrenching his hands. He is watching Arimotto's face with a sharp look.

Nilakanta is unaware of what is going on in Gobha. He could not extract a single word from the soldiers who had accompanied Arimotto, in spite of repeatedly asking them. But from Arimotto's demeanour, he guessed something sinister might have occurred.

Why didn't Arimotto bring his parents and bride with him? After all, he had travelled to Gobha to marry and bring them back. What could have transpired to force him to return without them?

Since his arrival from Gobha, Arimotto has not spoken to anybody. Except Samol.

Oh, this Samol!

Nilakanta swears internally.

It is only because of Samol that he cannot put his plan into action. He cannot even speak freely with the king. His piercing look makes the former chief minister quite uncomfortable.

'Let the time come. He will be the first to be slain,' Nilakanta tells himself.

Meanwhile, Ratnavali is busy arranging earthen lamps for the ceremony. Dressed in a captivating muga-silk mekhela and a riha made from eri-muga yarn, she looks like a fairy. She has intentionally chosen this attire for Fingua Kunwar, her secret lover.

During the king's absence, her father had kept Ratnavali at Fingua Kunwar's palace, where they rekindled their romance. The distance to Finguagarh over the highway was quite far, but the former chief minister knew a shortcut through the forest, which he used for his travels often.

Ratnavali felt like she was living in a dream these past few days. Ever since Arimotto conquered the kingdom, Fingua Kunwar has not visited Betona. She couldn't visit him either when Arimotto was present in the capital because her father had forbidden it – she was to serve the king.

Although Ratnavali does not dislike Arimotto overall, whenever she thinks about Fingua Kunwar, she grows angry at the king. Her father has repeatedly cautioned her against telling Arimotto about their relationship, or else she would have told him everything by now. Ratnavali has been overjoyed in recent days, enjoying the intimate company of Fingua Kunwar after a long separation. His touch feels magical, lifting Ratnavali to heaven. His passionate words stir a tempest in her heart. She cannot help becoming captivated by Fingua's charm and the wonderful love he showers on her. By contrast, Arimotto's beautiful eyes, tall stature and strength lack any playfulness or any expressions of love. Ratnavali wonders if the king even knows how to express love. He never seems to notice her beauty or compliment her. He only talks about Gangavati.

Is this Queen Gangavati more beautiful than she is?

Impossible.

Ratnavali has never seen a Laloong girl before. But hasn't she seen the Boro–Kachari girls of the neighbourhood? Gangavati must certainly be similar to them. But she will never be able to compete with Ratnavali.

Lost in these thoughts, she continues to light the earthen lamps. Arimotto, sitting in the front yard and immersed in joo, seems completely indifferent. As the sound of drums reaches her ears, Ratnavali sets down the tray of burning lamps and steps forward, standing at the doorway adorned with lamps. Fingua Kunwar has brought her muga silk from the south bank and jewellery from the Bhuyan kingdom.

Ratnavali looks breathtakingly beautiful.

Just as she is about to smile, Fingua Kunwar becomes serious and turns his attention to Arimotto, leaving Ratnavali shocked for a moment. She then resumes arranging the earthen lamps, feeling somewhat upset by his behaviour.

Fingua Kunwar did not speak to her.

What would have happened if he had?

Arimotto would come to know.

But how does it matter!

Is Arimotto a *ghorapak*? Or a *baak*? The evil spirit supposed to live on fish? Will he take Ratnavali to the lake and bury her upside down? Even her father?

Ratnavali laughs at her thoughts.

Arimotto turns around, his gaze fixed on the beautiful girl who is laughing to herself. Suddenly, a new thought seems to play in his mind.

While drinking joo with Fingua Kunwar, Arimotto cannot stop thinking about Ratnavali. Even as he makes his way from the courtyard to the amusement ground, thoughts of her occupy his mind.

As the puppet show begins, Arimotto sits with Fingua Kunwar for a while. Then, he addresses him, 'Allow me to go into the palace for a moment. Please enjoy the puppet show. I hope you won't be offended. I have made a decision, and all of you will learn of it soon.'

Arimotto leaves.

By this point, the joo has taken hold of him. The rows of earthen lamps appear like a border of lights. His footsteps seem to search for solid ground. Yet his steps have not faltered. With determined strides, Arimotto enters the palace, oblivious to Samol following behind, and Nilakanta further behind.

'Ratnavali,' Arimotto calls loudly.

Samol, feeling irritated, says, 'Deoraja, let me call her. Please have a seat.'

'Oh, Samol, why did you leave the puppet show? They were depicting the tale of King Harishchandra. I didn't watch it. I don't believe in Harishchandra's story. I'll never be King Harishchandra. Do you understand, Samol? Being King Harishchandra is pointless.

I intend to live well. I shall live happily,' Arimotto continues, with a mix of seriousness and inebriation.

Shortly after, Ratnavali, having arranged her dress neatly, comes running, ready to watch the puppet show. 'You summoned me, Deoraja?' she asks, looking at Arimotto's intoxicated gaze.

'Yes. I have something to say to you.'

'Please tell me, Deoraja.' Ratnavali says, surprised.

Arimotto looks deeply into her eyes and speaks, 'Today, right now, I shall marry you.'

Ratnavali is stupefied, struck by extreme disbelief and immeasurable horror. Who in Baidyagarh would dare defy King Arimotto's wish? Who could stand barehanded in the lion's den and say, 'I shall fight with the lion'?

She stares at the king, unable to comprehend the situation. Even Samol seems stunned by the unexpected turn of events. Nilakanta, on the other hand, stands at a distance, his heart dancing with joy. All he craves is power, unlimited power, regardless of whether it comes from Arimotto or Fingua Kunwar.

Standing in front of Ratnavali, his gaze fixed on her, Arimotto continues, 'There are people present, as well as a priest and your father. What else is required for a wedding? I shall marry you according to your customs, by lighting the sacrificial fire. Samol, call Acharyadev and make arrangements for the wedding. I know you have no objections. Where is your father? Samol, summon the officer in charge of the stables.'

'I am right here, Your Majesty,' says Nilakanta, rubbing his hands with joy as he steps forward.

'Good. Do you have any objections to my marriage to Ratnavali?' Arimotto enquires.

Ratnavali looks at her father with great hope, silently pleading for his support.

'Objection? There is no question of objection, Your Majesty. This is our great fortune. Go, my darling, get ready for the wedding. Let me call a few married women,' Nilakanta quickly walks away without meeting his daughter's eyes. Ratnavali remains motionless like a rock at the doorway of the Baidyagarh palace.

Arimotto enters the palace, as Samol waits outside. Ratnavali sees no way out. Without her father's support and having no close allies, she feels utterly helpless. What could she do in such a situation? Take her own life? Run away to Fingua Kunwar?

But there is no way to take her own life or elope. She can't escape Samol's watchful eye.

How can Ratnavali escape from Samol's sight and flee?

The chief minister stands up. Standing in front of Ratnavali, he says in a hard, cold voice, 'Please come inside. Get some rest before the ladies arrive.'

Outside, the final chapter of King Harishchandra's story begins, and the women watching the puppet show start to cry. It feels like their tears have snatched away Ratnavali's. She is sitting on the floor on a flowery rug, her head resting on her knees. Some married women, after singing wedding songs and fetching the ceremonial water, have ritually bathed and dressed Ratnavali in her wedding finery.

Now Nilakanta walks in.

'I'd appreciate it if you ladies leave us alone for a while. I wish to exchange a few words with my child,' he says with folded hands.

The women cover their heads and go out. Nilakanta sits down near Ratnavali and tenderly moves his hand over her head, saying, 'Don't be miserable, my child. You will be able to live a very comfortable life.'

Ratnavali looks up, fixing her dry eyes on her father's and asks softly, 'Why did you do it, Father? Why didn't you tell the truth?'

'For your good, child. What will you achieve by marrying Fingua? He is the king of four villages, while Arimotto has Komota and Gobha. Fingua has not been able to acquire even one extra village to date. On the other hand, Arimotto came from Gobha and conquered this kingdom. His domain will expand further, and you will live as an empress. Look at me, what could I become here? A horse-keeper. But now, I will be the father-in-law of a king. What more could we ask for, my child?'

Ratnavali stares at her father's face with surprise, and suddenly, everything becomes clear to her. She finally understands the motive behind her father's actions.

Her eyes well up with tears. 'Father, you have sold me to become the king's father-in-law?'

'Don't speak like that, my child. Why would I ever sell you? Isn't it for your well-being? Aren't you going to be a queen?'

'Is being a queen all that matters? You didn't think about anything else?'

'About Fingua? Those thoughts will fade away from your mind. If you give importance to those thoughts, you will lose the fortune in your hands right now. Forget about the king of four villages, child. It will benefit you, and you will realize it later.'

A disdainful smile surfaces on Ratnavali's face. 'There is no heart inside you, father. That's why you are capable of doing this. You could sell your own daughter.'

Before Nilakanta can say anything more, Samol appears before them, announcing that it is time to take the bride.

The king is sitting before the sacrificial fire, attired in silk. The married women are assisting Ratnavali as she sits beside him. Through her veil, Ratnavali watches Fingua Kunwar, who is sitting with his head lowered, wiping his eyes with the scarf thrown over his shoulder.

The smoke from the sacrificial fire is burning their eyes. Ratnavali knows that Fingua Kunwar is crying for her. Acharya Bidyanidhi has begun to chant the mantras, and as he pours clarified butter with the spatula, the sacrificial fire roars in a blaze.

Watching the fire, Ratnavali says to herself, 'I swear on the god of fire that I will forever continue to acknowledge Fingua Kunwar as my husband with body and soul. Someday or the other, I will go away to Finguagarh. I truly will.'

The acharya begins the ritual of offering Ratnavali to Arimotto in the name of Prajapati Brahma and in the presence of the god of fire. By the time the wedding ends, it is almost dawn. Despite the hurry, every wedding ritual is faithfully carried out, except that the married women are sitting quietly, not daring to observe the fun-filled rituals with the king.

Samol comes and stands next to them. 'Ladies, you may leave now. Her Highness needs rest.'

Once the women leave, Samol pays his respects to the new queen, 'I wish to meet His Highness, Chief Minister.'

'Please do not address me thus, Your Highness. My name is Samol.'

'I am not used to it, Chief Minister. Isn't it possible to meet His Majesty once?'

'I shall call him right away, Your Highness.' Samol leaves.

A few moments later, the king walks in, followed by his father-in-law. 'You asked for me, Ratnavali?'

'Yes, Your Highness. I have a question.' She stands up.

'Go ahead,' Arimotto says, surprised.

'Shouldn't a husband offer a gift to his newlywed bride, Your Highness?'

'He should, although there is no such custom,' Arimotto says, taken aback once more.

'I am going to make a request, Your Highness,' Ratnavali says calmly.

'Please go ahead.'

'Your Highness, please have my father driven out of this palace, this capital and this kingdom.'

TWENTY-THREE

In Konsari's melodious yet solemn voice, the description of Ayodhya before Rama began his journey into the forests comes alive. Sita's distressed entreaty, fearing possible separation from her husband, weighs heavily in the air inside Konsari's bedchamber. Inside Gobha's palace, she recites the Ramayana in her room, and sitting on an amsa carpet spread on the floor, Xunzira listens intently.

She listens regularly, whether she understands or not. On occasion, Konsari briefly explains the stories, while at other times, she only recites without additional commentary. Xunzira never asks any questions. Unlike before, she has also stopped talking. It's as if she has become still after the death of her husband, Phuleswar. Her only son, Samol, is also absent, having moved to Komota with Arimotto.

Samol never thinks about Xunzira.

As if he is Arimotto's shadow.

When Xunzira complained, Samol would laugh and say, 'Do you ever think of me? Only Konsari *Ayong* is your own. It's perfect. You live with ayong. I will live with my Deoraja.' Little did Xunzira imagine that those words, spoken in good humour, would one day become reality.

The palace of Gobha has become lonely and silent without Xunzira's enlivening chatter. Despite her typical involvement in day-to-day affairs, something seems amiss, as if the joy of life is nowhere to be found. Two extremely isolated women sit silently together, as if the need for communication has expired. The silence transmits between the two elderly women the words they want to say yet have no desire to express.

For quite some time now, Konsari has developed the habit of reciting the Ramayana in her room in the evenings. A few days before Arimotto left Gobha for good, she visited a *tol*, a school for Sanskrit in the Bhuyan kingdom. Konsari was excited to learn that the ruler of Bhuyan kingdom, Kusumbor Bhuyan, had established the school. She travelled there to enquire about the possibilities of setting them up in Gobha and its subordinate territories. During her visit, she also met the great scholar Mahendra Kondoli and Ragho Acharya, who had come there for an inspection. Before returning, Kusumbor Bhuyan gifted Konsari several manuscript copies, written on the barks of the saanchi tree by eminent poets of the time, and other books as presents. Ragho Acharya gave Konsari a copy of the Ramayana composed by his guru, Madhav Kondoli.

To some extent, these books have provided a sense of stability to Konsari and reduced the void in Arimotto's absence. Now, reading is not merely a means of using up her free time. It is also an aid to forget herself and keep all her anxieties at bay. She hopes to seclude herself in the barren valley of profound indifference.

Despite Arimotto's departure, Konsari has continued her welfare work, as usual without incident. From her outward demeanour and expression, nobody can read her inner anguish.

For on the outside, Konsari appears sombre. Composed. Engrossed.

At the end of the day's work, when Konsari returns to her bedchamber for relaxation, her face loses all self-confidence, brightness and tranquillity.

In the solitude of her bedroom, she is simply a mother. Only Xunzira is able to witness this vulnerable side of Konsari, experiencing her anguish as they both suffer in similar ways.

Yet looking at Konsari, Xunzira seems to forget her own pain, prioritizing Konsari's plight. This bond between them makes

Xunzira want to remain by her pai's side as much as possible, and Konsari, too, finds comfort in having her nannao around, as if unspoken words flow between them.

Arimotto has been living outside the Gobha palace since he was ten years old. After twelve years at the samadi, he was ordained the king, occupied with responsibilities in Kumoi–Boghora. Konsari hardly had Arimotto near her during this time.

Strangely, she had never felt his absence before. The secluded palace, devoid of any loved ones, didn't bother her.

Then Arimotto left Gobha, driven by his desire to expand his kingdom. Lived in Komota for two long years. Konsari felt a deep sense of loneliness and depression that she hadn't experienced before.

Now she feels overwhelmed.

Everything seems to lack meaning, and emptiness engulfs the palace and Gobha. Konsari carries a sharp thorn of guilt, constantly reminded of how she obstructed her only son's path to happiness.

Konsari did not see Arimotto at the time of his departure. She neither had the desire, nor the strength to do so. Afterwards, she returned to the palace, where Sadhukumar was waiting for her in the lobby.

Noticing the sadness on his face, she could tell Arimotto had left.

But Sadhukumar couldn't tell with what ingenuity Konsari had managed to change the course of Arimotto's life.

She had not said anything to Sadhukumar.

He, too, stayed silent.

They both sat silently in the lobby for quite some time before Sadhukumar left for Amsai Marjong. Konsari came inside … to the vacuum.

After a three-month hiatus, Konsari received a letter from Arimotto, containing important news that she had been yearning for. She had never expected her son to communicate with Gobha again, as returning was out of the question. Konsari knows her son too well and is aware of the tempest that Gangavati's rejection has unleashed in his mind.

To Konsari, who had been constantly plagued by anxiety about her son in the past three months, Arimotto's letter brought both happy and sad news. In the letter, he wrote about his marriage to a girl named Ratnavali, but it also contained the pledge to give up his right to Gobha's throne. Arimotto had not invited his mother to Baidyagarh, but Konsari understood the message he intended to convey. Her son had uprooted himself from the soil of Gobha and wanted to start a new life with his wife, Ratnavali, without the presence of his near and dear ones from Gobha.

The letter placed Konsari on the periphery of two emotions: joy and sorrow. On one hand, she felt relieved that her son was trying to lead a more stable life, but on the other, she felt the pain of being separated from him. This pain was also associated with worry about Gangavati, considering the void in the young queen's life. Konsari couldn't help but feel engulfed by deep sorrow, wondering how Gangavati would live such a long life without a companion.

Didn't Konsari see Gangavati's inner being one evening? Didn't she see her deep love for Arimotto?

Three long months have passed since.

'Pai.'

It is as if Xunzira's voice has awakened Konsari from sleep. Konsari lifts her head from the Ramayana and looks at Xunzira.

'Yes, Nannao.'

'I don't like hearing the Ramayana, Pai. That Balmiki or whoever, why did he write a tale with so much sadness?'

'Who knows, Nannao? Perhaps these are not tales. Perhaps these incidents occurred at that time. If Balmiki hadn't actually seen Sita, could he have written about such tragic events so realistically?'

'Did King Ramchandra then take Sita along with him?'

'Yes. Many things happened after that. An evil man named Ravan stole Sita away. Ram, by killing Ravan in battle, rescued Sita. But later Sita was again banished to the forests.'

'Why, Pai?' Xunzira asks, surprised.

'There were rumours among the people that Sita had an affair with Ravan, which reached King Ram's ears. To avoid the people's ire, he abandoned the pregnant Sita in the jungle. There, the hermit Balmiki came across Sita and took her into his hermitage. Her two boys named Lava–Kusha were born there.'

'Is King Ram so despicable? Why do people revere him so much then? Why do they worship him?'

'Perhaps because he has also done a lot of good things. Moreover, does anybody regard women's sufferings as sufferings at all?'

'Our Deoraja is way above King Ram. The hermit Balmiki ought to have written tales about our Deoraja. What good did King Ram do, Pai? He deserted his wife in the jungle upon listening to other people. But one thing surprised me, Pai: Was the hermit inspired by you to write this Ramayan or whatever? Even your husband sent you off with our Deoraja. Our little one, too, almost grew up in a jungle. Do you think Balmiki wrote about Lava–Kusha after noticing Samol and our little one, Pai?'

Xunzira's words force Konsari to laugh.

'No, no, Nannao, do you think Balmiki is from this era? He wrote the Ramayana about twenty thousand years ago. Let alone us, even our grandfathers and grandmothers were not born then.'

'Strange. The events of those times and these times are so similar.'

'Only time changes, Nannao. Does the nature of people change? Do plants and trees, forest deer and birds change their traits? Man also is an animal, after all. Why would men change? Whatever change takes place, it is only external. The interior remains the same, understand? Society keeps men upright by suppressing them with rules and customs. Even in its midst, however, the same incidents occur on a regular basis. These things are not written down because there is no Balmiki. People are not even aware of it.'

'I will request the acharya of Komota to write about you when he next arrives. Even he is a learned person like Balmiki. Or else … who did you say the man is, who wrote this book in the language we understand, Pai?'

'Madhav Kondoli.'

'Yes, I shall request him to write it. Despite knowing about you, why did he write Balmiki's book afresh? He could have written about you instead. Why would he write … it is about Laloongs, after all.'

'What you just said, keep it to yourself, Nannao. Tell no one. You will be ridiculed. Am I really Sita? You talk nonsense.' Konsari laughs.

'I say what needs to be said. You don't recognize your worth. You only acknowledge the worth of others. Tell me how you are inferior to Sita.'

Before Konsari can say anything, a khamsamai appears in the doorway.

'The queen of Khola is here,' he announces.

Konsari becomes alert.

'Gangavati has arrived. Go, Nannao, go and look … no, no, not you … let me go and invite her in. Go arrange for some refreshments. Arrange for her to freshen up as well.'

Closing her book, Konsari steps out anxiously. Why has Gangavati come here? At this odd hour?

She wasn't supposed to visit Gobha.

Didn't Gangavati swear she'd never maintain any relationship with Gobha?

So why is she here?

What could be the issue?

With these thoughts running through her mind, Konsari enters the parlour.

Gangavati is sitting with her head lowered. Standing in the doorway, Konsari looks at her, stunned by her appearance.

Who is this young woman, as frail as a shrivelling tree? Gangavati, the queen of Khola? Whom Konsari had seen three months ago?

After returning from Komota, Arimotto, ignoring every argument of his mother's, had stuck to his own decision. So Konsari had travelled to Khola. To meet with Gangavati.

When she set eyes on Gangavati in the palace of Khola, Konsari had been fascinated. How gentle! How decent! How lovely! Like a fragrant *kanchan* tree in full bloom, washed down with a light shower. Tidy and fresh. But moistened by rain.

Gangavati had only recently returned from the trial. She had been surprised to see Konsari. But without displaying any reaction, she had welcomed her with her royal dignity and gravity. Offered due hospitality.

Konsari had not gone to Khola on official business.

She had gone discreetly.

Looking straight into Gangavati's eyes, putting aside every formality, Konsari had said, 'I have a few things to tell you, Sajjoh.'

'Please come inside, Maah. You don't have to sit in the lounge.'

Gangavati had taken her into her private suite. They both sat down face to face.

Then Gangavati had raised her gentle eyes and looked at Konsari. She had said, 'Now tell me, Maah. What have you come to say?'

Even without hearing Konsari, Gangavati seemed to understand that what Konsari wanted to say concerned the decision about her relationship with Arimotto.

'I've come to tell you about such things, Sajjoh, which you may not have heard. Because when those incidents transpired, you were not even born.'

One by one, Konsari recounted each event, right from her marriage with King Pratapchandra to the birth of Arimotto. She told her everything about her transformation from Chandraprabha to Konsari. By the time she finished, the sun was setting.

Gangavati was sitting with her head bowed. 'Tell me, Gangavati, can we betray the trust of a society that has given us so much? Should we do so? Will you be able to participate in such betrayal? I am giving you the right to decide everything, Gangavati. Please think about it. Then do whatever you think is appropriate.'

Taking Gangavati's leave, Konsari had gone away. Alone in her room inside the palace, Gangavati was facing a grave crisis. Completely shattered, torn between confusion, conflict and love.

Where is the Gangavati that Konsari had seen three months ago? It is as if another woman named Gangavati is sitting in the lounge of Gobha's palace. Washed out by severe fatigue and sorrow. Charmless.

'Sajjoh.'

Sensing Konsari's presence nearby, Gangavati feels startled and stands up.

'Come with me, Sajjoh. We shall talk in my room.'

Konsari turns around with tired steps. Gangavati follows her, deep in thought.

As they sit face to face inside the bed chamber, Konsari looks straight at Gangavati.

It is as if the fresh kanchan tree has withered in these three months. Gangavati appears tired and sad. Arimotto was correct: if the heart is taken away, can anyone stay alive?

'Is there any news from Mriganko, Maah?' raising her head eventually, Gangavati asks.

'Yes, Sajjoh. I have received his letter today. After a long time. He is well.' Konsari could not gather the strength to speak about his marriage.

'When is he likely to arrive, Maah?'

'He did not write about that, Sajjoh. He has informed about giving up his rights over Gobha. He will need some time to get over his sufferings, Sajjoh.'

Gangavati's expression turns gloomy.

She had forsaken Arimotto. She had forsaken him forever. Logic and considerations had forced Gangavati to forsake her heart's call. Curbing all her desires, all her dreams inside her heart, she had written a letter to Arimotto with a firm hand.

Didn't Gangavati anticipate Arimotto's state of mind upon receiving that letter? She did. Yet Gangavati was convinced by Konsari's reasoning. She couldn't find any reason to tarnish her most beloved man with the stigma of betrayal. Offering a lavish banquet for her clanspeople, Gangavati had returned once again, assuming the grave responsibilities of queenhood by giving up her claim to womanhood.

But now, Gangavati has become confused all over again. Arimotto's child, growing in her womb, is ready and waiting to uproot Gangavati's resolve. As she fixes her gaze on Konsari's eyes, melting with motherly affection, she says calmly, 'I am going to become a maah. What shall I do?'

Konsari is flabbergasted, staring at Gangavati's face without a word, her eyes filling up with tears. What will Konsari say now? What should she say? After a long silence, Konsari takes one of Gangavati's hands in her own and says, 'Sajjoh, I would advise you to contact Arimotto in these times.'

'But he has sworn never to set eyes on me again, touching the waters of Brahmaputra and in the name Fa Mahadeo. He has vowed never to return to Gobha.'

'Such vows are meaningless. They deserve to be broken. But before taking this decision, you must know another truth, Sajjoh.'

'What truth, Maah?'

'Arimotto got married, Sajjoh. His bride's name is Ratnavali.'

It is as if Konsari has tossed a shawl of darkness over her bright, hopeful face. To conceal her teary eyes, Gangavati lowers her head.

Then she gets up, pays her respects to Konsari and says calmly, 'I wish to take your leave, Maah.'

'You are leaving? Please don't, Sajjoh. Stay here tonight. You must not leave at this late hour.'

'I must follow the society's norms, Maah, since I've decided to live within it. Please don't worry. Don't feel depressed. I shall remain at Khola. Please don't talk to Mriganko about this.'

'But—'

'I can understand your confusion. But it is pointless ... I now realize why Mriganko married so quickly. Perhaps you, too, have understood. His resentment towards me drove him to it, but he has found a foothold somewhere. At least he has not destroyed himself. Let him be, let Mriganko live happily. Let me not enter his life and turn it upside down.'

'How are you going to raise a fatherless child in this society, Sajjoh?'

'But you are there, aren't you, Maah? If I fail, if I become weak, I shall seek your support.'

Konsari stands up, pulling Gangavati to her bosom. Two soulmates, defeated at the hands of time, drift away in a river of silent tears, unnoticed by anyone.

TWENTY-FOUR

In a beautifully decorated recreation room within the Baidyagarh palace, Arimotto and Fingua are enjoying a moment of relaxation. Nearby, Ratnavali is busy stitching gold beads onto a silk garment destined for the king's court attire – a skill she has acquired from a foreigner from the west.

Nowadays, the kingdom receives frequent visits from travellers hailing from the west, as well as people belonging to various professions. Arimotto has already permitted some of them to settle in Baidyagarh, resulting in a significant increase in the kingdom's trade and commerce. While agriculture remains the primary occupation, Baidyagarh's advantageous location has led to rapid development.

'King Arimotto, I have never seen a ruler as popular as you,' Fingua Kunwar remarks, setting down his bowl of joo.

Arimotto smiles in response but chooses not to speak. Instead, Ratnavali chimes in, 'Popularity is one thing, but has the kingdom truly progressed, honourable Kunwar?'

Arimotto turns his attention to his wife and asks, 'What do you mean, Ratnavali? There has been growth in cultivation, trade, commerce – in fact, all around. The people are leading happy lives.'

'Perhaps Her Highness means the expansion of the kingdom, Your Majesty,' Fingua explains. He has become a frequent visitor to Baidyagarh, making great efforts to establish familiarity and informality within the household. Ratnavali openly converses with

Fingua, a practice that Arimotto encourages, as he believes in breaking free from restrictions. Baidyagarh's traditions and customs have not yet been significantly influenced by teachings from Gobha society. Arimotto laughs at Fingua's comment, 'So, Ratnavali is now considering the kingdom's boundaries as well? I had assumed that, apart from clothes and ornaments, she couldn't think of much else.'

'You always tease me about that, as if I don't have other interests. But really, has our kingdom's territory expanded even by the length of a reed in all these years?' Ratnavali responds.

Fingua Kunwar adds, 'I believe Her Highness is speaking the truth, Your Majesty. As a popular and powerful king, you should not be content with such a small kingdom.'

'But Kunwar, have you attempted to expand your own kingdom?'

'Forget about me, Your Highness. Am I a king? I only have control over four villages, that's all. I don't have military strength. I don't even have your courage and valour.'

'I tell him the same thing, honourable Kunwar. As a valiant conqueror, should he be satisfied with such a petty kingdom? The bigger the kingdom, the greater the progress. He has forsaken the vast kingdom of Gobha. In the last eighteen years, he hasn't visited it even once.'

'Don't bring up Gobha, Ratnavali. It makes me sad to talk about it.'

'But Gobha is where your parents are, aren't they? Ratnasinha is now seventeen, and Lokhaitora has also grown up. They wish to see their grandparents. Why don't you take them along?'

'Let go of this subject, Ratnavali. I'm not the king of Gobha any longer. I have no ties to the place.'

'Why don't you maintain any ties? What could have happened that made you vow never to return to Gobha?'

'Ratnavali, I've told you several times not to ask anything about it. In spite of that, why do you bother me with the same question? I'm happy and content with my family, my children. Why can't you remain content as well?'

'Please don't talk like that, Your Majesty. What could be more fortunate and blissful than being your wife? Have I ever complained? I am just saying that you, so great a warrior, seem content with the insignificant Komota. In King Durlov Narayan's days, Komota was enormous. The petty Bhuyans were merely Durlov Narayan's chief ministers. They became independent during King Indra Narayan and Durlovendra's reign. Viewing you as a weak king, none of them has accepted your supremacy in the last eighteen years. Don't I feel bad seeing the Bhuyans openly blustering around without paying any toll to you?'

'Why do you feel bad? Who told you about the status of these kingdoms during Durlov Narayan's rule?'

'Who should tell me? Is it a secret? I'm astonished because you weren't like this when you came from Gobha. How brave you were. Didn't you yourself tell me about growing the kingdom further right after our marriage? That you would establish a kingdom larger than Gobha?'

'I did. And it was justified at the time. But I'm not thinking about expanding the kingdom anymore. Now, I seek peace.'

'Of course you still want it. Only weak rulers talk about living in peace.'

'What do you mean? I have no strength? Do you want to find out? What do you want? A kingdom? The power of the Pancha Goureswar, like Durlov Narayan had? Alright then. You want more kingdoms, do you? You want to rule like a *bor-rani*, an empress, by making the independent chief ministers your subordinate? It will be done. I shall do it. I shall expand the kingdom as far as you want. Sometimes I feel frustrated thinking about you. Gangavati was different. She opposed stealing even a pinch of another's land. She did not support me when I came to conquer Komota either.' Forgetting about Fingua Kunwar's presence, Arimotto becomes irritated.

'If she was so good, why did you marry me?' Ratnavali breaks down in tears. Arimotto soberly considers her words for a moment. Some moments pass in silence as Ratnavali wipes her tears and tries to compose herself.

'Have I said anything wrong?' she finally asks, breaking the silence. 'You get annoyed whenever I speak. You should expand the kingdom. Tell me, is King Pratapchandra a greater warrior than you? Why can't you become the king of kings like Pratapchandra, who conquered Majuli from Komota?'

Arimotto freezes, his joo-drunk eyes suddenly sharpening. He stares at Ratnavali with a piercing gaze. 'How did you learn so much? Who told you all of this?' His words carry a serious tone.

Ratnavali feels uncomfortable, realizing that mentioning Fingua Kunwar might raise suspicion in Arimotto's mind. 'It was I who said it, Your Majesty. Do you recall what I told you during one of my visits long ago? Perhaps Her Highness heard it at the time,' Fingua jumps in.

'Oh, did you? But I don't remember,' Arimotto responds, surprised.

'How would you remember if you are always under the spell of joo to the point of being out of your senses? Do you have any thoughts about the kingdom? You have certainly forgotten about me. It's always Lokhaitora and Ratnasinha on your mind. There is no other topic of discussion besides the children. What a king,' Ratnavali says, attempting to lighten the mood.

The atmosphere eases once again, and Ratnavali and Fingua Kunwar feel relieved. They've successfully averted suspicion. After a while, Fingua Kunwar speaks up, taking a more indirect approach. 'The day you acquire a kingdom spanning Majuli to Bornodi and assume the title Bor-Raja, I shall accept your supremacy and remain a subsidiary ruler. With your strength, I shall acquire a couple of nearby villages.'

Arimotto looks at Fingua. 'Right now, my military strength is limited, Kunwar. It is impossible to expand the kingdom with this force.'

'Your Majesty, it's impossible when you believe it's impossible. Didn't you conquer this kingdom after coming from remote Gobha? The strength of one's mind drives the expansion of kingdoms, Your Majesty. Perhaps you don't realize how popular you are in this kingdom. The Boro–Kacharis living in the area and across the western region consider you as their own. They've discovered a connection with you. Those regions may not be under your dominion, but their inhabitants are your devoted subjects. You can easily conquer them if you so choose. You will not gain any special recognition for taking them over. However, if you defeat Pratapchandra and seize his vast empire, all the western rulers will automatically accept your rule. When the merchants of my realm return from trade and praise the glory of Pratapchandra, I feel miserable. I tell them that they don't know how valiant our King Arimotto is – the king of Komota can easily defeat ten Pratapchandras.'

With deceptive compliments, Fingua Kunwar has incited the inebriated Arimotto's thirst for victory. The slumbering tiger is slowly waking up. Fingua Kunwar is finally seeing the signs of success from his long-drawn effort, while Arimotto remains ignorant of the hidden intentions. For eighteen years, Fingua Kunwar has been tirelessly working to ignite the fire for battle within Arimotto. Arimotto's popularity has thwarted Fingua's ambitions to expand his own kingdom, leaving him content with only four villages.

Though spoken as flattery, Fingua's words hold some truth. Arimotto enjoys immense popularity among the Boro–Kacharis and other inhabitants of this kingdom. Arimotto is unlike any other ruler. He came from Gobha but became one with the local people, assimilating to their culture and lifestyle. Fingua Kunwar, assuming Arimotto would rule remotely through a representative, had started his own preparations to take over the kingdom. However, these conspiracies failed, and Arimotto settled in Baidyagarh, where he married Ratnavali. Ever since that day, Fingua has been burning with envy, waiting for the right opportunity to act.

After Ratnavali drove her father away from the kingdom, he sought refuge with Fingua, who had already planned his future scheme during Arimotto and Ratnavali's wedding.

'Father—' Lokhaitora comes and stands near Arimotto. 'The acharya had given me a grammar exercise. May I go and show it to him?' she asks in a soft, quiet voice.

Arimotto, lost in thought and sipping joo, smiles. 'You want to visit the acharya. Why are you asking for permission?'

'Mother says I am grown up now and must not leave home without permission.'

'Of course she'd say that. Because she had never ventured out of her house at your age, you see,' the king laughs aloud.

Ratnavali observes the laughter and feels as if a fire has erupted in her heart, filling her with intense loathing. For eighteen years, she has tolerated Arimotto's presence and borne two of his children without ever feeling close to him. The vow she took during her wedding remains strong. She is not the king's wife; Fingua Kunwar is the one who truly loves her.

He has maintained a clandestine relationship with Ratnavali ever since her wedding, and her feelings for him have grown significantly. She wonders what her life would have been like if she had never met Fingua. But his regular presence, his friendship with Arimotto and his covert expressions of love have reignited her feelings twofold. Fingua's overwhelming love gives her the strength to continue ignoring Arimotto.

Arimotto remains oblivious to the hidden desires and conspiracies of Ratnavali and Fingua Kunwar. They've patiently waited for an opportunity, and now they see a glimmer of hope as Arimotto shows an interest in expanding his kingdom. His popularity has thwarted Fingua's ambitions to expand his own kingdom, leaving him content with only four villages. But with this new development, they hope to change the course of events.

Over these years, Fingua Kunwar has diligently worked to incite Arimotto's thirst for battle and conquest, despite his focus on family and stability. Now, he finally sees the opportunity to fulfil his ambitions.

Pratapchandra is no longer as powerful as he once was, having shifted his focus away from the governance of his kingdom. He now spends most of his time on charitable activities and rituals. As a result, the frontier provinces have gained significant independence, with chief ministers effectively ruling their regions. However,

Pratapchandra remains a powerful figure, and his kingdom's structure remains almost intact, thanks to the skilled administration of his Prime Minister, Sogor.

After careful consideration and information gathering, Fingua Kunwar has skilfully convinced Arimotto to head eastwards on a victorious campaign. Through continuous indirect comparisons between King Pratapchandra's might, the grandeur of his expansive kingdom and Komota, Fingua Kunwar persistently strives to awaken the dormant warrior within Arimotto. A battle against Pratapchandra would likely result in Arimotto's defeat. It has been eighteen years since Arimotto last engaged in warfare, and he has not expanded his military force. The combination of newly trained soldiers and the older ones raises questions about Arimotto's ability to confront Pratapchandra effectively.

The loyal soldiers from Gobha have settled into family life after marrying local women, and they may not possess the same vigour and valour as they once did.

Arimotto's assessment of Pratapchandra's might relies heavily on Fingua Kunwar's opinion, whom he trusts, loves as a friend and relies on. Despite Samol's efforts to change Arimotto's perspective on Fingua, he has not succeeded, as he lacks the latter's eloquence.

If the king were to be killed by Pratapchandra, Fingua would achieve his goal. Arimotto would never accept the role of a subordinate king and would fight fiercely until his death. This would enable Fingua to rule as a feudatory king under Pratapchandra.

As the conversation takes place, Fingua Kunwar, Ratnavali and Arimotto hear the bhitor maji's voice announcing the arrival of the general. Fingua and Ratnavali wonder what important message the general brings at this late hour. They are concerned about whether a spy may have overheard their previous conversation inside the guest room.

Arimotto, aware of the reason for the general's visit, mentions that it likely pertains to the new arms samples. He instructs Ratnavali to serve dinner to Fingua and departs, leaving him and the queen alone.

Fingua enquires about the whereabouts of Ratnasinha and Lokhaitora, Arimotto's children. Ratnavali assures him that they are alone. They close the door and Fingua embraces Ratnavali, who had for a long time been craving his touch.

TWENTY-FIVE

The temple grounds resound with the evening prayers and within the sanctum sanctorum, the priest, hailing from Kanyakubja and educated in Banaras, recites the mantras with precision.

Seated in the temple, Pratapchandra observes the evening prayers, his countenance bearing traces of prolonged irregularities. Although his deep-set eyes remain fixed on the priest's face, it is evident that he is lost in thought.

Of late, Pratapchandra has been dedicating his evenings exclusively to the temple courtyard, where he immerses himself in scripture recitations and engages in religious discussions with intellectuals.

The kingdom is home to numerous Brahmin scholars, whom Pratapchandra has assisted in establishing permanent residences by providing land and dwellings. Much like his great-grandfather, Pratapchandra primarily pursues wisdom, which complements his role as the ruler. Prime Minister Sogor manages the majority of administrative duties, while Pratapchandra is engrossed in religious dialogues and philanthropic endeavours for the welfare of his subjects.

The once victory-obsessed and arrogant Pratapchandra, fixated on his Aryan lineage, has evolved into a selfless and benevolent ruler who abhors violence and earnestly seeks knowledge. However, his disinterest has led to the weakening of the kingdom's administrative machinery, despite his growing popularity.

Pratapchandra lacks the focus required to establish an efficient administrative infrastructure for the effective governance of his vast realm. His days and nights pass in passive indifference.

Even though he resides in a lavishly adorned royal palace, surrounded by maids and servants, the solitary king remains without a family to call his own.

With a wife who resembles the goddess Lakhimi, along with children and grandchildren, Pratapchandra could have led a joyful and contented life. He could have reigned over a vast and prosperous kingdom.

The kingdom sprawls widely, yet prosperity remains elusive. Years of neglect have rendered Pratapchandra's once-mighty infrastructure fragile. His expansion of the empire involved subduing the Bhuyan kingdoms and other minor provinces, which now exist under the control of feudatory chiefs. These chiefs are gradually growing more assertive, and the kingdom's security system has eroded due to Pratapchandra's apathy and lack of determination. Military strength is dwindling, and the chiefs are increasingly disregarding Pratapchandra's commands.

Sogor's challenge is to oversee every facet of the kingdom as Pratapchandra remains oblivious to most affairs. Even when Sogor attempts to enlighten him, Pratapchandra refuses to listen. Once, when Sogor tried to forcefully give him some information, the king became irritated. 'Manage the administration of the kingdom yourself, Prime Minister,' Pratapchandra said. 'I don't like to discuss administrative matters. You are a veteran. Unless you need any formal sanctions from me, look after everything yourself. At times, I feel like retiring and then assigning the responsibility of the kingdom to you.'

'When you speak like that, it makes me unhappy, O Son of God. I am merely your servant. I do not desire any more power and authority than I already have. I would beg to offer you some advice, Your Highness, if you will permit me to cross my limit.'

'Limit.' A sad smile spread over Pratapchandra's face. 'Does the question of limit still exist between you and me, Prime Minister? I am a lonely old man. What, pray tell me, is my limit?'

Prime Minister Sogor remained silent for a long time and then suggested, 'Please adopt a son, O Son of God. Adopt a young boy eligible to be the king of the Jitary dynasty. Ordain him as the crown prince of this kingdom. It will augur well for your subjects. Your loneliness will cease, too.'

Upon hearing Sogor's words, King Pratapchandra had appeared shocked. He stared at Sogor speechlessly for a long time and then responded gravely, 'Why should I adopt a son, Prime Minister? Am I childless?'

'You are not childless, but someone whose son's whereabouts are unknown even before his birth is akin to being childless.'

'My son's whereabouts are not unknown, Prime Minister. We know where my son is. Other officers or the citizens of this kingdom might be unaware, but you and I are in the know.'

'Yes. But what is that child's identity, Your Highness? That child has not been brought up as King Pratapchandra's son. That son does not know your name, O Son of Aryans. Does not recognize you. It may sound unpleasant, but it is the truth.'

A spark of severe ridicule flickered and instantly disappeared from Pratapchandra's eyes as he stared at the Prime Minister.

'Prime Minister, you accompany me to listen to the scriptures at the temple these days, do you not? I don't suppose there is any dearth of intelligence in you to not be able to realize the true implications of the scriptures. You quite well know the story of Ramayana, too. Did Ramchandra, who had banished his pregnant wife, re-marry for want of a child? Did he acknowledge anybody as an adopted son?'

'He did not, O Son of Aryans,' Sogor tried to pacify the agitated Pratapchandra.

'So? Why should I adopt a son? I shall not. I am preserving this kingdom for my son. The day he arrives, I shall take up asceticism and hand over the kingdom to him. If he does not accept, you are going to be the ruler of this kingdom after my death. Or else let this kingdom fall to ruin and reduce itself to wreckage.'

Pratapchandra had grown emotional. The Prime Minister sat quietly without responding. After a long time, the old king said,

'My dear mother used to call me Ramchandra. I often feel that this name has some connection with my cursed life, Sogor.'

'This is why a Kshatriya should not delve too deeply into the scriptures and epics. You can lose your direction in their hazy terrain. If you chose asceticism, you will have deviated from the Kshatriya caste. You are a king. You were born with royal virtues. Your primary obligations are the governance of the kingdom and its protection. It is not proper to reel under sorrow and neglect royal duties. The Ramchandra of Ramayana may have been beset with grief after Sita's exile, yet he did not forsake his kingly duties. Instead, he made preparations for an *ashwamedh jajnya* with the aim of universal conquest. If you wish to deliberate on the epic, then, Your Highness, you must agree to abide by this example. Moreover, King Ramchandra was not alone. He had the support of his brothers and their families, too. Who do you have, Your Majesty? You are old now. You need your near and dear ones during these times.'

'Why? To light my funeral pyre?' Pratapchandra had laughed.

'If you feel that way, I am helpless.' In utter despair, Sogor had given up. After that, the Prime Minister had not broached this topic again. Leaving the king to do as he wished, Sogor took on the rudder of administration in his hands.

But another challenge has now risen to face Sogor. Encouraged by Pratapchandra's apathy, a battle for power among the principal officeholders is about to break out within the kingdom. They have split into factions with the goal of overthrowing Sogor, who is navigating the situation with dexterity and patience. His long years of experience as a Prime Minister, profound political wisdom, power of judgment and the support of his loyal officers have all helped him save the kingdom from breaking into fragments.

When he notices Pratapchandra's forlorn, fatigued, age-shrunk countenance, the Prime Minister melts with affection. Watching the king pass a lonely life in the vast palace, his heart twinges with pain.

Many years ago, Sogor had tried to dispel this loneliness. He had tried to persuade Pratapchandra to marry again. But the king had turned down that proposal in clear words.

Embracing the memories of his wife, Pratapchandra carries on. Sometimes, it seems to Sogor as if, in the king's mind, Queen Chandraprabha is still alive. As if Pratapchandra is passing the time imagining his wife's presence near him. He has confined himself to a fantasy world. Sogor has given up trying to bring him out of this unreality.

What is the point? If this brings him peace, so be it. Decades have passed by in this manner. Queen Chandraprabha's memories have become the stuff of legend in Pratapchandra's kingdom. Many a tale has been told about the beautiful queen, who was given away to the Brahmaputra in a dream at the command of the river goddess.

Chandraprabha's existence has turned into a fairy tale.

Sogor doesn't know anything about Chandraprabha's life anymore. At first, he used to gather information through spies sent to Gobha on the king's orders. They even heard of a son being born to her. But after that, there has been no further news. Again, on Pratapchandra's orders, Sogor had stopped sending spies.

Chandraprabha and her son are undoubtedly still alive. Surely her son has attained maturity by now. She herself has never attempted to establish contact with Pratapchandra. It is only natural. Sogor had witnessed the queen's self-respect and resolve. She would not have revealed to her son his father's identity. For had she done so, it would have led to a faint possibility of that son seeking out his father.

But he hasn't arrived yet.

There is also no chance of his coming.

In his final days, Pratapchandra continues to wait for his son, a situation that concerns Sogor deeply. He feels for Pratapchandra's emotional turmoil, one that had once brought disaster into his life. So, despite the burden of his age and the exhausting responsibilities of managing the kingdom, Sogor continues to uphold the kingdom's administration. He is shielding Pratapchandra with all his might, but even his own strength is now waning.

As the feudatory chiefs, especially the Bhuyans, have begun asserting their sovereignty, the revenue for the administration, development and security of the kingdom has dwindled. The political landscape in the surrounding kingdoms is also changing. The Ahoms in the east and Kochs in the west are starting to emerge as significant forces.

At this time of multiple crises in Pratapchandra's kingdom, Sogor has come to the temple premises to discuss an issue. Evening prayers have just concluded. Pratapchandra is in the temple yard within the palace grounds, listening to the melodious recitation of verses from the Samaveda. In response to Sogor's greeting, Pratapchandra raises his head and calmly says, 'Sit down, Prime Minister. Because your usual time of arrival has passed, I assumed you would not come.'

'A problem prevented me from arriving on time. I cannot listen to the verses even now. I've only come to invite you to the counselling room, O Son of God.'

'Counselling room? Now? Why?'

'For discussions regarding security.'

'Is there a threat to our security? But right now, I'm listening to the recitation of the Samaveda verses.'

'The recitation must be halted, Your Highness. The kingdom is in a state of emergency. Your presence in the counselling room is essential.'

'What is the crisis, Prime Minister?'

'The king of Komota, Arimotto of the west, has attacked our kingdom.'

Arimotto!

It's not the crisis in the kingdom but the name of the invading king, Arimotto, that seems to have struck Pratapchandra with astonishment.

'Arimotto? The king of Komota? Are you absolutely certain, Prime Minister?'

'Absolutely certain, O Son of God. Please come. The major general awaits your presence inside the counselling chamber. Allow me to leave. I shall send orders for the senior officers' attendance right away.'

With Pratapchandra in a state of wonder and confusion, Sogor walks back after paying obeisance.

TWENTY-SIX

The advisory council has been meeting frequently. Pratapchandra stays busy in serious discussions with the major general, Prime Minister, chief sentinel and other high officials of the kingdom. The adverse reports from the messengers have cast a gloomy spell over the counselling chamber.

Arimotto's massive army is advancing from the west, not at a slow pace but with great velocity, like a tempest. Pratapchandra's soldiers have not been able to thwart Arimotto's attack or obstruct the opposing army's progress, not because of the vulnerability of Pratapchandra's army, but because of the feudatory kings' refusal to cooperate.

They have accepted Arimotto's supremacy almost without any resistance. In return, they've gained the authority to rule their kingdoms as subsidiary kings, autonomously. As a result, Pratapchandra's permanent army is beginning to retreat, being defeated at every step. The feudatory chiefs' lack of support makes it impossible for the permanent army to engage in a prolonged fight. Although a couple of provinces have offered help, the majority seem resistant.

During the reigns of Pratapchandra's father, Sompal, and paternal grandfather, Tamradhwaj, most of the provinces of his great-grandfather Dharmapal's kingdom had become independent on their own, especially those belonging to the Bhuyans. However, during Pratapchandra's reign, the Bhuyans, having lost their sovereignty once again, were forced to become feudatory chiefs. A couple of Bhuyans migrated to the south bank of the Brahmaputra and created new settlements, becoming sovereign rulers of small kingdoms. Towards the end, the Bhuyans, whose glory had faded in the face of Pratapchandra's heroism, were gradually raising their heads, taking advantage of the old king's weakness. After witnessing Arimotto's aggressive advance, they have completely surrendered their loyalty to the Aryan king.

So what if they are subsidiary rulers? After all, they are kings.

Not feudatories under Pratapchandra.

At least, the best among the worst.

Arimotto is relentlessly advancing, taking possession of Pratapchandra's extensive domain piece by piece. His expedition is made comfortable by the hospitality and military support of the feudatory chiefs, resulting in a small number of soldiers being killed. On the contrary, the strength of his military force has increased due to the support of the smaller rulers who have willingly accepted his supremacy.

Arimotto's soldiers are becoming excited.

While Pratapchandra's army is beginning to despair.

Arimotto has almost reached the fortified capital.

As a result, Pratapchandra has convened this untimely council to deliberate with the officers on their next move. However, in the midst of this critical moment and the serious discussions, Pratapchandra is repeatedly becoming unfocused.

The name of the king of Komota, devouring his kingdom from every side, is disturbing Pratapchandra with another thought.

Arimotto.

It's such a familiar name.

Who is this Arimotto?

Is it Arimotto or Orimotto?

What does Arimotto mean?

Could this Arimotto, by any chance, be his exiled son?

But that can't be possible; Pratapchandra's son's name is Mriganko.

He was certainly informed that Chandraprabha had named her son Mriganko.

After returning from Mayapur, Pratapchandra had tried several times to collect information about Chandraprabha. Some spies had been caught, and others returned unsuccessfully. However, after learning that Chandraprabha's son was officially named Mriganko, that she had wiped off the vermilion from her forehead and middle parting and assumed a different name for herself, Pratapchandra had stopped sending spies altogether. He understood exactly what Chandraprabha was trying to prove by adopting a new identity.

At first, Pratapchandra broke down, but later he became impassive. Realizing that Chandraprabha had abandoned her old identity and begun a new life, he began to cling to his memories as his only refuge. He wanted to erase from his mind Sadhukumar's wife, the queen of Gobha, and Chandraprabha's new identity.

Pratapchandra has traversed the rest of his years in despairing inertia. At times, he has misgivings about who exiled whom. Despite owning such a vast kingdom, he feels exiled himself.

Chandraprabha seems to have attained a fulfilled life. She is living as someone's wife and the mother of a child, even if it is in a small, impoverished, petty kingdom. But there is no dearth of honour, is there? Pratapchandra is aware that she is living with dignity in the palace of Gobha. He is sure of it.

Perhaps there is still grief in her heart. Perhaps the scars of humiliation have not yet disappeared from her mind. Apart from that, what other pain does she have? Is there any grief? Is she in excruciating agony from self-reproach, like him? But Chandraprabha has not committed any crime. Pratapchandra is the one who has done wrong. He abandoned his pregnant wife and gave her away to a non-Aryan king. Is there anything more painful than guilt? What else, aside from guilt, could gnaw at one's peace of mind? One's respite? Happiness?

'What is our duty now, O Son of God?'

When he hears Sogor's voice, for a moment Pratapchandra stares at him before sitting upright. After remaining still for some time, he says, 'Arimotto must be obstructed, Prime Minister. The feudatories of the west have surrendered. Let it be so. Our army has retreated temporarily, but it does not indicate defeat or the end of battle. Bring together soldiers from other fronts, gather arms and weapons from various sectors and assemble in the capital. Recruit temporary soldiers and confiscate the subjects' personal weapons. The chief sentinel has already been entrusted with the responsibility of food, clothes and so on. Increase the food reserves. Reduce leisure hours and dispatch soldiers in various directions. It is night now, and there is no possibility of Arimotto attacking at nighttime. If everything we have planned can be accomplished during the night, we shall move forward and attack him unexpectedly before daybreak tomorrow. Order the boatmen to be ready at the shores and keep the elephants and horses ready, too. I shall lead in the next battle.'

'The time for you to lead in the battle has not arrived yet, O Son of God. The fort of Pratappur is still secured. It is not necessary for you to take up arms until my death,' the prime minister beseeches.

'I know. My faith in you is still intact, Prime Minister. I also know that if the treacherous feudatories had not weakened our strength, it would have taken less than an hour for you to thwart Arimotto's progress. But it is the hour of crisis now. The soldiers are losing their morale. When they catch sight of me on the battlefield, they will gain courage and confidence. Please do not be anxious about my safety, Prime Minister. I may be aged, but I am not infirm. I still have the power to defeat a young warrior like Arimotto in battle. Go and appropriately execute the orders I have issued. Arimotto has, at present, become confident about victory. He is exhausted after the long journey as well as the hard labour. At such times, the soldiers are likely to be inattentive. From my long experience, I can say that an aggressive technique is the best at this juncture. Because they have to concentrate on self-defence, the opponents often lose the opportunity to counterattack and become disintegrated, too.'

Signalling the end of the meeting, Pratapchandra stands up. At that precise moment, a gatekeeper, out of breath, comes into the room. He somehow pays his obeisance and says, 'The chief sentinel has sent a message – the Komota army is attacking our fort.'

The sudden, unexpected news leaves the officers in the counselling room momentarily frozen, even Pratapchandra. But in the next moment, everyone springs to life, engaging in breathless discussions. The officers leave with brisk steps, while Pratapchandra makes his way to his private armoury to dress in war robes and collect his weapons. The major general, appropriately clad in combat gear, heads towards the main entrance, and Prime Minister Sogor gets busy passing necessary orders to the officers.

Pratapchandra emerges from the palace, accompanied by his bodyguards, and mounts a horse. As he raises his head and fixes his gaze on the main entrance, the exterior is illuminated by innumerable torches. The shrill cries of excited soldiers and the agonizing shrieks of injured ones create an awful environment, shattering the serenity of the night. Invoking Lord Mahabhairav, Pratapchandra raises his cane.

The main road inside the fort comes alive with the combined sound of horses' hooves and the war cries of soldiers. The Aryan–Kshatriya's thirst for victory boils in his blood, undeterred by age, filled with unfathomable fury and unrestricted fervour for combat.

By the time Pratapchandra and his soldiers arrive at the main entrance, it has buckled under the collective force of elephants. Pratapchandra stands still for a second, then dashes into the midst of the battle-crazed soldiers. Upon noticing their king, the troops, who were beginning to lose hope, regain their battling spirit. Under the orders of the major general, they fight united, with all their might.

Arimotto's army begins to gradually retreat as Pratapchandra's army goes wild in a battle spree. Intense sentiments of patriotism seem to transform every soldier into a powerful lion, weakening Arimotto's forces with their heroism.

Certain that defeat is imminent, Arimotto's army starts to retreat on the general's command. However, as their leader advances, the retreating soldiers stop in their tracks and attack Pratapchandra's men with renewed vigour without waiting for further orders.

Amidst a few battle-hellish moments, Arimotto and Pratapchandra face each other as captains of their respective armies. A few more moments pass. Pratapchandra hurls a sharp spear with infallible aim. Although Arimotto tries to dodge the blow, the spear hits his helmet, knocking it off. Arimotto's face, crimson with fury, glows in the light of torches, leaving the Aryan king spellbound.

To his astonishment, sitting on the horse in a man's attire is Chandraprabha. It is none other than Chandraprabha.

A brief distraction occurs.

Arimotto's spear penetrates Pratapchandra's body.

Pratapchandra falls off his horse, and the frenzied soldiers freeze for a moment. Despite his injury, Pratapchandra cries out in distress, urging the Prime Minister and major general to stop the battle. Soldiers on both sides stand still, and Arimotto, from his horse, looks at Pratapchandra in awe before commanding his soldiers to halt. He dismounts and kneels down beside the injured king.

In the midst of the tense scene, the major general carefully removes the spear that has pierced Pratapchandra through his armour, and with one hand, he raises the bloodied king to a sitting position. Every soldier on the ground is awestruck as they gaze upon Pratapchandra's wounded body.

'Why did you ask for the battle to stop, King Pratapchandra?'

The king looks at Arimotto's face. Then in a calm and exhausted voice, he asks, 'Who are you, Son of Aryans?'

'I am not a son of Aryans. I am a Tiwasha. Laloong. A non-Aryan.'

'Are you … Chandraprabha's son?' Pratapchandra asks in a voice trembling with hope and emotion.

'No. My mother's name is Konsari. But I have heard that earlier her name used to be Chandraprabha. My father's name is Sadhukumar. But why are you asking these questions, King Pratapchandra?' Arimotto asks in surprise.

Pratapchandra stares at Arimotto's face for a while. Then he speaks in a trembling voice, 'Is your real name Mriganko?'

'My real name is Arimotto. Mriganko was my given name. But I have discarded that identity. But what is the meaning of such questions, King Pratapchandra?'

'It does have meaning, Arimotto. But there are no words to express it. Perhaps there's no time for it either. You do not know your real identity, Arimotto. You are my son, my and Chandraprabha's son. Sadhukumar—' Arimotto raises his hand, gesturing to Pratapchandra to stop talking. For a few breathless moments, he looks intently at Pratapchandra. At first, his face turns red with profound anger. Then a fleeting smile of severe sarcasm spreads across his face. Lowering his hand, Arimotto speaks calmly and gravely, 'You are injured, King Pratapchandra. You need care. Please go back to your palace. Upon my word, I shall not attack this fort. I shall retreat. But please do not mislead me with irrelevant words. Diplomatic tactfulness is certainly required in battle, but what kind of diplomacy is this, King Pratapchandra? What kind of tact?'

Prime Minister Sogor comes forward. 'Please forgive me, King Arimotto. This is not diplomacy, but it's quite natural for you to mistake it as such. To determine the truth of His Majesty's words, you must know many more facts. Please be our royal guest, King Arimotto. King Pratapchandra is not a coward who would resort to mean tactics to defeat his enemies.'

Arimotto looks at Prime Minister Sogor's age-shrunk, gloomy face, and his mind is thrown into turmoil. The tug of war between belief and disbelief makes Arimotto restless. Taking his eyes off the Prime Minister, Arimotto observes the old, injured being treated by the royal medic. Is there any sign of dishonesty visible on his aged face? Any streak of deception?

No, there is nothing except sadness in the eyes of this exhausted old man.

'I have accepted your invitation, General. But my soldiers will wait outside the fort, and only my bodyguards, Prime Minister and major general will accompany me.'

'As you wish. The major general will keep you company. I am proceeding to the palace with His Majesty.'

Lifting Pratapchandra on a stretcher made of cloth tied to two bamboo poles, Prime Minister Sogor walks away with quick steps. Pratapchandra cannot be carried on horseback so as to avoid further bloodshed.

The royal medic rides away speedily on a horse. After consulting with the accompanying officers and issuing necessary orders, the hesitant Arimotto goes to the interiors of the fort with the major general.

TWENTY-SEVEN

Konsari descends from the carriage with Samol and stands in front of the main gate of Pratappur fort, which has been toppled by elephants. An aged Konsari in a black kasyong phaskai. With a gaze that seems to recall events from a previous life, Konsari looks through the broken gate with a bemused, forlorn expression, peering deep into the interiors of the fort, into the palace inside. Here, right here, Konsari had lived as Chandraprabha in another life. A delicate maiden named Chandraprabha, her pink feet adorned with anklets of tiny bells, had sauntered over this palace's veranda in that other life. Bedecked with a gold-embroidered riha-mekhela, a mist-like translucent scarf brought from Manipur and her body covered in gold jewellery, a newlywed bride called Chandraprabha had flooded a love-obsessed man named Pratapchandra with emotions. Embarking on a peacock-winged dream boat, Chandraprabha had sailed to a heaven of happiness.

And then the dream came to an end. Chandraprabha drifted away in the midnight waters of the Brahmaputra. Setting ablaze her own lifeless body on the shores of the Luit, Chandraprabha rose from its ashes – as Konsari. On her way to a new life, she threw into the heart of the Brahmaputra the ashes of her burnt body. Her past. The identity of her previous birth. Everything.

The river refused to accept the old identity thrown into its waters. It was instead returned to the sandy shores. Picking up that worn-out tag after aeons, Konsari has returned to the land of her previous birth, to set eyes upon the injured Pratapchandra, who is waiting for death.

By the side of Mayapur.

By the side of Mahabhairav.

After reading Arimotto's letter delivered by Samol in Gobha, Konsari had, at first, been shocked by the unexpected blow. Clutching Arimotto's letter in her fist, Konsari had sat speechless for a long time. Then she had raised her eyes to look at Samol, who was standing by her side. 'Why did Arimotto do this, Samol? I had forbidden him from expanding his kingdom eastwards. Because he had promised to abide by my instructions, I had permitted him to move westwards, much against my wishes. Why didn't he listen to me, Samol? Why did he fail to remember his mother?'

In response to those questions, Samol recounted to her the events of the last eighteen years. After telling her everything about Nilakanta, Fingua, Ratnasinha and Lokhaitora, he explained in detail about the expedition to the east and the battle with Pratapchandra. By the time the story came to an end, the dam in Konsari's heart had given way. After hearing about Pratapchandra's years of agony and Arimotto's remorse over slaying his father, Konsari felt weak. The frozen affection of a vulnerable mother concealed inside Abi Konsari, who had been performing her obligations with the same patience, sombreness and ease despite not seeing her only son for eighteen long years, was melting. At the same time, an unknown, young-looking woman named Chandraprabha began weeping inside Konsari's heart.

'There aren't many days left for His Majesty Pratapchandra's life to end. The spear wound did not heal. Although the bleeding has stopped, according to the royal medic, poison has entered his bloodstream. Deoraja is distraught. When I found out, I was also devastated. It would be best if you stayed close to Deoraja right now, Ayong,' Samol said, looking at his aunt.

Xunzira, who had lost her mind upon seeing her son after eighteen years, had also said, 'Go, Pai. Our child is in deep agony.

He has unknowingly slain his own father. He did not sin consciously. Our child may believe he has perpetrated a sin though he has not. Who else can explain that to him other than you? Furthermore, these are the last hours of His Majesty Pratapchandra. Good or bad, he has been your king. He was punished for his wrongdoing. Remove all bad feelings from your mind, Pai. Please go see him in his final hours. His Majesty Pratapchandra is so eager to see you. It would be a sin not to go.'

There was no need for so many words. Konsari's mental resolve had already crumbled.

'Please board the carriage, Ayong. The road is long. It will be painful for you.'

Without any protest, Konsari had sat in the carriage to visit Pratappur.

She is exhausted by the torturous journey now. By the burden of grief. The burden of opening the closed door of nostalgia and stepping onto the land of the sun, after ages.

'Come along, Ayong.'

At Samol's voice, Chandraprabha seems to awaken from her grave. Keeping her delusion at bay, Konsari steps inside the fort, heaving a sigh.

A throng of people have gathered outside the palace. All the officers, palace staff and people who have arrived from different parts of the kingdom to learn about the dying king's condition are speaking in low tones and looking sad.

Konsari's heart quivers.

Is it the end of everything?

Has Pratapchandra left the world without seeing Chandraprabha?

Seeing them approach the palace, people are turning their heads to look at Konsari. The erstwhile officers and staff are stunned as they look at her. Who is this strangely attired woman? Why does she seem so familiar? Where had they seen this face? When had they seen her?

Groping in the darkness of the mind, they are trying to compare Konsari's face to the face of a woman who has become a memory.

'Her Highness!'

Suddenly, a frail, withered old woman comes running out of the palace. She flings herself at Konsari's feet and begins to weep.

'Where have you been all these years, Your Highness? Who has kept you concealed and where? His Majesty has prepared to leave. I knew. I knew for sure … God Brahmaputra had not taken you away. Does God Brahmaputra ask for beautiful girls he sets eyes upon? Lies … everybody lied … that you were immersed in the Luit. For that reason, everything is in ruins here … Queen Mother had said to His Majesty, you have immersed Lakhimi, the goddess of wealth … in the river … you have invited a curse into your life. Queen Mother went away lamenting, Your Highness—'

The woman is besieged with sorrow. Konsari stands like a rock statue.

Chandraprabha! Queen Chandraprabha, who had been sacrificed to Brahmaputra! Everyone gathered there stands dumbfounded with astonishment.

Queen Chandraprabha, who had become a legend, has returned in person.

After some time, Konsari comes to life. She places her hand on the weeping woman's back, saying calmly, 'Get up, Bokuli. Don't cry.'

Walking beside Bokuli and in front of the dumbstruck onlookers, Konsari enters the palace. As Chandraprabha.

Inside the bed suite, Arimotto is sitting near Pratapchandra, who is lying with his eyes closed. Standing nearby are the royal medic and Prime Minister Sogor.

Chandraprabha stands in the doorway. She peers into the interior of the bedroom. Instantly, becoming still with endless awe, once again.

Everything is the same.

Every object is exactly where Chandraprabha had left it. As they were. Only their colour and sparkle have faded.

The colours of the vibrant paintings by skilled artists have faded, and the metal borders of the latticed ventilators have lost their gold-like lustre. The silk drape embroidered with gold and silver threads hanging from the door is tattered and worn. The beaded chains that hung from the vents above the doors have snapped, have become disorderly. The Tibetan carpet, which was designed with various motifs, has also become worn and faded. An ancient, colourless room. Ruins of a dazzling past. The corpse of a garden of love. A past. A painful past.

Yes. The past. Is there anything in the room that could be called the present? Is there anything here akin to life?

Only memories remain. Mere reminiscences.

One end of a silk scarf hangs from the mature cane chest, touching the floor. The way Chandraprabha had left it while leaving.

On the low ornate wooden table by the side of the bed still lies the silver girdle she wore around her waist. Chandraprabha had two girdles. She had considered wearing the silver one but changed her mind and had instead worn the gold girdle. The silver girdle had been left on the wooden table by her. Pratapchandra's body is still wrapped in the blanket imported from the Bhot hills with which Chandraprabha and Pratapchandra used to cover themselves while sleeping.

A faded, threadbare, colourful blanket.

On a gold-studded bedstead.

On the body of a mighty king.

Chandraprabha's eyes well up.

Silently wiping her tears, she goes inside.

Nobody sees Chandraprabha enter. Everybody's gaze is on Pratapchandra's face.

Suddenly, Pratapchandra's eyelids quiver. He pronounces very softly, 'Mahishi.'

Chandraprabha trembles.

From another birth on the other shore of a century, who is calling for Chandraprabha?

Pratapchandra?

The extremely powerful Mayamotto, who exiled his wife in an instant?

Is this the voice of Pratapchandra?

Chandraprabha's own Pratapchandra's voice?

She is standing still.

Her feet appear to be sinking into the floor, as if Chandraprabha is slowly being buried under the heavy earth of sorrow that she has borne with bated breath. Bokuli, standing at the doorway, sobs loudly. Startled, Arimotto, Sogor and the royal medic turn around together. Arimotto sees his mother after eighteen long years. The royal medic and Chief Minister Sogor see Chandraprabha after what seems like an age. All three of them look at her speechlessly. A tempest of sorrow is wreaking havoc on Arimotto.

Years ago, Arimotto had left his mother back in Gobha. The mother who is now wearied by age, withered by self-neglect and pale with sorrow. How did Arimotto manage to live away from this mother in Baidyagarh? His mother has been wasted by eighteen years of agony. No, not eighteen years. Much longer than that. From before Arimotto saw the world until today, his goddess-like mother withered bit by bit, by the hidden torment of countless days and nights. Forgetting his mother's forbiddance, Arimotto killed his own father – to pour fuel on the inferno of torment.

He kneels down in front of his mother. So do the royal medic and Chief Minister Sogor. 'Our obeisance, Your Highness, the Queen,' they both speak in tones laden with grief, touching their foreheads to the ground. Arimotto is silent. He is sitting with his hands over his face. His murderous hands are drenched in torrential tears.

After standing like a statue for a while, Konsari lays her hand on Arimotto's head. 'Please rise, Chief Minister. Rise, Royal Medic.' Sogor and the royal medic rise and, without a word, go out. They know there is no need to say anything. Chandraprabha, who has returned after one birth, is not the vivacious adolescent queen drifting away in the river.

This Chandraprabha is made of burnt gold. A mature woman with the wisdom of life. Perhaps a completely unique person. A one-of-a-kind individual. It is not necessary to open up one's heart before this Chandraprabha. There is no need for undue formality. Clutching one of his mother's hands with both his tear-stained ones, Arimotto rests his head upon it. Then he breaks down in silent tears. Chandraprabha is quiet. She is merely collecting the river of tears flowing from Arimotto's broken heart, with both her hands. A few distressed moments pass. Pratapchandra's eyelids quiver once again. In a very feeble voice, he again mumbles, 'Mahishi.'

Arimotto rises. Whatever was to be said has been said. Whatever was to be learnt has been learnt. Is there any language more powerful than touch? What can be more soothing than a mother's touch? Where can such a haven be found? Leaving his mother behind in the bedroom, Arimotto goes out with steady steps. There is no one in the room now. Chandraprabha advances towards Pratapchandra.

Resting both of his arms on his stomach, Pratapchandra is sleeping. His bare chest is covered with a thin cotton cloth, and the worn-out blanket lies over it. Pratapchandra has become as worn-out as the blanket. His once crimson-bright, gold-tinted complexion has paled, and his tall, muscular physique has shrunk. His previously smooth skin is now wrinkled, and his face bears the marks of age and persistent torment.

Chandraprabha places her trembling, shrunken right hand on Pratapchandra's forehead. His eyelids quiver once again, and slowly he opens his eyes and looks at Chandraprabha standing close by. His pallid eyes seem to sparkle with a few dots of light as he gazes at her. Then he says, 'I have grown exhausted waiting for you, Mahishi.'

'I know,' Chandraprabha replies calmly, tears drowning her eyes.

'There is so much to tell you. But there isn't enough energy to speak, Mahishi.'

'It is not necessary, *Aryyaputra*. This room has said everything on your behalf.'

'Aryyaputra. Son of Aryans! You have chosen this word for my peace of mind, haven't you, Mahishi?'

'If this word has given you peace, I am satisfied, Aryyaputra. It is not for your sake. I have used this word because I still have the authority to do so. I am not the wife of the king of Gobha, Sadhukumar. Yet I am not Chandraprabha either. My name is Konsari. Mother of Arimotto, the adopted son of Sadhukumar.'

Chandraprabha's words seem to act like a life-infusing mantra, and, instantly, Pratapchandra is revived back to life. Chandraprabha still belongs to Pratapchandra! He is still Queen Chandraprabha's Aryyaputra! Pratapchandra has not lost anything. Like coral on the seafloor, all the wealth belonging to Pratapchandra is restored.

The last rays of the sinking sun illuminate Pratapchandra's face. Lifting a tired hand, he places it over Chandraprabha's. He says slowly, 'You have set foot in this house. All my sins have been atoned for, Mahishi.'

Tears are blurring the scene in front of her. Chandraprabha takes Pratapchandra's hand in both of hers and stays in that position for a long time. Then, in a solemn tone laden with deep sorrow, she says, 'Misfortune, Aryyaputra!'

Streams of tears flow from the corners of Pratapchandra's eyes, and Konsari's chest is wet from the flood of her silent tears. The tears wash away all arrogance, every resentment and the loneliness of accursed births.

TWENTY-EIGHT

'Any evil deed committed unknowingly is not considered a sin in the religious scriptures. It is merely an offence deserving mercy,' says Acharya Prabhakar, seated on a grass mat. Arimotto, Konsari and Sogor are also seated on similar grass mats in front of him, all of them grief-stricken and worried.

'But, Acharya, I have not yet been liberated from the wound of guilt,' Arimotto says tiredly.

'It is natural, Arimotto. The mind does not always follow logic. The mind is also ruled by emotion, and emotion is governed by incidents. Therefore, incidents need to be controlled. An incident that is not under one's control can lead to a misfortune. An incident that is under one's control, and yet occurs, is an offence. You have committed an offence by ignoring your mother's prohibition, Arimotto. If the question of overall welfare had been involved, then disobeying your mother's prohibition might have warranted forgiveness. But you have disobeyed your mother to satisfy your imperial ambitions. This offence deserves to be punished.'

'I have no reservations about accepting punishment, Gurudev. On the contrary, I long for punishment in exchange for peace of mind. But who will punish me? Who is the adjudicator, Acharya? My father, in order to compound my guilt, convened the royal assembly and entrusted this kingdom to me. Acknowledging his murderer as his son, my father divulged every detail of his past to society and bestowed the grave responsibility of the kingdom on my shoulders. The burning pyre of guilt is constantly searing me, Acharya. I need to be punished. Perhaps, only punishment can grant me a little peace.'

'The actual authority for giving punishment is in God's hands, Arimotto. How could men, flaunting wisdom after learning only half the truth, have such power? Even so, you've been punished enough already. Acting upon late King Pratapchandra's command, they have acknowledged you as the ruler of the kingdom and have come to pay their respects to you. They did not, however, attend the ritual you had arranged and performed for the peace of your father's soul. For a judicious king like you, this is punishment enough.'

'This punishment has multiplied the torment in my mind twofold, Gurudev. Every penance directive you have prescribed has gone unfulfilled. Along with the subjects, the gods refused to cooperate with me. Every ritual became a disaster with one flaw or another. They remained incomplete. What should I do now, Acharya? What is my duty?'

'I've known you since you were a child. I have heard everything from your dear mother. Leaving aside the scriptures – I can tell you from my discretion – apart from disobeying your mother's forbiddance, you are not guilty of any other offence. You are merely a victim of your circumstances. You are a king. Royal commitments also include warfare. In a battle between two kings, if one of them is killed by his opponent, it is not considered an offence. Would you have harmed the late King Pratapchandra if you had known him to be your father? There's also the fact that your father has not accused you. The life that he had led prior to his death was almost identical to death. It is true that the wounds you inflicted had pushed him to death, but his reunion with his wife and son after many years apart allowed him to pass on to the other side with complete peace of mind. It should be regarded as good fortune indeed. Clear your mind of any feelings of guilt, son.'

'The acharya is right, Your Majesty. The officers of the kingdom have divided into groups in the absence of the late king. The law and order of the kingdom are in peril. I am an old man myself and unable to supervise all areas. It will augur well for everybody if His Highness focuses on the administration of the kingdom, forsaking all hesitation,' the chief minister said.

'I have no desire to rule a kingdom that was acquired by killing my father, Chief Minister. I've decided to leave this kingdom and return to Baidyagarh.'

'How can it be, Your Majesty? A kingdom without a king cannot continue to exist. It would be shattered to pieces. Please withdraw this unjust resolution, Your Majesty. Please do not let gloom and darkness descend upon King Pratapchandra's vast kingdom.' Chief Minister Sogor becomes restless.

'I think the chief minister has spoken rightly, Arimotto. To abandon this kingdom in these critical times would be a decision that will go against the rules prescribed for a king. It would not be proper for you to leave this kingdom until its state of affairs is stable. Moreover, if you could undertake a few tasks for the welfare of the people, it will not only bring you peace of mind but also restore peace and confidence in the minds of the people.'

'Even I believe the acharya's decision is appropriate, Arimotto,' Chandraprabha says.

'But, Maah—'

Interrupting Arimotto, the acharya says, 'If you live in this palace, self-reproach will torment you all the time. All of us know it. If you leave for Baidyagarh, you can escape from the pain. But escaping is useless. One who has the courage to face the truth and live with it is called a hero. Give up any thought of running away, Arimotto. The chief minister is a wise and experienced person. You should follow his advice. As a guru, I would like to recite a few sentences from the scriptures here, Arimotto.'

'Please go ahead, Acharya.'

'You are not a common man, Arimotto. You are a king. Your personality should reflect majestic traits. According to the Shukra principles, just as God Indra, king of the gods and the ruler of Amaravati, provides safety to the gods, a king too must protect his subjects. While a king should be as merciful as fragrant breeze, he should, at the same time, rule his subjects with rigidity. Much like the sun dispels darkness, a king should aim to remove the shadows of fear and establish truth and faith. A king should administer justice for crimes just like the god of death, Yama. Like fire, a king should cleanse all that is unclean and take pleasure in all the wealth that rightly belongs to him. Like the moon which bestows happiness, it is essential for a king to possess the qualities that fascinate one and all. Similarly, a king should safeguard the wealth and properties of the kingdom like Kuber, the king of wealth. Putting into practice the sacred ethics and principles incorporated in the Vedas, Smritis and other religious scriptures, he should rule his subjects judiciously and attend to activities aimed at the welfare of the people. You are the nurturer of your subjects, Arimotto. You would be able to command your subjects' loyalty and respect only when you are ordained with the majestic qualities of a king. The scriptures say – a king's beauty should be more than that of Manmoth, the god of beauty. It is not merely physical beauty, Arimotto, but mental as well. A king's strength and valour should be on a par with the strength and valour of the god of war, Skanda. He should be like Bhimsen in warfare, like Kritanta in fury, like Arjun in fame and like Dabanol in enmity. Like the pure breeze blowing from the Moloy mountains, a king should be chaste and righteous. Similarly, a king's diligence in work, tolerance, adaptability and generosity should be on a par with the universally venerable king Shibir. Humility towards religious gurus is also included as one of the virtues of a king. Like Yudhisthir, the epitome of piety, he should be truthful as well as humble and affectionate to his subjects. He should take a dip in the surging river of science and acquire the powerful notions of verse, speech, debate, logic, scriptures and philosophy of millions of years. This is the ideology of the Aryans, son. The guilt of killing your father is tormenting you. You are moribund with sorrow, but you cannot afford to drift away in the tide of grief like common people. Royal ethics does not acknowledge such weakness. Remove the robe of grief, son. Control yourself like a gallant king. Drowning yourself in sorrow, standing indecisively on the crossroads of sin and virtue, just and unjust, you have no right to shove the subjects of your father's kingdom, the people of Komota, towards uncertainty.'

Acharya Prabhakar concludes his speech and looks at Arimotto. 'I am your guru, your acharya, in the position of your father. I have said what I have realized as appropriate with my little knowledge of the scriptures. The ultimate decision is yours.'

Arimotto stays silent. He continues to sit with his head down, bewildered in that moment. All of them sit quietly for some time. Then Konsari speaks, 'Arimotto, after everything that the Acharya has said, there can be no scope for any apprehension. Follow his instructions and do your work. The chief minister is always available. Bring your family from Baidyagarh and stay for a while. You can make a decision about where you want to stay at any time.'

Before Arimotto can say anything, Samol comes in and stands before them. 'Deoraja, I have to tell you something.'

Everybody turns to look at him.

'Come, sit down, Samol,' Konsari says.

'It's the deoraja who has to get up, Ayong. A barika has arrived from Baidyagarh with a message.'

'Call him here, Samol,' Arimotto says, raising his head to look.

'But it's—'

'Never mind, go.'

Samol goes away. After a while, he returns with a barika, visibly exhausted from the journey. The barika had accompanied Arimotto from Gobha. He is very, very loyal, as close as a relative.

'What tidings have you brought, barika?' Arimotto is now alert, noticing his devastated appearance.

The barika waits for a moment uneasily. Then he says, 'I have brought tidings from Baidyagarh, Dcoraja. They are not favourable.'

Arimotto stiffens. Looking sharply at the barika for a second, he says anxiously, 'Why, what has happened?'

'Fingua Kunwar has seized possession of Baidyagarh, Deoraja. It has been ten days.'

Arimotto stares at the barika's tired and glum face. He then stands up. 'Where is my family, barika? Have you brought their news or not? Tell me and tell me quickly.'

'Yes, Deoraja. I've come bearing very bad news. How to say it, Deoraja … I am afraid.'

'Don't be afraid, barika, come on, speak quickly.'

'Her Highness has taken the side of Fingua Kunwar, Deoraja. She opened the gate of the fort at midnight, claiming it was your command. And—'

The barika touches his head to the ground and breaks down.

'I don't know where Ratnasinha, Lokhaitora and the queen are, Deoraja. I don't know anything else – I somehow managed to escape to bring you the news. Our Gobha was the best, Deoraja. Why did you leave such a lovely Gobha and come to Baidyagarh, Deoraja? Why did you come here?'

Isolated from his relatives, family and society for eighteen long years, the barika topples every barricade of protocol and becomes the re pasari of the samadi again. Arimotto's insides are being crushed by the heart-rending weeping.

TWENTY-NINE

Inside a room in a remote corner of Baidyagarh's palace, Ratnavali sits on an ordinary wooden seat. At one end of the room, Lokhaitora is seated on an ordinary bed. The clothes on both women are filthy. Their hairdos have become dishevelled. It is apparent that their days and nights have passed with neglect and anxiety.

Ratnavali's face shows evident signs of unease and discomfort. She frequently rises from her seat to peer through the room's porthole. She repeatedly approaches the door to place her ear against it in an effort to hear the sounds coming from outside.

There is no way to go outside to find out what is happening.

The door has been bolted from outside. Two armed guards are standing outside the door.

From what she can see through the porthole and the sounds she could hear by eavesdropping, Ratnavali is able to piece together to a certain extent what is going on outside.

She is feeling ill at ease.

Very ill at ease.

Fingua's strange behaviour has driven her to the pit of anxiety. She is devastated, trapped in a whirlpool of conflicting thoughts.

This is not how things were meant to be.

Shortly after Arimotto had embarked on his expedition, Ratnavali had been ecstatic about the prospect of a happy conjugal life. Despite her sadness at learning of Arimotto's death at the hands of Pratapchandra, the hope of gaining freedom from captivity and marrying Fingua Kunwar had fuelled Ratnavali's sparkling exhilaration.

After eighteen years of playing the faithful wife charmed by Arimotto's good looks and qualities, Ratnavali had heaved a sigh of relief on receiving the news of her husband's death.

Now she properly realizes how irritating and unbearable it is to be caught in the clutches of a non-Aryan king migrating from Gobha in the north banks.

Arimotto may have been a hero. Maybe he was handsome. However, he was no match for Fingua Kunwar, who deserved the title of Panch Gourheswar. He was a master at the art of satisfying women completely. He possessed all essential qualities. What did Arimotto have?

An unsuccessful king submerged in joo, sighing over some Laloong queen named Gangavati. A man with no ambition. An ordinary man who was getting older and living a happy life with his wife and children. A regular man.

Fingua Kunwar isn't like that. He dreamed of a vast empire and had showered Ratnavali with his love. He had remained unmarried for so long solely because of her, spending days tormented by the sorrow of not having her as his own.

Why shouldn't Ratnavali have stood by him? Why shouldn't she have supported him?

Soon after receiving news of Arimotto's death, she ordered that the fort's main gates be opened for Fingua.

Noticing the regular visitor, the guards and officers stationed at the main gate did not suspect any foul play. Being unaware of Arimotto's death, there was no question of any suspicion.

Very easily, almost without any resistance, Fingua Kunwar had taken possession of Baidyagarh. The palace interiors had appeared ghastly, with blood and dead bodies.

Following that, Fingua had entered the palace. Ratnasinha had fought with a fistful of soldiers. Ratnavali had told her daughter to stay inside, as she had impatiently waited outside for Fingua in the parlour. After waiting for years, she had boldly embraced him. He had also embraced Ratnavali, but there was no warmth in the touch. No evidence of mind-sweeping passion. At that very moment, Lokhaitora had come to stand in the doorway.

Her daughter's wounded look is still haunting Ratnavali.

What did those eyes lack? There was disgust, shock, disrespect, despair. When he noticed her daughter, Fingua Kunwar released Ratnavali from his embrace and laughed quietly. Icy – a terrifying sound.

Before Ratnavali could react, an officer and some soldiers entered, carrying Ratnasinha as a captive.

'Keep him confined. Do not let him go unless I say so.'

Ratnavali was astounded when she heard Fingua's command. Looking at her captive son's astonished and disrespectful eyes, she said, 'What are you saying, Kunwar? You are going to keep my son imprisoned?'

'It is necessary. Ratnasinha is not a small boy. He is a youth skilled in warfare. He has to be imprisoned temporarily. Don't worry. After everything comes to order, I shall release him.'

'Please free him, Kunwar. I shall explain everything to him. He will understand.'

'Understand? What will I understand, mother? What will you explain? What will you explain about this traitor, who pretended to be our father's friend before stabbing him in the back? I have understood. Everything is clear to me now. These soldiers sneered at me when they told me about you. You don't have a weapon with you, do you? Take one from Fingua. Stab me in my chest. Stab Lokhaitora's chest.'

'Do you hear, Ratnavali? Your son's words? Am I going to free this son? With what faith?' Fingua said.

'But—'

'Later. Tell me whatever you have to say, but later. You are unfamiliar with the rules and customs of warfare. I am busy right now. Go. Go inside. Take Lokhaitora with you. When I'm free, I shall come to you.'

The soldiers forcibly dragged Ratnasinha outside. After commanding an officer to place the queen and Lokhaitora in the same room, Fingua left without a glance at Ratnavali.

Since then, both mother and daughter were in the same room almost like captives.

Fingua Kunwar had locked up Ratnasinha somewhere inside the fort. Ratnavali had no idea where. In the previous twelve days, Fingua had entered this room only once. Today. But there was neither the preparation nor the appropriate situation to enquire about her son.

Fingua arrived with two pieces of shocking news.

The information Fingua Kunwar had received from his spies was incorrect. Arimotto had not been killed in the battle against Pratapchandra. It was the old king who had been killed instead. Arimotto was on his way back. He could arrive at any moment. He had ascended to the throne of Pratapchandra's kingdom. Not by winning the battle, but by virtue of being the legitimate son of Pratapchandra. Arimotto was not the son of the king of Gobha. In reality, he was the son of Pratapchandra. Arimotto was not a Tiwasha. He was an Aryan. He was the descendant of the Aryan–Kshatriya King Dharmapal.

Astounded, Ratnavali took in the worried and animated expression of Fingua Kunwar. She had even forgotten to ask about Ratnasinha.

'Please don't feel bad about my keeping both of you confined in one room in this manner, Ratnavali. These are dangerous times. I chose this course with your security in mind. Don't worry about Ratnasinha. He has been taken care of appropriately. We shall abandon this fort and depart today itself. I don't have the power to fight Arimotto. We have to consider self-defence. We shall go away either to the kingdom of Koch or to Karnapur, taking with us all of Arimotto's money and wealth. I'll take refuge there, build up a strong army and then return.'

Fingua Kunwar left without affording Ratnavali the opportunity to speak. He left Ratnavali drowning in an ocean of anxiety, alarm and bewilderment.

Ratnavali is aware that Fingua Kunwar is currently snooping around every nook and cranny of the palace. He is siphoning out of the fort all of Arimotto's treasures, every weapon he can find. Fingua Kunwar is getting impatient. He is working hard to locate the treasures carefully hidden in the palace's secured and secret chambers and to flee Baidyagarh as soon as possible.

What should she do now?

Should she wait for Arimotto and risk death or should she leave with Fingua Kunwar before he arrives?

Will he accept Ratnavali after his return? Is it possible?

Doesn't Ratnavali know what kind of an individual Arimotto is? Will he, who abandoned a vast kingdom like Gobha over a slight resentment, be able to forgive Ratnavali?

Never. Not a chance.

'I shall go away. I shall flee with Kunwar. What will I do when I return to this place with the person I've waited so long for – the person for whom I had cursed my spouse by remaining here? Apart from contempt and death, what else am I going to receive here? How could I live here while enduring the disdainful looks of my son, daughter and husband? I shall go away. I'll live with Fingua Kunwar, if I can. If I have to die, so be it.'

Arriving at a final decision after much deliberation, Ratnavali turns to face her daughter, who is sitting motionless on the bed some distance away.

Holding both her knees, Lokhaitora is resting her head on them.

The girl has changed so drastically in these few days!

Her full-grown body has thinned from not eating. Her face, as bright as the moon, has turned pale. She hasn't even slept properly. She has been sitting silently with a stoic expression.

Despite her best efforts, Ratnavali has failed to extract a single word from her daughter.

When Fingua's soldiers dragged away her brother, in front of them, Lokhaitora had run in a frenzy from the doorway. She had begged them not to take away Ratnasinha, crying. And then looking at her mother, who was standing nearby, she sobbed and said, 'This is who you are? So wicked? So ruthless? If you had nourished such sins in your mind, why did you give birth to us? Why did you raise us? Why didn't you strangle us to death as soon as we were born?'

Ratnavali lacked the courage to look her daughter in the eyes.

Not even now.

Her heart starts racing when she notices Lokhaitora sitting like a ghost. Her heart pounds when she thinks of her son being held captive somewhere. Her selfish ambitions weaken. She feels like she's about to become a mother once again, overcome by the urge to hold Lokhaitora in her arms. Thrown behind like a nightmare, her relationship with Fingua and the past, she wishes to return to the old family life, which was filled with peace and happiness. But she has been instrumental in blocking that path of return. She has exposed her foul interior to her son and daughter.

How could she live here?

If she lives with Fingua Kunwar, at least there is no fear of being torn apart by sharp, hateful looks. Ratnavali has given up hopes of a blissful conjugal life with Fingua. His distastefully rude behaviour and irritating face gleaming with greed have dashed those dreams.

His eyes no longer radiate the rainbow of love; instead, they exude a killer instinct and the irresistible avarice of a mean creature for trivial wealth. Ratnavali despises Kunwar.

Yet she has decided to go away with him, fleeing the venomous glares of her loved ones.

When she thinks of Arimotto, Ratnavali's heart twinges somewhere. Arimotto, the descendant of the legendary king Dharmapal, son of the valiant Pratapchandra. Ratnavali had looked down with contempt on this very Arimotto. She had felt frustrated upon comparing him with Fingua Kunwar, the owner of one fort and four villages, one who claimed to belong to the royal family of Gour but had no lineage or ancestry. Having been carried away by Fingua's sensuous touch, she had dismissed the self-assured Arimotto's sense of responsibility and affection, his magnanimity.

Ratnavali had been blind. Because she was blind, she had failed to notice Arimotto. She had evaluated him based on his domain and judged him by his lineage. Now there is no means of correcting the situation. Consoling every bit of remorse in her heart, Ratnavali must leave, for the sake of survival.

Startling Ratnavali out of her whirlpool of thoughts, Fingua Kunwar barges in. She stands up fearfully.

'I thought you had forgotten all about me, Kunwar,' Ratnavali says with resentment.

'I've not forgotten. Everything must be wound up, and the fort abandoned before Arimotto's arrival. I don't have much time,' he says somewhat carelessly, looking around.

'I, too, am prepared, Kunwar. It would be best to leave as soon as possible.'

'Correct. Ratnavali, do one thing: please remove all jewellery from your body.'

'My jewellery? Why, Kunwar?' Ratnavali asks, surprised.

'There's a reason. Come on. Remove them.'

Staring at Fingua Kunwar in astonishment, Ratnavali removes her ornaments one by one.

Wrapping them in a bundle, he hangs it from his waist before saying, 'Lokhaitora, get up and come here.'

'Why are you calling her? Let her keep her jewellery, Kunwar,' Ratnavali says uneasily.

Fingua is not paying attention to her.

'Lokhaitora, listen to what I've said, come, get up.' Fingua repeats in a voice of command.

'What kind of a person are you? You are coveting the ornaments of a little girl?' Ratnavali says, annoyed and terrified.

'Little girl? Lokhaitora?' Fingua looks at Ratnavali. Then he begins to laugh.

'Of course she is a little girl, Kunwar. She is my daughter.'

'Your daughter. Not mine. To you, this almost grown-up young woman might appear as a little girl, not to me.'

'Your words are shocking, Kunwar. She is like your daughter.' Ratnavali shivers inwardly. What does Fingua Kunwar intend to do?

'She is like a daughter. But she's not my daughter, is she?' Fingua Kunwar looks at Lokhaitora. 'Get up before I force you up.'

Clutching Fingua Kunwar's hand, Ratnavali begs, 'Leave her alone, Kunwar. Come, let us leave. I am feeling awful. Terrified.'

'Why wouldn't you? With the kind of deed you've done, you're bound to be scared.'

'I don't understand what you're saying, Kunwar. I don't want to, anyway. Come on, let us go.'

Fingua fixes his gaze on Ratnavali. Then through a piercing smile, he asks, 'Where do you want to go? With whom do you want to go? With me? Will you accompany me? You expect me to rely on and bring with me a woman who can betray her own husband? I am not such a fool, Ratnavali. I am bringing Lokhaitora with me. I will settle down with her. King Arimotto would never kill his son-in-law, after all. What do you have, Ratnavali? What am I to do with your aging, wasted body?'

Before her startled eyes, the weapon in Fingua's hand flashes. Ratnavali's blood stains the earth of Baidyagarh, turning it scarlet.

THIRTY

'It was noon when we had arrived at Baidyagarh. Inside the fort, decayed dead bodies lay scattered all around. Fingua Kunwar had fled with the entire treasure of the kingdom, and taken Lokhaitora, too. There was no sentinel at the fort. No officer, maid or servant. There was absolutely nothing. We were standing surrounded by the stench of the dead bodies in the vast fort. I cannot put into words what our feelings were, Jokanko,' Konsari says, heaving a sigh after returning from her past life.

Jokanko, listening spellbound while reclining on a bed in Konsari's room inside Gobha's palace, seems to wake up from his grave.

He looks at Ratnasinha, who is asleep nearby. Two teardrops are stuck to the corners of his eyes. Xunzira is absent. Perhaps she has gone to the kitchen quietly. To prepare food for Jokanko and Ratnasinha. Jokanko looks at Abi Konsari with fatigued eyes.

It is daybreak.

Morning light filters in through the bamboo lattices, falling upon Konsari's face. She resembles the pallid sculpture of a woman from an ancient temple. Jokanko stares at Abi Konsari as she sits on the bed near him, laden with centuries of unrevealed suffering.

Within this feeble-bodied woman, seemingly happy and tranquil are concealed so many words. Countless epitaphs. How does she remain so composed with such a burden in her heart? What kind of power does she wield?

Yet Jokanko has not succeeded.

His soul has been shattered by his mother's grief. The recent events have trapped him in a whirlpool without a way out.

He had come to the palace of Gobha in search of his roots. He had come to find Abi Konsari.

But what a bereaved past it had been She had introduced him to the pasts of herself, his afa, Sadhukumar Azo, Pratapchandra, Xunzira Asi, Lokhaitora, Jokanko and Ratnavali. Whose suffering should he let go of and whose pain should he accept? The grief and torment of self-reproach have piled up like a mountain inside him.

He has not slept the whole night. When Konsari wanted to pause halfway through, he grew agitated. 'Tell me, tell me everything, Abi. Please don't get up in the middle. I will rest later. I will rest only after hearing the entire story.'

Konsari had turned over the pages of the past, without any thought of rest for the night.

'Are you feeling poorly, Syu?' she asks, worried by his pale face.

'I am struggling to keep going, abi. I am not ill. My heart is going to burst.'

'I can imagine, Jokanko. Is it possible to have a human heart that does not throb with the pain of loved ones? We felt the same way you do now, Syu. Our hearts were broken as we witnessed Baidyagarh's plight and Arimotto's anguish.'

'And then what happened, Abi?'

'Let me explain briefly. How long shall I dwell on my sorrows? Ratnavali was discovered within the palace. Her lifeless body lay in a pool of sticky blood. The spear of Fingua Kunwar had pierced her through the chest and back. We also discovered Ratnasinha, who was imprisoned in a remote part of the fort. He told us everything. Rage, grief, and despair had changed him and he'd grown extremely frail. His mother's actions had so hurt him so deeply that he would keep punching his forehead and sobbing while he spoke about her. 'Mother has been killed,' he kept saying. It's fine, Father. It's fantastic. Nobody can be as unfortunate as someone who has a mother like her. Come on, let's go. Fingua Kunwar has taken away our Lokhaitora with plans to ruin her. We have to look for her and bring her back. We must hack Fingua to pieces and drink his blood."'

'Ratnasinha had gone insane with fury and distress. As had Arimotto. They both went to find Fingua and Lokhaitora with Samol and some soldiers while the acharya and I kept watch over Ratnavali's dead body.

'People who were working in various jobs in the capital had been hiding around in the surrounding villages. They soon returned on hearing that we had arrived. With their help, the corpses were shrouded and arranged in rows in a field that was cleaned up. The maids and attendants also brought us water to drink while cleaning the interior of the palace. They gave us milk and fruits. We also covered Ratnavali's body with a chador and placed it on a mat outside the room where we'd found her.

'No one recognized me. Everybody kept staring in awe. The people were astonished to hear that I was Arimotto's mother. And why wouldn't they be? If the king had a mother, wouldn't she have visited Baidyagarh at least once in these past eighteen years? But they did not know how unfortunate their king's mother was.' Konsari smiled weakly.

'Please don't say that, Abi. My heart aches.' Jokanko's voice choked with pain.

'What should I do, Jokanko – some people are born into this world solely to suffer. But never assume that I have accomplished nothing in this life. I've achieved many things that others strive for. I had Arimotto. I have Gobha. And you. Tell me, Jokanko, what do I not have?'

'That's true, Abi.'

'I had these thoughts while sitting in front of Ratnavali's body at Baidyagarh. For hours, Acharya Prabhakar Bidyanidhi consoled me with various philosophies from the scriptures. I have never met anyone as well-versed in the scriptures and patient. While your azo is not as knowledgeable about religious doctrines, his wisdom and patience are incomparable. During times of distress or peril, if he is close, I draw courage from him. And fortitude. You've probably heard how he has taken over the karam arrangements. He has not cried a single tear. Or broken down. But I know, as do you, how much pain he is in. Has he uttered a single word against you? He understands that you are not to blame. Your actions were entirely unintentional. You must go to him, Jokanko, so that your mental agony is relieved. Your azò arrived at Baidyagarh just as I was about to fall apart from sorrow, sitting by the corpse of Ratnavali. We had sent a barika to him with the news hours before we left Pratappur for Baidyagarh. Arimotto and the others returned shortly after the king of Gobha arrived. With Lokhaitora.'

'They found her? Was Fingua killed?' Jokanko grows excited.

'Fingua could not be found. He was not in Finguagarh. He'd vanished into thin air. Lokhaitora had died by the time they found her. She had ended her life by jumping into a pond near a Brahmin family's home close to Finguagarh. She had somehow evaded Fingua's clutches and taken refuge with this family. But she had left a detailed letter addressed to her father. I am sure you can imagine its contents. Do not ask me about the unknowable parts, Syu. I do not have the energy to narrate them.'

'You don't have to, Abi. I understand.'

Konsari remains still for some time. Jokanko is also silent, speechless from the unfathomable grief of learning about the tragic lives of the previously unknown, unheard-of relatives.

'Syu, I am sure you can imagine Arimotto's state of mind. It was just before sundown. Ratnavali and Lokhaitora's dead bodies were lying on the palace courtyard. Arimotto, Ratnasinha, I, Samol, the king of Gobha and the acharya sat on the ground. The preparations for the funeral were ongoing. Rows and rows of funeral pyres were set up on a field across the palace. Sons and relatives flocked to the overflowing ground to light the pyres, as thousands more arrived, the sound of their cries rocking Baidyagarh. But Arimotto had not cried. Neither had Ratnasinha. I only noticed their eyes turning blood-red. At one point, all the funeral pyres caught fire simultaneously. Everything reduced to ashes. Ratnavali's body was consumed by fire. Lokhaitora's did as well.

'That night, I went to Arimotto's chambers after talking to Deoraja and the acharya. He was sitting with his head bowed and hands on his forehead. When I stroked the top of his head, he slowly looked up. There was not one teardrop in his eyes. His blood-red eyes raised themselves to mine. "Everything is over for me, Maah. What should I do now?" he said to me. I sat down beside him, with no answers to his question. But I still had to tell him many things.

'We knew that Ratnavali's betrayal and his grief over Lokhaitora's death would destroy him completely, just like killing his father had done. Even at the time, we had noticed the foreboding of destruction in his eyes. The same anguish had caused Ratnavali to lose her mind. Tell me, Syu, is there a son who could stand seeing his own mother in that state? Which brother would not become insane if this happened to his sister? We sent the acharya to Ratnasinha. I went to meet my son. We had concluded that Arimotto might be relieved if we told him about you and Gangavati. Ratnavali had betrayed him. She had deceived him for eighteen long years. We decided to tell Arimotto about Gangavati and his other son in order to relieve him of the agony of this deception and Lokhaitora's death.

'"Why did Ratnavali do it, Maah?" he asked me. "What did I deprive her of? What did she desire? What else did she want after giving birth to Ratnasinha and Lokhaitora?'

'"Is it easy to understand what goes on inside someone else's head? She must have had some unfulfilled desire that you couldn't figure out."

'"Perhaps. But why didn't she tell me, Maah? Would I have bound her with shackles? No, Maah. I understand now. Every woman is the same. Greedy. Despite living a life of abundance, their greed never stops. The greed for an empire outweighs the husband. The greed to become the queen of a vast, powerful empire is greater than the children."

'"It is but natural for you to feel this way. Because you are not aware of many other things," I said. Arimotto looked at me on hearing these words.'

"What else is there to know, Maah? What else do I not know? Tell me. Give me all the grief that I am yet to earn. Before leaving this world let me learn what other misery Fa Mahadeo has in store for me," he said.

'"What I'm about to tell you relates to sadness as well. But those words will prove to you that your analysis is incorrect, Arimotto," I replied.

'Arimotto looked at me after I finished. He did not say anything.

'Then I told him about Gangavati. Eighteen years ago, what had made Gangavati change her decision of accompanying Arimotto to Komota – why she had not arrived despite making a promise to him. I recounted everything one by one. The things which I recounted to you, I told him too. He had heard some of it in Pratappur, but he was not aware of my life in Gobha after I returned from Mayapur. Who would tell him? Who knows about it except for me? Then I had told him about you.

'I said, "Gangavati could have related everything to you. When I learned that she was about to become a mother, I relieved her of all restrictions and asked her to contact you. But Gangavati didn't tell you anything. You'd got married by then. She had realized that you married Ratnavali in retaliation for her betrayal. She must have been unhappy. But to her, your happiness was more important than her pain. She did not want to disrupt your life by telling you about her motherhood. She has spent these eighteen years thinking only about you, Arimotto. She is nurturing her son, without the father's identity, all by herself."

'I cannot erase from my mind the sorrow-filled eyes of Arimotto as he listened to me, Syu. He continued to stare at me before bursting into tears. He shed many tears. For Lokhaitora. For his dead father. For Gangavati. For you. Perhaps he had cried for Ratnavali also, Jokanko.

'I let him cry.

'I let him lighten the burden of his heart with tears.

'Then I told him, "You must forgive Ratnavali, Arimotto. Did you marry her out of love? Did you ask her what was in her mind before marrying? Did you give her the love she deserved after marriage? Ask yourself, Arimotto. You will find the answers."

'We remained in Baidyagarh until the karam was over. Afterwards, the king of Gobha returned. I had chosen to stay there for a few more days. I felt it would not be proper to return to Gobha leaving Arimotto and Ratnasinha in Baidyagarh.

'Gradually, Arimotto became stable. Then one day, he announced his decision in front of Acharya Prabhakar, me and Ratnasinha.

'He had initially told Ratnasinha about you and Gangavati. He had disclosed everything without concealing a single word. Ratnasinha was listening attentively. I did not notice any signs of anger or revulsion on his face. He seemed to have transformed in those few days. He was no more the pampered son of a king. He only asked one question after hearing everything, "What are you going to do now, Father?"

'In reply, Arimotto remained silent for a long time before saying, "My late father has left me the right to his kingdom. Then there's Komota. I have no desire to govern both these kingdoms. I want to free myself of the responsibilities of a king. I have given much thought to Acharyadev's words. I discovered that while I once had the qualities of a king, those qualities have faded now. I lack the mental strength to rule a kingdom. I don't have any peace of mind. There is no respite, either. I have discussed this with the acharya. I've decided to give charge of Komota to you, Ratnasinha. Samol will be in charge of my father's kingdom. Chief Minister Sogor is aging now. He requires help. After learning of my identity, the feudatory chiefs have resolved to remain loyal as before. Every challenge confronting the kingdom's administration has been resolved. Samol is capable of administering my father's kingdom. I could have given you this responsibility, Ratnasinha but you are inexperienced. It will be difficult for you to manage such a vast kingdom. Rule over Komota. Earn the experience. After that, you will be capable of ruling both the kingdoms from Komota itself, if you so wish. I shall return to Gobha, Ratnasinha. I shall go back to my native soil. I have decided to build a monastery there. I've requested the acharya to help me find twelve devout Brahmin families. I shall establish those Brahmins there. After fulfilling every responsibility for the people's welfare assigned by the acharya, I shall adopt a life of asceticism."

'Asceticism? What do you mean, Abi?' Jokanko asks in surprise.

'You have not understood, have you? We don't get to hear this word here. Asceticism means denouncing everything, freeing oneself from attachment to even one's family and going away to the woods in the name of God. I never thought, Jokanko, that he would take such a decision. His words had startled me. I said to him, "Please do not take such a decision. You have two children of your own, Arimotto. You have your ma and afa. Is this the age for asceticism? Go back to Gobha, Arimotto. I shall invite the chiefs of *daskhool-barokhool* and explain everything before them. Settle down to a family life with Gangavati, Arimotto."

'He told me, "Ma, when I was ignorant of all the facts, I was angry at everyone. I felt resentment towards everybody. The reasons for which you had forbidden Gangavati to marry me, I have come to understand them. Living eighteen years of my life in Komota, I have learned about Gobha's society. I have come to understand what it has given to you and me. I have realized what my afa had given me. I do not wish to gain Gangavati by giving up that identity, Maah. I know, even if my afa desires to bequeath the responsibility of Gobha to me, I won't feel entitled to take it up. I shall go back to Gobha. But I shall not accept responsibilities for Komota or Komoi–Boghora. Deoraja should confer it upon someone from the clan who rightly deserves it. I shall establish a hermitage in the Dhoumora hills and settle there. Please do not force me to change my decision, Maah. I'll feel hurt.'

'I became helpless after listening to him, Syu. I looked to the acharya for some solution.'

'"What is your opinion, Acharya?" I had asked.

'After sitting quietly for a long time, the acharya had said, "Arimotto is a mature man, Aai. He has experienced life's ups and downs. The primary emotions of grief having subsided, he has come to this decision after a lot of contemplation. If you forbid him, surely he will abandon this decision. You are Arimotto's mother. It is understandable that your son's desire to become an ascetic is unbearable for you. You are, however, also the mother of a valiant king. After a king lives through the prime of his life, he can decide to give up the right over his kingdom. He can free himself from every attachment and become a sage. Or he can delegate to his young son the right of ruling the kingdom and consider retirement. King Banamal Barman, after his son completed his education and attained adulthood, had delegated the authority over the kingdom to him and accepted retirement. Similarly, at his old age, King Joymal Barman had also given the responsibility of the kingdom to his son Bala Barman and turned to spirituality. There are various examples like this one. If this desire has been born in Arimotto's mind as well, you must logically decide if your interference, even if out of motherly concern, is correct. I am incapable of giving any opinion, Aai."

'I felt confused, Syu. I could not decide what to do next. Arimotto remained firm in his decision. After a few days, he returned to Gobha, having fulfilled all his obligations. Samol had also expressed a desire to accompany his king. He repeatedly requested Arimotto not to bequeath the responsibility of Pratappur to him. Arimotto had told him, "You have served me long enough, Samol. But I am not a king anymore – what will you do by living with a sage? Go, take over the reins of Pratappur, bring Xunzira Asi with you and live as a sovereign ruler. If you live there, I will know the responsibility passed on by my father has not been neglected."

'Samol wept a lot before leaving.

'Lying at Arimotto's feet, he sobbed uncontrollably. Arimotto wrapped him in his arms. He did not cry. Perhaps he had freed himself from all attachments already, Syu. After sending Samol off to Pratappur, Arimotto returned to Gobha with twelve pious Brahmin families and a few people skilled in constructing shrines. On his return, he visited Gangavati. Only once. I'm sure you can imagine what kind of a meeting it would have been after so many years. You can also imagine how deeply Gangavati would have been hurt when Arimotto revealed his decision to become a sage. She told me everything later on. For the first time, I saw her cry, Jokanko. Even after that, Gangavati would go to the Dhoumora hills occasionally to catch a glimpse of Arimotto from afar. She never made herself known. She did not want to attain happiness for herself by preventing Arimotto from fulfilling his wish, Jokanko. Until then, one of Arimotto's works had remained incomplete. The construction of a monastery. And it remained unfinished. Due to some flaws, the monastery had been lying half-done. He had been devastated about not being able to complete it. When I went to see him later, he told me, "I did not get God's mercy, Maah. I could not fulfil even a single directive of the penances Acharya had prescribed."

'"What can you do, Arimotto? Leave everything to God's will," I said.

'Then he told me, "That's what I have been doing, Maah. Please do not come again. Please also tell Deoraja not to come. I would like to stay here all alone."

'"But tell me, Jokanko, could we let him live in the Dhoumora hills on his own? We sent some bodyguards to set up villages around the hills and settle there. Arimotto was not aware of anything. We had made arrangements for his security and food very cleverly. The guards, under the guise of neighbouring villagers, helped him. They kept him safe. That is why Gangavati forbade you to attack any kingdom on the west. But you did not pay heed to her. Like Arimotto, you unknowingly killed your father, ignoring your mother's dictate. Misfortune, Jokanko. Nothing else," Konsari finishes, heaving a sigh.

Jokanko bows his head.

There is nothing to say.

All words have left him.

Only one question remained.

What would he do now? What *should* he do?

After a long time, Jokanko raises his head and looks at her. He speaks in a calm, grim voice, 'What should I do now, Abi?'

'What can I tell you, Jokanko? I am an ordinary woman without any knowledge of the scriptures. But, based on what I've seen and learnt in life, I can tell you one thing: it is pointless to adopt asceticism. Running away from life's calamities is wrong. Looking at the positive aspects of life, one should keep the feet firmly planted on the ground. Try to live like that, Jokanko.'

Konsari places her hand on Jokanko's head.

The sun is rising outside the window.

THIRTY-ONE

Morning.

The shrine of Goddess Basundhari, situated atop Basundhari Hills, is illuminated by an uncountable number of lamps. The south bank of the Borpani river echoes with the sound of khrums played by the panthais. Every year, before the advent of the Assamese spring festival, Bohag Bihu, people of various tribes pay homage at the Basundhari shrine collectively. The Tiwashas never celebrate Bohag Bihu without first worshipping Goddess Basundhari. Otherwise devastation in the shape of an epidemic is likely to befall the land, it is so believed. The ruler of Khola had bequeathed the management of the Basundhari shrine to the royal family of Sohori. Despite being a feudatory kingdom, it was granted the right of autonomy. Until now, Sohori has been carrying out the responsibility of organizing the annual Basundhari phuja. But Sohori is no longer the Sohori of the past. It has grown into a significant township located between the Kopili and Kolong rivers. All because of Jokanko. It had been quite some days before he shifted from Khola to this township. Jokanko did not wish to live in the deserted palace of Khola. Konsari had requested that he live either at Gobha or at Amsai Marjong, saying, 'Who else do we have, Jokanko? Your azo is aging. He cannot work like before. Come and live here. Let the king of Gobha relax. You are the only one who will have to look after this vast kingdom.'

Jokanko had understood Abi Konsari's feelings. He had shouldered every responsibility. But he refused to live at any of the palaces of Khola, Gobha, Kumoi or Boghora. He needed a new place to begin a new life, forgetting the past – a place without the ruins of his old memories. After a lot of contemplation, he had chosen Sohori.

Jokanko has built a fort in Sohori, with the help of skilled workers from Komota. The new capital has been built in the style of Baidyagarh.

After shifting to Sohori, it is for the first time that Jokanko has taken the initiative of organizing the Basundhari phuja. In comparison to previous years, Jokanko has made plans to celebrate the phuja with greater pomp and grandeur. He has also invited all those neighbouring rulers who have never attended the phuja before.

Special arrangements have been made for the kings to sit on one side of the shrine. In the midst of the kings, Jokanko, who has become famous as Jongal Bolohu, is seated on a special chair.

The religious ceremony has not yet begun. Panibhari Doloi, the priest in charge of carrying water, has gone to the Borpani river to get some. Five panthais, each playing a khrum, are leading Panibhari Doloi from the front.

Thousands of worshippers from various villages, sitting in the shrine-yard and watching Ma Basundhari, are occasionally stealing a glance at the gallant hero Jongal Bolohu in awe and admiration. Jongal Bolohu is clad in a thenus woven with muga silk. His upper torso is bare, and a silk shawl draped over his shoulders covers his fair-skinned, sturdy body.

'It appears as if the phurimoso god has descended from the sky, doesn't it?' one of the dolois sitting at a distance says.

'Exactly. Phurimoso. You are right. We are fortunate to have such a king.'

'Our Laloongs have never had such a gallant hero ever before, I dare say.'

'But Fa, Deoraja Arimotto was also a brave hero.'

'Was Sadhukumar Deoraja a lesser hero? I have heard Abi and Azo talking about him. But I have never seen a more valiant hero than Jongal Bolohu, I swear.'

'It seems when he runs, even the hurricane Bordoisila cannot keep up with him. They say, in a battle even the tiger will be defeated.'

'Can you see how he has grown the kingdom?'

'True. His cultivation at Kondoli can feed the people of seven kingdoms.'

'And the fort? Who has ever seen or heard of a fort like this? First a ditch, then a plinth as high as a hill, again a ditch, again a plinth – I bet even an ant can't creep into the capital.'

'A huge fort has been built, I would say. Everyone from our village has taken a look at it from outside. They were not allowed to enter, though.'

'Why? We were allowed.'

'Not anymore. It seems two or three Kochari kingdoms, which Deoraja had made his subsidiary by defeating them, are plotting against him.'

'What battle will these Kacharis fight against us? Do they have a valiant king like ours?'

'You are right. But King Bodosa of Dimabong is supposed to be very valiant, too.'

'Maybe, but he is a king who is of our fathers' age. He is old. How could he compete with our deoraja?'

'Hey, is our deoraja never going to marry?'

'It seems not. He is supposed to have said, because he killed his own afa mistakenly, that he is never going to marry.'

'You really are well informed, Doloi.'

'It's because the king's bhitor maji is from our village. He does say a few odd things. That is how I know. Sometimes I also get to enter the fort because of him.'

'Have you seen Abi Konsari?'

'No. She never comes here from Gobha, you see. Only Xunzira Abi lives here. She is quite aged. One day she called me and enquired about my afa. Said they were from the same village.'

'Her son has become the king of such a vast kingdom – wonder why she doesn't go?'

She doesn't want to leave her land. Even the deoraja does not let her, they say. She goes now and then. Do you know there are many people from our clan there? Let's go once and have a look. After crossing Bornodi, we can mount the elephant. We will also visit Agnigarh and give offerings at Mahabhairav Temple.'

Not only the dolois but even the assembled crowd are talking about Jongal Bolohu's good looks and qualities, as well as his welfare mission for the people. He has not heard anything, obliviously watching the preparations for the phuja. Even though he has not heard anything, he is aware of what the people may be saying about him. His squad of spies is so powerful that he is abreast of everything that goes on inside and outside his kingdom. Jongal Bolohu has meticulously planned his kingdom so that even the neighbouring king, Gajaraj Bodosa, is becoming fearful. Before his arrival at Bohori, Jongal Bolohu had been successful in bringing a few small Kachari kingdoms under his domain. However, after the killing of his father, he has not expanded his kingdom any further. He has decided not to do so. Instead of wars and battles, he has become inclined towards building a prosperous kingdom. He wants to live in peace. Except for Dimabong, he has established cordial relationships with all other neighbouring kingdoms. With the combined strength of the neighbouring kingdoms, Gobha and Khola, he has become immensely powerful. Jongal Bolohu is glad about this significant progress. At the same time, his head bows in gratitude for Abi Konsari, Sadhukumar Azo, Samol Ayong, brother Ratnasinha and Xunzira Asi.

By dispatching trained people from distant Pratappur, Ayong has been teaching him new skills. From Komota, Ratnasinha, too, is sending people skilled in various vocations, also helping in the development of trade and commerce. Without his support, Jongal could never have been able to build such a stringent administrative system, and the kingdom could not have prospered either. Azo has also taught Jongal a great deal. His political wisdom and geographical knowledge have helped make him proficient at enabling progress and fostering security. Abi Konsari has instilled in him the strength of mind.

And Xunzira Asi?

Perhaps he will never be able to repay this affectionate woman's debt, even with his life. Xunzira Asi's nurturing since his childhood has brought him to this point.

His mother Gangavati had barely noticed him. Jokanko's mother had been an extremely absent-minded, melancholic woman since he could remember.

What an unusual childhood he had had. It seems, unlike other children, Jokanko was never allowed to participate in the celebrations of his desire. He was never permitted to enter the nuber, as an unwed mother's child. However, Jokanko had not known the actual reason for not being allowed entry. During festival celebrations, the major general and Xunzira had cleverly kept him away.

Unlike the other boys, Jokanko had never stayed at the samadi. He grew up all alone in a palace that did not have an abi, azo, afa, *khah-ee*, *kajal*, nannao – nobody. His mother, who lived her life apathetically, delegating the administration of the kingdom to the major general and care of Jokanko to Xunzira, had spent her days all by herself, reading religious books and lost in thought. Xunzira Asi had taken care of him. As much care as a mother could possibly provide. Xunzira Asi had taken him for excursions and told him stories. Jokanko had learned everything that had to do with society from Xunzira Asi. To Jokanko, life appeared to be normal. It had never occurred to him that there was anything unusual about his birth or style of living.

Perhaps because he grew up in this manner.

In none of the moments of the uncountable days and nights spent in Khola's palace, from childhood to youth, had Jokanko ever imagined what a strange future awaited him.

How happy he had been.

While travelling on the expansive road of life that appeared very smooth, apart from the dream of kingdom expansion, Jokanko had never frolicked with any other dream.

But where was the opportunity to frolic!

The major general, devotedly grooming Jokanko to make him eligible to become a king, had never allowed him any break to dream of anything else. If his mother had taken upon herself the responsibility of Jokanko, perhaps things might have been different. Perhaps his mother would not have encouraged him to nurture the thirst for victory.

But his maah had delegated the entire responsibility upon Xunzira Asi and the major general while she exiled herself into an unreal world of deep apathy.

Xunzira Asi emanated affection. Despite teaching Jokanko the ways of society, her primary concern had been his health. She had given Jokanko her undivided attention and profound love.

After his royal installation, when he went to pay obeisance to his mother, he had also bowed before his asi.

He hardly had the leisure even to think! From morning to night, the major general was training him in warfare and the administration of the kingdom. Jokanko knew that he was the son of a queen and would be crowned the king of Khola one day.

But without Jokanko's knowledge, so many incidents had occurred at the time. Arimotto had returned and settled in the Dhoumora hills. Jokanko had known nothing. Nothing at all.

After becoming king, he had begun to rule the kingdom with great enthusiasm. Sometime later, he had aspired to expand the kingdom. Going to seek permission for the expansion of the kingdom, for the first time, Jokanko had seen his mother in another form.

Raising her head from the pages of the book, Gangavati had stared at him with a pointed look. Then in a voice laden with grief, she had said, 'Even you?'

'Even you? What do you mean by that? I am the one who is going. Did anyone else also come to seek permission?'

Jokanko had laughed. He had not understood what his mother wanted him to say. Never tried either. He was then swaying with the dominant desire to grow the kingdom.

Gangavati had not laughed. She had said calmly, 'You want to engage in a fight to expand the kingdom? Why? Is the land of Khola not sufficient for you?'

'How does sufficient or insufficient matter, Maah? You know how large Khola is. Do you expect me to be content with this one small village?'

'You should be content, Jokanko. What is the use of wars and battles?' Gangavati had said. 'But if I forbid you, would you listen?'

'But why ever would you forbid me, Maah?' Jokanko's voice had manifested the signs of an ambitious king's intolerance, irritated by refusal.

Gangavati had tried her best to persuade him, but he was not a boy to pay heed at all. His mother's indifference, Xunzira's excessive love and affection, and his hectic life that was confined to training had transformed him into an adamant, angry and obstinate youth. Except for Xunzira, perhaps the tender, loving heart concealed within Jokanko had never been noticed by anyone, not even his mother.

He did not pay heed to her words, even to Xunzira Asi's words. Finally, his mother granted him permission on one condition. Jokanko would not attack the allied kingdoms, nor invade any of the western realms. Jokanko never had any intention of invading his allies anyway. But he was surprised when he was prohibited from attacking the western kingdoms.

'Why are you preventing me from going to the west, Maah?'

'Do not try to learn the reason, Jokanko. But never, for any reason, attack any of the western kingdoms. I will be hurt. Terribly hurt.'

Right then his mother's face had turned so gloomy that he didn't have the heart to repeat the question. Following his mother's words, Jokanko had advanced eastwards and conquered Kondoli. Then he returned after gaining victory over a few small Kochari kingdoms. It was on his way back that Jokanko, ecstatic over his victories, was reminded of his mother's cautionary words.

Why did his mother forbid him from travelling west? Who is in the west? With whom did his mother not want him to fight? King

Arimotto is in the Dhoumora hills. Jokanko had heard about his heroism even on his way. Does his mother fear Arimotto? Did his mother forbid Jokanko from going to the west for fear of losing her only son to Arimotto's hands? Yes, possibly, this must be the reason.

Thinking about his mother's fear, Jokanko had laughed in his mind and, in the middle of his return journey, decided to attack Arimotto in the Dhoumora hills.

After killing Arimotto, Jokanko had carried the severed head on a platter eager to show it to his mother. Upon noticing Mriganko's severed head in her son's hand, Gangavati had gone berserk. Right in front of the people and officers assembled to welcome Jokanko, she had berated him with curses.

'This is your afa, Jokanko! You have severed your own afa's head and brought it? You disobeyed me? *Thadok! Kafut lawa!* I shall never forgive you. With these hands, which you have used to kill your father, you will never be able to drink a drop of water at your hour of death. You will die drinking water like a cow with your mouth. The weapon, whose power caused you to forget your promise, will desert you in the time of your need. You—'

'It is time to offer the gold flower, Deoraja.' The priest's voice rouses Jongal Bolohu from the nightmare. He stares at the priest in confusion. 'The ritual is about to begin.'

'Oh, yes, of course.'

Offering the tray containing betel nuts and the gold flower, Jongal Bolohu looks at the idol of Aai Basundhari and pays homage. The priest adorns the four-armed idol of Aai Basundhari with the gold flower offered by Jongal Bolohu and the smaller gold and silver flowers offered by other kings. The floor is white from the milk and water used for bathing the goddess and the gods Ganesha and Kartik. The feet of the idols overflow with flowers and tuloxi leaves. From Ganesha's right hand, above his rat, hangs a garland of fragrant flowers. He holds his elephant trunk in his left hand. The light from countless earthen lamps in front of the idols of Kartik, who is wearing a garland of wild flowers, Ganesha, and Aai Basundhari, illuminates the temple premises. The priest offers ceremonial food, which the loro has cleaned in the waters of the Borpani. The priest's never-ending chants create a haunting ambiance in the soundless Basundhari shrine.

Gradually, Jongal Bolohu, who had become restless, relaxes. The strangeness of being Jongal Bolohu, his father's killer, is fading, and he is returning to normalcy. Though agitated at times, he does not lose control of his senses like he used to previously. If he did not have a grandmother like Abi Konsari, what would have been his plight, Jokanko wonders.

After initially learning that he had killed his own father, Jokanko had lost his mind. The thought of taking his own life was beginning to take root in his mind.

Without Abi Konsari and Xunzira Asi, Jokanko would have died long ago.

Abi Konsari had said, 'Syu, don't brood, go on doing your work. The more you work for the welfare of society, the more you will be at peace with yourself. Fa Mahadeo and Ma Kalikha love only those kings who worship society. Do not indulge in warfare. However far you have extended the kingdom, it is more than enough. Now think of keeping the kingdom secure and work for its advancement. Whenever you feel down, ponder over Acharyadev's words. Think about your abi, azo, afa and your mother's grief. Leave the judgement of your kharam on Fa Mahadeo, Jokanko. Immerse yourself in working for the people. Everything will settle down.'

Slowly, everything did settle down. As the popular king of a secure and prosperous kingdom, Jokanko lives a peaceful and happy life.

'Please accept the sanctified flowers of the ritual, Deoraja. It's time to pay homage.'

Taking the blessed flowers from the deori, Jongal Bolohu prostrates in obeisance to Aai Basundhari. Once this ritual is over, the Mikir *Barobhoni*, *Barobangthais* from Balisora, Polashguri and Choubori villages will worship at the foot of the shrine with sacrificial offerings.

Without waiting for the prasad, Jongal Bolohu bids farewell to everybody and comes out. The loro doloi himself will deliver the prasad at the palace. Before eating it, Jongal Bolohu will pay obeisance to the divine sword, the *deo langkhui*.

Speeding his horse through the dry, jungly autumn path, Jongal Bolohu is now returning to the palace. The westerly wind thrashes his face. A peculiar sound wave from the horses' hooves treading over dry leaves wafts all around. The villagers living in the villages on either side gaze in awe at the group of horse-riders leaving a trail of dust clouds behind them.

Halting his horse in front of the fort's central gate, Jongal looks around. A slight hint of a smile appears on his dust-smeared face. Not only the palace, Jongal Bolohu has also also built the security structure of the capital with great expertise. The Dabalang and Digholi lakes on the east, Kolong river on the west, the lakes Naw-bil, Molan Toli and Dholi-bil to the north. No enemy would succeed in attacking the palace easily, pervading the security structure surrounded by deep water bodies, rivers and ditches.

Towards the left of the central gate and the main street, Jongal Bolohu has constructed a raised platform to watch various entertainment and sporting events. The sentries can also use it as a watchtower.

Jongal Bolohu enters the palace, deeply satisfied. Xunzira is sitting just outside. On seeing him, she says, 'How could you survive without lunch until now? Or did you devour any human being out of hunger?'

'Not yet, Asi. I am so hungry, I could eat you! Please serve me some rice. I am on my way to the chambers.'

Inside, there is a library just before the bed suite. The room next to the library is his private armoury. Jongal closes the door upon entering. Then setting down the sanctified flowers and pushing aside a heavy storage case containing spears, he opens a secret door.

It is a tiny room with an earthen lamp glowing brightly in front of a wooden casket. Pouring oil on the lamp and pushing the wick forward, Jongal pays his respects and opens the long casket.

He touches the handle of the sword lying inside a case and pays obeisance before placing the sanctified flowers by the sword's side. Then he closes the casket, pays obeisance again and leaves.

Xunzira is preparing to serve him lunch.

THIRTY-TWO

'A spy coming from Sohori wishes to see you, Fa Bodosa,' a sentry says.

Gajaraj Bodosa of Dimabong instantly becomes alert. The Kachari ruler is sitting in the counselling chamber of the palace. The major general and a guest, Dhaneswar, are sitting near him. The king had met this person from the west on his visit to Mohong. After hearing that Bodosa ruled Dimabong, Dhaneswar had paid his respects to the king by offering a spacious split-wood boat, earthen pots made from the soil of Dharamtool, a pair of bottle-necked earthen jars, a drumful of tender seeds for cultivation and two eri shawls.

Pleased, the king enquires about Dhaneswar's identity. In reply, the man says, 'I am a landlord from the west. I enjoy visiting different countries. That is why I come to Mohong to trade in various items. I earn some money and I also get to travel.'

'Excellent. I am delighted to accept your gifts, especially the boat. Our craftsmen are not skilled in building a boat of this size out of split wood. Our boats are only made of solid wood.'

'They can, once they learn. It's not a tough task. Only a few items are required. I can teach them myself,' Dhaneswar states.

'That'll be great. The only modes of transportation here are boats and elephants. A few kings of our neighbourhood possess a few horses, though. But I don't. Our young men don't find them smooth enough. They are only comfortable with boats and elephants. I shall be very happy if you could stay in our kingdom as a guest for a few days and teach our boys the craft of boat making.'

'A petty landlord like me does not have the courage to disobey your command. I shall teach whatever I know. I am an unmarried man, and my home is where I live.'

This is how King Bodosa had happily invited Dhaneswar to stay in his kingdom. Initially, Dhaneswar had stayed for a few days and then left, but only after doling out instructions to collect the equipment required for constructing boats. A few days later, he returned with the tools and a few men skilled at making boats. After a few more days, Dhaneswar left for the west again. Then, a few days later, he returned with a man skilled at pottery. On both occasions, Dhaneswar brought peculiar gifts for the Kachari king. The king was so pleased that Dhaneswar was shifted from the guest house and given a place inside the palace. Dhaneswar never went back. He settled in Dimabong by marrying a Kachari girl. Now, he has become the king's most trusted confidant. Bodosa discusses each and every problem with Dhaneswar. And why shouldn't he? Is there anyone as wise as Dhaneswar? Who else in Dimabong is as knowledgeable as him? Who else is as widely travelled? As a result, nowadays, Dhaneswar is always present at the regular counselling assemblies. To the major general, it appears as if the king never takes a single step without Dhaneswar's advice.

The major general becomes irritated, noticing the king's heavy reliance on Dhaneswar. It is a fact that ever since Dhaneswar's arrival, the kingdom has made significant progress. The major general has been able to forge modern weapons. Dhaneswar has contributed to the kingdom's progress by importing high-quality seeds for growing paddy, pulses, vegetables and fruits. His counsel is not to be ignored either. Yet for some unknown reason, the major general dislikes him.

Despite everything, he is of unknown origin. Who knows where he came from in the west or what kind of man he is? When the major general notices his twinkling eyes, unpleasant thoughts arise in his mind, as if there's some hidden intention beneath Dhaneswar's camaraderie. But he cannot divulge his thoughts to anybody. Otherwise he runs the risk of causing harm to himself. King Bodosa, too, would never believe him. Where is the proof after all? On the contrary, by marrying a local girl, he has become all the more trustworthy to the king.

The man is an expert at talking. Not only does he show due respect to the king, he also shows respect to the major general and other officers, making them feel elated. But things appear to be changing slowly. Without holding any office, Dhaneswar is growing more powerful. These days, his behaviour and gait reflect the gravity and personality of a high-profile royal officer. On top of that, Dhaneswar is a man from the interior of the palace. Who would dare challenge him? Despite his agitation and grievance, the major general is compelled to discuss every critical and confidential matter of the kingdom right in front of Dhaneswar. In between discussions, the king often asks, 'What do you say, Dhaneswar?' Even today, as soon as it was announced that a spy from Sohori wanted an audience, King Bodosa said, 'Since he wants an audience after returning from Sohori so late at night, there must certainly be some important news. What do you say, Dhaneswar?'

'Certainly, there has to be. He would not have the courage to disturb you at this hour without any reason.'

'Call him,' Bodosa said.

The spy returning from Sohori comes in and bows. He cannot be identified as a Kachari. Attired in thenus-tagla, he looks exactly like a Laloong youth.

'What news have you brought? Speak,' the king asks.

'I have some strange news, Fa Bodosa.'

'Strange news? Let's hear. Speak, it is alright to talk in front of Dhaneswar. He is one of our own.'

'So be it, Fa Bodosa. A highly unusual piece of news. It seems the king of Sohori, Jongal Bolohu, has obtained a divine sword from the waters of the Kolong. Aai Basundhari appears to have showed it to him in his dream.'

'Then I'm sure you were lying drunk with joo at the time, weren't you?' the Kachari king says, annoyed.

The spy is saying bizarre things. Obtained a divine sword from the waters of the Kolong? Utter nonsense!

'I swear upon Shibrai. I have not drunk joo, Fa Bodosa.'

'Then where did you hear this strange news?'

'As you know, the Sogra Misawa festival of the Laloongs is currently underway. There, in the midst of the Khumkhati dance, I overheard some dolois talking about it. It seems that as long as that sword is with him, no one can defeat him.'

'Where is this sword?' King Bodosa asks, slightly worried.

'I could not figure out where the sword is. But I have learned that it is hidden somewhere within the palace. The king worships the sword every day. It seems Aai Basundhari has said that no one must know where the sword is kept. Otherwise it would bring disaster. It will also be disastrous if the sword is not worshipped daily. That is why the king never stays out overnight these days. However, even if he does, he possibly carries the sword with him.'

'Go. Take some rest. I have a feeling you, too, performed the Khumkhati.' Fa Bodosa laughs.

The spy bows and leaves. All at once, the Kachari king becomes solemn.

'Major General, does the spy's news seem credible?'

'I have not been able to make out whether it's credible or not. It might even be false propaganda spread by Jongal Bolohu to demonstrate his strength. He is a very clever king.'

'What do you say, Dhaneswar?'

'The major general's speculation is not something to be ignored. But if the news has any truth, then it is dangerous for our kingdom.'

'You are right. If Aai Kalikha or Aai Basundhari has actually given Jongal a sword, it would be difficult to thwart him,' the king says.

'As it stands, what he has done without the sword is becoming tough enough to obstruct. He has already succeeded in capturing half of our subsidiary kingdoms. If the rumors about the divine sword are true, perhaps it won't be long before we become his subsidiary, too,' Dhaneswar says.

'But it is in the air that Jongal Bolohu has decided not to expand his kingdom any further. After killing King Arimotto and feeling devastated on learning that he was Jongal's own father, he has decided not to indulge in warfare anymore. In all these years, he has not done so. He is only concerned about the progress of his kingdom,' the major general counters.

'Maybe. But how long will it take for someone to change their mind? If he has actually obtained the sword, I am sure Jongal will want victory all over again,' Dhaneswar says.

'Major General, Dhaneswar is right. We better be vigilant. Our venerated dynasty of Bangla kingdom and Arikhidima cannot remain at the feet of the Laloongs,' King Bodosa says, growing excited.

'Please do not get worked up, Fa Bodosa. It is unwise to take any decision hastily. First let me investigate everything in detail to determine how much of the news is true. If it is, then all we should do is strengthen our security arrangements. If we notice Jongal Bolohu preparing for an attack, we shall think of our next move,' the major general says.

'Though the major general's opinion is acceptable, there is cause for further thought, Your Majesty. Is it prudent to wait for Jongal's attack? His strength has now surpassed ours. Khola, Gobha, Pratappur, Komota, all these are with Sohori. However much we increase our strength, would we be able to withstand Jongal's attack?'

'It cannot be said for sure that we would not, honourable guest,' the general says, feeling extremely irritated.

'But we cannot also say that we could, honourable general. Until the other day, our Royal Highness was the most powerful king. After Jongal Bolohu became king, our Royal Highness fell to the second position. There is no alliance with the Ahoms either. On the other hand, Jongal, with the aid of Pratappur, Gobha and Khola, went on to become a powerful king. It is really depressing.'

'Right – you are right, Dhaneswar. Because of this Jongal Bolohu, Dimabong's glory has extinguished. Thinking about it seems to set my body on fire. Something has to be done, Dhaneswar. Major General, think of doing something sensible. Jongal cannot be allowed to enjoy kingship in this manner.'

'First let me collect information, Fa Bodosa. Then we could contemplate doing something accordingly,' the major general says.

'The general is correct. Send secret agents to Sohori and fetch every detail. After collecting news about arms and ammunition, forts, number of soldiers, everything – only then the strategy of destroying Jongal Bolohu must be planned,' says Dhaneswar.

Noticing Dhaneswar's dexterity in almost making the king decide to attack Jongal Bolohu, the major general grows exasperated.

'Proceed with the work as Dhaneswar has said, Major General. Jongal has seized our most productive kingdoms from us. He cannot be allowed to stretch his arms towards Dimabong. I have been patient so far. But not any longer. Something must be done this time.'

'As you command,' the major general says helplessly.

'Let the council wind up for today.'

The king leaves.

Bowing to the king, the major general, too, walks out worriedly.

'Let me take leave, too, Your Majesty. Tomorrow, I expect the weapon that can be concealed inside a bamboo stick will be finally ready for display before you.'

'I am happy to hear it, Dhaneswar. We could enlarge our armoury only because of you. Once completed, this weapon could be given to the spies. Carrying a sword draws attention. But it is necessary as well.'

'Of course, Your Majesty. More weapons will be forged with your blessings, and the blessings of Shibrai. I cannot rest until I see you back in top position. The love and respect you've shown me is unforgettable. Since I married, I've become a part of this kingdom. I don't even feel like an outsider anymore, Your Majesty; I've started to feel like a Kachari.'

'You've learned our dialect. You dress like a Kachari. It's just that you look different. You could almost pass for a Kachari, though.' The king laughs.

'Allow me to take your leave, Your Majesty. Please rest.' Bowing before the king and contemplating the next strategy, Dhaneswar leaves the room with a sense of satisfaction.

King Bodosa, seething with the desire to recover his lost glory and defeat Jongal Bolohu, retreats to the privacy of the palace chambers.

THIRTY-THREE

'Everything we had heard about the divine sword is true, Fa Bodosa. I have thoroughly confirmed the veracity of the news,' the major general says.

'Do you see, Queen? You did not believe me, did you? Now, do you hear? You did not believe it even when Dhaneswar said so. Now?' the Kachari king says to his wife.

He has called the queen to the secret conference today, with a particular goal in mind. The major general is not aware of the purpose. Only Dhaneswar knows.

'Yes, I have heard. What is to be done now, Major General?' the queen says.

The queen is not very fond of Dhaneswar. His exaggerated flattery displeases her. She is also peeved by the overabundance of importance the king pays to Dhaneswar. A couple of times, she has even voiced her displeasure. But the king would not pay heed to her. That is why the queen now directs the question to the major general, ignoring Dhaneswar.

'Your Highness, the Queen, it is true that Jongal Bolohu obtained a divine sword. But, as of now, he has no plans to attack any kingdom,' the major general says.

'Then? What is the point of worrying so much about the sword?' the queen asks irritably.

'The sword is not the only reason, Your Highness, the Queen. Jongal has been expanding his kingdom little by little. He is allowing people of his own clan as well as from others to set up villages and settle on the frontier forest and the unused land.'

'But those lands are in his realm. He has settled those people for agriculture. The land is fertile. It yields a good harvest,' the major general opposes.

'Those are superficial reasons, honourable general. You are a simple man. That's why you cannot think of harmful things. But I've seen a lot while travelling as a trader. The people have outwardly been settled for agriculture, but they all belong to the king's army. With little effort, our secret agents can confirm it.'

'Dhaneswar is correct, general. Despite so much land, why settle people on the frontiers of Dimabong? Being the major general of this kingdom, are you supposed to take things so literally?' the king says, plainly irritated.

'But it is not only in the proximity of Dimabong, people are being settled in every such vacant land within the kingdom. New implements and tools are being harnessed. New seeds are being imported and sowed,' the general says, flushing with insult and embarrassment.

'The major general is repeating what the spies have reported. He has not spoken from his imagination,' the queen says, feeling annoyed.

'The queen and the honourable general have misunderstood my words. Please forgive me for speaking the unpleasant truth, Your Highness, the Queen. I have not said that Jongal Bolohu will break any of the conditions. I simply stated that because of his sword and other abilities, he would always consider us beneath him,' Dhaneswar replies modestly.

'Only when friendship is established will we know whether he will consider it,' the general says irritably.

'I'm sure the general does not presume that I oppose the friendship? I have already accepted the proposal of friendship. I am only worried about the possibility of becoming his subordinate after the alliance. Although I am a guest in this kingdom, I no longer consider myself to be one. It is my motherland now. I am worried that our Majesty, the King, will be slighted. The general seems a little too soft on Jongal Bolohu.'

'Are you raising doubts about my loyalty, honourable guest?' the general roars, losing his patience.

'Oh, please do not think like that. Doubt you? Of course not. I will never ever have the audacity. I made this remark noticing your generous belief that Jongal Bolohu would never make us his subsidiary. Should the enemy be trusted so much?'

'General, your anger is unfounded. Dhaneswar is correct. You are far too generous. It is your binding duty to consider the security of the kingdom. Jongal harbours tremendous strength and power. He is skilled and intelligent. He also possesses both manpower and military power. Moreover, he has the divine sword. It's possible he might consider us his subordinate even if we're friends. Certain things can be predicted ahead of time. It is not necessary to wait for things to happen,' the king states seriously.

'Then what do you suggest we should do, Fa Bodosa?' the affronted general now asks calmly.

'I would certainly start with friendship. But right away, I am thinking of two other things. To ensure we are not looked down upon by Jongal Bolohu even after we build a friendship, we will marry off our youngest daughter, Sukumola, to him.

'What are you saying? You are going to give your own daughter to a Laloong king for your vested interest?' The queen is taken aback.

'I have no choice. This sacrifice must be made for the welfare of the kingdom. I am not the first king to marry his daughter to an enemy king to foster goodwill. There are numerous examples of this. It is a common custom to establish friendship through marriage to rule a kingdom. I have summoned you here specifically for this purpose. I don't want to make any decision without informing you.'

'As a mother, I cannot agree to such things.' The queen is enraged.

'How could you possibly disagree? You are more than simply a mother; you are the queen of this kingdom. Would you be happy to see Jongal Bolohu unleash terror and destruction upon our people? Would you be happy to watch me insulted? A king's daughter will be given to a king. How does Laloong–Kachari make a difference? Dhaneswar and I have thought of carrying out this plan after a great deal of contemplation.'

'Now I understand. Where the root lies,' the queen says, heaving a sigh.

'What are you trying to say?' The king retorts angrily, realizing that the queen is pointing towards Dhaneswar.

'I am not trying to say anything. What is the use of making an issue out of nothing?' The queen is irritated.

'Alright. Since you have agreed, let me move on to the second point. But first, you must swear upon Aai Gamadi that you will not speak a single word about what we are going to discuss with anyone.'

Forcing the flabbergasted queen to pledge her agreement, the king says, 'We are going to give Sukumola in marriage to Jongal, but Sukumola must be able to do certain things for her own kingdom. She must send us information about the internal affairs of Jongal's kingdom.'

Listening to the king, the queen is startled.

'What kind of a condition is this? Tsk, tsk – do not speak such words. You are going to use our daughter as a spy? You are going to tell her to betray her husband? No. I shall never accept this condition. There is no need to give her in marriage. If Jongal makes us his subsidiary, let him. And honourable guest, why do you broach this topic? You are a guest. Behave like one. You don't have to worry about the welfare or otherwise of the kingdom.'

'Why are you annoyed with Dhaneswar? This idea is not his – it is mine. Don't say anything to him. Moreover, I have not said anything wrong. Sukumola must be prepared to make this sacrifice for the interest of the kingdom. If we have all the information about Sohori, Jongal cannot make us his subsidiary. We can live in peace as friends.'

'But when Jongal finds out, will he spare Sukumola's life?' the queen asks in despair.

'Why would he find out? It should be done without his knowledge. Sukumola is an intelligent girl. She will be able to figure it out.'

'Instead, why don't you collect information using another strategy?' the queen pleads out of desperation.

'If it were possible, do you think I would have thought of Sukumola? Jongal has kept the divine sword hidden somewhere inside the palace. Much as I have tried, I could not uncover where it has been kept. We would need this information, too, wouldn't we?'

'But will Princess Sukumola give her consent?' the general asks doubtfully.

'Why not? She is a king's daughter. My daughter. She is a girl who is not afraid to sacrifice her life for her country.'

'You want to marry her off to Jongal to die. You only want Dimabong. Not your daughter.'

'You speak as if I don't consider her my daughter. You must understand, Queen. A small sacrifice is essential to save the kingdom. Sukumola does not have to live her entire life as a spy, you see. After she has provided the necessary information, we will not bother her anymore. She can live with Jongal happily. We will also live here peacefully. The marriage proposal must be sent to Jongal before the Hangseo Manaowa festival this spring. You can leave now. Go and tell Sukumola that I want to see her.'

After telling the queen to leave, the Kachari king begins discussing the friendship proposal with the general and Dhaneswar.

THIRTY-FOUR

Inside her bedchamber in Gobha, Konsari sits alone, spinning yarn with a tortoise-shell shuttle. Her hands, once fair and glowing, have now withered even more and her skin has become wrinkled with age. Only her long nose and elongated eyes still hold a few faded sparks of her former beauty.

In this vast palace devoid of family, Konsari lives with the khamsamais and sentries. There used to be Xunzira, who was always by her side. However, then she had sent her nannao to live with Gangavati to raise Jokanko.

Sending Xunzira to the deluded and lonely Gangavati, burdened by society's reproach and concern for Arimotto, had brought Konsari a sense of relief at the time. If she could, she would have gone to Gangavati herself or brought the queen of Khola to live with her. But both of them had to bow their heads before society's norms. The bond between the two lonesome and helpless women is now maintained solely by Xunzira.

Thinking about Gangavati, Konsari still squirms from sharp stings of self-reproach. She identifies herself as the cause of the destruction of two lives and writhes in agony at the thought. But it isn't merely two lives; she wonders if her decision brought about many more cursed days and nights as well.

What if Gangavati had joined Arimotto in family life in Baidyagarh? Society might have labelled Konsari and Arimotto traitors, condemning her Aryan identity, but many more unbearable incidents could have been avoided.

Konsari believes it is nothing but misfortune that has plagued her life, and she considers it cursed. Nowadays, she refrains from social activities and stays at home, finding solace in the shuttle and religious books, attempting to leave behind all the anguish.

Xunzira often visits, spending the day with her pai before returning home. She cannot bear to stay away from Jokanko, especially at night when he becomes restless, haunted by thoughts of his father's killing.

Fortunately, Jokanko has become more stable these days, focusing on the administration of the kingdom. The society's criticism is slowly diminishing, and he is now acknowledged as the chieftain by every Laloong kingdom, thanks to his able leadership, heroism and dexterity. Hearing the praise for Jokanko from the subjects brings immense pleasure and solace to Konsari. She feels as if she has finally found some peace after enduring numerous ups and downs throughout her life. In the last phase of her life, she has discovered a leisure bereft of accidents – a freedom she never experienced before.

'Abi, Abi—' Jongal Bolohu calls out loudly, walking into the room with confident steps. 'I know for sure that you are sitting with this shuttle. Oh! Why are you so fond of spinning yarn? The sight of it exhausts me.'

Hugging Konsari and planting a kiss on her head, Jokanko settles down beside her. 'Can I swing the sword like you? Let me swing the shuttle instead. I'm an old woman,' Konsari laughs.

'Don't call yourself old. I'll get angry. Come on, put the shuttle down.' Jongal takes it from his grandmother's hand. 'You have forgotten that you have a syu, haven't you?'

'So you've come to remind me, have you?' Konsari laughs again, caressing Jokanko's cheeks with her hand.

'Of course. You never visit Sohori at all, even though it was once a subsidiary of Khola. Your grandson is the king there, after all. But do you remember that Khola was once a subsidiary of Gobha?'

'Never. It was never a subsidiary at all. Don't lie. My daughter-in-law's kingdom was sovereign.'

'Maybe, but it was never equal to Gobha. You speak very highly of your daughter-in-law's kingdom, don't you? But not about Gobha,' Jokanko laughs.

'Of course I would. Now, tell me, where do you belong? Khola or Gobha?'

'I belong to you. I am your subsidiary.' Jokanko embraces Konsari. She laughs heartily and then becomes serious. 'In Laloong society, there is no subsidiary as senior as me, Syu. Kings are there only to rule the kingdoms. No one is above society, except God.'

'If you know so much, why don't you visit Sohori? Doesn't your syu ever come to your mind?'

'Of course I remember my syu. I feel like going, too. But somehow it never happens, child.'

'Come today. Let me take you. Xunzira Asi lives alone. You, too, live alone. Come, both of you can live together. On the other side, Azo also lives alone. What a situation.'

'Take your azo instead. He never goes anywhere. Going to Sohori will cheer him up.'

'As if he will go. Is Azo any less? He gave me the charge of Gobha. You gave me Khola. Is it possible to rule such a vast kingdom?'

'You have to. Your afa and azo were such gallant heroes. Well, everyone says that you have become an even bigger hero than them.'

'Yes, everyone says that. But do you?'

'I always think of you as my stupid little syu. It never occurs to me that you are a king, my pet.'

'Alright. You don't have to think of me as a king. But am I little? Look at my arms. Even if you clasp them tightly, it will feel like the touch of an ant to me. Understand, Abi?' Jongal Bolohu roars with laughter, and so does Konsari.

After spending some lighter moments with her grandson, feeding him his favourite food, a relaxed Konsari faces Jongal Bolohu. 'Now tell me, Jokanko, why did you come?'

'How did you know that I have come with a purpose, Abi?' Surprised, Jokanko asks.

'I have come to know you, Syu. Am I not your abi? If I can't read my syu's thoughts from his face, am I fit to be his abi?'

'That's why I love you so much, Abi. You know so many things. You understand so many things. If I had met you in my childhood, things would have been so much better. Maah was hardly there. Had there been no Xunzira Asi—'

'Don't recall those memories, Syu. What's the use of recollecting unpleasant thoughts?'

'Nowadays, I don't recollect them, Abi. I don't dwell on anything unpleasant. But still, at times, they do come to my mind, and the thoughts make me miserable, Abi.'

'Whenever you feel miserable, put yourself in the midst of people. Come to me. Go to Azo. Talk to Xunzira. Aren't you feeling better after engaging yourself in social activities? Keep working for the people. Gradually, your miseries will recede more and more.'

'True. By following your advice, I have earned a good reputation, Abi. Even Azo's advice has done me good. That's why I have not invaded any kingdom, despite having the divine sword given by Ma Basundhari in my possession. And I shall not.'

'A very good resolution, Syu. Ma Basundhari did not give you the deo langkhui to massacre people and expand the borders of your kingdom. It has been given to defend yourself only.'

'You know, now and then, I touch the deo langkhui with my fingers, Abi. It's incredible! When Ma Basundhari appeared in my dreams, she said that I would recover a sword from the waters of the Kolong river. At first I had dismissed it as a dream. But Xunzira Asi insisted that I go. She suggested I search the waters after taking a bath in the river. "If you really find it, then there is nothing like it. Even if you don't find it, there's nothing to lose, right?" I was so surprised to find the sword that I'm not sure how long I remained in the water. Abi, do you believe that the sword possesses some strange power from Ma Basundhari?'

'There are certain things that give you peace if you don't judge them by logic and argument but accept them with faith. We are people with slanted eyes. How much do we really know about this world? We haven't seen God, but isn't there some kind of power somewhere? How else can this world go on with such precision? How can the sun always appear on time? What about the moon? You found the sword through a dream. It would be wise to believe that the sword does have some divine power. This belief will provide strength to your mind, too.'

'It's true, Abi. When I go to the Basundhari temple to pray after worshipping the sword, I feel mentally strong. I often go to the Mahadeo temple to light lamps. Before anyone rises, I run away and then return quietly. My body remains sound, and my mind feels sound, too.'

'How do you go so far? Don't you feel exhausted?'

'Not at all. Do you think I eat only steamed fish-fingerlings like you? I eat full-sized grilled catfish, do you understand? And a whole roasted chicken at a time. Do you think I am a tiny bird like you?'

'God almighty – am I a panthai like you? I am a rickety old woman.'

'You dare to call yourself old again?'

'Alright, I won't. Let's set jokes aside for now. Now tell me, what is it that you have come to say?' Konsari enquires.

'Something quite serious has happened, Abi. The king of Dimabong has sent a marriage proposal for his youngest daughter to me.'

'To you?' Konsari looks up at Jongal, her politically wise eyes becoming piercingly sharp.

'Yes. You know that I have decided never to marry. I am confused by this unexpected turn of events, so I have come to ask for your opinion. I will not marry. That is for sure. But the reason behind this proposal from the king of Dimabong is a matter of concern.'

'The matter is not difficult to understand at all. The proposal of marriage is to establish friendship, certainly.'

'But our spies have learned that Bodosa is upset because I have become too powerful. If he is upset, he should be thinking of fighting. Why does he want to marry off his daughter?'

'Perhaps he is upset. Since he doesn't have the strength to fight you, he wants to establish friendship. It's a good approach. Instead of fighting and expanding kingdoms, it is always preferable to be friends and live peacefully. We have been able to live peacefully until now because of your cordial relationship with the Jaintias and Mikirs, as well as your good relationship with other neighbouring kingdoms. The conflicts have always been with the Kachari kingdoms, with whom you have been at war. They have also fought against you. You know, Syu, friendship would be good for all.'

'But, Abi, I don't think friendship with the king of Dimabong is the right thing to do. He is no longer as powerful as I am, but he used to be as powerful as the Jaintia king. He only became weak after fighting with the Ahoms.'

'Did the Kacharis go first to fight with the Ahoms? It is the Ahoms who are sneakily encroaching upon other people's land. The Ahoms are located in the east, and you are in the west. The Jaintias are on the hills. He must establish a cordial relationship with someone to increase his strength. They are offended by the cunning of the Ahoms. Moreover, they don't want to invite trouble by provoking them. There is no battle going on with the Jaintias as of now; they share a good relationship. That leaves only you. Many customs of our society are similar to theirs. Perhaps that is why he wants to marry off his daughter to you. Would a young girl be given to an old man instead of a young man? It's not as if he has no love for his daughter.'

'But does he have good feelings for me in his mind?'

'It is but natural not to have good feelings. You may be right. Behind the facade of marriage and friendship, he might have some bad intentions. But you cannot reject the marriage proposal. You are not an ordinary panthai, are you? You are a king. However bad the intentions might be, it is cowardice for a king to reject a marriage proposal. No king ever does this. Haven't you seen for yourself?'

'Indeed, I have. And therefore I have not been able to decide what to do. I don't have even the slightest intention of getting married, Abi. Look, Abi, my afa, without knowing that he was his afa, killed my azo, Pratapchandra. I, too, killed my afa without knowing what I was doing. Even though you have coaxed me into believing that these were merely accidents, my mind refuses to accept it, Abi. I don't have any desire to take my dynasty forward.'

'Can destiny be altered by one's wishes and desires? Whatever is in your kharam is destined to happen.'

'Even you talk about kharam these days, Abi? Do you believe in fortune and misfortune?'

'I am growing weaker, Syu. Leave my words aside. Get married. I have heard quite a lot about the beauty and virtues of the princess of Dimabong. Perhaps she is the girl who has been chosen for you. I've heard that the other one is already married. Besides, you also have the deo langkhui with you. The kingdom is well protected. What harm could Bodosa cause you? Furthermore, wouldn't he be concerned about the well-being of his daughter? Any harm to his son-in-law is harm to his daughter as well, isn't it?' Konsari says.

'True, Abi,' Jongal Bolohu says thoughtfully. After deliberating for a long time, he proceeds to his kingdom, deciding to accept the proposal.

At the capital, the messenger with the marriage proposal is still waiting.

THIRTY-FIVE

Throngs and throngs of people.

The Kochua ground, adjacent to Jongal Bolohu Fort, is bustling with activity. Beltola lies in the west, Mikir Hills to the east and Jaintia and Kachari Hills to the south and southeast. Kings from all the kingdoms south of the Brahmaputra, along with other invitees, have filled the rows of visitors' camps erected on one side of the expansive field. Perhaps not a single subject of the kingdom remains indoors today. Thousands and thousands of people have gathered under the extensive awning that stretches from one end of the Kochua field to the other.

It feels as if fairies and demi-gods have descended from the heavens, harmonizing with the exhilarating spring season in Sohori. Everybody's spirit pulsates to the rhythmic beats of khram panthai, khram khujura and *tokor*. The khorlas and panthais of the Magrawali clan, adorned in flamboyant costumes, perform the Muinary Kanthi dance, holding each other's waists and matching step for step. The cadence of tumding togor and the soulful melody of muhuri spread animated joy among the youth across the sprawling field. The aroma of delicious cuisine wafting from the cooking shed adds to the excitement of the festivities.

Today is Jongal Bolohu's wedding day. The otherwise secure capital has been thrown open for everybody. Even the central gateway of the fort, where Jongal Bolohu's royal residence is situated, is wide open today. However, only select people have been permitted to enter the fort. Leaving the venue at Kochua field, people have come to stand in front of the entrance, gaping in awe at the elegantly decorated interiors of the fort. Jongal Bolohu is yet to make his appearance at the venue. He is giving company to the specially received invitee kings inside the fort, while his brother, Ratnasinha, stands with him as the groom's companion. Samol, the king of Pratappur, supervises every arrangement at the wedding.

Meanwhile, Xunzira, Sadhukumar and Abi Konsari have no responsibilities today. Sadhukumar sits among the people, drinking joo profusely. Xunzira and Konsari have joined an elderly group of women, sharing humour and laughter with them. Xunzira is floating in delight. She has not witnessed a wedding in ages and has not experienced happiness in a long time.

Ever since that day when Sadhukumar brought young Xunzira to the palace at Gobha, she has witnessed numerous tragic incidents. Her husband passed away, and Samol went away to Baidyagarh. Whatever joy she once had came to an end. Today, after so many years, she will be able to see a wedding – not just any wedding, but Jokanko's, whom she has raised from infancy. It's the wedding of the powerful Jongal Bolohu, acknowledged as Jela by all.

'Don't drink so much joo, Nannao. Why do you forget that you have aged?' Konsari says, teasing.

'Please don't stop me, Pai. I don't care even if I die. I am so happy today. This motherless child's life will finally find satisfaction. He was insisting that he wouldn't marry. Tell me, Pai – if he had remained unmarried, what would society have said? This is better. What if she is a Kachari? She is a king's daughter, after all. You seldom get to see such a beautiful khorla, though she cannot be compared to you. You are as magnificent as the full moon.'

'Come off it, Nannao. People will laugh at you. What rubbish,' Konsari laughs.

'I swear. Let people laugh. Is there anybody who can match your beauty? You know, even today, people cannot take their eyes off you. Even I. Not to mention the old deoraja.'

'Nannao, you have lost control over your tongue. Put down … put down the bowl of joo.'

'Today I shall say whatever I want to, Pai. Just think about what you have done to Deoraja. He has grown old thinking and thinking about you. Yet you don't pay any attention to him.'

'Stay quiet, Nannao. Look what you are blabbering – an old couple with one foot in the grave! You'll get a thrashing from me.'

'A thrashing from you would be most welcome. People will say, "Look, Abi Konsari is thrashing the old woman!" They don't know that the old deoraja, ever ready to lay down his life for you, is still staring at you. Look, look at him.'

Xunzira giggles like she used to. As does Konsari. Waves of happiness wash over her heart.

'Come, Nannao. Let's go look at the bride. We can also make sure the bride's party has been properly served food.'

'Yes, Pai. I have been there so many times since yesterday. Yet I don't feel satisfied.'

Finishing the remaining joo in one gulp, Xunzira gets up. They walk out to a sea of inquisitive eyes through the middle of the awning.

Inside the bridal camp Sukumola, the bride, is sitting with her head bowed, with her near and dear ones from Dimabong around her. Bedecked in a bridal outfit and jewellery gifted from the groom's side, Sukumola looks resplendent. Yet, although the sparkle of a new bride is evident from her attire, her eyes show neither the dreams nor emotions of a woman about to get married.

If anything, there is rigidity. Born of pure determination. Of profound sorrow.

After all, she is going to be sacrificed for her kingdom. She has to share her life with a foe, setting aside all her dreams and desires. Can she succeed? Can she fulfil the enormous responsibility given to her by her father? Can she make powerless the valorous Jongal Bolohu?

Sukumola is lost in profound contemplation. She has not prepared herself mentally to daydream about the life of a new bride. However, Sukumola can't help but feel a deep curiosity about Jongal.

What does he look like?

What is his character like?

What are Jongal Bolohu's thoughts on the brink of this political marriage? Does he consider the king's daughter his enemy? Or were the same feelings of repulsion and hatred stirring within him, as they were in Sukumola?

In the royal palace of Dimabong, Sukumola has listened to numerous tales about Jongal Bolohu's heroism and appearance. From a young maid named Moukhati, who hailed from a Kachari village near Sohori and worked in the Dimabong palace, Sukumola has heard stories about Jongal Bolohu that seemed like fairy tales. A beautiful image of the unmarried, youthful king has already been painted on Sukumola's young heart.

Until recently, nobody had apprised Sukumola of Jongal Bolohu's misdeeds. But gradually, her father began to reveal the dark side of Jokanko. Listening to these revelations had filled Sukumola with intense anger. Over time, a deep-seated hatred had taken root in her heart toward the malevolent Jongal Bolohu, who sought to bring ruin to their kingdom.

On one occasion, her father had summoned her to the secret council chamber, where their esteemed guest Dhaneswar and the major general were present. He disclosed Jongal Bolohu's plans to attack the Kachari kingdom and said, 'The Bangla kingdom and our ancestral Arikhidima dynasty cannot afford to be humiliated by the Laloong, Jongal Bolohu. We must take action, my dear. Unless we weaken him, Dimabong will one day become subordinate to Sohori.'

'What do you intend to do, Father?' Sukumola asked with concern.

'We wish to establish an alliance with Jongal Bolohu, dear. If we offer you in marriage to him, then Jongal will become our ally.'

Sukumola was taken aback by her father's proposal. 'Are you truly suggesting that we can forge an alliance by marrying me off to that wicked man? You intend to give a Kachari girl to a Laloong?'

'I do not take this decision lightly, my dear. But I am left with no other choice. As the king of this realm, I must make this sacrifice for the welfare of our people. Furthermore, the customs and traditions of Laloongs and Kacharis are quite similar, differing only slightly when it comes to our dialects. As the princess of this kingdom, you must be prepared to make this sacrifice, my dear. Haven't you heard of the heroes and heroines of our land who gave their lives for our nation? Heroes like Rangadao, Degadao, Demalik and Halodao, who fought for our country, and fearless women like Wairang Ma, who stood up for the nation, sacrificing their lives? Just as we pay our respects to their memory, one day, our people will also revere your name. Not everyone has the privilege of making a sacrifice for their country. You are truly blessed, my dear, which is why you have been entrusted with this noble duty of safeguarding the kingdom.'

Her father and the esteemed guest, Dhaneswar, shared many more details with her. As she listened to their words, Sukumola felt a sense of pride, akin to a soldier entrusted with the responsibility of defending their kingdom.

After a few days, the wedding date and time were finalized. However, Jongal Bolohu presented a condition – he would not come to Dimabong for the wedding; instead, the Kachari king must journey to Sohori to give away his daughter in marriage. With no other option, the Kachari king reluctantly accepted this condition. The flames of anger had begun to consume him, and Dhaneswar's words only fuelled that fire. All of the Kachari king's doubts were dispelled when he summoned Sukumola once again to the secret council chamber, where only Dhaneswar was present, and the major general was absent.

Seating her beside him, her father said, 'In the name of Brai Shibrai, Aai Gamadi, swear that you will never reveal what I'm about to tell you to anyone.'

Surprised, Sukumola, now transformed into a patriotic soldier, took the pledge and said, 'Tell me what you wish to convey, Father.'

Her father continued, 'In the name of Shibrai, promise me again that you will adhere to my words without fail.'

'I swear in the name of Shibrai, Kalikha, Kamakhya and Ranachandi – I shall abide by what you tell me.' Soon after that, however, her father's words had startled Sukumola – she would have to work as a spy for the Kachari kingdom while living as Jongal's wife. This was an unfeasible proposition, she protested.

But then their guest Dhaneswar had intervened. 'It is natural to feel upset, Princess, but you could help save the kingdom from a grave disaster. Is the king asking you to harm Jongal Bolohu? You know about Jongal's insatiable hunger for other kingdoms. We are not equipped to match his strength. He is not as modest as the Kacharis. No matter how much we try to maintain family ties, Jongal will never abandon his desire to acquire Dimabong. Once he secures a kingdom as prosperous as ours, he will undoubtedly move on to seize the Ahom kingdom. Not to mention his alliance with the Jaintia king. He even has eyes on the fertile pastures and forests upstream. If he truly regarded us as his equals, wouldn't he have come to Dimabong for the wedding? Which Kachari princess has ever gone to the groom's house for her marriage? Isn't that an insult? Doesn't this prove that he sees us as inferiors? His Highness has endured great insult. He has been compelled to camp in Sohori to solemnize your marriage solely for the sake of his kingdom. If His Highness can do this much, why can't you? Are you not a heroic woman yourself?'

The honourable guest and her father continued to make compelling arguments that ignited a blaze of revulsion and patriotism in Sukumola's heart. She is carrying the same fiery resolve within her now. Jongal Bolohu had accepted the marriage proposal under one condition – the wedding must take place in Sohori. He would not travel to the Kachari kingdom for the ceremony. As her father accepted this insulting proposal, Sukumola felt crushed. Yet she wholeheartedly followed her father's every directive, vowing before Aai Ranachandi at the capital's gateway, 'I shall never forget my country, even as I become Jongal Bolohu's queen. In the name of

Shibrai and Aai Gamadi, I swear to never think of myself as Jongal's wife but as a soldier dedicated to my country.'

'The groom's grandmother has arrived. Move, move, make way for her.'

As Sukumola is lost in her thoughts, she hears a commotion created by some women and looks up to see Jongal Bolohu's grandmother and aunt standing at the doorway.

'We have come once again to have a glimpse of our *pohari* darling before the wedding,' Xunzira says cheerfully, under the grip of joo. The women make a big fuss to make them comfortable.

Xunzira and Abi Konsari come in and sit near Sukumola. Lifting Sukumola's face by her chin and gazing spellbound, Xunzira exclaims, 'Oh my poor dear, the bride seems withered. Haven't you eaten anything, Pohari, my pet?'

'The custom forbids eating, they say,' Sukumola replies softly, her head bowed.

'I knew that no one would let you eat. Look, I have brought these rice cakes hidden under my scarf for you. Eat them quietly. Nothing will happen,' Xunzira insists.

'There's no need,' Sukumola says, hesitant.

'What do you mean there's no need? So what if you are getting married? That doesn't mean you must starve. I have fed Jokanko too secretly, you know? Now don't let anyone find out.'

'Who is Jokanko?' Sukumola asks softly.

'Oh my *gossai*! You don't know who Jokanko is? Jongal – it's Jongal. Here, come now, eat.'

'Nannao, don't force her. Do you think my darling is like Jokanko, who can't go a few hours without food? You don't have to eat, Sukumola. You must have become familiar with Xunzira Asi because of her frequent visits here. She is intoxicated with joo right now because of her son's wedding. I'm sure you know who I am – I'm your abi. But I don't live here. I live in Gobha. Only Xunzira lives here. She has raised Jokanko since he was an infant. She dotes on him. Please regard her as your mother. She is very affable. I hope you understand?'

'Yes, I do, Abi,' Sukumola answers with a bowed head.

'You are the one who will have to look after our Jokanko, understood, Pohari? He is a very peculiar boy. But his heart is as soft as cotton wool. He was against getting married. He used to get a fright even hearing a girl's name. Now we'll see what he does. I dare him to ignore such a beautiful girl and go out of the palace,' Xunzira laughs again.

The women who were maintaining some distance from the king-groom's grandmother now come closer, encouraged by the laughter. The bride's camp resounds with laughter and fun. Sukumola is sitting with her head lowered, feeling quite perplexed. She cannot sense any trace of enmity from these two friendly old women. Sukumola feels uneasy yet pleased.

'It's time to take the bride to the marriage ground.' Fa Bodosa arrives and stands at the doorway. A splash of tears drowns her eyes instantly. Her mother has not come to the wedding, even though she loves Sukumola the most. Despite her father's persuasion, her mother has refused to come, saying, 'I shall never go to the wedding where my daughter is going to be sacrificed.' At the time of Sukumola's departure, her mother had wept like a possessed woman.

'Don't cry, Pohari, don't cry. We are with you,' Xunzira says, caressing Sukumola's heart with her words. Tears soak the gold-embroidered bridal attire that was brought by Samol.

In the midst of the women's wedding songs, Sukumola emerges from the bride's camp. The rituals of the wedding begin according to the Dimasa–Kachari custom. Under the awning, the groom's group sits on one side, and the bride's group on the opposite end, as per the customs.

Following tradition, the priest invites the groom's parents to sit, but it is revealed that Jongal has no mother or afa. The assembly falls silent, and sorrow sweeps over the minds of Jongal's relatives and the dignitaries from Khola and Gobha.

'The groom has no mother or afa, honourable *gissia*,' Sadhukumar says.

'Let Asi come. Asi will do it,' Jongal says gravely.

Xunzira melts with compassion, tears streaming down her face. Konsari quietly instructs her to go, as she sits down, feeling content and fulfilled. Then, at the direction of the gissia, Gajaraj Bodosa sits down in the place reserved for the bride's family.

'Who is the gissia?' Konsari asks Sadhukumar, who is sitting near her.

'Head priest. The Dimasa–Kacharis worship the ancestors of Banglaraja and Arikhidima. According to the position of these deities, the Dimasa kingdom comprises twelve parts known as the *daikho*s. Their religious rituals are performed in the *madaikho*, which is similar to our nuber. Every daikho has a *jonthai*, who is the head priest. The principal priest of the twelve daikhos is called the gissia, a very respectable position.'

'Now the *haingra* and *haingidima* – the oldest man and woman from the groom's side, must take their places,' the gissia says.

Sadhukumar and Konsari get up and sit near each other. A strange sensation shakes them both all at once. Without any rhyme or reason, Konsari's cheeks become hot.

Then Samol and Ratnasinha take their places at the gissia's direction, followed by the jelas of the clan and the other people.

Ratnasinha watches Konsari, Sadhukumar and Xunzira sitting in front, his eyes filling with tears. Endless sorrow, wrath, resentment, remorse, despair – pulling him to pieces. He is taking sips of the rarely available joo-*lamphoo* from the gold-plated bamboo tube.

He wants to die.

He feels like disappearing into the infinite darkness, mortified by his mother's sins. Agonized by his sister's horrific death. By his loneliness.

But at the same time, the boundless affection and the harbour he receives from these relatives soften him. He knows that after leaving Sohori, the rainbow in his mind will fade away. He will have to sink back into the abyss of loneliness and suffering. Despite his best efforts, he can't escape. The wild flames of his past will chase him until he dies.

He wants to escape by drowning himself in wine.

If he wants, he can go to Gobha or Pratappur. Many warm hearts are waiting with open arms to welcome him. But he no longer has the mental strength to attempt a normal life. Nobody can tell what is going on inside his mind. Abi Konsari, his brother Jokanko – no one. He has not laid himself bare in front of anybody. He wears down entirely within himself.

Why did his mother do such a thing?

Why didn't she think about him? About his sister?

He suddenly feels a hand on his shoulder. Startled, he turns his head to see Samol.

It is as though Ratnasinha's father is looking at him. He lowers his head. A few drops of hot tears fall on his silk scarf and vanish.

The bride and the groom now rise to pay obeisance to their families, though Jokanko does not bow before the bride's father. As per custom, a sovereign king can't bend before another. So it has been decided they will publicly pay obeisance to everyone. The two of them kneel in front of the massive crowd assembled under the huge awning. The gissia begins to give the blessings:

> *Amgadojang amgadike*
> *Pjghun badainha jayotri bohoroha*
> *Bonjoo bastharoha mander*
> *Batharoha amgadaojang.*
>
> (We have seated Sukumola, the youngest daughter of Fa Gajaraj, king of Dimabong, along with the deoraja of Khola, Sohori, Jela Moongsa Jongal Bolohu, in the season of Autumn, in the night of Sot, the last month of the year, in the days when the shimolu flowers are in bloom, the modar flowers are in bloom. By inviting all friends and relatives, inviting all the neighbours and laying seats on the huge courtyard, reclining on the pillars of the awning, in this pleasant moment and in front of their father and paternal grandfather, mother and maternal grandmother, we have sanctioned their union. Whatever this couple decides to raise – be it cattle, poultry, paddy – everything will flourish ...)

> … *khamro khamkha songren songkha, yaushi gongji sainyaba jaosi sainyaba. Shibarai ribani basain khahi jalai bhoji gara dijijang yaupi gajauni yaokhrai renhi gupuni yaokhrai renhi yaosi gongji dibuba blaisa dibleng dibuba* …
>
> (… counting on fingers, on the day provided by Lord Shiva, in the night provided by Lord Shiva, young and old have arrived together, building a golden bridge, a silver bridge after covering a long distance and crossing many rivers. They have not met with any obstacles on the way. Like a fleet of birds, like a pack of deer, they crossed the hills, crossed the rivers. It is uncountable. They are not bowing before me – they are bowing before Lord Shiva himself …)

Touching her head to the ground, Sukumola pledges before Aai Heremdi and Brai Shibrai.

'I set my head on this land – this land does not belong to me, but to the people of Dimabong. I am dedicated to sacrifice my life for the land of Dimabong – I will give my life for the land of Dimabong …'

By now, it is noon.

THIRTY-SIX

'Come, come, Dhaneswar. You have arrived at an excellent time,' Fa Bodosa said with a smile as he noticed his guest enter.

'Are there any good tidings, Your Majesty?'

'We have received a letter and many gifts from Sukumola today. It has been a month since the wedding, and I was feeling sad at not receiving any news for so long. It seems the gifts have been sent by my son-in-law. Jongal has also sent a letter. I'm delighted, Dhaneswar. It appears Jongal is not who we imagined him to be. Sukumola also writes that all is well. She is quite comfortable, she says. A woman named Xunzira lives with them. She is very loving and caring, it seems. Hopefully, things will go on in this way. Sukumola won't have to experience any unpleasantness. Ever since I asked her to spy for us, my mind has been constantly restless. She even cried a lot on her wedding day.'

As he listens to the king, Dhaneswar's face darkens for a moment. Almost immediately, however, he says with a bright smile, 'You are absolutely right, Your Majesty – it's really unfortunate for one's daughter to have to engage in such activities. I pray to God that whatever you are thinking comes true. I myself was quite worried this past month, although I haven't told you yet.'

'What are you so worried about?'

'Your Majesty, I can only speculate, but it seems they deliberately wanted to keep us at a distance. They didn't want us to get too familiar with the inside of the fort. It appears they consider us mere guests, not equals or dignitaries. They might be trying to display their superiority over us.'

'You might be right, Dhaneswar. Your observations are astute. I must admit, I didn't pay much attention to these details during the wedding festivities.'

'Your Majesty, it is not my place to say this, but I believe it is essential to be vigilant in political matters. We may be from a smaller kingdom, but we should never let others look down upon us or take advantage of us.'

'You are wise, Dhaneswar. Your concern is valid. From now on, I shall be more cautious in dealing with them. Thank you for bringing this to my attention.'

'Your Majesty, I hope I haven't offended you by speaking so frankly.'

'Not at all, Dhaneswar. On the contrary, I appreciate your honesty and sincerity. It is vital for me to have advisors who can speak their minds without hesitation.'

'I am honoured by your trust, Your Majesty.'

'Let us enjoy the festivities for now. We can discuss other matters later. This is a happy day, and I don't want anything to mar our joy.'

'As you wish, Your Majesty. I shall remain by your side during happy or challenging times.'

'Thank you, Dhaneswar. Your loyalty means a lot to me.'

And so, they continued to celebrate the joyous occasion, putting aside their worries for the time being.

'I believe Jongal does not trust us. He is afraid we learn about the internal affairs of the fort, which is why we were denied entry. Did you notice the large number of guards he had stationed outside the bride's camp, Your Majesty?'

'You are right, Dhaneswar. I hadn't given much thought to this. He didn't come here to get married because he does not trust us. We were not allowed to enter the fort either.'

'But My Lady Sukumola is comfortable there, Your Majesty, so it would be wise not to think about this humiliation too much.'

'Why can't I, Dhaneswar? Your words are not enough. It doesn't matter that Sukumola feels comfortable. She made a vow in Shibrai's name.'

'She is a young woman. They have gifted her a lot of clothes and jewellery. And given her love and care. To top it all, Jongal is a handsome man. These things are enough to make her feel content. Can we match such opulence with our own limited means? The wedding exposed our weaknesses. Why did he give so much jewellery and clothing? Was it to make us appear inferior?'

'It could be. Perhaps he has a reason behind holding such a grand wedding, too.'

'Your Majesty is so clever, unlike me. Yes, I realized only now that perhaps Jongal wanted to invite the kings from every direction to exhibit his strength and power. Other than being a good opportunity for gathering all of them together, Jongal also conveyed the message that all the kings are with him. We are powerless in the face of his strength. It is making me feel very inferior.'

'Of course you feel that way. Why wouldn't you? His intentions are not good. He aims to subdue all other kings and become a sovereign himself.'

'Your Majesty speaks the truth. A month has passed since the wedding, yet he hasn't visited Dimabong with Sukumola. Instead, he sends gifts. It's his arrogance, bolstered by possessing the divine sword and a fortified kingdom, surrounded by water. He believes himself to be invulnerable.'

'Let's see how long his conceit lasts! We must find a way to deal with it. Any ideas, Dhaneswar?'

'Your Majesty, what possible way can I think of? We are dim-witted people. But what if we could somehow obtain the divine sword?'

'You're right. The sword fuels his arrogance. Without it, he would lose his strength. But it is said to be hidden so well that no one has seen it.'

'My Lady Sukumola may be able to find it. It is rumoured to be hidden inside the palace.'

'But what if she faces danger? Do you think Jongal will spare her if he finds out?'

'Princess Sukumola is an intelligent young woman. Can't she do even this much for her kingdom? I've got an idea. None of us has visited their place yet. Jongal has not sent any invitation, either. It would not be proper for Your Majesty to go without an invitation; your dignity and pride are involved. However, there is no such reservation as far as I am concerned. Jongal has sent so many gifts, and we must also send gifts in return. Why should we remain inferior? Allow me to carry them. Please write a letter, instructing her on what she needs to do; I shall give it to her in secret. I shall also try to gather information by discreetly investigating the fort.'

'Well said, Dhaneswar. I shall make arrangements to send you very soon.'

'However, without offending Your Majesty, I'd like to say something else.'

'Please speak.'

'It would be wise not to let anyone know about our discussion, Your Majesty. Even walls have ears, and Jongal's spies may be lurking everywhere. We must avoid the risk of Jongal overhearing our plans. Our general is loyal, but somewhat simple-minded. It's best not to inform him in advance.'

'You're right. We'll be discreet. Is there anything else?'

'Your Majesty, if a few spies could be assigned under my command, I can take them with me. They could prove invaluable later for sending news. The major general's loyal men might not serve the purpose.'

'Then where would you find such spies? All our soldiers and spies are devoted to him.'

'I have a keen eye for people, Your Majesty. These are the eyes of a trader. I left my land and property when I took refuge under you, as I haven't come across any individual as generous as you. That is the reason Jongal Bolohu's behaviour surprises me. Can't he maintain a cordial relationship with a king like you? Can't he show due respect?'

'What can be done, Dhaneswar; after all, not everyone possesses equal wisdom. I have married off my daughter to a very evil man. God knows what is going to happen.'

'Fear not, Your Majesty. Everything will turn out well. Have faith.'

Dhaneswar shifts the conversation to other topics, his task now accomplished.

THIRTY-SEVEN

'You know, Pohari, Jokanko has a strong fondness for fish curry cooked with *samsoori* herbs. He also enjoys tongkhrai cooked without oil and the dried fish dish *nafrong*, prepared with *samailoor*, *pamjari* and *damlong* herbs cooked in alkali. Today, let me teach you how to prepare them,' Xunzira says, her gaze fixed on Sukumola, who is sitting near the hearth.

'Sure, Asi. But can I cook as deliciously as you?'

'Why not? When you cook with love, even the simplest fare becomes tasty. Let me share something with you: you should personally feed your man. That's how love grows. That's why I'm teaching you to make Jokanko's favorite dish. When your man returns weary, sit by him, talk to him and serve him food with love and care. It will make him fond of you.'

'My mother also gave me similar advice before my departure, Asi.'

'Of course she would. A mother's happiness lies in her daughter's happiness. I don't have a daughter of my own. My son is living so far away as a king. I find contentment in taking care of you all.'

'Why don't you also live with Ayong at Pratappur, Asi? He is the king of such an enormous kingdom.'

'What would I do there? He is happily settled there with his family. The grandchildren have already grown up; they attended the wedding. Perhaps you didn't notice. I visit them now and then.

But my heart won't allow me to leave Jokanko. He is like a child without parents, and he has grown up under my care. Moreover, he is very particular – his heart is as tender as cotton wool, but he cannot tolerate deceit. Sometimes, he becomes despondent. I'm sure you've noticed this. So, I can't bear to leave him and go far away. But now, I think I can go. Once you are properly settled with a grandchild, I'll leave for Gobha. I want to spend the last days of my life with Pai, sharing our joys and sorrows. Poor Pai is also lonely, and that saddens me.'

'But she can come and live here, Asi.'

'She can. But she has many social obligations. As much as one desires, work never leaves us alone. And then there are the people's expectations and countless problems. Everyone turns to Pai for help. Jokanko is beyond their reach, you see. He has built such an impenetrable fortress that even an ant can't creep in. It frightens them.'

'Truly, Asi. I had never seen such a fort before. I wonder how it was built.'

'God knows where he acquired the skills to construct such a fort. Paba is so knowledgeable, and he's only interested in work. It's only since you arrived that he's slowly changing, you know. The way he loves you is evident. Did you see how he dug a beautiful pond nearby for you to bathe? There are many other ponds around this fort, and it holds so many wonders that even I haven't seen until now. I think I should go out with you. We can explore together. Now, hurry and fetch some dried fish from the *hookari* above. We must finish cooking quickly. Have you noticed how impatient he becomes for food when he arrives? But, of course, how would you know? He doesn't show it in front of you. You see, if his meals aren't served on time, he becomes very restless. He has been like that since childhood. Now, get up and bring down the fish.'

Sukumola gets up and brings the fish from the smoking rack above the hearth. She hands it to Xunzira and then sits down next to her, following her directions absentmindedly.

More than six months have passed since her wedding, and countless days and nights have been lived within Jongal Bolohu's fortress. Sukumola is gradually adjusting to her new life. The initial rigidity is fading with each day, thanks to Xunzira's love, care and conversations. These have greatly helped Sukumola adapt to the unique lifestyle of this foreign land.

Xunzira's affection and care often remind Sukumola of her own mother, who is equally loving and skilled in everything.

Sukumola has developed a fondness for Xunzira. Despite her deep-rooted aversion to Jongal's kingdom, Xunzira has won her over.

And Jokanko?

Over these past six months, Sukumola has experienced a complex array of emotions. The first day she set eyes on Jokanko at the wedding site, she was struck dumb, left in awe. So handsome. So strong. So composed. For a fleeting moment, she forgot her initial purpose and felt the emotions of a newlywed bride. However, she quickly snapped back into her resolute soldier self, ready to lay down her life for her country.

With a stern countenance and her head bowed, she moved over and sat beside Jokanko. Jongal Bolohu seemed equally solemn, never once glancing at Sukumola. When the priest offered blessings for a joyful and peaceful married life in front of a vast assembly, Sukumola felt an unsettling sense of strangeness. She hadn't come to this kingdom to live a happy, tranquil life as Jongal's wife. Her presence was a political necessity dictated by her homeland, relinquishing her womanhood to this sinister man dressed as a groom in the service of her nation. As the priest and elders bestowed blessings for parenthood upon them, Sukumola quietly vowed, 'I swear in the name of Shibrai – I shall never forget my kingdom. I will not let this evil man harm my kingdom. I shall relay every detail about the security structure of this kingdom to my homeland and fortify it. I shall render Jongal Bolohu, the enemy of my country, defenceless.'

Even at the end of the wedding, when Sukumola and Jongal knelt together, she reiterated her pledge quietly to herself. Then the intimate nights arrived. When Jongal first touched Sukumola, she shuddered with revulsion and wept silently during the moments he overwhelmed her with his affection.

In the meantime, Sukumola succeeded in dispatching minor pieces of information about the fortress's interior to her father. She managed to do so discreetly through trustworthy messengers who brought gifts from her father's kingdom. However, over time, when she was unable to detect any signs of the Kachari kingdom's enemy within Jongal Bolohu's affections, Sukomola began to hesitate. Jongal never displayed any inclination to attack the Kacharis through his actions or behaviour. He never disrespected his father-in-law, and Sukumola could discern no political or power-hungry motives in his affection.

Could her father have misconstrued her husband? Or had she herself misunderstood him? Had Jongal cunningly lured her into a facade of affection while secretly planning an attack on the Kachari kingdom? This possibility seemed more likely.

Despite her hesitation, Sukumola continued with her mission in earnest. Her father had instructed her, 'Report to me whatever you observe or hear. I will determine which matters require the most attention.'

Sukumola diligently followed her father's instructions, writing to him about everything she observed or heard whenever the opportunity arose. Yet opportunities were scarce, and her father couldn't dispatch messengers too frequently to avoid arousing suspicion from Jongal. Sukumola had to be cautious and write two letters each time – one for show, containing news about her well-being, and the other secretly carrying critical information.

Her father had explained that once she had conveyed all the intelligence about the military both inside and outside the fortress, the fort's layout and internal design, she wouldn't need to do anything else.

She hoped for that.

Being a spy weighed heavily on her conscience, and she found it disgraceful and disloyal. Whenever Xunzira displayed affection or Jongal showered her with love, Sukumola felt overwhelming remorse.

'Asi … Asi!'

When Sukumola hears Jongal's voice, she grows cautious so as to not get caught writing letters. Xunzira laughs. 'Look at how he is yelling for me. He is hungry. He does not know how to behave like a king, you know. Get the meal ready. Let me go and call him in.'

Xunzira goes out.

'Where is Sukumola, Asi?' Jongal asks, the moment he sees Xunzira.

'Oh, my child does not seem to want me anymore these days. He only wants Sukumola.' Xunzira laughs.

'You tease a lot, Asi. Please call her. I want to show both of you something.'

'Won't you have your meal?'

'Later. First let me show you what it is. Come over to the queen's bathing pond with Sukumola. I shall be waiting there.'

Without waiting for Xunzira's reply, Jongal goes out, bustling with excitement.

Upon reaching the pond with him and Xunzira, Sukumola stands spellbound. Floating on the pond is a magnificent small canoe inlaid with gold. The canoe itself is tied with a gold shackle.

'What a beautiful canoe!' Sukumola exclaims like a young girl. Jongal Bolohu laughs aloud at her bright, happy face.

'You like it?'

'It's so beautiful. Who wouldn't?' Sukumola laughs.

'It's for you. Don't let Asi step on it.'

'Why? Just because you say so? Every morning and evening, I'll be the one to sail on it, dressed up in gold-inlaid clothes,' Xunzira says angrily.

'But don't forget to sing with your toothless mouth. Be careful, the river god might kidnap you for your beauty,' Jongal says seriously.

Sukumola giggles, forgetting her surroundings.

'Look at the way they are laughing – these two always make fun of me.' Xunzira laughs, too.

Some moments pass in enjoyment before Xunzira says, 'Both of you take your time. Let me go and lay out the meal.'

Giving both of them an opportunity to spend time alone, Xunzira leaves.

Laying a hand on the gold shackle, Sukumola says, 'Such a beautiful shackle! Such a beautiful canoe! Where did you get so much gold? Who built it?'

'You like it, Sukumola?'

'Of course. I like it very much.'

'I have not given you anything. So I had it built for you after a lot of thought. You remain confined to the fort. Sail around in the boat now and then. You will feel good.'

'I am happy even otherwise. Xunzira Asi is with me.'

'Are you happy when I am not here?' Jongal asks, fixing his eyes on Sukumola's.

'What are you saying!' she laughs.

'But I don't even feel like going out anymore. I just want to sit near you. Are you trained in Maiyong's magic?'

Sukumola blushes self-consciously. 'I don't know any magic. It's you who knows it. You have imprisoned me here with your magic. You don't even let me go home.'

'Because I don't want to let you go. How can I live without you?'

'How did you live before?'

'God knows – it really surprises me when I think about it. And how did you live in Dimabong?'

'Perhaps I had been seeing you in my dreams.' Sukumola giggles.

Before Jongal can say anything, Xunzira is back. 'Come inside, both of you. Someone called Dhaneswar has arrived from Dimabong. Sukomola's father has sent some things for you.'

The brightness on Sukumola's face extinguishes all at once. Stepping over the dream-like moments, she transforms into a valiant heroine once again.

THIRTY-EIGHT

'Our princess is living blissfully in Sohori, Your Highness, the Queen,' Dhaneswar says. The queen's face lights up. She has been spending unhappy days, not having had a glimpse of her daughter ever since she went away to get married. More than grief, concern for her daughter is making the queen suffer a lot.

The queen does not understand politics. Why did they have to give away their daughter to build an alliance? Was there no other way? Isn't it enough to sit face to face and talk things out openly? What was this custom? How could Fa Bodosa give away the daughter he doted on to a man of another clan living in a strange land? Could there be happiness when obtaining sovereignty in exchange for a daughter? That is why the queen has no peace of mind at all. She wonders how Jongal is treating her daughter and how her daughter is coping amidst strangers, all alone. She has not been able to pay a visit even once because Jongal Bolohu has prevented her from coming, that is for sure. Perhaps the girl is imprisoned inside the fort, immensely sad about not being able to visit her mother. But now, after hearing that her daughter is happy and content, a smile creeps onto her face.

'Please tell me, honourable guest, about all that you have seen and heard,' she asks cheerfully.

'Your Highness, the Queen, you have no reason for feeling anxious. They are looking after My Lady Sukumola very well. They took great care of me, too. She has also sent a letter addressed to you. From what I could see and hear, apparently the two of them are getting along very well. The king has gifted her with a gold-inlaid canoe to sail around. It's even anchored with a gold shackle.'

Taking out the letter, he lavishes more praise upon Jongal Bolohu and Sukumola's married life. When the queen goes indoors happily, Dhaneswar turns grave. The king asks in surprise, 'What is it, Dhaneswar? What are you worrying about?'

'I am worried and upset, Your Majesty.'

'Why? What happened?'

'If I am compelled to tell lies, won't it make me upset, Your Majesty?' Dhaneswar says, heaving a sigh.

'Were you speaking lies just now?' the king asks anxiously.

'They can't be called lies entirely, Your Majesty. My Lady Sukumola appears to be living quite happily, but from what I noticed and heard, it could also be considered false.'

'I don't understand, Dhaneswar.'

'It is difficult to understand. Even I didn't understand initially. She seemed happy, but I observed that she lives like a captive. She is constantly under the watch of a woman named Xunzira, never allowed to be alone for a moment. Shouldn't the queen of a kingdom have the right to be alone sometimes? The letter I gave was just for the queen's eyes. There is a secret letter for you. She had to employ many tactics to write that letter – it hurt me to see that. It seems even Jongal doesn't trust her, keeping constant track of her movements.'

'Perhaps it's out of love and affection for her.'

'Maybe. But don't we also have love and affection? Do we constantly watch over our women?'

'Would he have gifted her a golden boat if he didn't love her? I think you are misinterpreting things, Dhaneswar.'

'I pray to God that each and every one of my observations is a misinterpretation. But is Jongal a man of love? Isn't he the killer of his father? He is a very clever man, Your Majesty. He wants to captivate My Lady Sukumola with the gold canoe. If he truly loved her, would he keep her captive inside the fort? She has never stepped outside. If Princess Sukumola went out, wouldn't she realize Jongal is preparing to attack our kingdom?'

'What are you saying, Dhaneswar? How did you come to know this?'

'Your Majesty, am I not capable of collecting this information for the sake of my kingdom? As you know, I was with my own group of spies. After I was given permission to move around, I observed everything I needed to. I pretended to be a simpleton, claiming I had never seen such a capital before. If we are not careful – we'll be in danger.'

'You have made me really worried, Dhaneswar,' the king says, staying silent for a moment.

'The facts are disturbing, Your Majesty. But a way has to be found. I have drawn up a map of every street, fort and river. Though I could not collect information about their arms and ammunitions or the strength of the army, I shall find out soon – by hook or by crook. It is my responsibility, Your Majesty. I'll help you even at the cost of my life.'

'I am fortunate to have a friend like you, Dhaneswar. You are doing a lot for a foreign kingdom.'

'Please do not call it foreign, Your Majesty. It breaks my heart. I have been fed on the food grown in this land. I'm not sure if I can ever repay the debt. Forget about me – I am a very ordinary man. The welfare of the kingdom is the welfare of all of us. But the way Jongal is growing in strength, the way his army is multiplying, it won't be long before he attacks our kingdom. Has he eyed any other kingdom apart from Kachari, to this day? Now, we have become family. Then what is the purpose of multiplying soldiers and practising for war? I doubt if he has accepted you as family at all. Has he visited our kingdom even once? Has he allowed Princess Sukumola to visit? Your Majesty, this time I asked if he would accept an invitation from his father-in-law. But he avoided the topic. Had he displayed to me the respect and honour befitting a visitor from his father-in-law's kingdom, I would have understood that he had adequate reverence for you. I was made to stay outside the fort. I didn't set eyes on him during my stay there, but the general visited him ten times. I can't understand what there is to talk about at such length. There is hardly any disorder or disquiet within the kingdom. However, people who covet others' kingdoms would have matters to discuss with the general frequently, what else? Haven't I observed you? How many words do you exchange with the general?'

'I must, Dhaneswar. If Jongal is not weakened, we'll be in trouble.'

'Would it be wise to think of the extreme, Your Majesty?'

'What are you trying to say?'

'Despite being an enemy, Jongal is our son-in-law after all. Too much ill feeling would be ominous for us.'

'You are considerate, Dhaneswar. I feel like appointing you my Prime Minister at times. And I shall. Try to acquire fluency in our dialect. Otherwise people might be offended. After all, you are an outsider. You may be respected as a guest, but as a Prime Minister, you may not be accepted.'

'I am very grateful for your magnanimity, Your Majesty. This petty trader has no lofty goals.'

'You might not, but I do – to have a wise and reasonable man like you as our Prime Minister will be to our advantage.'

'You speak like that because of your affection for me, Your Majesty. My competence will be revealed only through my work. What is my contribution anyway? At this hour of crisis faced by the kingdom, of what assistance am I to you? I have only taken from you – I have not been able to give anything in return. The day I am able to make this kingdom absolutely secure is the day I will feel that I have contributed something. I have made it clear to Princess Sukumola also, Your Majesty, that if you succeed in tracking down the divine sword and sending it to us, only then will the threat from Jongal subside. Otherwise, there is fear of great peril for our kingdom.'

'What did Sukumola say?'

'She has agreed to search for it and will inform us once she discovers it. I'm sure she must have mentioned it in her letter. She is a very talented girl, not forgetting her own country even though she is buried in gold and has become a queen, Your Majesty.'

'Truly – I feel sorry when I think about her. Where have I sent my poor girl …'

'Thinking about it breaks the heart, Your Majesty. Friendship with Jongal has increased our strength. The Nagas and the Ahoms have given up eyeing our land, not to speak of the petty kingdoms – all owing to her sacrifice. We have received so much secret information because of her alone. I'm sure she has written more about it in her letter.'

'Let me read the letter. Listening to you has made me so worried that I had almost forgotten about it. Give it to me. I want to read it now.'

Fa Bodosa begins to read with deep concentration as Dhaneswar secretly plans his next move.

THIRTY-NINE

'Do you know the name of this hill?' Jongal Bolohu asks Sukumola, who stands near him on a stockade atop the hill. Absentmindedly gazing at the distant Himalayas, Sukumola turns around and replies, 'No, I don't. What is its name?'

'Rupeswar. It is also called Khulsing Makha. It is said that fairies from the heavens used to descend on this mountain earlier. There is said to be a treasure trove of gold and silver jewels here. I've heard everybody saying it.'

'Do fairies descend from the heavens?' she laughs.

'Of course. A fairy is already standing in front of me,' Jongal chuckles.

'What rubbish.' Sukumola blushes.

'Is it not true? You know, at times I think that if I had not met you, I wouldn't know that the world is so wonderful.'

'Am I so good?'

'You are, Sukumola. When your afa sent the marriage proposal to me, I had actually made up my mind not to accept it. I never wanted to get entangled in marriage. The marriage took place only because of Asi. Had I not listened to her, I would have made a great mistake. I would have lost a fairy like you from easy reach. Xunzira Asi always teases me that I have only now grown into a full man from a dwarf,' Jongal says, laughing heartily.

Jongal had not felt any special attraction towards Sukumola at the beginning. But her humility, loyalty and diligence won him over. Her beauty and good qualities captured the non-conforming Jongal, making him tender and pliant. Initially, Jongal had not fully trusted Sukumola, suspicious of the Kachari king's intentions, but he had received no suspicious information after the wedding. Sohori's spies kept a close watch on the activities of the Kachari kingdom's major general, but Jongal found no grounds for suspicion. He had not received reports of any worrisome discussions between the major general and the Kachari king since the wedding.

Soon, all suspicions abated. Jongal had followed Sukumola's every movement closely at first, remaining on his guard. But in time, Sukumola compelled him to let his guard down. Nowadays, Jongal feels ashamed of himself for his suspicions about this unassuming, gentle, loyal girl.

Presently, Jongal lets Sukumola move around freely within the fort. Frequently, Jongal also goes out on elephant-back with her. These days, Sukumola's company enthralls Jongal. Surmounting all suspicion, sorrow and hardship, Jongal Bolohu has become normal. He has transformed into a happy, content family person and a doting lover.

'I'm thinking of taking you to Dimabong in a day or two,' Jongal Bolohu says.

The absentminded Sukumola is suddenly alert. 'To Dimabong? With me? What is the reason behind such compassion?' Sukumola laughs.

'It has nothing to do with compassion – I don't have any compassion for you, understood?' Jongal says seriously.

'What do you mean?' Sukumola looks at him with fear.

'Did I frighten you? Honestly, I don't have any compassion for you. I have only love. As much as the skies,' Jongal Bolohu says.

'Shall I demonstrate how much love "as much as the skies" is?' Jongal moves closer to Sukumola. Forgetting the dignity of a king, he takes her in his arms.

Freeing herself from Jongal's embrace, Sukumola says, 'Yes, you do have love. I know, I know. But why do you forget that you are a king?'

'So what if I am a king? Don't I have any right to make love?' Jongal laughs. Then he says, 'Are you going to Dimabong or not? This time I am going to leave you there. Stay there for a year or two.'

'A year? Can you?' Sukumola laughs.

'I cannot, for sure. But can you? Tell me – look at my eyes and tell me – can you?'

Forgetting his status, Jongal draws Sukumola into his arms once again.

Sukumola is on the verge of melting. She is on the verge of turning into a river of love. She tries to dam up that river with all her life.

What is she supposed to do? What is she supposed to do with this bountiful love? Should she throw it away into the waters of the Kopili? Destroy the dignity of such trust? The dignity of such love? Dismantle Jongal's security, bit by bit? For the sake of her kingdom? For the well-being of her own kingdom?

For quite some time, the mental conflict has been making her restless. Her nights have been robbed of sleep due to intense anxiety. It has snatched away all the pleasure of the moments of passion.

Everyone is so concerned about her.

How loving they are.

As for Xunzira Asi and Abi Konsari, she is the darling of their hearts.

Recently, Jongal had taken her to the main home at Gobha and also to Amsai Marjong. Jongal's abi and azo had treated Sukumola with so much care and affection that it nearly brought tears of joy to her eyes.

And Jongal?

Perhaps there will be no room left in her heart for Jongal's love. He declares his love to be as vast as the skies, or even greater.

Sukumola is growing weaker. She feels like she's on the brink of losing her resolve.

Had she not sworn in the name of Shibrai, Sukumola might not have shared any information with her father. Sometimes, she's afraid she might forget her promise.

There's no relief.

Her mind knows no respite. The closer Jongal Bolohu gets to her, the more intense her inner turmoil grows.

Dhaneswar's visit has significantly amplified her inner struggles.

According to the guest, it appears that Jongal Bolohu might be planning to attack the Kachari kingdom. He has even brought a letter from her father, reiterating the same concern. Her father makes another puzzling claim.

Jongal Bolohu is said to possess a divine sword, and as long as he wields it, he is invincible. With aspirations of conquering all the kingdoms and becoming an emperor using this unusual weapon, he may be planning an invasion against the Kachari kingdom.

Reading her father's letter and listening to Dhaneswar, Sukumola had felt shocked.

'A divine sword? I haven't heard about the existence of such a thing.'

'It seems our son-in-law worships the sword every day. How would you know, Princess? Does anyone trust you?'

'Why won't they trust me? All of them love me so much.'

'Is trusting someone the same as loving them? You are the Kachari king's daughter. Why would he reveal his strength before you? Our king is only worried about this sword. It is excruciating to watch him. If you could track down the sword, it would be to our advantage. If we obtain it, there will be no need to fear any invasion from Jongal.'

Sukumola could not but accept as true what the guest had said. The man's words had managed to keep her heart from melting. Otherwise, she would have forgotten all about her pledge.

She had heard not a whisper about this sword from anyone in the palace. Perhaps they had all been forbidden from telling her. Perhaps what the honourable guest had said is correct. No one in Sohori trusts her. Not even Jongal. His love, his affection, everything is a facade. Jongal is clearly planning an attack on the Kachari kingdom. Although he has taken her all over the kingdom to show his trust in her, she was never shown the sword lying at home. Jongal was the enemy of the Kachari kingdom. Even hers.

'Are you feeling unwell, Sukumola?' Jongal asks anxiously, seeing her perspiring face resting on his chest.

'It's my head,' wiping her face with both her hands, Sukumola said.

'You are bound to feel unwell. I have brought you too far. I know you are not used to travelling on elephant-back. I should have guessed. Close your eyes for a while. You will feel better,' he says affectionately.

Sukumola does so and falls asleep on Jongal's lap, exhausted.

FORTY

Aai Sareswati rongphool maloti,
Tomaloi mani jao paro.
Pahora namoke suworon koriba,
Jen uzjonia naro.
(O Ma Saraswati,
white and fragrant like the jasmine flower,
we are offering you a pigeon.
May the forgotten verses
return to memory like a school of fishes.)

An elderly man sings to the rhythm of the single-stringed *tokari* in praise of Ma Saraswati. Jongal Bolohu, Xunzira, Abi Konsari and Sukumola sit on the raised platform of the Rongchuwa ground, listening to him. In front of them, people have gathered to join in the fun.

Sohori is bursting with high spirits today. Jongal Bolohu has opened the royal treasury to distribute alms to the poor and is spending lavishly on food and entertainment. He has invited groups of dancers, singers, drummers and other performers from faraway places. All the village heads have been invited to watch the amusements.

The panthais are participating in various sports like *bhota khel*, cock-fighting and top-fighting. So are the teenagers. They are cheering. Laughing. Dancing. Singing. Enjoying the revelries. Feasting together.

Jongal is beside himself with boundless happiness today. Xunzira and Konsari are also overjoyed. Jongal is going to become a father, and Konsari will set eyes on her great-grandchild, while Xunzira will behold her grandchild. Barikas carrying loads of gifts and goods have been dispatched to the Kachari kingdom.

On one side of the Rongchuwa ground, a number of large, whole *rohita* and catfish are being grilled using long skewers over large earthen furnaces. Jongal's favourite dish is grilled fish.

With a bowl of joo-sa in front, Jongal is listening to the ascetic's soulfully melodious song. Sukumola is sitting close to him. Restless. Agitated.

A few days since returning from the Rupeswar hills, an incessant hailstorm of agony seems to have descended upon the young queen. She had fallen asleep as soon as she reached Sohori. Feeling anxious, Xunzira and Jongal Bolohu had nursed her.

When she had felt better, Xunzira had asked Sukumola some embarrassing questions. Then she had said thoughtfully, 'I have other doubts. Don't run around too much.'

After several days, when Sukumola began to experience severe bouts of vomiting, Xunzira confirmed her suspicions and laughed heartily. 'You're going to have a baby, just as I suspected,' she said. 'Now, rest and let me send the news to your father and share it with my son. I need to prepare a gold-studded outfit.'

Xunzira left, and Sukumola remained stunned and frozen for a moment. Then, a wave of joy washed over her.

When Jokanko returned, he showered Sukumola with even more affection. The following day Abi Konsari, who was equally caring and attentive, arrived.

'This time, I'll stay in Sohori, Jokanko. I won't consider myself inferior to my daughter-in-law,' Konsari playfully teased Jokanko.

Xunzira joined in, saying, 'Take this opportunity to enjoy a bowl of joo, Pai.'

Konsari laughed and replied, 'You think I'm like you?'

'I'm a Laloong, not a mekdo' like you. If you had married our old deoraja, you'd be smarter than me,' Xunzira continued to jest.

Konsari retorted, 'Do you want a thrashing from me in your old age? The older you get, the less control you have over your tongue.'

Xunzira couldn't contain her laughter, bending over with mirth.

Despite these joyful and peaceful moments, Sukumola couldn't fully enjoy them. She was restless, consumed by confusion and conflict. Carrying the seed of an enemy in her womb, she felt trapped in a whirlpool.

Which path should she choose? Whose hand should she hold – her paternal kingdom's or that of her husband's? Whose refuge should she seek, and whose trust should she preserve?

'Have you ever heard the songs of Jona Gabhoru before, Sukumola?' Jongal Bolohu asks.

Emerging from her thoughts, she replies, 'I heard a few in my childhood. More like fables than songs.'

'Just listen to them. Are you worrying about something? You seem distracted.'

'No, not at all. I'm listening,' Sukumola tries to focus on the ascetic's songs while keeping her anxieties to herself.

Goruchor rajyote jona gabhoruwe tiri hoi rajpat khai;
Na xo kuworok thoise bondi kori tair maan balaban nai

'Do you know that Jona Gabhoru was also a Kachari king's daughter, just like you? He ruled the Goruchor kingdom, much like our abi,' Jongal tells Sukumola, glancing at Konsari and laughing.

'When have you seen me ruling a kingdom, Nannao? When have I ever imprisoned nine hundred princes?' Konsari responds cheerfully.

'There aren't nine hundred princes, only one – our old deoraja,' Xunzira chimes in playfully.

'I think I'd have to leave Sohori only because of you, Nannao. This old woman talks nonsense,' Konsari playfully retorts.

'You are a young woman, aren't you? But it doesn't matter even if you're not young. Your beauty could still captivate not just nine hundred, but thousands of princes, even now,' Xunzira remarks.

'Asi is absolutely right. You're still very beautiful, Abi. Isn't she, Sukumola?' Jongal adds.

'Oh, really, you people are intolerable. Listen, listen to what the ascetic is singing. I had never heard Jona Gabhoru's songs until today!' Konsari exclaims.

'Because you're a mekdo',' Xunzira says softly.

Everyone bursts into laughter, and Sukumola can't help but join in.

> … *Otikoi jilike balit balichanda,*
> *Otikoi jilike Xun;*
> *Tatukoi jilike Jona je Gabhoru*
> *Jene purnimare jun.*
> (Jona Gabhoru is as bright as the full moon, even brighter than silver and gold).

'Just like you,' Jongal whispers, making Sukumola blush.

'They will hear,' she whispers back.

'Should I speak a little louder for them to hear?'

'If you do, I shall go away.'

'No, no, stay here.'

The ascetic now starts singing the tale of Jona Gabhoru. She was the daughter of King Burha of the Kachari kingdom and ruled as a queen in the Goruchor kingdom. She had imprisoned nine hundred princes in solitary underground cells, all captivated by her beauty and seeking her hand in marriage. For her marriage, she had three conditions: a betel nut and leaf that didn't grow on trees, couldn't be cut with a knife and had no lime in it must be placed in her fist. The ancient iron mortar of her grandfather's days must be split into two at once with a wood-handled axe, and both pieces must be measured on the scale to prove their equality. The third prerequisite was creating a foot-long hole by defecating on the rock in front of Gabhoru's palace.

'Ye-e-e-e—'

Putting her hand over her mouth, Sukumola bursts into laughter, forgetting everything. Waves of her laughter stir all the others, too.

The ascetic carries on singing, full-throated. 'After succeeding in the three tests, the proposing prince must uproot the fan-palm tree spanning a vast area on the eastern side of her residence in one tug. The roots of the palm tree extend overground for about three hundred feet. Nobody knows how deep the roots go underground. Two hundred and twenty-four wild elephants have been tied to the tree trunk. The elephants must be driven away after uprooting the tree. The prospective groom will be taken prisoner if he fails to succeed in the tests.'

'If you had been Jona Gabhoru, I would have run away with you without attempting any of these preconditions,' Jongal says gently.

'Run away with me? You?' Sukumola bends over with laughter.

'Or I would have stayed back as a gobhia.'

Her stomach is about to burst with laughter.

'Don't laugh so much. It's not healthy for you,' Konsari says.

Sukomola sits down properly. All of a sudden, a powerful wave of disquiet washes over her. Standing at the crossroads of confusion and conflict, she writhes again, unable to share her feelings with anybody.

After thirty days of careful pursuit, Sukumola has discovered the existence of the sword in a secret chamber inside the palace. The honourable guest had said that Jongal worships the sword every day, but she had never seen him performing any ritual anywhere inside the palace. She had even kept a close watch on Jongal for a few days after the guest left but found no evidence of it.

When does he worship it then? Where is the sword? Jongal visits the Basundhari temple for prayers every morning. Is the sword inside the temple? Would a sword of this significance be kept in an insecure temple?

When Jongal leaves for the temple in the morning, she is usually asleep. Once she asked to accompany him, but Jongal refused, saying, 'I go running and return the same way. How can you go? There is no need. You can go on elephant-back when you want or visit Maha Deoshal later in the day. Why wake up so early?'

She had given up on waking early after this. Now, just when she is about to give up hope of finding the sword, this fact strikes her mind.

When she becomes certain about the existence of the sword, Sukumola's blood begins to simmer. Jongal had not trusted her. If he had, he would have told her about the sword.

Her father was right.

What the honourable guest said was also true.

Jongal is going to attack the Kachari kingdom. If not today, then tomorrow. Eventually, it will become a subsidiary of his own kingdom.

Worried and filled with hatred for Jongal, Sukumola passes on the information to her father. But soon after, joyful news arrives. Now she is left contemplating her next move.

'Sukumola, what are you thinking about?'

She starts at Jongal's question. 'Nothing really – I am listening,' Sukumola replies.

'Listening? Then tell me, what is he singing?'

'Isn't he singing about the conditions?'

'I knew it. You haven't been listening at all. What is keeping you so distracted? Are you thinking about your mother?' Jongal asks tenderly.

A splash of tears drowns Sukumola's eyes for no reason. 'Yes,' she says with head bowed.

'I know. It would be unnatural not to remember her. Our plan to visit your parents did not work out either. How about inviting them?'

'Do you think they will come?'

'Why won't they? The honourable Dhaneswar is due to arrive, isn't he? Send a letter with him and ask them to come. They must be aware of your condition by now. They won't be able to resist visiting us, mark my words. Now listen attentively. The tale is about to end.'

'… Prince Gopison of Nagaon decked himself up and set out to rescue the nine hundred princes and marry Queen Jona

Gabhoru. Gopison is the only child of his widowed mother. His widowed mother tried to prevent Gopison, saying, "Jona Gabhoru, is doomed, my son; you must not go. Her hair is lizard-tailed, her gait is awkward and she is arch-footed. She walks, looking back at the people. She is a voracious ghost, carrying a massive load of rice grains in her lap and gulping them down. Her teeth are jutted, her smile is hideous, her head is crawling with lice, her cheeks are swollen, she is as dark as coal and there is a black mole on her forehead – curly-haired, repulsive."'

'Oh, Shibrai – so hideous.' Sukumola falls down laughing. She forgets that she had become a soldier of her country a little while ago.

'Do you think Gopison was dumb like our Jokanko? He understood very well that his mother is lying. If it had been our Jokanko, he would have gone off to sleep, drinking joo.' Xunzira laughs aloud.

'Asi, he told me that he would have either run away with her or stayed as a gobhia. He also wouldn't have accepted the conditions, he said.' Sukumola bursts out laughing once again.

'Who is this hero? Wanting to be a gobhia? You need to be cured by a faith healer from Maiyong,' Xunzira laughs.

The ascetic sings on: 'Gopison did not listen to his mother. He approached Jona Gabhoru, fulfilled the conditions, released the twelve hundred wild elephants, killed Jona's heroic brother Abhimon and took away Jona Gabhoru by marrying her.'

In those moments of gaiety, the chefs at the Rongchuwa ground start to serve the grilled fish before them.

FORTY-ONE

'Aai.'

Sukumola, forgetting her physical condition, rushes to embrace her mother as she crosses the palace doorway. In front of everyone, she breaks down sobbing in her mother's arms. Her mother is crying, too, her emotions a tumultuous mix of grief and delight. If not for the invitation from Sohori, she might never have the chance to visit her daughter. When the messenger from Sohori arrives with numerous gifts, food and the news of Sukumola's impending motherhood, a rush of sorrow and joy overwhelms her.

It has been more than a year since her daughter left for an unfamiliar land to forge an alliance. Ever since the wedding, anxiety for her youngest daughter has been gnawing at the queen mother. She'd never imagined such a marriage could bring good news. It hardly seemed like a marriage, more a political alliance between a powerful, aging king and a young, potentially powerful one. As both a queen and a mother, she had found it challenging to accept this union.

This was the reason she vehemently objected to the marriage, shedding countless tears. But no one paid heed to her protests, not even Sukumola herself. Accepting defeat when the queen gave up food and took to her bed, her daughter had come to her. Raising her mother from the bed, she sat opposite her and said, 'Why are you grieving, Aai? If my marriage with the king of Sohori is beneficial to my kingdom, tell me, why shouldn't I do it? My afa is such a great king. If his kingdom fell under the control of some other kingdom, and someone from another land were sat on his throne, would you be happy? Could you bear it? As for me, I could not, Aai.'

Looking at the calm, sober face of her daughter about to be sacrificed for her kingdom, the queen's heart felt like it was crumbling to pieces. Was she not aware that though she gave so many reasons to her mother, Sukumola herself has been shedding silent tears?

The queen had been helpless before her husband and daughter's logic and decision. Determined not to watch her daughter being sacrificed, she did not attend the wedding in Sohori. She did not give her blessings.

Since then, the queen had spent every day and night worrying. Despite the king's and Dhaneswar's assurances that Sukumola was happy and content, the queen's mind couldn't accept it. She couldn't shake the feeling that Sukumola was not well, that she endured unhappy days in the unfamiliar kingdom.

She had wanted to visit her daughter many times, but the king would not permit it. 'Have they invited you? You're the queen of a kingdom like Dimabong. Why should you visit another king's house, even if it's your son-in-law's, without a formal invitation?' the king said, expressing his displeasure at his daughter and son-in-law's lack of visits.

After receiving the news of Sukumola's approaching motherhood and the invitation, the queen has succeeded in arriving in Sohori, overthrowing all such obstacles. She has come bearing every provision necessary to cook and feed her daughter herself, as well as plenty of gifts. Upon her arrival, she has entered into a hurricane of sorrow and joy from the doorway itself.

'You remembered me after so long, Aai? Why have you come to see me after so long? How did I offend you, Aai, that you have been punishing me like this?' Sukumola says, her head resting on her mother's chest, tears streaming down her face. Xunzira observes the scene with misty eyes.

After some time she said, 'Don't cry, Pohari. Come, come inside, bring your mother inside. She is exhausted from the journey. Please come in, Your Highness, the Queen. Honourable guest, please come inside.'

'Your daughter-in-law is not letting me go. She is blocking the way,' the Kachari queen says, moving her fingers gently over her daughter's hair.

'You too have started teasing me just like Asi, haven't you?' Sukumola laughs.

'Or else you would make me cry and cry.' Her mother smiles, her eyes pouring. Sukumola is in tears already. She looks at her mother and says, 'Of course I would. Who made you remember your daughter after so long, Aai?'

'Don't speak like that, my child. We are the women of the royal family. Can I come even if I want to? Even you forgot all about us after coming to your new home. You didn't visit even once.'

'We were planning to visit. Your son-in-law was supposed to go. But ...' Sukumola blushes and lowers her head.

'That's precisely why I rushed to your side, my dear.'

'So it took you two months to rush here.' Sukumola smiles while wiping her tears, then gestures to Xunzira and says, 'This is our *madoi*, about whom I had mentioned in my letter. Remember?'

'Oh, greetings, *Jamaijou*,' her mother says, looking at Xunzira.

'Greetings,' Xunzira replies, folding her hands.

'Come, please come inside. You too, honourable guest.'

Dhaneswar, who has been watching the mother–daughter reunion with masked irritation, folds his hands and smiles, 'Perhaps I should go to the guest house, Asi.'

'No, no, come inside. You came as a messenger earlier, but today you're our guest. You must stay here. Do come in.'

The khamsamai carries the visitors' luggage, and everyone enters the palace. Konsari is waiting in the lobby. She stands up as they enter. The queen stops in awe when she sees Konsari.

'Aai, this is our abi,' Sukumola says.

The queen, arranging her *rikowsa* over her head, greets Konsari with folded hands and says, 'Sukumola had written about you in her letter. Those who attended the wedding had spoken highly of you, too. It's a pleasure to meet you here.'

Returning the greeting, Konsari says politely, 'We were eagerly waiting to see you. Your arrival has delighted us.'

The queen and Dhaneswar take their seats, while Sukumola remains standing. Xunzira goes inside.

'I've heard so much about you, Aai. Those who saw you at the wedding said that there isn't a girl in our kingdom as beautiful as the king's abi.'

Konsari asks, puzzled, 'What is she saying?'

'She's saying there's no girl as beautiful as you, Abi,' Sukomola explains.

'Am I a girl, a *mattlasa*?' Konsari laughs.

Xunzira and a khamsamai come in with two bell-metal bowls filled with joo arranged on a bell-metal dish, two bowls of water and a small, round tray filled with betel nuts. Offering them to the guests, Xunzira says, 'You must be exhausted after the journey. Do please quench your thirst first – you can freshen up later on.'

Dhaneswar is staring at the pile of silver betel nuts and leaves arranged over a gold tray in the centre of the room, his eyes glittering with greed.

'How lovely these two bunches of betel nuts and leaves are. Where did you get them, Aai? How did you make them?' Dhaneswar can't help asking.

'These have been made here itself. They are put together by wrapping threads of gold and silver around them. Some of the utensils are of silver, others of silver inlaid with gold. Do you like them?' Konsari asks, smiling.

'Oh, yes, Aai. I am astounded. I had never imagined that I would be so fortunate to view such rare objects with my two eyes. I have seen many silver-gold objects in Our Majesty's palace. But here I have seen a silver market, a gold market.'

'I wonder how our honourable guest would have reacted if he had seen Pratappur.' Xunzira laughs.

'I have been to those places, Asi. During my days of trade. My own people are there, too. But they are ordinary peasants and labourers. Bell-metal bowls and dishes are their limit. However, I did not have the good fortune to enter the fort of Pratappur. Surely, a king's fortune and that of his subjects are not the same, is it?'

'Honourable guest, you must not weigh your fortune with gold and silver. Can gold and silver bring peace? Not even to the king. Only living together with unity and harmony can create peace,' Konsari says.

'Aai is absolutely correct. Living in unity is most important. Even I tell our king. Instead of becoming a great king by expanding frontiers, everybody should live in harmony. The subjects should be well looked after,' Sukumola's mother says.

'I tell Jokanko the same thing, too. Initially, he did not understand. He used to expand the frontiers by waging war. But now he does not wish to fight anymore. He is concerned with the welfare of his subjects, the growth of agriculture, trade and commerce,' Konsari says.

'This has been possible due to our old deoraja and Konsari Pai. There is hardly anyone as righteous as our deoraja, anywhere,' Xunzira says.

'I have heard about him, Jamaijou. Sukumola had mentioned him in her letter. Those who attended the wedding also said the same thing. My daughter has married into a very noble family. Do look after her as your own, Aai.'

'How can we look after her – she is the one who really looks after us. She is a very *lukhumi* pohari – a blessed daughter-in-law,' Xunzira says.

'But you have to stay for long, Aai,' Sukumola says.

'Not this time, my love. I have come to treat you to a meal. I shall stay for two days and leave.'

'Two days?' Sukumola goes pale. 'Why did you come for two days? You needn't have come at all.'

'Some days ago, a vulture dropped a piece of flesh on the frontyard. It is very ominous. A ritual to seek Aai Gamadi's blessings has been intended. On top of it, there has been no rainfall in this season of cultivation. So a phuja to worship Aai Herembeswari by erecting a *misenko* is also in the offing. I have to go, my child. What can I do? We are *hashri gojoni* – the deer of an enclosed forest. Can I stay back even if I want to? I shall be here again. On time. Then I shall stay longer. It has to be only two days this time, love.'

'I know. You don't love me.'

'Why are you hurting your mother, Pohari? Even if it is for two days she has come, hasn't she? Don't you realize the number of responsibilities the queen of a kingdom has? You are a queen yourself. Haven't you experienced it?' Xunzira lightly chides. Then, looking at the queen, she smiles, 'Your daughter is very sentimental, Pai. She gets upset even with us over petty matters, you know.'

'Asi – Aai will think it's true.'

'If you are a good pohari, take your mother inside. Let me arrange some snacks.'

'I don't want to have anything now, Jamaijou. It's evening already.'

'Are you going to stay on an empty stomach just because it is evening?'

'Asi is right. The jerks and jolts from the elephant ride have really made me ravenous,' Dhaneswar says.

Everybody laughs aloud.

'Please come inside. A separate room has been arranged for you. Please go there. Do freshen up by the time the food is served.' Xunzira signals to a khamsamai waiting at the doorway. Dhaneswar accompanies him.

Dhaneswar's delight knows no bounds. For the first time, he has entered the interior of the palace. During his earlier visit, he had stayed in a guest house outside the fort. Even there, he couldn't see much because he was always with someone or the other. That is why this time Dhaneswar has accompanied the queen to Sohori. He knows there will be no opposition from any quarter when it comes to the king's mother-in-law's retinue. It would be a good opportunity for Dhaneswar to inspect both the interior and exterior of the fort.

Dhaneswar moves toward his goal, step by step. With great dexterity, he succeeds in creating tremendous hatred for Jongal in the Kachari king's mind. Only a few more steps now. Suddenly, a khamsamai says, 'Honourable guest, these are your change of clothes.'

Taking the clothes, Dhaneswar looks at the khamsamai, who has an innocent face.

'Oh, there was no need for these clothes. I have brought my own,' Dhaneswar says.

'Asi has given them. She said they're new.'

'Your asi is indeed magnanimous. Very kind. This is why you all have been blessed with such a god-like king. But I haven't seen His Majesty. Isn't he in the capital?'

'Yes, he is. He has gone out of the fort.'

'Is it? I wonder where.'

'To warfare training.'

'Warfare training? Is he intending to go to war again?'

'We have no knowledge about all that,' the boy says sombrely.

'Oh, I am just asking. We are also khamsamais like you. It scares us to hear about battle, you know,' Dhaneswar laughs.

'Please rest.' The khamsamai leaves, greeting him with folded hands.

At that moment, Sukumola's mother is engaged in conversation with her daughter, having freshened up. After replying to her daughter's endless queries, she asks, 'How do you like it here, Sukumola?'

'I am quite comfortable. Everybody loves me a lot. But I am always worried about you all, Aai.'

'It is very natural. But it is useless to ruin your health by worrying. We all are quite good, too. No doubt your absence pains us. Even your afa grieves for you. Apart from that, everything else is going on smoothly. What can you do, my child – you decided to get married and move to a distant land thinking that it would be favourable. Now you must try to live with everybody cordially. I am really pleased to see your *abou* and madoi. They are very good people. Look after them well. They are old women. Treat them with love and care. You will be loved in return.'

'They are really very good, Aai. I try my best to take care of them. But they don't allow me to work much. Abi has taught me so many new things. She is not a Laloong, you know – she was the queen of Pratappur. You must be aware?'

'Yes – I am. I have heard about it. A very tragic life.'

'It's not tragic despite being tragic, Aai. Here, everybody looks up to her as a goddess. And as for her, because of the way she has been serving the people by becoming one with them, today everyone has completely forgotten that she was an outsider. She doesn't live here. She lives in Gobha. Despite your son-in-law's insistence, she does not live here, saying that it would inconvenience her people. She has been here for quite some time now. She is supposed to stay for a few more days. She takes great care of me, Aai.'

'What about my son-in-law?'

'He, too. I think he takes greater care of me than Afa does for you. He is such a great king. He is very busy. Even then.'

'It's really fortunate to gain a husband's attention. Is my son-in-law in the royal sanctum? It's evening already – he is not home yet?'

'I am not sure where he is exactly, Aai. After returning from the Deoshal temple and having his meal, he has gone out. He said he will be late before leaving.'

'Doesn't he tell you anything before leaving home?'

'Sometimes he does. Sometimes he does not. I have qualms about asking him, too.'

'It's better not to ask. You are a woman from another kingdom. And the friendship is new, too. He might be offended. It's different with ordinary people's wives. But a king's wife should not be very eager to know everything. Moreover, how are outside issues important to us? All that matters is being able to live in peace and harmony.'

'But over here, things are a little different, Aai. My mother-in-law herself had ruled a kingdom. Even Abi lives all alone in Gobha and looks into various issues of the kingdom. These days she even takes me with her to deal with public matters. However, I have gone only once or twice. Ever since my pregnancy, I have not been allowed to venture out alone. It's really boring.'

'But it's for your own good. Don't be unhappy.'

'Aai, aren't you going to look at my gold canoe?' Sukumola says suddenly.

'You can show the gold canoe to your mother later on. Now bring your mother. Let her have something to eat,' Xunzira says from the doorway.

At that very moment, Dhaneswar is peeping through the window in an attempt to figure out the set-up.

Leaving her mother to eat and going out to call Dhaneswar, when Sukumola notices him, she gives in to laughter. 'What are you looking at, honourable guest?'

'Oh, My Lady, please come on in. Let me tell you something,' Dhaneswar says excitedly.

'What is the matter, honourable guest?' entering the room, Sukumola asks, a little surprised.

Something happened, you see. I was resting. Suddenly noticing a shadow, I looked out of the window. Someone left in a jiffy. He was watching me.'

'Why should anyone watch you? Are you a young maid?' Sukumola laughs.

'You guessed right. My Lady is very intelligent. But I feel you have not realized the gravity of the matter,' Dhaneswar says gravely.

'I really have not understood.'

'But of course, how would you? Since you do not receive any information.'

'What information do I not receive? Please explain clearly what you are trying to say.'

'I shall tell you clearly enough. But tell me, are you really not aware of anything? About what is going on inside and outside the fort?' Dhaneswar mutters, as if telling a secret.

'What is going on? Please tell me now,' Sukumola asks inquisitively.

'Are you really not aware that your husband, the king, is practising warfare?'

'Practising warfare? Who told you?'

'Who would tell me now? I have known for a long time. I didn't let you know because there was no means. I thought, that is, His Majesty thought that it is within your knowledge. Nevertheless, he has sent a letter to you assuming that you may not be aware. That is why I myself accompanied Her Highness, the Queen, once again.'

Taking out the letter and giving it to Sukumola, Dhaneswar says, 'Her Highness is totally ignorant, mind it. We haven't informed her. She is very soft-hearted. She will be frightened. Make sure not to tell her anything.'

'I shall not,' Sukumola says, going through the letter hurriedly.

'Our hopes rest on you alone. His Majesty says that no one except you can save Dimabong. Noticing his faith in you, I am astounded. He says, "It's my good fortune and great pride to be the father of a daughter having such love for her country."'

Folding the letter, Sukumola looks up. 'So much has been happening, and I am totally in the dark.'

'How would you know, Princess? Unless you are told. Your husband, the king, has gone to practise warfare even today. I suppose you don't know, do you?'

'No, I don't. I was not informed.'

'Apparently, you are not trusted, My Lady. However, he cannot be blamed. After all, you are the daughter of an enemy king. He is preparing to attack his father-in-law's kingdom – why ever would he inform you? Would that make you happy? Moreover, you are not well, too.'

'Even then, I would have liked to know. But I have not heard a single word from anybody about a possible invasion of our kingdom.'

'There – now do you understand? Xunzira Asi may be in the dark – but what about Abi? She participates in everything, doesn't she? You ought to have heard something at least from her or some other people from inside the fort. If you think deeply, the whole matter is really very disheartening. You are the queen of this kingdom – yet no one informs you about anything. Is loving and trusting the same thing? But little do they know how intelligent you are. How courageous. They cannot even imagine what sacrifices you are capable of, for the sake of your own kingdom. Where can you find a woman of such substance? But let's not talk anymore, Princess. Let's go outside. You don't know who is watching and from where.'

'In fact, I had come to invite you for some refreshments. Please come, honourable guest.'

Sukumola goes out worriedly, concealing the letter.

FORTY-TWO

The royal palace of Dimabong finds itself encircled by the Tiwasha army. Long torches illuminate the hands of every soldier, casting an eerie glow. Flaming arrows, tipped with iron-wood seeds, rain down upon the palace, leaving crimson stains across the courtyard. Lifeless bodies are strewn in chaotic disarray. The unexpected onslaught of savage soldiers has left the palace's once secure fortifications in ruins.

The palace is engulfed in a raging inferno, the entire capital consumed by merciless flames. Blades, spears and knives glisten with deadly intent under the torchlight. Jongal Bolohu, donned in a rhino-skin vest, brandishes the resplendent divine sword while standing defiantly before the defenceless Bodosa. His laughter reverberates through the chaos. Amidst the cacophony of cries, moans, maniacal laughter and anguished screams, Bodosa collapses, life draining into a crimson pool. The divine sword impales him through his chest.

Sukumola, her breath coming in desperate gasps, writhes in agony, her cries for help echoing through the turmoil.

'*Sukumola* … *Sukumola*—' Someone is shaking her by the shoulders, and she opens her eyes with great effort to see an anxious face above hers.

'What is it, Sukumola? Are you not feeling well?' Jongal Bolohu asks with concern.

Sukumola stares at her husband through her delirium. It is not the same hideous, vengeful face she saw moments ago. It is the face of a husband. The adoring face of the concerned husband of an expecting woman.

'What's wrong, Sukumola? Why are you staring like this? Do you want some water? Should I call Asi? Abi?'

'Some water, please,' Sukumola replies wearily, emerging from her nightmare.

Jongal fetches a bowl of water, helps Sukumola sit up and take a few sips. He then gently wipes her face with a damp cloth.

'Did you have a bad dream?' he asks affectionately.

'Yes,' Sukumola responds, her eyes filled with tears.

Jongal pulls her closer, running his fingers through her hair, and asks, 'What was it about?'

'It was a very bad dream. I mustn't disclose it. I shall tell the tulsi plant.'

'Oh, you've learned all this from living with Asi, I can see. She is full of dos and don'ts. But I don't follow any of that. It's natural to have bad dreams in your state of health and such hot weather. Go back to sleep. Let me call for help. Let someone stay with you until I return from the Basundhari temple,' he suggests.

'No need. Please sit down.' She grasps Jongal's hand just as he is about to leave.

Sitting down again, he looks at Sukumola. Traces of fear and sadness still linger in her tearful eyes.

'Where were you yesterday?' Sukumola asks with agitation in her voice.

'Why do you want to know?' Jongal is surprised.

'Because of the dream. Where were you all of yesterday?'

'I was watching the new recruits train in warfare. Did you see me fighting in your dream?' Jongal can't help laughing.

'I told you – I mustn't say. I feel so miserable. I don't like battles and wars. Not at all.'

'I know. That's why I don't tell you anything these days. I've noticed that you get depressed when such matters come up.'

'Why did you have to recruit new soldiers again? We already have so many.'

'Soldiers don't remain the same forever, do they? We need new recruits. Toothless, grey-haired soldiers can't defend the kingdom!' Jongal laughs. 'Please go to sleep. Don't worry yourself with these thoughts. What did Asi say? These times are for thinking good thoughts, listening to good things. I'll send her. It's almost daybreak.'

After coaxing Sukumola off to sleep, he leaves. The moment he goes outside, however, she sits up again. Her face, once radiant like the soft morning sun, resembles the sky before a storm.

He is right.

The honourable guest is right.

Only Sukumola didn't believe it.

Jongal Bolohu is preparing to attack the Kachari kingdom. He is amassing soldiers, arms, ammunition. Sukumola is being held captive by his love, kept in the dark about everything.

For this very enemy of her country, Sukumola wants to melt away! She wants to melt away in love!

How foolish she is!

She had sworn in the name of Shibrai to safeguard her kingdom. She had offered to sacrifice her life for her kingdom. She had willingly chosen to be a Laloong queen to spy for her kingdom.

What has she done!

Her father had instructed her to discreetly send weapons from Jongal's private armoury, one by one. But she couldn't do that, as Jongal visits his armoury every day. She was asked to send detailed information about the inside of the fort, but how much could she actually send! Oh, if only she could have – how propitious it would have been for the Kachari kingdom! Her kingdom wouldn't have faced disaster at the hands of Jongal.

The honourable guest is right.

Sukumola's sense of perception is quite low. She lacks the ruthless, focused insight of a spy.

Her father says she won't have to do anything anymore. Sending the divine sword will be enough. It is the cause of Jongal's arrogance, the source of his strength. If Sukumola manages to dispatch the sword, Jongal will become powerless.

Sukumola gets out of bed and starts walking with tired steps. These days, her energy is dwindling. She gets tired easily, her weight increasing by the day. Her unborn child, ready to enter the world, is beginning to play in her womb. When the child in her womb makes its presence known through its movements, Sukumola is left bewildered, feeling a mix of unnamed emotions and agony. A sharp-edged question repeatedly strikes her heart: who reigns supreme?

Is it her husband or her motherland?

Which is supreme?

Motherhood or the duty of a soldier?

She has been secretly supporting her maiden home while living in her husband's – is it patriotism or treachery?

Despite being the queen of Pratappur, and Jongal's remorse, Konsari had returned to Gobha, entrusting the governance of the kingdom to the son of a maid.

Abi Konsari is grateful to her adopted kingdom. Committed.

And Sukumola?

Isn't her position far more powerful than Konsari's here?

She is the queen, the wife of Jongal Bolohu and the soon-to-be mother of his child. Which is supreme? Husband or motherland? Family bonds or the security of the kingdom's subjects?

As Sukumola contemplates her choices, her unwavering loyalty to her motherland takes precedence. She feels like a devoted soldier, willing to sacrifice everything for her country. Yet Jongal's affection also tugs at her heart, attempting to melt her resolve. As she gazes at his slumbering face, she senses the playful movements of their unborn child. She thinks of her marital family, showering her with the finest of provisions, and Jongal, eager to fulfil her every desire. She longs to surrender herself to this affection and gratitude.

After her morning bath, Sukumola prays to the sun and makes a solemn decision – this will be her final act. Once she delivers the sword, she will undertake no further missions for her father's kingdom. Once her duty is fulfilled, she will live as Jongal's wife and the queen of Sohori. She is determined to dissuade her husband from attacking her father's kingdom and make him swear in their child's name. Could he, after taking such an oath, invade her father's kingdom, even if he were the enemy king's daughter? Is Jongal truly so ruthless and inhumane?

It's challenging to believe that Jongal's strength is solely derived from the sword. He possessed courage even before acquiring it, didn't he? Yet perhaps her father is correct. Is his audacity to invade the Kachari kingdom also contingent on the sword? If Jongal succeeds in conquering Dimabong, he will become the greatest king south of the Brahmaputra. Khola and Sohori will eclipse even the Ahom kingdom. Ratnasinha already rules in the north, Samol in Pratappur and Gobha holds sway over its loyal provinces. Khola and Sohori maintain friendly relations with smaller kingdoms to the southwest of the Brahmaputra. They have forged close bonds with the Jaintia and Dimoruwa kingdoms. Sohori enjoys a warm alliance with the Bhuyans of Bordoba, who offered to erect the grand canopy for Sukumola and Jongal's wedding as a symbol of friendship. Sukumola and the people of Dimabong were captivated by the splendid canopy fashioned from spears. With such close friendships established, how difficult would it be to sway the minor Bhuyan clans? Sukumola is beginning to place her trust in her father's analysis.

If she hadn't stumbled upon hints about Jongal's secret activities, perhaps she wouldn't be so convinced. It serves her purpose well. If she delivers the sword to her father, Jongal's self-confidence will crumble. If he fails to locate the sword before his impending battle, Jongal will hesitate to wage war.

But won't he grow suspicious of her? Won't he suspect her involvement? Jongal is a peculiar man; would he spare her?

No, Jongal would never believe she was responsible. She will soon be the mother of his child. He would never fathom that she would undertake such a deed.

And even if he were to suspect her, there's little she can do. Having sworn in Shibrai's name, she arrived here through marriage. Even if she has to endure consequences while trying to honour her vow, she won't waver. She doesn't aim to destroy Jongal, only to safeguard her motherland. Her father even promised that, after securing the divine sword, he would never assail Sohori.

And why would he, anyway?

Is her father so inhuman? Could he do injustice to his own son-in-law? Wouldn't such injustice bring injustice upon his own daughter? Her father, too, is gallant. Not mean. He has taken resort to such means to save his kingdom. But which king does not take this path to save his subjects and his kingdom? Jongal's intelligence staff collect secret information from the Kachari kingdom even now, don't they? Didn't she overhear Jongal talk to the chief of intelligence staff?

It will be fine. If the sword is dispatched, both the families would be saved.

After invoking the sun god, Sukumola comes to her mother's room, where Abi Konsari, Xunzira Asi and her mother are chatting. As soon as she enters, Xunzira exclaims, 'Pohari, my child, aren't you feeling hungry today? Your mother is waiting to have breakfast with you.'

'Aai, let's go.' Sukumola smiles.

'Wait, come in first. I've brought some trinkets for all of you. Let me hand them out. I wanted to give Aai and Jamaijou their gifts. But they wanted to wait for you.'

Sukumola comes in and sits on the bed. Her mother picks up a floral-patterned bag made of cotton lying nearby. Placing a pair of gold earrings, a black mekhela with white flowers and a silk riha on a bota, her mother offers it to Xunzira and says, 'What can I give to you, Jamaijou – these are trivial objects. It'll make me happy if you accept them.'

'Oh my goodness – so beautiful! How could they be trivial? But this silk riha is of no use to me, Pai. I get along wearing the mekhela over my breast in the methoni style with the chador over it. What is there in my old body to cover with a riha? Pai, please give it to her.' Xunzira laughs, after taking the gifts, revealing her teeth blackened with *kajila*, the black gum made from burnt bamboo and used for coating teeth.

Sukumola and her mother cover their faces and laugh.

'How many bowls of joo did you devour early in the morning?' Konsari laughs, mildly hitting Xunzira on her head.

'It's not our joo, I promise. I've drunk *jugara* brought by Pohari's mother. A joo fermented for six months. Very delicious,' Xunzira giggles.

Laughing, Sukumola's mother arranges a floral riha woven with eri, a coarse yarn spun from muga cocoon, a pair of *rigu* and rikowsa, a gem-studded ring, an ivory comb and betel nut and leaf over a bota. Offering them to Konsari, she says with folded hands, 'Aai – these are for you. What can I offer to an angelic lady like you? It will give me great pleasure if you wear them without hesitation.'

'Pai, do these words go with you? You are the queen of such a great kingdom. What is Sohori compared to it?' Xunzira says.

'Is great and small measured by the size of a kingdom, Jamaijou? I have given away my own daughter to your family. You have been looking after her with love and care. Accepted her as your very own. That itself has humbled me. I am not a queen now, Jamaijou, I am a mother only.'

Konsari picks up the gifts from the bota and in turn places a necklace of gold beads, an eri scarf and a few cowrie shells. She says in a composed voice, 'Sajjoh, there is no such thing as great and small. Even your daughter is looking after us, looking after our son with love and affection – she is going to be the mother of our son's child. You are great yourself, which is why you can talk so humbly. May Fa Mahadeo bless you and your kingdom with peace and prosperity. Do keep visiting us. We, too, shall visit you. We are indeed very fortunate to have relatives like you all.'

Listening to Konsari, Sukumola's eyes brim with tears without any reason. She says softly, 'Aren't you going to give me anything, Aai?'

'Oh my god, what is our pohari saying? If your mother hasn't brought anything, what are our gifts for? I am happy with my vessel of jugara. That will do.' Xunzira laughs again.

'For you I have brought the most, my child.'

Taking out a scarf worn by men designed with floral motifs, an eri shawl and a knife with an ivory handle, and handing them to Konsari, her mother says, 'This cloth is called *jupai*. Young men wear it during Bihu. It may be worn at other times also. It takes a lot of labour to weave. These two items are for my son-in-law. The eri shawl is for Sukumola's *ajou*.'

'Deoraja is going to love it. I don't know what our Jokanko is going to do with the jupai – he is a wild man – god knows if he will understand the importance of jupai. However, he will love the knife, no doubt.' Everybody laughs together.

Offering the bag to Sukumola, her mother says, 'These are yours. There are a variety of things inside. You can look at them later on. Oh, by the way – you must wear our costume today. I myself shall cook and serve you a meal today. I have got something new for you. Let me show you what it is.'

Opening the bag, her mother takes out a pair of rigu, *rija*, *spai* and red *rikaousa* with black flowers to be worn as a veil and gives them to Sukumola. She then takes out a silk blouse with flower work on it. A short, Chinese-style, long-sleeved blouse.

'Oh, Ma Kalikha – whatever is this?' Feeling the blouse with her fingers, Xunzira exclaims.

'This is not our costume. It is worn by the Ahom king and the wives of high officials. It belongs to the other side of the Patkai mountains. It's called the *Xingkhap* blouse. It covers up the body very nicely. Looks beautiful, too.'

'Really, very beautiful,' Konsari says.

'It's very pretty, Aai. I wonder what it would be like to wear,' Sukumola says.

'It will suit you, Pohari. Your body is not dried up like ours, is it?'

Konsari covers Xunzira's mouth with her hand. Sukumola falls down laughing. Even her mother is laughing. She is feeling light-hearted. Her daughter's happy family life has lifted the heavy rock of anxiety from her heart.

'Come, Sajjoh – Sukumola, come, let's go and have breakfast.' Konsari rises.

'Please go ahead, all of you – I shall go and change into the clothes brought by Maah.'

'Wait, wait – don't lift the bag. Let me call a khamsamai,' Konsari says.

Sukumola excitedly brings out the bag of clothes gifted by her mother. Handing it to a khamsamai, Konsari and the others walk out. Just then they see Dhaneswar, who is sitting on a gold-inlaid stool with a tray of delicacies spread before him, waiting eagerly.

The lavish treat includes parboiled rice, rice cakes cooked in bamboo tubes, curd, honey, banana, grated coconut smeared with jaggery, guava, ripe mulberry, plum, honey-fig, ripe mango, sweet fruits, wild chestnut, steamed rice-cake, sweet rice-cake, pounded wet rice and rice cakes fried with salt and pepper. 'The honourable guest must be tired of waiting,' Xunzira says laughing, sensing Dhaneswar's restlessness.

'I am not tired, Asi. In fact, I can't seem to finish counting. There are so many kinds of fruits, so many varieties of snacks – even if my greedy tongue can control itself, my stomach cannot endure. As a matter of fact, I used to be a skinny landlord of the west. Even marrying a Kachari woman has been useless – a trader's stomach, after all. It's worrying me, but I can't seem to control my mouth.'

Sukumola is nearly falling over with laughter again. Xunzira has not been able to control her laughter either. Despite their best efforts, both Sukumola's mother and Konsari end up laughing heartily.

Dhaneswar is gnashing his teeth. Thinking, 'Laugh – go on laughing – you eyeless daughters of Laloong-Kachari. How long are you going to laugh – I am merely pretending to be humble, but I am not humble at all. I am a man who makes hay while the sun shines. Wait and watch how I spread my shoots from a small branch. It won't be long.'

'Is our son-in-law not eating?' asks Sukumola's mother.

'Of course he will. He'll be here any moment. He visits Basundhari every day, you see. Please sit down, Pai.'

Sukumola's mother and Konsari sit down. As does Xunzira. Two khamsamais serve the food in gold platters over the stools.

'I cannot bear to eat in gold platters. My heart begins to race. Gold platters and bowls in Dimabong and gold platters and bowls here – where do you get so much gold from?' Dhaneswar asks.

'But you know where the gold comes from, honourable guest. You are a traveller, after all. It's found in the river sand. Long narrow pieces of gold are obtained after washing it. It's a tough job. Our people do it and barter the gold to earn their livelihood. If you are so fond of it, we could get you married to a gold washer's daughter,' said the Kachari queen, concealing her irritation.

'No need, Pai. His eyes can barely absorb the dazzle of the dishes. Marrying a goldwasher's daughter would have affected his heart.' Xunzira laughs.

'Let him eat in peace, Xunzira.' Konsari gravely hides a smile. Then looking at Dhaneswar, she says, 'Gold plates and bowls are required to serve revered visitors, honourable guest. It's a king's house. Kings and officers from different kingdoms keep visiting here. Moreover, Jokanko is the apple of everyone's eyes. As you know, the flood of Kopili and Borpani rivers is wreaking havoc over Sohori. In the midst of such havoc, the king's cultivation process has been yielding enough paddy for stocking every year. He has made great strides in trade and commerce too, exporting items such as aloe wood perfume, sandalwood, ivory, buffalo, paddy and pulse. He has also brought in from outside skilled workers and craftsmen to the kingdom. With the help of Brahmin pundits who had migrated during his father's rule, he has opened up schools to facilitate reading and writing. During the monsoon when Borpani's waters flood Kopili, it overflows its banks. Digging canals from Kopili to Kolong has helped control the deluge significantly. The king is also trying to reduce inundation from floodwaters by way of fortification. You have been able to witness all of this because of his efforts.'

'What are you talking about, Abi?' Jongal comes in and, greeting his mother-in-law, sits down.

'I was talking about you, Syu,' Konsari smiles. 'Come, sit with us.'

'Where is Sukumola?' the king asks, sitting at a distance from his mother-in-law.

'She will be here any moment. Have patience. He only wants Pohari. Where has your hunger gone?' Xunzira demands.

Deeply embarrassed in the presence of his mother-in-law, Jongal says, 'I'm famished, Asi.'

Breaking open a honey-fig the size of a ripe pomegranate and licking its honey, Dhaneswar says, 'I couldn't wait for Your Majesty. In fact, these divine delicacies have prevented me from waiting. Why wouldn't Your Majesty's popularity grow? In Dimabong, whenever Your Majesty's name crops up, the people who attended the wedding say that Your Majesty is "*jooba smanpang, deba bonlepopung*".

'What does that mean?' Xunzira asks.

'It means that he is as tall as a fan palm, as wide as a silk cotton tree. Why wouldn't he be? The amount of labour His Majesty puts in, we cannot even imagine. Which is why I have become like a big fat pig, can you see?'

Dhaneswar points at his belly.

At that moment Sukumola, crossing the doorway, laughs out.

Jongal turns around.

The sight of her makes him awestruck. He feels captivated.

Sukumola is wearing a gold-inlaid silk *rigu rijapai* and red *rikowsa*, with a gold-coral beaded necklace brought by her mother around her neck, armlets and bangles gifted by Konsari and gem-studded *jangfai keru* brought from upstream by Jongal. Her tightly bound topknot dazzles with gold flowers. A tiger-nail pendant is hanging from a myrobalan-shaped beaded necklace. A silk floral blouse adorns her body.

'Oh my gossai – from where did this fairy appear?' Xunzira exclaims. Sukumola blushes self-consciously.

'Really, Asi—' She laughs.

'Asi is right, My Lady. You are looking like a fairy indeed.'

'A charm or amulet doesn't make a difference. *Shooo, shooo*,' Xunzira chuckles.

'Charms and amulets don't help, Asi. She must eat. Look how frail she's becoming from not eating,' Jongal whispers.

'If only she would eat. You have to coax her into eating. Come, sit down. Sit near Pai.'

Sukumola complies.

'Asi is right. The princess is delicate, and she must eat well to regain her strength. That's why His Highness is such a picture of health, like a tiger. He's privileged to dine on full-grown fish from Kolong–Kopili. We're not as fortunate. Speaking of fish, it reminds me that His Majesty, our King, expresses his desire for a pot-bellied catfish. He instructed me just before I came here, "Tell my son-in-law to send a catfish, if possible." I almost forgot. Thank goodness I remembered,' Dhaneswar, with a slice of ripe mango in his hand, says.

'Why does he suddenly want a catfish? Does he think his son-in-law's kingdom has nothing else to offer?' Jongal chuckles.

Sukumola, engrossed in her meal, feels her heart race with anxiety. She knows why the honourable guest has brought up the topic of the pot-bellied catfish.

'When does he mention the catfish, honourable guest? Why didn't I hear about it?' Sukumola's mother asks, sounding irritated.

'He couldn't tell you; you're too straightforward. You would never agree. So, he mentioned it to me privately. Have you ever seen our Royal Majesty ask anyone for anything? His son-in-law is family, and he finds him endearing. I'm sure he didn't mention it to anyone else. It's not really a request, more of a suggestion. In fact, I brought up the delicacy of full-grown catfish from the Brahmaputra when we discussed my visit to Sohori. He only mentioned it then. I once savoured it during my trading days, you know – it was cooked with ripe elephant apple. So delectable, I almost wished to die eating it.'

'Fortunately, you didn't,' Xunzira quips.

Laughter erupts from everyone, including Jongal. His heart brims with joy. The Kachari king is Sukumola's father, the very Sukumola who captivates Jongal with her beauty and virtues. His suspicions from the past days dissipate. The intelligence reports about the Kachari king's intentions are in line with the desire for peace and goodwill.

For the first time, the Kachari king has asked for something like a family member – a simple pot-bellied catfish. A delightful revelation.

Observing his mother-in-law, Jongal adds, 'The honourable guest can't put it any better, Aai. Such full-grown catfish from the Brahmaputra are rare to find. Even I cherish them. However, it won't be available immediately. We'll have to catch it by damming. Once it's in the dam, I can send it.'

'But of course, there's no rush; it can be delivered another time. I don't understand this sudden craving for a pot-bellied catfish at his age,' Sukumola's mother remarks.

'It's quite natural, Sajjoh. It's good to have desires. It's a sign of his good health,' Konsari chimes in. The queen finishes her meal and nibbles on betel nut wrapped in betel leaf with clove, lime and the bark of the bohot tree. Then she says, 'It's almost time to head to the kitchen. Otherwise I won't be able to finish cooking.'

'I'll stay with you, Pai. I'd love to learn a few recipes. You see, there's a child in our house who adores food.'

'A child? Whose child?' Sukumola's mother asks in surprise.

'It's my child, Pai,' Xunzira declares.

Sukumola's mother laughs along with everyone else. Then she stands up. 'Come, Kamaijou, let's go. I hope our son-in-law, the king, won't leave without having lunch.'

'I won't, Aai. I'll stay until lunch. But I have to go out after that.'

After his mother-in-law leaves, Jokanko turns to Sukumola. 'Come, let's go to the lakeshore.'

Sukumola follows Jokanko outside. Dhaneswar stays behind, sipping joo and watching as the khamsamais collect the dishes.

Seeing these objects makes him feel like stealing them. Even at Dimabong, seeing the gold and silver tempts him to steal.

Dhaneswar, however, never dirties his hands by killing a rat. He prefers to amass everything methodically, whether it's this fort, this kingdom or the gold plates and bowls – he wants it all.

FORTY-THREE

Three bamboo tubes engraved with floral motifs sit on a table. The queen of Dimabong, while pouring joo-sa into the tubes from the narrow end of a vessel shaped from the outer shell of a gourd with a hole in its belly, explains: 'Today, you must taste some joo-sa sent by your daughter and son-in-law. It's delicious.'

Lifting a bamboo tube, Fa Bodosa laughs. 'You are bound to find it delicious. After all, it's from your daughter and son-in-law's kingdom.'

'No, Your Highness, it really is delicious. However, it is no match for our jugara,' Dhaneswar says, picking up his bamboo tube.

'It seems even our Dhaneswar has been mellowed by the hospitality of our son-in-law.' The king laughs.

'As a matter of fact, I have not mellowed, Your Majesty, but the hospitality was very satisfactory. The first two times I had stayed outside the fort. The food was cooked by prisoners. This time, I had the pleasure of dining on food prepared by Her Highness, our queen and our princess's *madou*. It felt like I was living in heaven.'

'What special dishes were you served?'

'There is no end to the list, Your Majesty. To be honest, one of the dishes cooked by Her Highness, Our Queen, didn't appeal to me. But then it was't for me – it was specially prepared for your son-in-law, the king and our princess. I had requested some. But it did not taste good.'

'Whatever did you prepare?' the king asks the queen.

'Pa-sa.'

'Oh, it's no wonder our honourable guest did not like it. This dish is full of energy, you know, Dhaneswar. When we set out for hunting or war, we do not have the means to cook food. So we crush small pieces of fish or meat and mix with it the sap extracted from tender urium leaves. The sap dissolves the fish and meat. The locals call it Pa-sa. It provides a lot of energy when consumed.'

'Ugh – let it give as much energy as it wants, I shall never eat it for the rest of my life,' Dhaneswar resolves.

Noticing their guest's facial expression, both the king and the queen start laughing.

'Then there was meat of the *dorik* bird cooked with fresh coriander, jaggery, ripe tamarind dipped in mustard oil, salt and eggplant, duck cooked with bamboo shoot, dhekia ferns cooked with khorisa, a condiment made from the young and tender shoots of bamboo, fine and fragrant maniki modhuri joha rice, pungent curry of the xol fish, burnt cane-shoot and bitter bhekuri seeds rolled in banana leaf and roasted, tangy curry prepared with ginger leaves, fragrant arum and black pulses, fish and deer meat grilled, pork with sesame—'

'Enough, enough, I don't want to hear anymore – oh – so much in two nights and a day.' The king laughs again.

'It's true,' adds the queen. 'I am delighted, to say the least. Their hospitality was unparalleled. Our daughter is living happily there. For you, they have sent two sets of clothes woven with silk warp and a gold weft that is studded with gold beads. I genuinely enjoyed every moment of my stay there. Our daughter will have a wonderful life in Sohori. There is nothing to worry.'

'Didn't I tell you? You were the one who had worried needlessly.'

'But what made you crave pot-bellied catfish? Our son-in-law was amused. I wish the honourable guest had not spoken about it,' the queen says.

The king looks at Dhaneswar for a moment. Then he chuckles. 'Only someone who has tasted this catfish knows about it. I am tired of eating the *namxan* fish and *doumesser* meat from the hills. Our son-in-law's kingdom is in proximity of the Kolong river. It is close to the Brahaputra as well. That is why I mentioned it. Do you think it was impolite?'

'It was not impolite. However, wasn't it embarrassing?'

'In fact, Her Highness, our Queen is right. Nonetheless, didn't I take it upon me, later on? And I suppose His Majesty is not wrong either, is he? Eating fish from the rocky beds of hilly rivers and wild fowl could be quite boring indeed. Please forgive me, but I think asking for the fish was a good gesture. Our son-in-law is yet to visit our kingdom. It's possible this is because the feeling of attachment has not grown in him. His Majesty, our King, has displayed a bond that our son-in-law will undoubtedly appreciate. There will be visits to and fro. We can also see our princess frequently.'

'The honourable guest's words are irrefutable. I cannot disagree.' The queen laughs. Then she says, 'I'm going in. I have a lot to do. Are you going to have your meal here, Dhaneswar?'

'No, Your Highness. My woman will hack me to pieces. You know how blunt she is. No sooner did I go home than I went out again.'

'Alright then.' The queen leaves.

The king looks at Dhaneswar. 'Amused?'

'Not only amused, Your Majesty – he even said it. The queen concealed it in case it offends you, but I am your slave. How can I not say?'

'What did he say?'

'He wondered why his father-in-law only longed to taste a catfish? Did he think that we have nothing besides catfish in our kingdom? Then he laughed so hard – so hard – I felt like fleeing in humiliation. Why wouldn't our Highness, the Queen, feel bad? Can one endure such rudeness? After all Her Highness is soft-hearted. Forthright. She'd never been to Sohori before. She did not attend the wedding either. How could she understand what is going on? The queen was upset even without knowing anything as she listened to our son-in-law's words and noticed his laughter.

Imagine my plight, Your Majesty. Ever since the wedding, he has meted out insult after insult. At the wedding, he didn't bow before you. Except for the priests and the public, he did not bow before anyone else. He refused to let us into the fort. He did not pay a single visit here. You are a great king; without taking any offence, you took the initiative of sending Her Highness to their kingdom, you have expressed your desire for an ordinary catfish, in spite of all this, should he have ridiculed and affronted you before everybody? It was very disappointing, Your Majesty.'

'There is no doubt that it is disheartening. But what can be done? Our daughter is about to become a mother. Could we ever dream of hurting her?'

'No, no, she shouldn't be hurt. One should always wish one's daughter well. Even as I reflected on my way back, I thought it would be wise to overlook everything. Let our son-in-law attack, if he so wishes. What harm could it cause? At most, we will have to bow to our son-in-law's supremacy and continue paying taxes and revenue. Nothing more. Then again, I pondered, could I bear to see you as a subordinate king? You are a father; perhaps you could. But I am your servant, and not only do I address you as god, I genuinely believe that you are one. I cannot, for the life of me, bear witness to my god removing his turban and kneeling before someone. I would rather leap into the Dhanshiri waters with my family.'

'Why should you jump, Dhaneswar? I shall never allow that to happen. I am the descendant of King Hattsungsa, and I have never bowed to anyone. Tell me everything that you have seen and heard.'

'Everything of which I have informed you has proven true. The princess remains oblivious to everything. Upon our arrival, we found that preparations for battle were in full swing outside our son-in-law Jongal Bolohu's fortress. I encountered no obstacles this time, as I was accompanying the queen. That's why I took a comprehensive look both inside and outside the fortress. I even observed their battle drills. It's truly horrifying! So many warriors! I noticed a significant cache of arms stockpiled within the fortress. It was brought to my attention that even other minor kings have formed alliances, including the Bhuyans of Borduba.'

'You are correct, Dhaneswar. The Bhuyans of Borduba are advancing steadily. They must be confronted, much like a tiger with its neck in a noose, someday.'

'It doesn't seem very easy to crush them, Your Majesty. Looking at the extent of their friendship with Sohori! Didn't the Bhuyans erect with spears the main canopy of Princess Sukumola's wedding as a symbol of friendship?'

'Yes, yes. Thank you for reminding me. The Bhuyans must have joined hands with Jongal. It's a matter of great concern, Dhaneswar. Once upon a time, our kingdom spanned the Dikhow river to Kolong as well as the whole of Dhanshiri, you know. Initially, the Ahom king had asked us for land the size of a *tirilai laisini.* They never even had the courage to fight.'

'Tirilai laisini? What does it mean, Your Majesty?'

'As wide as a straw, do you understand? After migrating from the land of Norá, the Ahoms begged us for land as wide as a straw. Through shrewd strategies, they managed to expand their territory all the way to Namdang. Regrettably, we were compelled to relinquish the eastern bank of Dikhow and even forsake our capital, Dilau. Our beloved salt spring had to be surrendered to the Nocte Nagas. It pains my heart to recollect these events. I yearn for the day when our lost land will be reclaimed. I am resolute in my determination to resist. I will not permit the Ahoms, who migrated from the far side of the Patkai mountains, to establish a permanent presence in our territory. My resolve is not limited to regaining control of the salt spring; I also intend to impart a lesson to Jongal. Remember, we are descendants of the Hattsungsa dynasty. Do you comprehend? The offspring of a hero.'

'But how can you put up a fight on all fronts, Your Majesty? We're surrounded – Bhuyans in the north, Sohori in the west, Ahoms and Nagas in the east and Jaintias to the south. The Jaintias haven't shown any hostility. The Nagas are living peacefully after acquiring the salt spring and the Ahoms are busy with their own troubles with the Nagas, Borahis, Morans and Chutias. We'll get our land back someday with Aai Ranachandi's help. Jongal is the problem – he has the divine sword and strong allies in Gobha, Pratappur, Komota and the petty kings. Haven't I witnessed everything at Sohori? They have enough gold to wrap around the whole fortress. You can ask Her Highness, the Queen. She will tell you. I doubt we'll regain Dimabong if he attacks us. We're vulnerable, Your Majesty. Whose support do we have? There are enemies all around.'

'You are correct, Dhaneswar. We have grown weaker. What should we do?'

'What wisdom can I offer, Your Majesty? If you deliberate on the matter, a solution may emerge. I can suggest this: the one who strikes first holds the advantage. Initiating the battle is the key.'

'Indeed. I'm considering a similar approach. When we ascertain the timing of Jongal's invasion, we will move forward and confront him, preventing his victory.'

'But he is our son-in-law, after all. We can't harm him, Your Majesty.'

'True. Since we've given our daughter to him, we must not harm him. What should we do, Dhaneswar?'

'Please don't put me in an awkward position, Your Majesty. Honestly, I know little about warfare. However, based on what I've gathered from your wisdom, I have one suggestion.'

'Please, go on.'

'Your Majesty, imagine this: we cannot harm Jongal, which is just. Apart from his ambition to expand his kingdom, he is an admirable person. His greed led to his father's demise, and the divine sword has only fuelled it further. But if we could seize the sword and imprison Jongal through a surprise attack on Sohori, he might learn a valuable lesson. We can release him later, showing mercy. Without military strength and without the divine sword, Jongal can't harm us. In the meantime, I'll secretly build alliances with the Bhuyans of Borduba, petty non-Laloong rulers and Mikirs. Even if this is not kept secret, it won't harm us. Jongal won't suspect our true intentions; he'll think we want to befriend these rulers because they're his allies.'

'Absolutely right, Dhaneswar. I'll call the general and discuss it.'

'Of course, but it's risky to discuss it with the general in advance. Sohori's spies might catch wind of it. We risk not only losing our kingdom but the princess as well.'

'You're a wise man, Dhaneswar. I promise you this: one day, I shall appoint you the Prime Minister or major general of my kingdom.'

'It's not necessary, Your Majesty. I'm content as I am. I'm here to serve and learn from you. The honourable general is a wise and trustworthy man, though age is catching up with him. He's straightforward and kind-hearted, with a dislike for warfare. But he's a good man.'

'Being good is not enough, Dhaneswar. One must be courageous and intelligent. Since you've undertaken the responsibility of gathering information, haven't I been kept informed of the activities of the Bhuyans, Ahoms, Nagas, Khola Sohori, Gobha, Jaintia and Dimoruwa kingdoms? No, Dhaneswar. I shall appoint you my major general.'

'I won't question your judgement, Your Majesty. But perhaps it's best not to rush into granting me a title. If Dimabong ever faces danger, you can consider it then. Until that time, I can continue to gain knowledge and understanding from you. May I take your leave for today, Your Majesty? My impatient spouse will be eagerly awaiting me.'

'Of course, Dhaneswar.'

'You seem quite apprehensive about your wife,' the king laughs.

'You know Phoolkhuri inside out. She used to be your maid – very straightforward. I can't help but feel frightened. When I briefly stopped by at home, she warned me that I should return early. If I'm not back on time, I won't find Phoolkhuri at home. Instead, I'll find Aai Heremdi sitting with the large knife used for sacrifices.'

'Well, it's best to head home then. Come back tomorrow,' the king suggests.

Bowing to the king and plotting his next move, Dhaneswar leaves with a contented demeanour.

FORTY-FOUR

'Combat training concludes today, Sukumola,' says Jongal, preparing to leave.

Sukumola, in the later stages of her pregnancy, is lost in thought. She looks up on hearing Jongal's words and asks, 'Today's feast is to celebrate this occasion, isn't it?'

'Yes, it's a tradition. We all feast together on the last day of training. The new soldiers are welcomed, too. You can step outside to see; all the soldiers are gathering on the field within the fortress. I'll distribute rhino-skin *paroo*, langkhui and armour to each of them. I'd like you to join me. There will be plenty of entertainment. But given your condition, you should watch from a distance. It's not time yet; I'll let you know when it is.'

'Why have you recruited so many new soldiers?' Sukumola asks, somewhat hesitantly.

'New soldiers need to be recruited from time to time. The same soldiers can't go on forever. Can bald, toothless soldiers defend the kingdom? Haven't I told you this before?' Jongal chuckles.

'That's true, of course. But you've also invited the neighbouring Bhuyans and other petty rulers. Is there a war on the horizon?'

'Not for war, but sometimes I invite these rulers for my convenience. It helps maintain good relationships, prevents border conflicts and facilitates trade and commerce discussions. This is the first time I've invited them since your arrival. They were invited to our wedding, but we haven't met since then. I wasn't inclined to invite them this time, but the Garos from the hills are causing trouble in the southwestern kingdoms of Chaygaon, Looki, Beltola and others after a long time. Messengers have arrived seeking our help. That's why the kings have been invited. We need to discuss whether or not to send soldiers.'

'You don't invite my father to such meetings, do you? He's our neighbour too, isn't he?'

'No, it's somewhat different when it comes to my father-in-law. As you know, Dimabong didn't have a good relationship with Khola-Sohori before. While there was no direct conflict with the other Laloong kings or petty rulers, we weren't particularly friendly either. A cordial relationship has only developed recently, after our wedding. He was supposed to be invited this time, but the meeting had to be arranged hastily. If he had been invited abruptly, without my first consulting the other kings, who knows what kind of situation my father-in-law, the king, might face? He's not a petty king, after all. How many kings are as great as him? A king with the courage to confront the Ahoms. He deserves respect and a more substantial gathering, but that's not possible during this rainy season. I'll invite him in the spring. He can also meet his grandchild. I must be on my way now. After distributing the shields and swords, the royal assembly will convene, and then the feasting ensues. Oh, there's one more thing – my father-in-law requested a catfish, and I'm disappointed that we haven't been able to catch one. We've tried damming several times, but the catfish has eluded us. This time, we built a large dam at the mouth of the Kajoli where the Kolong flows into the Brahmaputra. We can get fish for the feast, and if a pot-bellied catfish surfaces, we can send it to the king.'

Sukumola gazes at Jongal's face, which radiates enthusiasm and excitement. She finds it peculiar. On one hand, he's preparing for a potential attack on her father's kingdom, and on the other, he's eager to send her father a catfish and showering Sukumola with affection. However, he hasn't trusted her. Why would he lie to her like this? Is his story about the Garo invasion, the assembly and the catfish all a fabrication? Her father's words ring in her mind, 'Once we have the divine sword, we'll feel secure about our kingdom. We've received news that Jongal's seemingly friendly relationship with us is a complete deception. It's clear he's planning to attack Dimabong, though we're not sure when. Please send the sword as soon as you can. Leave the casing as it is. Jongal won't know. Even if he does, he'll never suspect you. Recently, didn't Jongal's stepbrother, Ratnasinha, the king of Komota, visit Sohori? Jongal will suspect him of taking the sword. After all, he's not his own brother, and Ratnasinha is known to be aggressive and undisciplined. I've heard he has become morally depraved. Please don't worry. Once we have the divine sword, everything will be alright.'

Sukumola has no reason to doubt her father's words. It's true that Ratnasinha visited them recently. She's heard Abi Konsari lamenting his moral decline. Jongal won't suspect her if he doesn't find the divine sword.

'What are you thinking about, Sukumola?' Jongal's words startle her.

'Oh, nothing really. I just didn't feel myself for a moment.'

'Lie down, my dear. I'll tell Abi and Asi to stay with you. Don't move about unnecessarily. You don't need to go to the feast in this heat. It's scorching out there, and you won't be able to bear it. Can I leave?'

'Yes, you may.'

Jongal leaves after caressing her. Sukumola lies down, a weary figure. Konsari and Xunzira enter. Seeing them, Sukumola tries to get up, but Xunzira exclaims, 'Don't get up – don't get up. This is not the time for formalities, Pohari. We've told you many times. Why don't you listen to us?'

'What's wrong? Are you not feeling well?'

Sitting beside Sukumola and taking one of her hands, Konsari asks, 'Just a little. But I'm feeling better now, Abi.'

'Then why are you upset, dear?'

'I'm worried, Abi. I'm scared.' Sukumola's eyes fill with tears.

'Why are you crying, Pohari? What's there to be so scared

about? It's a God-given gift, and God himself will bring it into the world safely.'

'Xunzira is right, my child. Don't let negative thoughts enter your mind at this time. Come, get up. Come and sit outside. Nannao, tell someone to bring some tender coconut water for her. It will make you feel better. Get up, my child. Lying down will only make you worse.'

Sukumola gets up. At that moment, a khamsamai, carrying tender coconut water, arrives.

'Give it to me. Hold the fan,' Konsari instructs Xunzira.

'Abi, Deoraja has asked you to visit the gathering of soldiers on the ground. The kings from Dimoruwa and Borduba have arrived. He's invited you to join them. Deoraja will be busy elsewhere.'

'Alright. I'll be there.'

'Should I tell them to keep your carriage ready? Deoraja has asked you to take the carriage.'

'Indeed, instruct them to have it prepared. I'm on my way,' she says, gently helping Sukumola into a seated position. Handing her the coconut water, she turns to the khamsamai standing nearby and says, 'Please, stay close to Her Highness. Fan her. These summer days seem never-ending.'

After downing the coconut water in one go, Sukumola responds, 'She doesn't need to stay here, Abi. I can manage. After resting a while, I'll go outside and sit.'

'Are you certain? Very well. If you require anything, ring the bell. Be careful getting out of bed,' her caretaker advises.

'I will, Abi.'

With that, Konsari and the khamsamai exit the room. After lying down for a bit, Sukumola musters the strength to stand up. She slowly makes her way out of the room, feeling fatigued.

In the distance, sounds of merriment and celebration drift in. The soldiers sit in orderly rows on the field. As Sukumola gazes at the scene, she contemplates their impending journey to Dimabong. Armed with swords provided by Jongal Bolohu, these soldiers will soon turn the soil of Dimabong red with the blood of Kachari soldiers. Jongal's very hands, which now caress her tenderly, will strip the yellow turban from her father's head.

Sukumola is overcome by a suffocating pain. Beads of perspiration form on her forehead.

Resolutely, she returns indoors. In the palace's backyard, the khamsamais are occupied with packing items destined for Dimabong.

Noticing Sukumola at the entrance, a helpful individual hurries to fetch a chair for her. She sits down, her gaze absentmindedly fixed on the bamboo baskets, earthen pots and cane chests. After some time, a group of men enter, carrying a massive, pot-bellied, full-grown catfish suspended from a bamboo pole. Instantly, the inner courtyard erupts with commotion. Khamsamais from various corners of the palace gather around to catch a glimpse.

Sukumola stares unwaveringly at the catfish sprawled on the courtyard. This fish is destined to save her father's kingdom from impending danger, secretly carrying the divine sword from Sohori's palace to the royal palace of Dimabong. That's why her father has slyly brought up the topic of a pot-bellied catfish with Dhaneswar.

Suppressing her excitement, Sukumola tries to remain calm. In time, the khamsamais return to their respective tasks. Only three of them remain in the courtyard, as most of the palace's occupants are busy at the training grounds, community kitchen and royal assembly.

Sukumola rises with remarkable composure and begins walking towards her room. Silence envelops the surroundings, with no audible conversation or footsteps. She briefly pauses in front of Jongal's armoury, straining to hear any voices or approaching footsteps before cautiously opening the door.

Her heart races, and she breaks into a sweat, overcome with a mix of excitement and the fatigue of her late-stage pregnancy. Inside the armoury, shields, lances, swords, daggers, spears and bows-and-arrows are meticulously arranged. A barrel containing a bundle of spears stands on one side.

Sukumola's attention is drawn particularly to the barrel, as she has observed Jongal standing near it on two occasions, engaging in prayer and other rituals. With no time to waste, she pushes the spears aside and peers into the barrel, only to discover that it does not house the sword she seeks.

Panic sets in. Where could Jongal have hidden the divine sword? Sukumola repeatedly inspects the spears and then notices a hidden door concealed among them. Despite the door's considerable weight, she summons all her strength and manages to move it.

The barrel falls away, unveiling the door. Sukumola waits a moment, a sharp pain piercing her back. She clenches her teeth and endures the pain, then pushes open the door to enter.

The room she discovers is small, solitary and tranquil. A wooden platform occupies the eastern side, bearing a long wooden box. An earthen lamp still casts a soft glow, though the flowers on the platform have begun to wither.

Sukumola reverently pays her respects to the platform. As the pain in her back resurfaces, she once again grits her teeth, waiting for it to recede. With trembling hands and perspiration on her brow, she opens the box and gazes at the sword resting inside. She gently touches the sword's sheath to her forehead, paying her respects again, and then draws the sword from its sheath. After carefully placing the sheath back on the platform, Sukumola emerges from the room with the sword, offering her respects one last time.

With the door securely closed, she pushes the barrel back into position with all her might. An intense pain sears through her, and she sinks to her knees beside the barrel. Tears fill her eyes as she bites her lip to stifle any sounds of agony. As the pain subsides, Sukumola rises with the sword.

She can't afford to dwell on her suffering. The pot-bellied catfish is invaluable, a rare treasure. This opportunity might never present itself again. Concealing the sword beneath her clothes, Sukumola somehow fights the pain in her body, moving swiftly to her room.

There, she wraps the sword with a two-and-a-half-foot-long cotton towel and picks up a knife. Ignoring the torment at every step, she makes her way to the backyard and takes her seat, reserved from earlier. All three khamsamais are busy wrapping the catfish with banana leaves.

Addressing the khamsamais, Sukumola says, 'Please go and fetch Abi. Inform her that I'm feeling worse than before. And bring me a bowl of water.' Two khamsamais promptly follow her instructions. Turning to the third, who appears bewildered, Sukumola adds, 'Could you also fetch me a fan? I'm truly feeling quite faint.'

The khamsamai hastens away. With nimble hands, Sukumola inserts a knife into the catfish's mouth, deftly separating the tightly joined, sharp inner teeth. Then, using a larger knife from the ground nearby, she hammers the sword into the fish.

Afterwards, she returns to her seat, having made sure the sword's handle fits perfectly into the pot-shaped neck of the fish. It is undetectable.

Before the khamsamais can return with water and a fan, Sukumola has already begun to whimper in pain. They observe her perspiring face, their confusion evident. One of them hurries off to inform Xunzira, who arrives in a trice.

Soon after, Abi Konsari joins them. Sukumola, with Xunzira's assistance, has made her way to her room and lies down on the bed. Konsari helps her loosen her clothes.

First, Konsari enquires about her discomfort, asking, 'Did you lift something heavy or slip somewhere?'

Sukumola responds, 'It was a minor slip, Abi.'

Konsari calmly examines and assures her, 'Don't be afraid. Ma Kalikha will protect you. Just relax, I'm here with you. Nannao, go and make the necessary preparations. Send a message to Kopahi bai.'

Sukumola asks, 'Should I call Jokanko?'

Konsari shakes her head. 'No need. What does he know anyway? He's occupied with something important, and we shouldn't disturb him.'

'Very well, Pai. I'm on my way. Pohari, would you like some water to drink?'

'No,' Sukumola replies in a feeble voice.

Xunzira leaves.

Wiping Sukumola's face with a wet cloth, Konsari says, 'You must think of me as your mother. You mustn't feel shy. During these times, a woman gains the strength of Ma Kalikha, do you understand? God has created men. Then again, He has allowed the wives of these men to create men. It's a great responsibility. A great task. Because of this significant task, He has granted us great courage, too, even strength. He has provided us with nourishment in our breasts, much like Goddess Earth. It's just that we often don't reflect upon it. When we do think about it, we realize the immense strength of women. Embrace your strength, child. There will be some pain, but as soon as the baby arrives, you will forget all your suffering. It's God's way. God is the saviour and the destroyer.'

Sukumola gazes at Konsari's confident, wide eyes. The agony intensifies, but her mind remains serene.

With an abi like her, what sorrow or pain couldn't one possibly endure?

Three hours after Jongal returns home having completed his work, Sukumola becomes a mother, and he a father. The pot-bellied catfish is on its way to Dimabong, carried on the back of an elephant.

FORTY-FIVE

It is raining when the two men from Sohori, carrying a variety of foods along with the catfish, dismount from the elephant and stand at the entrance to the palace of Dimabong.

Fa Bodosa has just finished breakfast and is getting ready to go to the royal assembly. Once word of the arrival of the two Sohori visitors spreads, the palace bustles with excitement. The attendants get to work, taking care of both the men. They all understand the significance of visitors from Sohori in the king's palace. The attendants carry the parcels and keep them on the raised plinth inside the palace. The fish has finally arrived.

As soon as they set eyes on the fish, the maids create an uproar. The Kachari queen comes outside. The two men bow before the queen.

'What tidings have you brought? Is all well with my daughter, your queen? Is all well with the others, too?'

'All's well with everybody, Your Highness. Our Deoraja has sent a pot-bellied catfish for Fa Bodosa. It was caught by damming the mouth of the Kajoli river.'

'Is that so? Let me have a look at the fish.'

A few men lift the fish and carry it near the queen. The queen is flabbergasted at its sight.

'What an enormous fish!'

Before anybody can say anything, Dhaneswar barges in.

Looking with astonishment at the baskets and chests kept on the plinth, he walks up to the queen and bows.

'Your Highness, the Queen, I have to see His Majesty. I have something very serious to tell him.'

'He is getting ready to go to the royal assembly. Please have a seat in the lobby outside, honourable guest. Let me go and inform him. Look, our son-in-law has sent such a huge fish.'

On seeing the catfish, Dhaneswar's eyes widen in surprise. A servant is beginning to untie the cords and unwrap the banana leaves from the fish.

'Wait, wait – don't remove the leaves. Let His Majesty arrive.'

'One can look at the fish better if the leaves are removed, I suppose,' the queen says irritably.

'Sure. One can. But Your Highness, it would be better if the leaves are removed in front of His Majesty. I have never seen such a huge catfish in all my life. It's a delight to watch even the unwrapping of the sheaths. Wait, wait, don't unwrap. Your Highness, His Majesty—'

'Wait, let me inform him. Please go have a seat, honourable guest.'

'It's not necessary, Your Highness, the Queen. I would rather take a good look at the catfish. I wonder if I will ever get to see such a fish again. It's not one of those common rockwater fishes, you know.'

The queen goes inside in exasperation.

'What is the commotion about?' the king asks.

'Visitors from Sohori have arrived. The honourable guest has come, too. He has something serious to tell you, he said. Our son-in-law has sent a huge catfish. It's larger than a large hog.'

The Kachari king is startled.

'Sent a fish? A catfish? Where is it? Let it be brought here.'

'What nonsense. Why will the fish be brought here?' the queen says, astonished.

'It's important. No – let me go myself.' As he rushes out, the king's steps falter, and then, with grave strides, he walks outside.

The two messengers come and pay obeisance to the king. Returning their greetings absentmindedly and after exchanging a few pleasantries, the king looks at the fish. The servants working inside the palace are standing here and there, eagerly waiting to watch the fish unwrapped.

'It's really a huge fish. I've had a great desire to relish one for a long time. I am really pleased that my son-in-law remembered,' the king says.

'A feast was arranged for our newly recruited soldiers. There was an assembly of kings, too. For that reason, when the mouth of the Kajoli river was dammed, this catfish was found,' one of the men from Sohori narrates with great enthusiasm.

'Is it? In fact, it is our good fortune, I must say. Please take a breather. Enjoy the food and drink. We shall talk later,' the king says.

'As a matter of fact, we shall not spend the night here, Your Highness. We have to go back.'

'You need not go back. You are tired from the journey. Moreover, it's raining heavily. Let the rain stop. How could we allow visitors to our kingdom to return in this way?'

Summoning the officer in charge of attending to visitors and sending the two messengers to the guest house, the king calls for the head chef. 'Take the fish inside. Don't unwrap the leaves. I shall look at it later. Let me talk to Dhaneswar first. Come, Dhaneswar. Come inside.'

For the first time, the king invites Dhaneswar into the main residence of the palace. Astonished, the queen also follows them.

Disappointed, the people who were waiting to watch the fish being unwrapped, get busy putting other things in their proper places. A few of them carry the fish inside the room.

'Aren't you going to see what your daughter has sent?' sitting with Dhaneswar inside the room where the fish has been kept, the king says.

'I shall, but later. First, let me hear what tidings the honourable guest has brought.'

'Her Highness is absolutely right, Your Majesty. It must be relayed in the presence of the queen.'

'What important news have you brought, Dhaneswar?' the queen asks.

'Nothing new, Your Highness. His Majesty is already aware of most of it. But you are not. Our kingdom is in great danger,' Dhaneswar says.

'What danger are you talking about?' the queen asks in great surprise.

The king looks at Dhaneswar. Nervous that Dhaneswar is about to disclose something which has been concealed from the queen for a long time, the king says, 'I think you must not speak about it before her, Dhaneswar.'

'No, Your Majesty, it will be unpardonable if Her Highness, the Queen, is not apprised of the present situation. A moment ago, I received information that His Highness, Jongal Bolohu, having concluded combat training, is indulging in feasting and also holding a conference with the neighbouring kings.'

'So what?' the exasperated queen cuts in.

'It's very serious, Your Highness. At the conference, everybody has resolved to attack Dimabong unitedly to make it their subsidiary.'

The queen stares at Dhaneswar for a while. 'Honourable guest, who has given you authority to collect information about what is going on at Sohori?'

'I have,' the king speaks angrily.

'Why? Don't we have our own people in our kingdom?'

'What are you saying? Isn't Dhaneswar our own? He has settled here by marrying one of our girls. He has helped us in so many ways,' the king says, feeling irritable.

'No, Your Majesty – Her Highness, the Queen, is not wrong. After all, I am not a Kachari. It's your magnanimity that you have accepted me as one of your own people. But I am merely a guest, am I not? At your single command, I shall have to go away with my wife and children. How does it matter if my wife is a Kachari? Her position is that of a maid, after all. The queen is not at fault,

Your Majesty. She is not aware of my activities, is she? Had she known, she would have understood.' Dhaneswar's voice falters with feigned emotion.

'It's true. Had she known, she would have understood. Let me explain to her then. But before that, she must swear on Aai Heremdi not to tell anybody.'

The king turns to face the queen. After the queen swears secrecy, he narrates everything right from the beginning. The queen takes it all in with great astonishment.

Dhaneswar's almost inaudible sobbing fills the room, casting a gloomy atmosphere. The queen's heart brims with fury.

Having disclosed everything, the king says, 'Now tell me – what must we do?'

'How am I supposed to know what is to be done? I am finding your words hard to believe. I have been to Sohori myself. I did not notice anything wrong either in their behaviour or their words.'

'The queen is absolutely right, Your Majesty. Even I was won over by their behaviour. But is behaviour the ultimate concern, Your Highness, the Queen? Just think, His Highness Jongal Bolohu had killed his own afa, King Arimotto, to gain victory over his kingdom. Even King Arimotto had killed his afa.'

'I know. However, they had killed without knowing the full facts,' the queen says gravely.

'Whatever may be the reason, they had killed their own fathers, after all. And thereafter, have you ever noticed any sign of remorse in Jongal Bolohu's behaviour? King Arimotto, after abandoning his kingdom, was spending his days on top of the Dhoumora hills in the name of God. But King Jongal Bolohu continues to govern his kingdom. That, too, very successfully. Can anyone hunger after another's kingdom without any greed for power and expansion? His Majesty, our King, is also a king. But have you ever noticed any craving for other kingdoms in him? If His Highness, Jongal Bolohu, is the epitome of goodness, why doesn't he return the petty kingdoms he had seized from us? Why doesn't he let go of Kondolini?'

'Who said he won't? After all, we have become a family only recently,' the queen says with great frustration.

'If he is willing to give back our land, in that case, wouldn't we have had an inkling about it? We may not have known. But the princess would surely have known. Has she ever intimated anything like this to you? Assuming that I am not your family, is there anyone closer to you than the princess? Moreover, she is about to become the mother of Jongal Bolohu's son, isn't she? Yet she regularly sends information to us. It is because she has been able to see the reality for herself.'

'You are right, Dhaneswar. These women don't seem to understand at all. How great our kingdom had been! And now it has become feebler than an old *jhumar* deer. I established a family relationship with the hope that everything would be well. But his eyes are fixed on our land. Dhaneswar, please attend to the visitors from Sohori satisfactorily and make arrangements for them to return today itself. I am on my way to the royal assembly. The gissia must be summoned. To worship Aai Gamadi. Wait, let me first take a look at the catfish.'

The king gets up, and so does Dhaneswar. Fa Bodosa pulls out the sword by opening the catfish's mouth.

'She has sent it! My darling daughter has kept her promise!' the king says excitedly.

'What? What is this?' the queen asks.

'A sword. The divine sword. This is the root of Jongal's tyranny. Now let me see how he dares to touch the soil of Dimabong. I myself shall make him my subordinate long before that.'

'What are you saying? You are going to attack your son-in-law's kingdom? Our daughter lives there. She is going to become a mother any day. Even so, you are going to cause harm to her?' the queen asks in surprise.

'How would I cause harm to her? Am I going to slay the king? So what if he is our son-in-law – he is an enemy. He is amassing soldiers to make us his subordinate. Assembling kings.'

'Why don't you talk to our son-in-law face to face?' The queen becomes agitated and fearful of impending warfare.

'What is there to talk about? Who knows – he might even come to attack us tonight itself. And what is the use of talking to a man whose greed for land knows no bounds? All these years I had lived in fear of him. Not anymore. The divine sword is in our hands. There's no more fear.'

'But—'

Before the queen can say anything more, a maid speaks from outside, 'Someone else has arrived from Sohori.'

'Go and see who it is. Tell them to take the fish away.'

The king goes inside to conceal the sword.

The queen walks outside. A man comes up and, after bowing, offers some coconut balls, a variety of rice cakes and a pot of honey to the queen.

'I have come with good tidings, Your Highness. Queen Sukumola has given birth to a boy.'

Holding the parcel of snacks in her hand, the queen stares impassively. Tears obscure the view in front of her.

Torrential rain lashes the palace courtyard.

FORTY-SIX

Thoodei nana thoodei
Tuyakha thi khate mosrong wise unang
Thooyade thooyade bhoudisa mai jinanang
Thoodei, thoodei.

Sukumola is humming a lullaby, cradling in her lap her pink-skinned baby wrapped in a *khitapsa* sent by her mother.

Konsari and Xunzira are sitting next to her.

'Your voice is very melodious, Pohari,' Xunzira says. 'Come on, sing another one.'

'He has fallen asleep, Asi,' Sukumola replies self-consciously.

'Let him sleep; we are awake, aren't we? Let's listen to some more songs while we drink joo. Songs we've never heard before,' Xunzira says with a laugh.

'Do sing, my child – it's really pleasing to the ears,' says Konsari.

Putting the baby to sleep, Sukumola begins to sing softly once again:

Moinab moinase thijaoba
Moinab kugebeng guaross
Bator batose thijaoba
Bator buku dogoi se
Nannah lai dere nung majangnang—

'I don't know the rest of it,' Sukumola giggles.

'It was so pleasant to hear, child. What name are you going to give the little one, dear?' Xunzira asks.

'I'm not sure. You all can decide on a name. However, there are two names in my mind. Pet names. Baragusu and Bubao.'

'What do they mean?' asks Xunzira.

'Baragusu means the first bloom, and Bubao means the bud of a flower.'

'Really beautiful names. I like Bubao better,' Konsari says.

'Even I. It's a pity, Pai – we shall not see him grow up.'

'Why do you say that, Asi?' Sukumola says sadly.

'She doesn't mean it. When she is drunk on joo, she always talks this way,' Konsari laughs. 'Go, my child, go and have something to eat. I shall look after him. One feels famished at these times. Because one has to feed the baby. Even then, make sure that you don't eat too much in one go. Eat less but frequently. It's good for your health.'

'But Asi keeps feeding me all the time,' Sukumola says.

'You must eat whatever she gives you. Xunzira knows very well what you need to eat. Now go.'

Sukumola and Xunzira leave the room. Konsari sits looking at the baby sleeping on the bed.

A great-grandchild.

Bearer of their dynasty.

Very dear. Very desirable.

King Pratapchandra, too, is blended in this little face. As are Arimotto and Jokanko.

Whenever Konsari looks at the baby's face, these faces seem to flash on and off. The eyes are wide, but the nose is a bit broad. The complexion is golden. The arms and legs are plump.

In this baby's body, the Aryan and non-Aryan have merged.

Aryan blood flowed through the veins of King Pratapchandra and Konsari. Arimotto had represented that blood. Ratnasinha is of the same lineage. However, Jokanko bears two distinct bloodlines – non-Aryan Tiwashas and Aryan Kshatriyas. This infant has drawn the blood of the Kacharis, another non-Aryan clan.

This child is similar to this land. Like this country.

Enriched by the fusion of various streams.

Konsari prefers it this way.

When she was banished and the people of this land had open-heartedly embraced her, Chandraprabha witnessed for the first time a new society – one that was greater than even a king. People outrank kings here. She had seen how small kingdoms exist peacefully by adhering to the rule of harmonious co-existence. From Lali Hilali songs, Chandraprabha had learned how to integrate different societies into one. In Pratappur and her father's kingdom, Chandraprabha had only observed the avarice for victory. Land greed. Among other lofty kings, Chandraprabha had seen ruptured images of thirst for victory, pride in being Aryan and wild satisfaction from humiliating others. Between these two kingdoms, Konsari had chosen Gobha. And so, Konsari replaced Chandraprabha. She had made efforts to blend into Gobha's society. Even now, Konsari wants to breathe her last on this land. Hoping to blend into the soil when she dies.

On her way to becoming Konsari from Chandraprabha, she had to ford many rivers of sorrow. She had to witness Pratapchandra and Arimotto suffer terrible pain. She had to bestow on Gangavati a lifelong agony. Isn't Jokanko also suffering because of Konsari?

If Konsari had not prioritized society, Arimotto and Gangavati might have lived a conjugal life in Baidyagarh. Arimotto and Jokanko need not have suffered the mortification of killing their fathers. Those mishaps would never have occurred.

All this has happened because of Konsari. It's all thanks to her determination to transform into Konsari from Chandraprabha.

And Sadhukumar?

Isn't Konsari to blame for rendering Sadhukumar's life futile? Everything she has done for this society – can it fill up the void of a life wasted?

No, it cannot. Konsari knows this. Nonetheless, she feels there has been no error. She has not committed any blunder by making society her priority.

After going through innumerable gloomy days, at last, Konsari seems to have put her feet on a sunlit courtyard.

There is well-being all around.

Jokanko has emerged from the humiliation of killing his father. He is living a happy and peaceful life with Sukumola. He is concentrating on the welfare of the society. There is also goodwill with the Kachari king. There is no hostility between them.

Looking at Jokanko's content, serene expression, Konsari feels a sense of peace. Perhaps the thirst for victory in Dharmapal's dynasty will fade over time. Recognizing the rule of harmonious co-existence, perhaps Jokanko will govern his kingdom similarly to Sadhukumar. If everybody is happy and prosperous, Konsari will also be happy. And eventually, she will rest in eternal peace on this kingdom's soil.

Konsari startles when the infant moves its body. Placing the baby on her lap, she gently pats it to sleep again. Looking at the baby's face, Konsari unwittingly sighs.

Her son Arimotto's descendants will be passed down through this child. Ratnasinha's lineage has come to an end. His mother's actions have ruined his life.

His mother's betrayal and debasement had deeply shaken Ratnasinha to his core, eradicating his respect for people. His trust. His faith.

Arimotto, who had placed Ratnasinha on the throne of Komota, had chosen to live as an ascetic in the Dhoumora hills. Shortly thereafter, Ratnasinha launched an attack on Fingua's fortress, ultimately taking Fingua's life. Following this, he spiralled into a river of sweet wine.

Konsari had made multiple attempts to support Ratnasinha, even attempting to arrange a marriage for him and set him on a more stable path. However, these efforts proved futile, as Ratnasinha had sworn off marriage entirely. His heart held neither respect nor love for women, as he sought to leave his past behind. Yet the nights in Baidyagarh resonated with the sounds of the anklets of intoxicated prostitutes, a testament to Ratnasinha's internal turmoil.

Konsari had journeyed a long way from Gobha to help Ratnasinha, but hadn't she herself fallen into an abyss of suffering during that time? Her son's death and a series of other tragedies had left her completely devastated.

While Jokanko had the support of a mother like Gangavati and Xunzira, Ratnasinha was left to navigate his challenges alone. Occasional visits from Samol, who came from Pratappur, and infrequent visits from Konsari were the extent of his social interactions. Even Jokanko, upon learning of Ratnasinha's plight, had visited him. Ratnasinha, on occasion, made trips to Gobha and Sohori. However, the isolation of Baidyagarh, coupled with its painful memories, took its toll, leading to his mental disarray. Ultimately, his coercive relationship with Acharya Prabhakar's granddaughter incurred the wrath of his subjects. By that time, Acharya had already passed away. Despite his royal status, Ratnasinha now leads a solitary life, seemingly oblivious to the world, as an unmarried bachelor.

The line of heredity is on the brink of ending.

Konsari is aware of this.

She keeps herself updated on all the latest developments, sharing them with no one.

Konsari refrains from letting sorrowful tears taint the family's current stream of happiness. Perhaps by containing all the pain within, she has turned into stone, transcending all emotion.

For the first time in what seems like an eternity, she feels a sense of freedom. There is finally a sense of relief in being able to cradle the soft body of a baby.

'Have you fallen asleep with the baby, Abi?' Jongal enters and says cheerfully.

'No, Syu, I'm awake. Have you eaten anything?'

'Yes. I'm delighted to see you this way, Abi. I was growing weary of watching you spin yarn and read scriptures. Please let me hold the baby.'

'Are you sure? You won't accidentally smother this tiny baby with your strong hands?'

'My hands might be tough, but what about my heart? That arrogant Jokanko is no more, rest assured.'

'You've truly changed, my syu. Sukumola has finally set you straight,' Konsari laughs.

'She's a wonderful person, Abi. It would have been a great mistake not to marry her!' Jokanko exclaims joyfully, cradling the child in his arms.

Before Konsari can respond, a khamsamai approaches and stands before them.

'Abi, someone has come from Dimabong bearing gifts for the baby – he wishes to meet Her Highness.'

'Go, inform Her Highness. I'll be there shortly. Call Xunzira Asi here.'

'He says he won't stay overnight. He must return immediately; there's a religious ritual.'

'Let me go, then. Syu, do you think you can look after the baby? You'll be free once Xunzira is here.'

Concealing the secret letter brought by the messenger, Sukumola engages in conversation with the chief administrator of Dimabong's palace while examining the gifts sent for the baby.

At that moment, countless canoes, crafted from both solid and split wood, silently glide down the rivulets, stealthily making their way towards the Kopili river in the direction of Sohori.

FORTY-SEVEN

It's a dark monsoon night.

Every brook, every stream gurgles with water while countless boats make their way into Sohori through small rivers and canals. With the current pulling them downstream, the oarsmen deftly manoeuvre the oars held at both ends. Using long bamboo poles, the boats carefully clear their way. Kachari soldiers occupy the boats in the front, while hooded boats at the end of the line carry supplies like raw soft rice, packed rice, rice powder, grilled potatoes and steamed pulses wrapped in edible leaves, salt and oil. They also carry helpers and medics. In a boat ahead of the one carrying the soldiers are Dhaneswar, Fa Bodosa and the major general. Dhaneswar, studying small maps drawn on the *bhurjapatra* Himalayan birch in the light of earthen lamps covered with thin banana tree barks, explains the route they need to follow.

The boats come to a stop at a specific location where the soldiers split into two groups: one group goes with the major general, and the other with the king and Dhaneswar. Holding the bhurjapatra up to the lamp, Dhaneswar instructs, 'Let the major general attack the regiment near the fortress. If we can defeat its soldiers, capturing the fortress won't be too difficult.'

'Put out the earthen lamps. Take the firefly-filled papaya stems. Wrap them with cloth. Follow the map as you move ahead,' the king commands.

The segment led by the major general moves forward to attack the picket near the fort, while the remaining soldiers, armed with spades, axes and other weapons, follow the king and Dhaneswar, wading through the swampy waters towards the fortress.

'We only need to dig the southeastern section of the fortress,' Dhaneswar says. 'The soil is sandy on the western and northern sides. I have already inspected it. It will cave in when dug. And on the southeastern side, it is like clay, so there will be no issues.'

Although they begin to burrow into the fortress surreptitiously, it isn't long before they catch the attention of the sentry. Instantly, the horrifying hour of battle begins.

On hearing the commotion, the ever-alert Jongal sits up on his bed. He picks up the sword from the head-side of the bed and strides out. At the same time, the chief sentry of the palace comes rushing in.

'Some people are digging into our fort, Deoraja!'

'Who? Ahoms? Bhuyans? Jaintias? Dimoruwas? Nellys? Lookis? Ranis? Mikirs? Or … or … is it the Kacharis?'

'Kacharis.'

'Kacharis?' Jongal falters. Could the Kachari king be attacking Jongal's kingdom? Is that even possible?

Why not? The Ahoms would never cross the Kachari kingdom to get into the Khola Sohori. Not even the Bhuyans, Jaintias, Ranis, Lookys, Dimoruwas – none of them. Never.

Kacharis. It's got to be the Kacharis. Yes.

The principal gatekeeper is hurrying towards him.

'Deoraja … Kachari soldiers … Kachari soldiers are attacking the regiment guarding our fortress. They're digging into the fort and could enter any moment now. The soldiers inside the fort have gone out to fight them. There's no hope of getting support from the soldiers outside the fort.

'It's alright. Don't panic. We have the deo langkhui, the divine sword. And we have the blessings of Ma Kalikha. No one can harm us. You go ahead, and I shall be on my way.'

Hue and cry have filled the palace. Xunzira, Konsari – everyone has come outside.

Jongal has returned to the bedroom, where Sukumola is sitting on the bed.

'What has happened?' she asks anxiously.

'Your afa is attacking our fortress.'

'My afa? But why? Why is he doing it?'

'Your afa wants our kingdom. After giving us his daughter in marriage, now he is coming to take advantage of our friendship.' Jongal is growing frantic.

Konsari and Xunzira walk in, visibly out of breath.

'Abi, Asi, stay with him. Sukumola, please go and cook some rice. Simple rice will do; I don't want to go out on an empty stomach. Ma Kalikha has forbidden me to go to battle without eating, as I have told you before. Now go,' he commands.

With that, Jongal walks out and enters his armoury, quickly putting on his jacket.

Meanwhile, Sukumola is lighting up the kitchen hearth. As she waits for the water to boil in the bell-metal mihdo, she sits with her head resting on her knees. Restless. Disturbed.

The letter from her father the night before has left her sleepless.

'Sukumola, you've done so much for our kingdom. Maybe you felt guilty about spying for our kingdom, but only Brai Shibrai knows the true extent of the good you've done for us. Jongal Bolohu is currently preparing to attack our kingdom, unaware that you've sent the sword to us. We are on our way to invade his kingdom. The sword of victory is in our hands, and Jongal can't harm us. Our kingdom is secure. However, we want to teach Jongal a lesson. We want him to understand that he is not invincible. He won't come to any harm, but he must realize that it's wrong to covet the land of others. You had left for Jongal's kingdom, pledging in the name of Shibrai and Aai Heremdi, for the sake of your country. Do one last thing for us. When Jongal prepares for battle, do not give him any food.'

'Sukumola, Sukumola,' Jongal calls as he enters the kitchen.

Sukumola always cooks Jongal's meals. After learning how to make his favourite dishes, she had taken this responsibility upon herself. It would give her great delight to serve a variety of dishes to the food-loving Jongal.

'Sukumola, your afa has attacked our kingdom. I'd never imagined, even in my dreams, that he would ever lay siege to his son-in-law's kingdom. However, he has only seen my image as a son-in-law. He hasn't seen Jokanko, the warrior. He has no idea I have the sword of victory. No one can hurt me.'

'But I heard you're the one who is planning to attack Dimabong?' Sukumola lifts up her head to look at him.

'Who told you this?' The excited Jongal comes to a halt. He gives her a piercing stare.

'I heard it from the khamsamais.'

'And you believed them? Is that why you're cooking rice and sitting here so miserably?'

'I can't help but feel miserable,' Sukumola replies with tearful eyes.

Moving closer to Sukumola, Jongal holds her hands, looks into her eyes and says solemnly, 'Look at me, Sukumola. Do you believe that I am capable of such a thing?'

Sukumola lowers her head.

'You are the mother of my child. You are the love of my life. Can I ever hurt you? In the name of Fa Mahadeo and Aai Basundhari, I've never even considered attacking the Kachari kingdom. Serve me rice, Sukumola. I shall be back, fully geared.'

After Jongal leaves with hasty steps, Sukumola's lets the tears roll. Everything becomes clear to her. Her father's intentions become apparent as well. Standing in front of the vessel used for cooking rice, she breaks down, completely oblivious to everything around her. She doesn't know how long she has been crying, when suddenly, she is startled by Jongal's agitated voice.

'Sukumola, who has taken away my divine sword? Who has pierced this spear into my heart? Where has my sword of victory gone?'

Sukumola continues howling in response. Jongal enters the kitchen and stares at Sukumola for a while before saying, 'Why are you crying? Whose impending harm brings tears to your eyes? Is it for me or for the Kachari king? I don't have the sword of victory with me, only its sheath. Let it be. Never mind. Jokanko is not afraid of battle. Give me food. What is taking you so long? Stop crying. Abi, Abi!'

Suspicion weighs heavily on Jongal's mind, as if the sound of Sukumola's crying echoes the resonance of betrayal. Sukumola makes no move to serve the rice. Instead, she weeps with her head buried between her knees. Jongal stares at her for a moment, then walks towards the hearth. He removes the cover of the cooking vessel and stands there in shock. Inside the vessel, small pebbles are boiling, resembling the sound of rice cooking. Everything becomes clear, crystal clear.

Jongal pulls Sukumola up by her shoulders. 'You took away the deo langkhui, didn't you? Did you send it to Dimabong? To have me killed? Are you cooking pebbles instead of rice so that I'll be defeated in battle on an empty stomach? Are you not going to serve me rice?' Sukumola continues to cry, offering no other response. He lingers over Sukumola's lowered face and tearful eyes for some time before asking calmly, 'Why did you do it, Sukumola? What harm have I caused you?'

It is that terrifying calm before a storm.

Sukumola goes silent.

Jongal's hands tremble with the thirst for revenge, the instincts of a killer awakened within him. The unpredictable Jokanko has emerged.

By the time Abi Konsari arrives running, Sukumola's lifeless body is lying by the fireplace.

The enemy's cries echo from the other side of the fort.

'What have you done? What have you done, Jokanko?' Abi Konsari exclaims in shock.

'It's all over for me, Abi. Sukumola betrayed us for the sake of her country. She took away my sword of victory,' Jongal's voice falters, but then his fury reignites. 'I will go into battle. I know the Kachari king is well informed about our kingdom. That's how he has advanced so far. But I'm not dead yet.'

Leaving Konsari rooted to the ground, Jokanko leaves, carrying his weapons and the sheath of the divine sword.

It is time to fight the final battle.

FORTY-EIGHT

Through a deserted forest road, the Kachari queen and Dhaneswar's wife, Phoolkhuri, are riding on the back of an elephant. The dark, moonless night is made gloomier by the sound of swamp deer. It's nearly dawn, and the elephant carrying both of them, as well as the ones carrying the bodyguards, have arrived at the border of Sohori.

'Why didn't you inform me earlier, Phoolkhuri?' the queen says, her voice laden with sorrow.

'If only I had known, Aai. Do you think the trader tells me anything? I only overheard them speaking when they were about to leave for battle. I lunged at him with a dagger, but he tied me up and took it away. Isn't he accompanied by a bunch of corpse-eating vultures? They've been deceived. After restraining me, he gleefully revealed everything. He plans to kill our Fa Bodosa. He will also kill our son-in-law. He has orchestrated everything with the Ahoms. He intends to rule Dimabong, Gobha and Khola-Sohori while remaining subordinate to the Ahoms. The son of a wretched trader. Look at his greed. If he is caught, no one should kill him. I will cut him to pieces. Then I will drink his blood. I am a Kachari woman. I can kill for my country. I can die for the country, too. Aai, Fa Bodosa has made a grave mistake. He should never have trusted a stranger.'

'I had tried to dissuade him many times, you know. But he didn't listen to me. He even married you off. We are still-water fish. Where can we go after breaking the dam? Would this have happened if they had listened to us?'

'But Aai, I will break the dam. I will cut him to pieces and feed him to the crows and vultures.'

'Speed up, *Mout* Agoui,' the queen pleads to the elephant keeper.

'We can't go any faster, Aai. We have to cross streams and brooks, and there are thorny bushes and plants that sting and cause fever. We also have to watch out for the devil's nettle plants.'

'No matter the thorny bushes. Let the devil's nettle sting, for that matter. You be quick. As I was leaving, the *datonkor* bird was chirping above my head. I also saw an otter dive into the water. Something ominous is about to happen. Very ominous. I have offered a fowl to Aai Heremdi. May she protect us all. Move faster, Agoui, or everything will come to an end,' the queen pleads again.

In fact, everything is nearly coming to an end at that moment. The Kachari soldiers have taken over the interior of Jongal Bolohu's fortress. From the raised platform of the Rongchuwa ground, the kings of Dimabong and Dhaneswar survey the scene. Torches illuminate the inner grounds of the fort that are smeared with the blood of Laloong soldiers. No, the blood of Kachari soldiers has mingled with theirs. Jongal and a handful of soldiers have managed to escape the fort after slaughtering many Kacharis. A group of Kachari soldiers, loyal to Dhaneswar, is chasing after them, as directed by their commander.

'I hope you've instructed them to only capture my son-in-law. Are you certain he will not be harmed?' the king asks anxiously.

'Of course, Your Majesty. Why would they? Haven't you given them prior instruction?'

I certainly have. I'm really worried, Dhaneswar. I don't know why, but I have a strange feeling. I feel like I've made a mistake, Dhaneswar. The number of soldiers you claimed to have amassed – I didn't see so many of them.'

'They are not salaried soldiers, Your Majesty. Most of them have returned to the samadi or to their homes in the villages.

They'd have arrived on time if they had known we were going to strike first.'

'In that case, things are bound to be different. I could see my son-in-law fighting from here. So full of strength, so skilled – it exceeded my imagination. His weapons broke into pieces, yet he killed so many soldiers with his bare hands. But seeing the way he fled, it depresses me. Perhaps he didn't even have the chance to eat a morsel of food. You know, he can't bear going without food. I wonder how he is holding up in the fight.'

'It is indeed depressing, Your Majesty. You think this way because you are wise. But if our kingdom had been under attack, wouldn't you have had to fight in the same manner?'

The king falls silent, his gaze inadvertently fixed on the station adjacent to the fort. From there, the sounds of shrill laughter and painful screams reach their ears – the echoes of war drums.

Jongal races with lightning speed towards the Kolong.

Unarmed.

Helpless.

The soldiers pursuing him are growing tired, occasionally stopping to shoot arrows at him. But not a single arrow has struck Jongal as he swiftly manoeuvres from one side to the other.

After a long and arduous run, he finally reaches the Kolong river. His throat feels parched. As is the inside of his heart – his unseen soul.

Tears fill his eyes at the thought of Sukumola and their baby.

Sukumola, who had betrayed him.

The same Sukumola whose dark tresses he used to bury his head in, finding solace and sleep. Sukumola who had nestled in his chest as they drifted off to slumber.

The passionate days and nights now seem fictitious. The relationship between a husband and wife has lost its sanctity.

While pretending to be in love, Sukumola had secretly poured poison into his drink. It was the same Sukumola whom Jongal had loved. Loved with every fibre of his being.

He has left the Kachari soldiers far behind. They are no match for him when it comes to running.

But he has not eaten anything. And without food, he feels very weak.

His lips have dried up with thirst.

Lying on the bank of the Kolong, Jongal cups his hands and draws a palmful of water. In the blue light of dawn, he is startled to see his palms.

Coated in blood. Both of them. How to drink water!

He lowers his head and begins to lap the water directly from the river, like a cow. In that moment, his mother's voice, the voice of Gangavati, echoes in his heart and mind.

'… This is your Fa, Jokanko. You have beheaded and brought your own Fa's severed head? You have disobeyed my orders. *Kaphut lawa.* Scoundrel! I shall never forgive you. At the time of your death, you will be deprived of drinking water with these two hands – the hands with which you have killed your own father. You will die drinking water like a cow. *This weapon, whose power made you forget your promise, will abandon you when you will need it the most …*'

Two hot tears roll down Jongal's face and mingle with the waters of the Kolong.

'I understand – I understand everything, Maah. You are watching over me from the skies as a star, you are crying for my afa …'

A group of Kachari soldiers is drawing closer. Shooting arrows. Jongal plunges into the Kolong and continues to move downstream underwater.

The soldiers chase him along the riverbank, launching arrows and throwing weapons into the water. But Jongal has disappeared.

After a while, he resurfaces to breathe and glances towards the banks. In an instant, a lance flies towards him. Reacting swiftly, he submerges himself again.

The Kachari soldiers are perplexed. Dhaneswar had ordered them to kill Jongal by any means necessary, but all their arrows, spears, lances and swords have been exhausted. No blood has stained the waters of the Kolong. Jongal continues moving downstream, remaining submerged.

By this time, the Kachari queen has climbed up to the Rongchuwa. Dhaneswar wants to flee as soon as he sees Phoolkhuri, but one of his legs is knocked down with a blow of her sword.

The Kachari king looks surprised.

The queen and Phoolkhuri advance towards him. Kneeling before the king with her head touching the ground, Phoolkhuri weeps like a madwoman as she tells him everything.

Holding the soldiers of the security regiment captive, the major general and a few bodyguards are climbing up to the Rongchuwa, silently listening to the revelations. Without waiting for the king's orders, they encircle Dhaneswar, who lies sprawled some distance away, with swords and spears. The trader falls to pieces from the jabs and stabs of spears and swords, and gets trampled.

'General, go, go immediately; they will kill your son-in-law. I have come to realize … I have realized everything … It was a great mistake … it was a great mistake,' the king says tearfully.

At that moment, Jongal rests at a spot on the riverbank after traversing a great distance underwater.

All sense of hunger and thirst has escaped him, his body and mind completely seized by exhaustion.

Everything has become irrelevant.

This kingdom, this family, this land – everything has lost its meaning.

The tender Sukumola, under the guise of love, had stolen his battle weapon from him. No, not only his weapon, but also the meaning of his existence.

Why did Sukumola commit such an act? What had Jongal deprived her of? What misery had he inflicted upon her? What was his offence?

No, Sukumola should not be solely blamed; it was the consequence of his own sins. He was the killer of his father. He had been cursed by his mother's imprecations. Could a son who had been deprived of his mother's blessings ever achieve true victory? Could the goddess of good fortune, Lakhimi, remain in the house of such a son? Or the god of happiness, for that matter?

The Kachari soldiers charge at him. Their fatigue is evident as they struggle to keep up with him along the banks of the Kolong. Driven by their ambition to rise through the ranks from common soldiers to officers, they keep running, their growing fatigue making them increasingly furious. They have discarded their bows now, their quivers empty.

Jongal leaps into the Kolong. Kajolimukh is just a little further way.

If he can reach the Brahmaputra, he will have the opportunity to cross over to the opposite bank. Samol awaits him there, along with his brother Ratnasinha.

Jongal will return again.

Jongal will never surrender.

Jongal is not afraid of anything.

Nothing at all.

Jongal's determination to reconstruct his shattered mind, destroyed by Sukumola, burns within him. He will survive for the sake of Bubao, his precious child. With the aid of Ayong and his brother Ratnasinha, Jongal will return, fully armed, to reclaim the seven-tiered fort, the capital surrounded by a moat – Khola-Sohori.

But where is the way? How can he escape?

The mouth of Kajoli has been dammed by Jongal himself, using long bamboo poles intended for delivering fish to his father-in-law. There seems to be no way back.

On the bank, eleven Kachari soldiers stand, their eyes filled with bloodlust. They uproot a few bamboo poles embedded near the bank. One of them hurls a spiny bamboo with a sharpened end at Jongal, who is trapped within the dam.

Meanwhile, Fa Bodosa, accompanied by his queen, Phoolkhuri and a few bodyguards enter the palace bereft of any remaining male members. In the kitchen, Konsari sits motionless with the baby on her lap, next to Sukumola's lifeless body on the ground. Thumping her breast, Xunzira wails in deep sorrow. The margi khamsamais, too, are crying.

At the doorway, the Kachari queen turns into a statue. As does the king, Phoolkhuri and the soldiers.

Konsari lifts her head and stares. The Kachari queen collapses upon Sukumola's lifeless form. The fortress of Jongal Bolohu, now turned into a graveyard, shakes with the sound of heart-rending wails.

FORTY-NINE

Xunzira is feeding the crying baby, dipping cotton wool into diluted buffalo milk. Konsari sits on the floor with her head between her knees. The Kachari queen and Phoolkhuri sit identically.

The palace is silent.

Sukumola and Jongal's lifeless bodies have been placed in the courtyard, where they lie covered in cloth. The Kachari king and the major general sit nearby, their heads bowed in grief. Rows upon rows of shrouded corpses stretch out before them. It is hard to tell which was a Kachari and which a Laloong. Both Kachari and Laloong soldiers are sitting all over the fort, their heads lowered.

It has all become clear to everybody.

Profound sorrow has robbed their voices.

The main gate is open.

Throngs of people pour in. The kings from neighbouring realms have arrived, but there is no one to greet them today. They find whatever space they can and settle in. People fill every corner, both inside and outside the fort.

The silence is only broken by the sound of heart-wrenching cries and, occasionally, the cutting of bamboo.

All eyes are fixed on King Bodosa, hundreds of invisible spears of loathing and contempt piercing his being. The Kachari king is siting with his head bowed.

His eyes are dry. But he is concealing a sea of tears within his heart.

At every turn, the voice of the Kachari queen echoes in his mind.

'What did you accomplish? What came of all this? What did you gain by killing a hero like our son-in-law? By sacrificing our daughter? What did your greed bring you? More land? More trees? Two more rivers? More gold? More weapons? Did you gain these people? The people who bowed before you as family? These people are going to loathe you now. They will spit on your name, Fa Bodosa. What will you do with a land tainted by their spit? What?'

In the courtyard, Sadhukumar has just arrived. Xunzira wails like a possessed woman and kneels in front of him. 'Oh, Deoraja, they stabbed my golden child to death. They fleeced his skin back with thorny leaves until he died—' Another chorus of lament quakes Jongal's city.

'Get up, Nannao. I have heard. It is nobody's fault. It is our kharam. What can you do?' he tells her calmly.

King Bodosa stands up and approaches Sadhukumar, kneeling before him. His voice trembles with tears as he asks, 'Have you truly realized what happened, Deoraja?'

'I have, king of our family. Please rise. You have lost your daughter. We, too, have lost our grandson. What is destined to happen will happen.'

'Deoraja, the time has come to take them to the funeral,' the jela baro says gently.

Sadhukumar goes inside without looking at anybody. Konsari sits like a rock with the baby on her lap. Sadhukumar stands beside her, gazing at her tired, worn face, marked by age and suffering.

Konsari raises her head.

She continues to stare blankly.

There are no words left to say.

No more questions to ask.

Sadhukumar sits beside Konsari, silently taking her hand in his. She asks him, 'Why did you break your promise and enter the house, Deoraja?'

'Was it possible to stay away, Your Highness?'

'Impossible, Deoraja. Impossible.' With her head resting on Sadhukumar's hands, Konsari finally lets out her tears, a release after countless years of pent-up grief.

FIFTY

Is there an end to life?

Does the stream of life cease to flow?

Is there an end to hope?

Trees perish. They grow back into saplings.

Men perish. Leaving behind their hopes and dreams for the next generation. Now Jongal has done it.

Just like Arimotto had left him.

Just like Pratapchandra had left Arimotto.

This tiny Bubao!

This tender bud continues to support the collapsing fortress of life with his two tiny hands.

Still keeping alight a dim lamp of life-spirit in Sadhukumar are the Kachari king, the Kachari queen, Xunzira and Konsari …

The queen and king of Dimabong had knelt before Konsari and begged for Bubao.

'I shall need time to think it over, Bai,' Konsari had replied. 'Let the rituals be completed. But what does it matter whether he lives here or in Dimabong? It's your land after all.'

'Pray, do not speak like that. Pray, do not. I don't want this land. Fire has already consumed my greed for land. We shall return to Dimabong. This land does not belong to us. We are simple people, easily hurt by simple words. We do not have the authority to walk on the ground where your feet rest. Just give us Bubao. We shall go back with him,' Fa Bodosa had said.

'What are you going to tell him when he grows up and finds out that you murdered his father?' Konsari asked.

'I don't have the answer with me.' The king of Dimabong lowered his head.

'Give me time to think. Let the karam rituals get over.'

Today, the karam has come to an end.

The once bustling township ruled by Jongal now lies deserted.

The bloodstains have been washed away, and the weapons scattered have been collected and stored.

The section burrowed by the Kacharis lies in its current state – exposed, ravaged.

At the spot where the princess used to bathe, the gold-inlaid boat still floats, anchored to its gold shackle.

In the drawing room, two bunches of gold and silver betel nuts and leaves remain displayed on a silver tray.

The only thing missing are the fresh flowers.

It is the putrid odour of the withered flowers that clings to the soundless room, hesitant to depart.

There is nothing else.

As they are about to enter, the king and queen of Dimabong come to a halt at the palace threshold.

Samol stands on the other side of the door, with the same hard, expressionless countenance, wearing the uniform of a common soldier.

'We have come to take Bubao, O noble king of Pratappur,' says the Kachari king, his hands folded.

'I am not the king of Pratappur. The son of Prime Minister Sogor has now ascended to the throne of Pratappur. My name is Samol. The administrator of Khola-Sohori. The servant of Deoraja Sadhukumar. Abi Konsari does not live here. Bubao is not here. Abi Konsari and my mother have left, taking Bubao with them. Before they left, they told me that you have no authority over Bubao because you have no answer to give to him.'

Lost and directionless, the king of Dimabong stands still, as if facing a hard rock.

Just then the phurimoso rises in the sky.